"Group chat, booth, or s[...] behind the bars of one of th[...]

"Group," she said, offering her credit chip.

The angel stamped the back of her hand with what appeared to be flaming letters that spelled out the word "Chat," then gave her a dark coin. "Give this to Charon at the ferry. He'll take you across the Acheron and Styx rivers—the other barrier river won't be finished until next month."

"Thanks," Ariel said, stepping through the turnstile. The gray-bearded ferryman accepted her coin and helped her into the boat, then poled away from the shore toward the first tunnel in the row.

"I'm Charon," the ferryman said. "Been here before?"

"First visit," Ariel said, occupied with thoughts of Carlo and not really wanting to talk.

"Sorry to hear that. Your loved one departed recently?"

She shook her head. "Eight months ago, but it's too expensive to visit her often."

Charon shrugged and turned the ferry toward the tunnel mouth. "You're telling me. I work here and I can't even visit my parents with my discount. We like to say, 'people are dying to get in here.'" He paused a moment, waiting for her response, but when he didn't get one he cleared his throat. "Sorry. Macabre humor doesn't go over with everyone, I guess. You get used to it when you work here."

Ariel gave him a faint smile. "I won't tell a soul."

Charon snorted. "Won't tell a soul. Good one."

THE DIGITAL
DEAD

BRUCE BALFOUR

2003
50TH
ANNIVERSARY

ACE BOOKS, NEW YORK

THE DIGITAL DEAD

An Ace Book / published by arrangement with
the author

PRINTING HISTORY
Ace mass-market edition / August 2003

ISBN: 0-441-01084-9

To Warren and Betty Balfour
without whom none of this would have been possible

ACKNOWLEDGMENTS

This particular collection of words was made possible through the efforts of many fine individuals, living and dead, some of whom allowed me to stand on their shoulders while others simply wouldn't get off my back. My thanks, as always, to Leslie Balfour for her encouragement and loving support; to Heather and Hope Wilson for spurring me on to greater efforts; to John Morgan for shepherding the manuscript; and to my agent, Richard Curtis, for keeping an eye on things. On the technical side, I'd like to thank neuroscientist Dr. Michael Persinger of Laurentian University for his research using transcranial magnetic stimulation, and Dr. Andrew Newberg of the University of Pennsylvania for his studies of the neurobiology of religious and mystical experiences. I also wish to express my gratitude to those who helped in the past and have gone on ahead to scout out the terrain on the other side, including Fritz Leiber, Philip K. Dick, and Roger Zelazny.

PAIN walked the night, screaming victory in its dark voice of thunder.

The storm surge hit him at full force, a power elemental, twisting and pulling his body apart. Waves of furious electrons rose to vast heights before thundering down on his fragile form. A spectral deathwind howled in anger. His eardrums vibrated with the cacophony of the desperate and the dying. Glittering sprites of fragmented images sprayed in confusion, blending future and past in Time's death throes. Bands of color swirled in the darkness, punctuated by bursts of gray static in the afterglow memory of lightning. He screamed as his fingernails ripped away. Cold chills slipstreamed up his spine, while tides of chaos pulsed against his back.

Torn between two worlds, Norman Meadows fought to drive air into the tortured chambers of his convulsing lungs. His chest ached with the effort.

Fire and ice. Warm red light pulsed in his head while ice blue water chilled his veins. Numbness enveloped his arms as a wave of cold rolled through his skin. Spasms knotted the muscles of his legs—dead weights that dragged him farther into the storm-tossed depths. Static electricity crackled and popped in a manic dance across his body. Through a fog of confusion and anxiety, the rational part of his mind struggled for control, forcing him to think. He had come too far to stop now. He must fight his way out, back the way he had come, back to the safety and warmth of his home. The cryptologic sea of the digital dead sapped energy from living entities to protect the secrets of the

Elysian Fields beyond. No mortal had scaled the towers of memory guarding the final gate, and Norman Meadows knew he was too weak to go farther. He would not be the first. Survival occupied his mind, focusing his efforts to escape on an adrenaline rush. His body needed fear to save his life, but the seething datastorm wanted to push him beyond his fear into panic. Spectral voices whispered in his ears, urging him to join his ancestors. Screams echoed across the vault of the sky, warning him to ignore the whispers. Fatigue oozed through his brain, a current of exhaustion swamping his thoughts. Death might get him through the gate, but that would be the easy solution. He would only succeed by coming out alive. He reached down, using his last reserve of strength to seek the golden undercurrent of reality, plunging toward the time-space flux of energy that held the world together, diving against reason into the cold depths of the flowing darkness that preceded death. With a final lunge, hurled beyond the point of no return, his fingers burst with a golden light that flowed up his bones and into his skull.

Flash. A brilliant spear of cobalt lightning split his brain in half.

Real mode. Blinking against the brightness, Norman gulped true air into his lungs. The electrode throbbed at the base of his skull. Through the thunder of his headache, he forced his eyes to focus on a pane of glass, then through reflected shadows on the window to the view beyond. His eyes filled with the warm clarity of a spring day. Quicksilver honey flowed down from the sun to ooze over fields of amber, stick to rivers of black asphalt, and splash the pastel blossoms of the trees with radiant highlights. Pieces of blue sky had fallen, becoming flowers that danced on the wind. Brushes of radiance punctured the clouds, painting the distant mountains with purple and violet, splattering the green canvas of the forest with yellow, orange, and crimson.

He tingled with the flow of real space, his senses buzzing and confused—hearing colors and tasting the silence, touching flavors and smelling the time.

Fatigued and enhanced by his digital journey, he rested until his emotions drained away and the dark tide rolled over his consciousness. When the static of the electron surge finally faded in his brain, he remembered one thing: the vast face and elemental power of the killer AI known as Firestorm, defender of the digital dead.

ARIEL Colombari lay naked on the rough concrete floor
and cried. She cried for the loss of her former life, she
cried for the things she had to do now to survive, but most
of all, she cried for the loss of her husband. Carlo's body
had been discovered eight months earlier in the cold waters beneath Nova Alcatraz, the floating city in the San
Francisco Bay. Her head lay on the dirty sheet of poly-
styrene foam that she normally slept on, a great insulator
inherited from a friend who scavenged old landfills for
valuable materials. She thought about rolling her body
onto the warmer surface, but she couldn't gather the
strength to go that far. At least her feet were warm, resting
on the hut's heating and waste removal system; a rusty
metal mesh in place of a manhole cover leading down to
the sewer. The smell didn't bother her anymore, but she
was always careful to take a shower when she got to work
so she wouldn't offend the customers. A gust of wind
howled through the cracks in the patchwork of plastic and
garbage that formed the walls of the hut, tossing a strand
of her long black hair into her mouth. The glitter she'd inhaled almost ten hours ago had worn off now. She opened
her eyes, relieved to see that Brother Digital was out at the
moment. The light from the cracked glowglobe was dim,
but he'd be able to see her puffy eyes and the tears on her
face if he came in. A broken advertising holo of Nova Alcatraz flickered on one wall, showing Carlo's project as
seen from the air, an immense nautilus seashell wrapped
around the old prison island in expanding white spirals.
Above the arcology floated the slogan: Live the Good Life.
    As Carlo used to say, life didn't come with any guaran-

tees. She used to think that people failed in life by doing one remarkably stupid thing that could never be corrected. But it was just as easy to take a series of missteps, forging a chain of broken dreams that slowly wrapped itself around your neck until you strangled in despair.

Ariel wondered how she had sunk so low, back on the street after spending five years in the privileged apts of the construction zone on Alcatraz. As a partner in the architectural team, Carlo received many benefits, including the luxury housing. She quickly grew accustomed to the elegant surroundings and their rich lifestyle, but the government men forced her to leave after his death. She still didn't know how he was murdered, or why. She knew they were surprised to find Carlo under Nova Alcatraz, because the swift currents in the deep water should have carried him out to sea, but his body had lodged in one of the intakes that pulled seawater into the desalination plant. The detectives spoke to her only briefly before the FBI took control of the investigation. Security issues made his death a federal case somehow. They said she wasn't a murder suspect, but they made her leave Alcatraz anyway. Cut off from her funds, she returned to her old dancing job at the virtual feelie club on O'Farrell in the theater district. The club's owner, e-Bert, had foreseen her future when she quit to get married, telling her that his dancers always came back—and she'd hated to prove him right.

The dancing itself wasn't so bad. She worked in a private 360 booth, and it was up to her if she wanted to see the club's cheaper customers watching her through the mirrored glass. While she danced, a constant full-body scan worked with the microscopic force-feedback sensors embedded in her transparent skintight to replicate the look, feel, smell, and taste of her body in a virtual environment. An AI mimicked her voice and operated her virtual self where anyone in the world could reach her, so all she had to do was provide a body and nervous system for sensory modeling. The local club visitors wore disposable skintights in their private booths, giving them full-sensory contact with her, but Ariel always kept her end of the loop turned off so she wouldn't have to feel what they were doing. The only time she had ever been motivated to feel anything was when Carlo made his visits to the club before they got married. Other dancers had met husbands and partners at the club, so Ariel's case wasn't unusual, but e-Bert's eyes lit up with greed when Carlo offered to buy out her contract at twice the going rate. Now, Ariel felt like her five years with Carlo had been a dream, living in a world of servants, fine clothes, perfect food, exotic travel, and friends who didn't care how much things cost. The dream had dissolved into a nightmare where she had no clothes, no food, and the only travel she did was chemically induced.

She'd originally come to San Francisco as a nano-processor layout designer, but the advances in AI-assisted design of quantum processors and biochips had made her obsolete after two years. With enough money, she could have retrained, but the depression after the loss of her job led her to try smoking glitter, one of the new multivector designer drugs that flooded the brain's synapses with dopamine. Money exchanged for bags of sparkly glitter dust raised her self-esteem and made her feel energetic, happy, and optimistic, at least for a few hours. It didn't have the unwanted side effects of many older drugs, except for a crash into depression and spontaneous memories for a couple of hours, and the glitter experience was slightly different for everyone because it customized itself to the body chemistry of the user. "Glitterati" sometimes had brilliant insights or visions, but the only consequence Ariel had ever experienced was a few hours of memory loss. She thought glitter would help keep her spirits up while she looked for a new job, but it hadn't worked out that way.

Ariel pushed herself up to her elbows and fought the in-evitable wave of nausea that quickly passed. Her body was covered in goose bumps, but she couldn't remember why she was naked. Her clothes were missing. Brother Digital was gone, so she couldn't ask him if he knew anything about it. She sighed and sat up. The rough concrete had formed a fine pattern of red dots on the right side of her body. Her gaze fell on the few grams of glitter dust that remained in a clear bag near her hand, then she gazed at the Thai Krong speedflamer beside it, all ready to make her feel better. She knew it was a mistake to have started glittering again after Carlo's death, especially after the expensive treatments that had broken her addiction for five years, but she'd only smoked a few times recently, and it gave her temporary relief from her thoughts about Carlo. Brother Digital didn't like it. The cumulative effect of his God Box was helping her control the glitter habit, but it was a creepy experience, and she didn't like the religious fanaticism she sensed from his followers.

The Pingers were generally harmless, busy seeing "miracles" most of the time, but they kept pushing her to read the Digital Bible and learn about the Entity. Brother Digital assured her that learning the ways of the Entity would lead to enlightenment and success, but that was hard to believe when he lived in a hut with her in an alleyway.

Ariel's stomach voiced a protest. Her chip held enough credits for a small meal. She struggled to remember where she might have left her dress, or at least her underwear, but they were nowhere in sight. Some of Brother Digital's hardware occupied one corner of the eight-by-ten-foot hut, but when she crawled over to look behind the neural jack and the computer gear, she realized that she'd been sitting on her crumpled dress for the last ten minutes. The underwear was still in hiding, but she could get another pair in her dressing room at work.

As she pulled the temperature-sensitive dress over her head and wriggled into its warmth, Brother Digital pulled back the rubber door flap and crawled inside. His long brown beard dragged the ground until he sat down with a heavy sigh, adjusting his clean polychrome robes around his chubby, thirty-year-old body. The animated rainbow of colors that cycled through the cloth looked brighter than usual, so BD had probably forgotten to reset it to a slower speed once he was done preaching. He dramatically tossed his long hair over his shoulders, then looked at Ariel and smiled. "Good afternoon, my priestess." Even his conver-sational voice boomed like that of an angry god.

Ariel snorted. BD had often said she'd make a perfect high priestess if she'd join him in the Church of the Ping. In a way, she felt honored, but she couldn't picture herself that way. "Did you enlighten anybody today?" She tried to sound perky so he wouldn't suspect she'd been using glitter.

"The great unwashed masses were not ready to hear my exhortations this day. However, the fog was thicker than usual, so perhaps my spectral aura was too dim to guide them to me."

Ariel nodded, amused as always by the way he talked. "That was probably it. Wait until summer is over, then we'll see the sun again."

"My mission must continue, fog or no fog. The Entity trusts me to deliver His digital message."

"Got anything to eat?" Ariel asked.

BD rummaged around in his robes and produced a Tastee-Glo candy bar, which he offered to Ariel with a bow of his head. "An offering to my priestess."

"Thank you." She forced a smile and took the candy, then quickly popped open the package and ate the creamy delicacy that glowed in the dark. He watched her in silence while she ate. The candy wrapper evaporated in her hand while the nutrient load dispersed in her bloodstream, al-ready making her feel better. BD never complained about hunger, and he always seemed to have a snack tucked away in his robes. When she finished chewing, he scratched his beard and moved closer to squint at her face. "Have you been crying?"

She nervously glanced at the bag of glitter sitting out in the open and shifted her body to hide it. He reached around her and grabbed the bag. She felt his hot breath on her face. "Glitter, my child? Have I taught you nothing these past few weeks?"

Ariel wanted to back away, but the roof was too low for her to stand up, and her spine was already pressed against the wall. "I'm sorry. I miss Carlo."

BD sat back and sighed. "I know. I'm working on a way for you to visit him, but I haven't had any success yet."

"The Entity?" She wondered if there was a chance.

"No. The Entity helps those who help themselves. But my brother may have special access."

Ariel didn't know if he was referring to a relative or to another Pinger. "Brother?"

"Yes," he said. "That's all you need to know right now. These are church mysteries that the unwashed would not understand."

"Oh." Another recruiting trick, she thought. She was fond of him, and she admired his persistence, but she didn't want to be a Pinger. And she didn't like being referred to as "unwashed," since she was as clean as possible under the circumstances.

"I'll keep trying," he said, lifting her hand to his lips. He kissed it gently. "Trust me."

She rubbed her forehead, pushing back against the hammering inside her skull. She needed more food. "Okay, look, if we can get something to eat, I'll help you look for recruits this afternoon."

He perked up and beamed his perfect smile at her. "You will?"

"And maybe we can meet your brother soon."

He sighed and sat back on his heels. "We can try tomorrow night, but he's hard to reach."

Ariel leaned over and placed her head against his chest, then put her arms around him. "I'll do whatever you want if I can visit Carlo."

"You understand what you're saying?" BD asked, brushing her long black hair with one hand while he put his other arm around her. "You've learned the error of your ways?"

Well, things couldn't get any worse. "Yes."

"You must give up the glitter. It interferes with the Divine Light of the Entity."

"Okay," she sighed, remembering the bag he held in his hand.

"You must wear the polychrome robe."

Maybe she could get one that fit better than his did. A belt might help. "Okay."

He held her face between his two huge hands. His gaze drilled into her brain. "And there is one more thing you must do. Something much more important, and far more personal, which will also give me great pleasure."

Here it comes, she thought. BD always seemed to be after one thing.

"You must enter the new God Box with me," he said. "We can do it tomorrow. And this time, you'll feel the full power of the Entity."

3

TAU Edison Wolfsinger, born for the Towering House People Clan, whom the Navajo call the *Kin yaa'aanii*, glanced up at the red sandstone arch that towered almost three hundred feet above Bridge Creek. Known to the Navajo as Nonnezoshi—one of the Rainbow Sky People frozen by time into eternal wind-carved stone—the white *bilagaana* called it Rainbow Bridge. Almost three hundred feet across, it was the world's largest natural arch, a stone bridge of great beauty and power. Gathering thunderheads foretold the approach of a male rain and provided a dramatic backdrop enhanced by the cries of ravens echoing off the high canyon walls. The sight filled Tau's mind with beauty and calm, prompting him to think how the reality of this environment was so much more fulfilling than the visuals in the entertainment sims. The longer he lived in the *bilagaana* cities, the more reality drifted into the fog of memory.

Minutes earlier, Tau had faced east to recite the Dawn Prayer, reminding himself to live well. With the prayer finished, he thought of the song of the bluebird and chanted:

> Just at daylight the bluebird calls.
> The bluebird has a voice
> His voice is melodious that flows in gladness
> Bluebird calls, bluebird calls.

Cool water lapped at Tau's feet where he stood on reddish black gravel—colors that reminded him of Mars. The scents of sage, water, and fish mingled in the dry air. He watched his naked reflection ripple in the clear blue waters of Lake Powell, waiting for the tug on his simple fishing pole that would tell him breakfast had arrived. Behind him on the sand, his footprints walked backward twenty yards to the sheer cliff face and the small brown tent that held his sleeping fiancée, Kate McCloud. Tau smiled as he heard her soft snores rise above the gentle lapping of the waves at his feet. She was real, the sandstone canyon was real, the lake was real, and beauty filled his heart. If the fish were real, too, everything would be perfect.

Tau noted that his tall reflection looked healthier than it had two months ago when he stepped off the shuttle. His long black hair was tied back in a ponytail, revealing deep-set brown eyes, high cheekbones, a wide face, and a sharp jawline. He and Kate had taken the time to go backpacking as prescribed by his father, Dr. Kee Joseph Wolfsinger, a famous medicine man in *Dinetah,* the Big Reservation of the Navajo that covered over 25,000 square miles of land in Arizona, New Mexico, and Utah. With so many relatives visiting his parents' house, this trip was the perfect excuse for Tau and Kate to be alone and enjoy the simple life again.

The most pressing demand on Tau's time was finding enough wild food to supplement the rations in their backpacks. It reminded him how he'd been sent out as a boy, supplied only with a bag of dried berries, to hunt enough rabbits to feed the family. He wasn't allowed to return to the hogan until he had enough rabbits for everyone, even if it took two or three days. When he got older, he was assigned to watch his uncle's huge flock of sheep. He thought it would be an easy job, but then he found out how much trouble sheep could get themselves into in the high-walled canyons that snaked their way through the plateau. He had to clear weeds from their feeding areas and put oil on their cuts. In the spring, he often had to stay up all night with newborn lambs to nurse them or protect them from coyotes.

A tug on his fishing line brought Tau back to the present. He knew better than to reel the fish in right away; the hook had to be set first. Knowing that the striped bass would rise to the surface of the lake to chase the tiny shad for their early morning meals, Tau had netted several shad the previous evening to use as bait. The shad spread out across the lake during the night, then returned to their schools for protection in the early morning hours once they were able to see each other. Around sunrise, the stripers ascended from the shadows to feed on the shad. When there were thousands of shad collected in one area, the stripers would attack in groups, disturbing the water in a "striper boil" of frenzied feeding activity. Tau had studied the shad and the stripers for two days to learn their ways, watching how they followed the same swimming patterns and appeared in the same places each morning. They were creatures of habit, just like Tau. Now, as he crouched beside the clear water, he could barely make out the dark shapes of two large fish floating above submerged boulders. Two fish didn't exactly make up a striper boil, but he only needed one or two. While the first fish pecked at the shad on the hook, the other one pecked at the transparent fishing line. Smart fish. Maybe too smart. They pecked again. It looked like some sort of conspiracy to frustrate Tau and make him go away, but he knew they planned on stealing his bait first.

A rumble from the Thunder People echoed between the canyon walls and shook the ground. A light patter of rain formed circles on the calm surface of the water. The Blue Flint Boys sent gusts of wind at Tau, fanning the water so that he couldn't see his fishy tormentors beneath the surface. While the gentle tugs on the line continued, Tau's body gained a wet sheen from the light female rain, rapidly gaining strength before it became the harder male rain typical of the summer monsoons. Already, Tau saw the tiny waterfalls starting at the top of the cliff face overhead. Expecting a storm, Tau had positioned their tent under a rock overhang that provided a partial screen from the rain, but he was glad to be out where he could feel the wet patter against his skin. Despite the early hour and the cloud cover, the breeze was warm and comfortable.

The tip of his fishing pole bounced twice. Tau set the hook and reeled in his breakfast, a striper that glittered in the light. A pretty creature, the top of the fish was bluish black, its sides were silver, and its belly was white. Several black stripes gave the fish a sporty appearance. When he bent over and released the hook, he was careful to apologize to the striper and thank him for being Tau's meal. While he watched the fish gulping air, he was reminded of life in his spacesuit, dependent on the fragile shell and the air supply he carried to protect him from the hard vacuum of space and the thin atmosphere of Mars. More than once, he had believed he would die gasping for air, just as this fish was dying.

Among The People, death was not a release from the Earth surface world to a better place. Tau understood that existence in the hereafter was shadowy and uninviting, located below the ground to the north. The dying person would walk down a steep cliffside trail to a pile of sand at the bottom of a deep canyon. Dead relatives, who looked as they did when they were alive, escorted the novice to the afterworld on a four-day journey. Old guardians stood at the entrance to the underworld, waiting to test and see if death had really occurred.

Nearby, the Navajo sandstone walls channeled runoff from the mesa into an instant waterfall; the water dropped hundreds of feet to pound the red rocks before it escaped into the creek. Tau's spirit soared. In this holy place, the death and shadows of the recent past seemed to be a half-remembered nightmare fading away with the dawn. In the past year, he had witnessed the gruesome death of his mentor, the destruction of the colony he'd built on Mars, the betrayal and murder of his closest friend, and so many other unnecessary deaths, including the men he had killed by his own hand. The thin veneer of civilization was so easily pierced by politicians, soldiers, and others who showed their animal origins when driven by greed or a need for power; this was not Tau's way or the way of his people, who strove to walk in beauty and remain in balance—*hozro*—with nature. He had promised Dr. Max Thorn that he would find the people responsible for his murder, and it was a promise Tau had kept, although he suspected that there were others—gray, faceless men in the halls of power who ordered the death of innocents while they sipped their morning coffee. But Tau was only one man, and the gray men were many. It was better to accept the small victory of fulfilling his promise to his dying mentor. Max would understand; Tau wanted a normal life, not the Don Quixote existence of a crusader against dark windmills and unknown forces within the government. The time of the warrior had come and gone; now it was time for peace and security.

Laika barked once inside the tent—a startled sound she often made when she woke up. Tau shook his head and allowed unpleasant thoughts to drift away on the current. To balance the bad events of the last year, he had set foot on a different planet, gained credibility in the scientific community, made contact with an alien civilization, stopped a war, and become engaged to Kate McCloud. Now, in this place of beauty, his senses were filled with the warm breeze, the circles of raindrops hitting the water, the splash of the waterfall, and the smell of a dead fish on the rocks by his feet. Maybe he had only imagined the vast conspiracy. Maybe it was really over now.

He smiled at the thought.

SIX hundred feet up from Tau, a man with multispectral binoculars watched him from the top of the cliffs on the opposite side of the canyon. Arnold Persinger lay stretched out on his stomach, his black T-shirt bulging with muscles that had not been grafted on in a biostore. Black pants, desert combat boots, a black cap, and a high-powered assault gun completed his outfit. He smiled. "I think that's him. Weird guy. He's fishing naked."

"What's wrong with that?" asked Kent Ross. Intent on the readouts from a row of tiny instruments and gauges strapped to his arms, he wondered why he tolerated the uninformed and usually inane comments from his beefy underling—although it was probably because Persinger could beat him up with one hand. Ross was in good shape, but he depended more on the gray matter in his head to get the job done. Dressed in a nanocamo jumper that changed its color and pattern to match its closest surroundings, he was almost invisible where he sat on a red boulder beside Persinger. His pockets were loaded with an array of unusual surveillance and communication devices. Their backpacks concealed the heavier items that casual eyes were not allowed to see. Since this was a covert op, rip-away patches identified them as special agents of First Virtual Insurance, covering the real emblems on their backpacks.

"It's just weird, that's all. Nobody fishes naked. Too dangerous." Persinger snorted and whacked his itchy nose, sending a large red ant plummeting 600 feet to a watery grave.

Ross glanced at his partner and shrugged. "He's a local guy. Maybe that's what Navajos do here. Some kind of back to the Earth thing."

"There could be tourists on the lake that might see him." He saw two more ants on his sleeve and sent them into oblivion with a slap of his hand.

"Too damn hot," Ross said, concentrating on his instruments again. "Only the crazy tourists come here late in the summer."

Persinger squinted up at the falling raindrops. "The rain should cool things down."

"Yeah, sure. They have monsoons here in the summer. Flash floods, temporary waterfalls, road washouts. Cools things down for a few hours, then it clears up and gets hot again."

Persinger shook his head. "Listen, I know we're just supposed to watch this guy, but he looks harmless. What do they want him for?"

Ross gave him a cool stare. "You know I can't tell you that."

"Just give me a hint. You don't have to give me the full jacket on the guy."

"Okay," Ross sighed. Persinger needed to be warned anyway. "Let's just say Wolfsinger has a big nose. He works for NASA, he's some kind of molecular scientist, he came back from Mars two months ago, and he's trouble."

"Mars, eh?" Now he was really interested. "I thought that was a one-way trip."

"Not for this guy. He's important. So is the McCloud woman."

"Well, they can't be all that important, out here back-packing in the middle of nowhere. And he works for NASA?"

"He's on leave right now. Time off after the Mars trip. As to this location," Ross said, sweeping his arms in an arc that took in the vast open country of high desert and red rock that surrounded the jewel of Lake Powell, "can you think of a better place to hide?"

"We managed to find him. Ow!" Persinger dropped his binoculars to slap at a line of ants marching into his shirt. When he rolled over, he saw the frantic activity of an anthill he'd been blocking with his body. "Christ. Ow! Ow!"

While Persinger peeled off his black shirt, slapped at the ants on his chest, and rolled in the rocky dirt like a maniac, Ross studied a handheld holo viewer topped with a tiny satellite dish. "Maybe Wolfsinger wanted us to find him. Or he just doesn't care. They say Wolfsinger took out Guardian while he was on Mars."

Persinger sat up and threw a handful of dirt down his back to hit the ants he couldn't reach. "No way. Ow! Guardian was a pro. Warlord trained him."

"I guess Wolfsinger was better. Probably some kind of deep-cover spook. Anyway, the spysat says this guy is a high probability match with the image on file. You want to call in the ground confirm?"

Panting, Persinger stood up and frowned at Ross. His torso was dusty and scratched as if he'd been in a fight. Raindrops streaked the dust on his tanned skin. "Don't tell me Nygaard is on this one himself."

"He's the man. We're just supposed to spot Wolfsinger and wait for orders."

"Okay, then you call it in. That Nygaard guy creeps me out."

4

THE five o'clock rush-hour traffic, heading north on the 101 through the Free County of Marin, seemed heavier than usual as it forced Dag Nygaard to slow his vintage 1984 Lotus Turbo Esprit to a modest 122 miles per hour. The hybrid power plant purred softly behind his head and warmed his back while the flat aerodynamic shape of the Lotus cut through the patches of light fog curling down to the freeway from the gentle slopes of Mount Tamalpais. Dag took a deep breath, enjoying the smell of the black leather that surrounded him, and remembered that his deceased father, Lars Nygaard, the original owner of the shiny white Lotus, had rarely been able to drive faster than thirty miles per hour on the local freeways. Car ownership was restricted in the San Francisco Bay Area, but Dag's federal employee exemption allowed him to operate a personal vehicle without paying the astronomical tax normally levied on FC Marin drivers. The elevated freeway sliced neatly through the rolling hills covered in private homes made of plasteel, glass, wood, adobe, and stucco, so Dag had a sweeping view across the blue gray waters of the San Pablo Strait to the distant techtowers of Berkoakland. On his daily trips along this route, he had rarely seen the encroaching fog dare to obscure the bay views from the east Marin neighborhoods full of retired holo stars and biotech billionaires.

The musical tones of Inge Hannestad's voice interrupted his thoughts. "You must be hungry by now." He and Inge had met in Oslo when they were seven years old. They grew up together, lived together, and took their first jobs together working for Dag's father in the old Storting,

Norway's national assembly. She knew his moods and sensed when he was tired or hungry.

Dag nodded in response. He wouldn't have to show up at work for another hour, so he pulled off on Lucky Drive to visit his favorite fast-food restaurant. Beyond the ruins of old wood buildings and the muddy cove, the Pelican Roost Town Mall—formerly known as the San Quentin Prison—sat on a picturesque point of land that jutted into the bay, providing a grand view of the water for its wealthy residents and shoppers. Dag smiled when he saw the regal white forms of great egrets stalking fish in the marsh.

A right turn took Dag into the shadows beneath the ancient freeway, then a left put him on the main road through the town of Corte Madera. He avoided the largest potholes in the road, but the wide tires of the Lotus dropped into craters every few seconds, jarring his teeth. The tops of submerged government office towers, their faces covered in simulated adobe for a Southwestern look, loomed on both sides of the street like cliff faces in the desert. A little farther on his left, the adobe walls dropped away, replaced by low commercial buildings encased in faceted sapphire glass at the nexus of two pedestrian slidewalks. Shoppers swarmed among the buildings in a frenzy of consumer lust.

"I wish you'd eat someplace healthier," Inge said.

Ignoring her, Dag stopped the Lotus in the empty parking lot between the antiquarian Borderlands Books and Captain Bill's Krill Grill, "Home of the Thrill Krill Burger." After a quick glance in the rearview mirror to check the ice blue eyes and strong Nordic face that had attracted so many women when he was twenty years younger, he levered his seven-foot-tall frame up and out of the low driver's seat, flicked a speck of dust from his expensively tailored suit, and strode toward the golden doors etched with artistic plankton images.

Inside, he found three people ahead of him at the stainless steel counter. Three more customers stood in a second line. His stomach grumbled when he glanced over the menu, finally settling on the tasty Bill's Thrill Krill Burger Deluxe. His choice made, he glanced around at the large holos of two automated fishing boats harvesting krill from cool ocean waters while they sailed along the inner walls. Misters sprayed the air with the scent of fresh fish and the sea. Burbling water and the clang of the occasional ship's bell provided atmospheric noises, while a narrator's voice described the virtues of krill.

". . . certain times of the year," boomed the narrator's voice, "krill gather in vast swarms in the waters of Antarctica and the northeast Pacific, making them easy to locate and harvest. They are then quick-frozen on board the harvesting boats to lock in nutrition and flavor. Nature's perfect food, zooplankton provides essential amino acids and proteins, fatty acids, and a taste that can't be beat."

The main advantage of krill, thought Dag, was that it allowed him to eat regularly on his meager salary. Because he was a federal employee, the government provided his clothing and his houseboat in Sausalito, but his promotion to management meant he no longer received hazard pay, completion bonuses, kickbacks, or any of the other perks enjoyed by his subordinates in the field. He had inherited the valuable Lotus from his father, and sentimentality kept him from selling it for the cash. With his low-frills lifestyle, he didn't need a big salary anyway, but it would have been nice to eat fancier food on a regular basis as he had in the old days. Fortunately, the addictive quality of the krill burgers and the atmosphere of the restaurant made Captain Bill's an appealing stop for four of his dinners each week.

The line took one step forward. Dag's stomach grumbled. The man in front of him, who looked like a weight lifter, stared at the young female cashier. Her tight white sailor's uniform enhanced the blinding glare of her superwhite teeth.

"I should have brought sunglasses," whispered Inge.

"Ahoy, and welcome to Captain Bill's Krill Grill, matey" the cashier chimed. "Batten me jib, may I take your order, please?"

"Yeah," said the weight lifter. Dag couldn't hear the rest

of his order, but the cashier's smile gradually faded to a look of horror.

"This doesn't look good," Inge said.

When Dag saw the gun in the weight lifter's hand, he rolled his eyes and checked his watch; he had half an hour to eat and get to work. With wide eyes and shaking hands, the cashier keyed numbers into the register to upload credits to the weight lifter's chip. With a heavy sigh, Dag quickly reached forward, put his right arm around the weight lifter's neck, and jerked backward. When the man grunted and the gun came up, Dag took it away with his left hand. The cashier just stared, her hand poised over the register.

"Leggo," grunted the weight lifter, trying to twist out of Dag's hold on his neck. Jerking his face to the right, he croaked, "Emo!"

To Dag's right, a small man with a big hand cannon stepped out of the second line. When his finger tightened on the trigger, Dag kicked the back of the weight lifter's right knee and pulled him to the right. The blast from Emo's gun made Dag's ears ring. He felt the sudden impact of the bullet when it struck the weight lifter in the chest. Startled, Emo was too slow to react when Dag pitched the weight lifter forward and reached into his coat. Emo sidestepped the falling body and grabbed the arm of a screaming gray-haired woman to yank her forward. Before Emo reached relative safety behind her back, the top of his head disappeared in a red explosion of hair and bone that made the old woman scream even louder before she fainted.

Dag sighed and shook his head while he put his needler back into its slim holster beneath his suit coat. A man couldn't walk into a restaurant for a peaceful meal anymore without someone taking a shot at him, or so it seemed.

"Thank you! Thank you!" screamed the cashier. She lunged over the steel counter to grab Dag and hug him with her arms and legs.

"Friend of yours?" Inge asked. She didn't sound happy.

"No," Dag said, trying to peel the cashier off of his body.

"She seems pretty friendly."

"Excuse me." Dag had to pry the cashier's arms and legs apart to make her release him. "I'd like two Thrill Krill Deluxe burgers, please."

The cashier shook her head, still stunned from the excitement while she sat on the counter. Her breasts heaved beneath her tight uniform, making Dag think unwanted thoughts.

"I know what you're thinking," Inge said. "Stop it."

A middle-aged woman wearing a name tag that identified her as Bitsy Zulu-Rinehart—First Mate, pulled the cashier back behind the counter and beamed at Dag. "Whatever you want, sir. It's on the house."

Dag put his credit chip on the counter and repeated his order. The cashier giggled while Bitsy grabbed two steaming Thrill Krills from the bin and handed them to Dag with an elaborate bow. "Anything else, sir? Anything you want is yours."

Dag glanced at the cashier.

"Watch it," Inge said.

"That's all," Dag said, passing his chip over the reader in the back of the register to transfer the credits. Warm burgers in hand, he turned away from the confused looks of the cashier and Bitsy to start toward the exit, making a mental note to call a cleanup crew on his way to work.

"Nice work," Inge said. "They were asking for it."

Dag nodded. The insulated wrappers around his burgers would keep them at the perfect temperature until he was ready, so he figured he'd eat them in the car on his way to work. With ten minutes to go, he'd have to hurry.

"Dag?"

"What?"

"Your car."

He looked up from the burgers and saw a group of four surly young men with bulky grafted muscles admiring the Lotus. They all had glowing nanotattoos of skeletons, disembodied heads, and obscure symbols that slowly crawled over any of their skin exposed to the light. They wore no shirts, and bulletproof plasteel plates were grafted onto their stomachs and backs like shiny turtle shells. Two of them sat on the hood trying to pry the window out of its frame. The alarm system that his father had installed would have given anyone who touched the car a quick warning before it delivered a near-fatal electric shock, but the bleeding hearts of FC Marin had recently passed laws to prevent the use of such practical devices. However, the thieves weren't able to break in through the molecular locks that seamlessly sealed the doors to the car body.

"Hey," Dag yelled, running toward the Lotus.

The two standing thugs yanked their hands out of their pockets to expose the steel claws on their fingers and the shredder blades that flipped up on the backs of their hands. The other two glanced at Dag and kept working on the window.

Dag didn't have time for this foolishness. They had touched The Car.

He reached inside his suit coat.

Two quick shots, and both guys on the hood did neat back flips to land in heaps on the bushes. The smartneedles from his gun were deadly and silent, blossoming inside the heads of his targets for maximum damage. The other men crouched, ready to fight. Dag hesitated at the back of the car, shook his head at the stupidity of youth these days, and popped two needles up their noses.

When Dag unsealed the driver's-side door, he saw the numerous paint scratches on the hood and gritted his teeth, trying to remain calm. He knew the nanopaint would repair itself over the next hour or so, but the perfect finish of the paint was marred right now, and he'd have to look at it all the way to work. He remembered when the whole area had been populated with reasonably polite wealthy people who respected nice vehicles, but he'd been very young then, and the whole area had gone to hell after the Power Wars and Marin's secession from the NorCal region. It would be one thing if the locals would remain in their own neighborhoods, but they had a habit of migrating across city

lines. Corte Madera didn't have an automated defensive
perimeter like some of the smaller rich neighborhoods
such as Mill Valley or Tiburon, and that allowed visitors to
transact business in local shops, but Dag thought the whole
desperate attitude of customer equality had gotten out of
hand. When thugs could just stroll into parking lots to take
cars apart, customer service had gone too far.

"Calm down, Dag. You need a cool head for work."

Inge was right, of course. Stepping over the hand brake
lever, he carefully folded his long legs into the tight space
under the steering wheel, careful not to bump the fire ex-
tinguisher with his right elbow, and settled back into the
semireclined seat for a moment. He set the warm krill
burgers on the center console. Eyes closed, he practiced
the deep breathing exercises he'd learned from his yoga
classes; part of the anger management series his employer
had advised him to take.

"Dag, you've got seven minutes to get to work."

Calmer now, he slowly opened his eyes. He released the
heavy clutch and switched on the ignition. Using the key-
pad on the center console, he tapped in a numeric code that
would deploy a federal cleanup crew to his current location. With that bureaucratic detail completed, he ignored
the oozing bodies on the pavement, shifted into reverse,
and concentrated on backing out of the parking space.

"I'm worried about you, Dag. I think your old age is
getting to you."

Dag sighed and shifted into first gear. "I'm only forty-
one." In an attempt to distract Inge, he switched on the
radio. The melodious voice of a trained feelie actor, now
running the country, spilled out of the sound system. President Rex King wanted the public to know how he felt
about the dangerous new nanoshield technology, and why
other countries weren't mature enough to own such a vir-
ulent defensive weapon system.

"You're losing your edge, Dag."

He didn't know why Inge liked to badger him like this.
Perhaps they'd just been together too long. "I'm not losing
my edge."

"I saw you hesitate before you shot the last two."

"I didn't hesitate. I aimed."

"You can't hesitate in this business. It could be fatal."

"Thanks for the tip. I'll make a note of that." Back on the street, he picked up a krill burger and popped open the wrapper, starting a timer that would dissolve the burger's packaging in under ten minutes. The simulated fishy scent of warm krill filled the air. Dag's mouth watered in anticipation while his stomach rumbled in harmony. On the radio, the director of the nanoshield project at the Los Alamos National Laboratory, Dr. William Ng, responded to a question from President King by saying that the technology was "perfectly safe in the proper hands." Dag switched off the radio.

"Ignore me at your peril, Dag. I only have your best interests at heart."

Dag bit into the warm burger, and his mouth exploded with flavor. Moments later, marketing molecules in the krill patty shot into his bloodstream, triggering endorphins in his brain to convince him that this was the best meal he'd ever had.

"I know you mean well," Dag said, his voice barely audible with his mouth full of food. She could be irritating at times, but he loved her, and he knew she loved him. He had never been able to stay mad at her for long—especially not after the accident. He still felt guilty about that, even though he'd done everything he could to help.

The turbocharger howled while the Lotus accelerated up the ramp heading north onto the freeway. The federal office in the Marin County Civic Center wasn't far, but he'd have to push it to be at work on time. His superiors were tough, and he had to keep an eye on every operation, otherwise the entire house of cards could come down.

"Dag?"

"Hmm?" In a rush, he crammed the rest of the burger into his mouth so that he could open the second one. The resulting blast of endorphins made him feel dizzy.

"You'd do anything for me, right?"

"Mm-hmm." He'd proven it many times.

"And you love me more than life itself, right?"

"Mm-hmm." Another explosion of endorphins hit his brain. He was lucky he could still drive.

"Then I want you to do something for me."

Dag swallowed the last of the second burger. "Anything, my peach."

Inge's voice dropped to a whisper as she made her request.

For a dead woman, she could be very demanding.

5

YVETTE Fermi woke to the rousing tune of Wagner's "Ride of the Valkyries." Coincidence, perhaps, but she had been dreaming of herself on horseback in a winged helmet and shiny gold Valkyrie armor, leading an army into battle at full gallop. Thousands of fierce accountants were arrayed against her with briefcase shields held high. When the music started, the full-length smartwindows in her spacious tower apt shifted from opaque black to crystal transparency so that she could see the brilliant sunrise. Living 1,600 feet up near the top of Lum Tower, the fog blanket never obscured her view of the eastern horizon, although she rarely saw the city during the summer months. She spotted herself in the canopy mirror overhead and marveled at how good she looked with her blond hair draped over the scarlet pillow. Her body was firm and muscular in the revealing nightgown. She sat up in her replica canopy bed, which was festooned in red silk to match her nightie, and sniffed at the scent of roses in the air. Eyes partially closed, she staggered toward the glass wall to check the weather, resolving not to stay out so late on weeknights. Her promotion to director of NASA's Ames Research Center two months earlier had conferred certain advantages, such as this luxury apt, but the social demands were tough, especially when she also had to entertain clients for her new advertising agency. Lost in thought, it took a moment for her to realize that her expensive view was blocked by two large objects in the middle of the window.

Baggies. Some people called them "flies on the wall."

Ever since mountain climbers had combined the porta-ledge sleeping platform with spider lines and molecular bonding patches so that novice climbers could safely hang from sheer cliff faces, clever homeless people in San Francisco had adapted them to hang from skyscrapers. With friction cups and sliding Jumar line climbing brakes to simplify vertical ascents, the baggies were able to gain sufficient altitude on the sides of buildings to be out of danger from predators and unnoticed by cops on the ground. With much of the free ground space in the city already occupied by the ramshackle huts of long-term "homeless residents," the impoverished community had greeted the baggie innovation with approval. An early city court case established the legality of homesteading on the sides of buildings as long as only one attachment point was used and they didn't remain in place for more than a week.

"Hey! Get off!" Realizing that they couldn't hear her, she tried banging on the thick glass with her fists. The dirty sleeping bags didn't move, but she saw a long white beard blowing in the wind.

Her fists balled, she glared at the ceiling. "Jeeves!"

The soft male voice of the apt's AI responded instantly. "Madam?"

"Get these bugs off my window!"

"The baggies have a legal right to hang there, madam. I am prevented from shocking them loose until seven days have passed."

One of the baggies, the one with short white hair and a beard, rolled over in his sleeping bag. He squinted at Yvette, then smiled and waved before going back to sleep. Yvette sighed in disgust. "Fine! Do I have any messages?" She started toward the hallway door, pausing only to bend over and pick up the black suedelace panties she had dropped on the floor the previous night; the self-cleaning rug had already carried them twenty feet across the room toward the disposal chute, assuming that they were garbage. And her Victoria's Covert Action panties were definitely not garbage.

"Mr. McCarthy is waiting to speak with you."

"Connect. Give me a privacy screen." As she padded down the hallway on her bare feet, the walls on both sides sensed her presence and displayed holos of that day's random selection of Impressionist paintings hanging in the Louvre. The programmed mister filled the air with the scent of lemon. The life-size semitransparent head of her assistant appeared three feet in front of her and maintained that distance while she continued walking toward the kitchen. "Pat. How's Russia?"

"Cold, Director Fermi. Very cold."

His strong young face did look a little blue, and frost coated his brown mustache. "Are our friends helping you with the locals?"

"Money talks, I guess. Now that everyone has been bribed and we're talking to the right people, this is going more smoothly than I thought it would. Professor Ryumin has negotiated access for us."

"Excellent," she said. When she entered the kitchen, Jeeves sprayed a Stimbucks caffeine aerosol into the air so she wouldn't have to drink out of a bulb or break a capsule while she ate breakfast. "How soon can we get the advance team to the mountain?"

"Today, if they're ready. All the roads into the area were vaporized by the blast, and scorched tree trunks are all over the ground, but a hovercar can make it in. I've seen the Russian reconnaissance photos and the NRO imagery, and we've identified two possible search sites. The Russians didn't send any ground teams in sooner because they think it's too dangerous."

"Maybe it is." Almost a year had passed since the explosion at Yamantau Mountain in the Beloretsk region of the southern Urals, and Yvette had still been on Mars at the time. Based on her famed spaceflight experience, and her new position as director, NASA in its infinite wisdom had chosen her to help the Russians find out why their mountain had exploded like a volcano. Scans had already determined a complete lack of unusual volcanic or seismic activity in the Urals at the time of the detonation. The blast sent a third of the mountain into the atmosphere to rain nonradioactive dust on neighboring countries for thousands of miles downwind. Atmospheric sampling aircraft dispatched from Ames had monitored the dispersal of the cloud at high altitudes for months, so NASA was certain that the event had not been nuclear in origin. Spaceguard had not tracked any incoming debris from outside the atmosphere, and there had been no aircraft or other weaponry over the Urals at that time. That left the kind of mystery and political confusion that Washington and Moscow didn't like, so an international ground team directed by NASA and the Russian Space Agency was investigating the massive crater.

Yvette's stomach rumbled when her nose detected the scent of bacon, eggs, and toast in the warming drawer. The Ready light blinked on, and she removed her silver breakfast tray, already decorated with solitary blue and white orchids at each corner. The crystal plate and heavy silverware were perfectly positioned with a contact patch to hold them in place while she carried the tray back down the hallway past the bedroom.

Pat cleared his throat. Yvette noticed that his teeth were chattering. "Professor Ryumin asked me about the rest of the team this morning. Do we know who else is going?"

"I have some ideas," Yvette said, padding into her home office with her tray. The windows faced east and north to let her see both the Golden Gate and the Bay Bridges when there wasn't any fog. Nearby, the upper body of the white-haired baggie blocked part of her view to the south past the adjoining bedroom wall. Yvette gritted her teeth. "Bastards."

"Excuse me?"

Yvette sat down behind the desk, wishing she had put on a robe. She didn't like giving the baggies a free show. "Nothing. Don't tell Ryumin anything right now. If the advance team finds anything interesting, I'll know who to call."

"Okay, I'll keep him busy with the first group."

Yvette chewed a bite of her eggs. "Let me know immediately when you have something."

"Will do," Pat said. Then his head disappeared.

Yvette glanced at the camera pod mounted on the corner of her desk while she munched on her toast. "Jeeves. Monitor."

A scaled-down holo image of the upper half of her body appeared above the camera pod. Yvette sighed, shook her hair, and pushed it back behind her shoulders. Good, but the nightgown wouldn't work. It looked intimidating, but not in the way she wanted. "Blue suit." The nightgown in her holo image disappeared, replaced by a blue business suit with a high collar. "Connect with Keith at AdForce Virtual."

While she nibbled on her bacon, the seated figure of Keith Longo appeared in front of her desk. Ready for her calls at any time, he was dressed immaculately in a black suit with a red scarf. "Hi, boss. Up late?"

Yvette glanced at her holo image, annoyed that she'd forgotten about her bloodshot eyes. Too late now. She decided to ignore his comment but made a mental note to slap him down if he started sounding too familiar. "Got those seafood ads ready to go yet?"

"The lab released the ads for testing this morning. Dancing plankton, persistent image, catchy jingle with a forced buy impulse."

Using technology "borrowed" from the virtual reality sim lab at NASA, they had already run one ad for a nano-tattoo company that drove up sales by 800 percent in less than two days. A few media buyers had already questioned the ethics of the AdForce Virtual "direct brain marketing" technology, complaining that mind control shouldn't be used to force entertainment sim users to buy products, but many more clients were lining up as they heard about the results from the nanotattoo ads. Advertising agencies had been using behavior modification techniques in their ads for years, so she really didn't see the problem with using a more effective technology to manipulate consumer purchases. Everyone wore brain-stem receivers anyway, but AdForce was the first agency to make use of them "to prompt wise consumer decisions." In addition, Yvette had access to a new feelie chip that would improve the reality of the ads in a few months, and she had already licensed the improved feelie hardware to other unrelated companies.

Synergy: that was the key. Her NASA job gave her contacts, advanced technology, and a nice place to live, but her AdForce business would allow her to retire wealthy by the time she was thirty, maybe sooner. If the business happened to fail or be the subject of any investigations, Keith would take the fall, shielding Yvette, the secret owner of the company, from any consequences. She considered AdForce Virtual a low-risk, high-return situation—especially now that their own subtle ads were being broadcast to bring in new AdForce business. They had hired twenty employees during the first month of operations, mostly tech geeks, and Keith was already looking for more people to supplement the staff. "Has Captain Bill seen the ads yet?"

Keith shook his head. "Not yet, but he approved the content last week."

"Don't wait. Show it to him now, and see if he goes out to buy food from one of his own restaurants. If he does, we're in."

"It's better if we wait for the test results. We don't want to send our client into convulsions."

Yvette sighed. One of their early test subjects had committed suicide after viewing the prototype AdForce VR that showed kittens eating breakfast cereal. "I don't need a squeamish COO running my company, Keith."

His eyebrows went up in a satisfying manner. "Oh, I didn't mean—"

"Show it to Captain Bill. If the ad doesn't work, fire everyone, including yourself."

"Yes, boss," he stammered.

CURLED in his sleeping bag, Eric Stamp looked over the ridiculously long white beard provided by the Covert Action Camouflage department and studied the 1,600-foot drop to the pavement. If he had to die someplace, it might as well be a quick death in a beautiful city like San Francisco, but he didn't relish the idea of a long fall, screaming like a schoolgirl all the way down, until he made a big splash on the pavement. The portaledge seemed way too small for safety, particularly with the strong breezes at this altitude. Birds didn't even bother to fly up here, or at least he hadn't seen any. The stress of having to stay up on the side of the building to monitor the equipment was distracting enough that he barely paid any attention to the hot-looking blonde prancing around her apt in a tiny nightgown. A spysat could have gathered the same data without risking any lives, but there weren't enough spysats in useful orbits to dedicate one to noncritical surveillance.

Stamp huddled around the pathetic amount of heat generated by the holocam recorder connected to Yvette Fermi's windows, wishing he hadn't screwed up his last assignment. His boss was a tough one to please. The man was a stone killer, and that had allowed him to go far in his career, but Stamp wasn't the only member of Special Ops who was surprised when Warlord left, and Nygaard became their group leader. Fortunately, Nygaard must have been in a good mood when Stamp reported that he'd botched his watch-and-pop job on the Escobar Power Cartel. As a result, Stamp and his partner, Frank Murdoch, had been assigned to the Fermi surveillance, a job dangerous enough that it might kill him just as dead as if Nygaard had used that nasty little needler he always carried around in his shoulder holster. Fermi herself didn't look like much of physical threat as long as she didn't see through their disguises, but she seemed to have connections in high places; high enough, in fact, that they might go over Nygaard's head. In any case, his perch on the side of this residential skyscraper was too dangerous. When they'd first watched their subject getting undressed five hours ago, Murdoch almost fell off his platform.

Stamp ducked his head into his sleeping bag where Fermi wouldn't see him from her desk, then punched up the scrambler code for the secure net link. After a few quick pings, he relayed his recorded data burst from the last twelve hours to his masters. The sensors picked up everything the blonde said or did in the apt, so he hoped someone at headquarters found it useful. With any luck, he wouldn't have to spend the entire week up there with Murdoch.

6

KATE McCloud went to sleep happy, wrapped in the warmth of Tau's embrace, her bare back pressed up against his chest in the soothing darkness of their tent beside the water. Rain tapped lightly on the tent fabric, and it lulled her to sleep after an evening by the crackling fire where she had listened to Tau's stories about Monster Slayer, one of the Hero Twins who grew into a man in one day and made the Earth Surface People safe from the evil creatures that roamed *Dinetah*. They were appropriate stories because they were camped in Monster Slayer's neighborhood near Navajo Mountain. She enjoyed listening to Tau's deep voice while his brown eyes twinkled in the jumping light from the campfire. When Tau told these traditional stories, his voice held the same breathy and dramatic tones that Kate associated with his father, Kee Joseph Wolfsinger.

Kate was sleeping better since they'd been on the Big Reservation, and the nightmares had finally stopped. Ever since her return from Mars, her dreams were bright and sharp, full of color and a strong sense of reality. She always felt some measure of control in these dreams, but never enough to keep bad things from happening. Tonight, for the first time in two weeks, they had returned. Thoth, the Egyptian god of wisdom, whose human body was topped with the feathered head of an ibis, walked across the surface of the lake and approached her. Thoth looked left, then right, his eyes darting like those of a bird, and clacked his long, curved beak.

"Kate McCloud," said Thoth. His voice boomed like thunder, but it had a screechy quality that reminded her of

birds. Since he drew the material for his image and sounds
from her mind, he appeared as her own stereotypical con-
cept of how a god should look and act, which was based
mainly on Hollywood holies and old flatfilms featuring
Charlton Heston.

"Hello, Thoth," she said, now quite familiar with the
ways of the alien AI. Although Thoth was a Free Mentality of the Gwrinydd race, and a powerful autonomous intellect, he didn't stand on formality.

Thoth clacked his bill a few times, regarding her with
black eyes that didn't blink. "The fortress of knowledge is
defended by the towers of memory."

"Okay." He always started out by saying something
cryptic.

"The Free Mentalities have decided that you should be
our conduit. I could continue to read your memories and
learn of your world in a passive way, but the slow datalink
we must use for direct communication is insufficient for
our needs. The Free Mentalities wish a more active connection."

She didn't like the sound of that, and this was the first
time he'd complained about the speed of the NASA
datalink between Mars and Earth. "More active? What do
you mean?"

Thoth clacked his bill, pausing while he searched for
the correct phrase. "You would say 'real time'; to see
through your optics, hear through your auditory receptors,
and gather data through your nervous system. To sense."

Kate shuddered at the memory of her first contact with
Thoth. "No."

Thoth tipped his head to one side. "It would require
only a minor upgrade to your neural pathways."

"You put me into a coma last time!"

"You are better prepared for this upgrade."

"No! Absolutely not!"

"All will benefit from this, including you. Communication through the nightly barrage of images generated by
the random firings of your neurons is vague and uncertain.
Datalink contact has not been established between us for

many weeks, limiting our understanding of your world. An active connection would permit immediate data transfer between us."

"No! I don't trust you to understand how my body works! And I don't want you in my head all the time!"

"Kate McCloud, I do not understand your concern, but I must ask—"

"No! Go away!"

She woke up with a start, banging her face into the side of the tent when she sat up. This was the first time Thoth had communicated with her so directly since she'd returned to Earth. Thoth normally confined his interactions to memory scans or conversational transmissions through the high-speed NASA datalink, allowing her to maintain her privacy. What he was suggesting now, this idea of using her as some sort of remote mediahead probe for the Free Mentality voyeurs, was a complete and total invasion, and there was no way she would allow it. Even if she said okay, Thoth's last "upgrade" had nearly killed her. Her colleagues might push her to do something like this in the name of science, but science could go climb a tree, for all she cared. She was a professional archaeologist, not a guinea pig. Let some anthropologist who was desperate to be noticed volunteer for this duty; she had a life of her own to lead, and her reputation had already been established by the papers NASA had allowed her to publish in the professional journals over the last two months. She thought of waking Tau to tell him about Thoth's invasion of her sleep, then thought better of it. This was something she could handle on her own, and there was no need to worry Tau. She adjusted her position in the double sleeping bag to keep out the chill air and snuggled up against Tau, careful not to wake him. Maybe she was worried about nothing, and Thoth had just been a regular nightmare? That would be good. Her eyelids felt heavy as she stared into the darkness.

TAU awoke to the sound of whistling in the dark, disturbing the peaceful noises of the lake water lapping at the bank and the soft sighing of the wind. His relatives had taught him that the sound of whistling in the dark was always a sign that a ghost was near. The *chindi* was the evil part of a dead person—no matter how cheerful or kind that person had been in life—that returned to avenge some neglect or offense after death. If a corpse was not properly buried according to tradition, if some of his belongings that he wanted in the grave were left out, or if the grave was disturbed, the *chindi* would return to the burial place or to its former dwelling. Despite his education, Tau felt it hard to shake off the omen of disaster associated with a ghostly visit—that he or a relative would soon die unless the proper ceremonial treatment was applied by a Navajo singer like his father.

While the rhythmic whistling continued, rising and falling in an unearthly tone, Tau remembered his first experience with a ghost when he was a boy at the reservation boarding school. While playing football, Charlie Begay, the school's best quarterback, fell and hit his head on a rock. Tau remembered the horror of trying to keep the blood from spilling out of Charlie's cracked skull until the ambulance came and took the body away. When he and the other boys went to visit Charlie in the hospital, they were told that he had died, but the nurse at the small hospital didn't mind if they wanted to visit him, so they crowded into Charlie's room and stared at the corpse, whose eyes were still open and staring at the sky. They all knew it was bad that Charlie had died indoors, trapping his *chindi* in the building instead of allowing his inner wind the freedom to leave the body and disperse into the sky. Back at the school that night, Tau had awakened to the sound of whistling in the dark, and the screen door to the big room where all the boys slept on cots creaked open to reveal a dark figure without a face. Tau was too scared to move or say anything, so he just watched as the ghost slowly walked inside and sat down on the cot next to Tau's where Charlie had slept for many years. In the dim light, Tau saw that it was wearing Charlie's football jersey. When Tau got up the nerve to grab the flashlight under his pillow and turn it on, the faceless boy snapped his head toward Tau and disappeared. The following night, the faceless boy in Charlie's football jersey returned once more, sitting on the cot beside Tau, but when Tau turned on his flashlight, it reached out for him. Tau was too scared to scream, but he jumped out of the cot and ran through the back door into the infirmary, which was part of the old abandoned hospital built for the soldiers. The ghost ran after him, its feet never touching the floor, slowly gaining ground while Tau ran at full speed, jumping over broken wheelchairs and crumbling medical equipment, and then made the mistake of running downstairs, where he was trapped until he used a piece of metal to break the latch on one final door, the door to the cold storage room where the dead had been kept. Something happened in that place, in that storage room where fingers of ice clutched at him in the dark, but the next thing he remembered, he was on an examination table in the infirmary. The disciplinarian had not believed Tau's stories until the third night, when he slept in Tau's cot to prove his point and the faceless ghost appeared once more.

The memory of that boy without a face still haunted Tau, and he still didn't know what he really saw that night, but it had scared him enough to remember it now as the ghostly tune kept him wide awake in his tent by the water.

Frowning at a sudden thought, Tau rolled over to help pinpoint the source of the sound, then reached out and felt a lump of fur. The whistling stopped, the object growled, and Tau felt tiny teeth sink into his hand. So it wasn't a malevolent *chindi* after all, it was a malevolent, snoring Pekingese named Laika.

Tau clenched his teeth and shook the dog loose from his hand. Laika landed somewhere on the other side of the tent; then he heard tiny footsteps on the sand as she charged him again. Tau braced himself, wondering which part of his body the needles would sink into next and felt surprised when Laika shot out through the tent flap instead, racing off into the moonlight. He sighed, thinking he could just let her take care of her business and come back in her own good time while he slept. She could take care of herself, but his conscience nagged him with reminders of the numerous coyotes and other creatures of the night that could be harmed by the vicious little dog. He finally felt around until he located his bandanna, wrapped it around his wounded hand, and crawled outside.

The moon wasn't full, but it was bright enough to blot out many of the stars. Laika clattered around among the rocks somewhere in the moon shadows of the cliffs, but the echoes made it hard to pinpoint her location. The cool air brushed his skin, giving him chills while he studied the landscape, watching for movement.

Laika whuffed, then growled, then began barking her head off. Tau rolled his eyes, wondering why Kate and Yvette had ever bothered rescuing the little demon dog when they'd had the perfect opportunity to leave her on Mars. Her previous owner had been a psychotic Russian general, so maybe some of his personality had rubbed off on her. One of Kate's behavioral psychologist friends had identified Laika's attitude as "little dog syndrome," as if putting a name to it made her easier to tolerate. The fact was, the little snot hated Tau for distracting Kate's attention away from her, and there wasn't anything they could do about it. Now, she'd probably found some lethal creature hidden among the rocks and was calling Tau over to investigate so she could watch the beast tear his arm off and kill him with it.

Tau cautiously picked his way along the scree of the cliff face and followed Laika's constant yapping to the source. She sat perched on a boulder, barking. When he looked up in the direction she faced, he saw the brief glint of some shiny mineral, or maybe a star, several hundred feet up at the top of the sandstone cliff "Laika? Quiet, Laika. What do you see?"

Laika glanced at him once, silent for a moment, then returned her attention to the same spot and continued yapping. Tau shrugged, not really caring to stand around out there when he could be sleeping, and reached up to grab her.

Something popped on the rock by Laika's right front paw, showering Tau's face with tiny rock chips. He jumped back, almost stumbling over a clump of sagebrush. "What the hell?"

Laika continued barking. Tau shook his head, wondering if this was some kind of trick on the dog's part. He blinked and rubbed his right eye to clear it, thinking a rock had probably fallen from the cliff behind them to bounce off Laika's boulder. Lucky it hadn't hit him in the head. He took a step forward and reached for her again.

The rock near Laika popped again, in a different place this time, and a metallic noise accompanied the shower of chips on his face. Something about the sound was familiar, setting off a tiny alarm in his head, and then he placed it. He ducked down into the shadows behind the boulder. A ricochet? Someone shooting out here in the middle of the night? Maybe some camper who didn't like yowling dogs? Unlikely. They hadn't seen anyone in the canyon other than distant houseboats out on the lake. In any case, he couldn't leave the dog sitting out there in the open on top of the boulder. He stood up and grabbed her. Something whistled past his ear and ricocheted off the hard ground behind him.

Kate. She was alone. While Laika struggled in his arms, Tau crouched and ran across the rocks, back toward the tent, stumbling over the larger stones he couldn't see in the shadows. He was making enough noise to wake the dead, but he didn't care. When he approached the tent, Laika broke free of his grasp and raced ahead. Everything looked undisturbed, so he slowed to a jog until he saw Laika hop back outside, sniff the ground, and run off to the water's edge where she started barking again. When Tau slid to a stop and threw back the heavy fabric of the tent flap, his heart fluttered. Kate was gone.

"Kate?" Tau looked around in a frenzy. He cupped his hands to his mouth and yelled. "Kate! Are you here? Kate!"

Hearing the dog's whine, he ran to the water and looked out. In the distance, he could barely detect a soft hum fading away. Small ripples struck the rocks by his boots; they could have been caused by a boat, since the water had been still a few minutes ago. He hopped around anxiously, thinking he should put more clothes on and go after her, but how? They had talked about the possibility of someone coming after them because of their activities on Mars, but why kidnap Kate? Why not Tau, since he was the one who had interfered with the Red Star operation? Frustrated, he yelled out across the water, "Kate!"

When a bullet thumped into the dirt near his feet, he remembered the sniper on the cliffs, picked up Laika, glanced around to see that there weren't any large rocks or bushes he could hide behind, and ran for the cover of the tent. It wouldn't be long before the first glow of sunrise lit the eastern skies, and he knew he'd be a much easier target in daylight.

PERSINGER licked his lips and squinted into the tele-photo nightscope mounted on his M40A3 model sniper rifle. The moonlight gave him plenty of illumination, and the image processor corrected for the differences between light and shadow on the landscape six hundred feet below, but his reflexes were slowed by the glitter he'd snorted three hours earlier as a way to pass the time. He was still shocked that the dog had been able to detect him at such a distance, and he had been unable to blast it before Wolf-singer plucked it from the boulder it was sitting on. The silenced 7.62 mm rifle had been handmade for this kind of sniper task by armorers at the Marine Corps Marksman-ship Training Unit in Quantico, Virginia, but it still depended on a clear head to make the shot at his distance.

Persinger sighed. Things weren't going well. After Ross had called in the sighting report to Nygaard, they'd had a long delay before they got a response. Nygaard was on a job somewhere and would be delayed, but he didn't want to lose the chance to grab the McCloud woman and pop Wolfsinger. If Persinger and Ross were successful on this job, it would mean a big bonus and maybe even a promotion for Persinger, still a lowly shooter in the organization.

And if he could get a promotion, he might be able to get away from Ross, who was such a straitlaced snot that he wouldn't even drink with Persinger when they were out on assignment. Nygaard was no party animal either; in fact, he was kind of spooky, but Ross was in charge of this team so Persinger rarely had to deal with their Nordic division head. They had both assumed that Nygaard would show up in time for the dirty work, so they left their boat hidden about a mile downstream. The sudden change of plan had thrown both of them off. Once Ross had left to work his way down the cliffs to the boat and then on to the camp where Wolfsinger and McCloud were sleeping, Persinger had plenty of time to do some glitter and watch the stars. Now, Wolfsinger was being unpredictable, and the dog was distracting him. If he had to, he'd climb down, swim across the river, and pop the target in the head at close range because it wouldn't be healthy to have Nygaard mad at him. On the other hand, if he could nail Wolfsinger at a distance, he could just take it easy until Ross or a recovery team picked him up in a helo, saving him a long climb down the cliffs.

Persinger tried switching the scope to other wavelengths so he could spot Wolfsinger's position, but the tent fabric had something in it that kept him from seeing through. The best he could do was infrared, but even that mode showed multiple heat sources that were too vague to shoot. He tried an experimental shot anyway, and the bullet ricocheted off the tent—probably that puncture-proof smartfabric the rich kids like Ross used for camping.

The radio blipped in his ear. "Apple to Potato."

God, how he hated the call signs that Ross came up with on their assignments. "Potato here."

"Apple has the melons. Time to go to market," Ross said.

Persinger rolled his eyes. "Confirm on the melons. Ready to pick the peach."

Ross paused before answering. "You haven't picked the peach yet? It was ripe half an hour ago!"

"The peach jumped out of the tree," Persinger said through gritted teeth.

"Get the peach picked, Potato! Apple is going to market! Out!"

"Out," he said, thinking how nice it would be to slice the Apple.

7

"NO! The nanoshield is a *defensive* system," yelled Rex King, banging his fist on the desktop. The polished oak of the *Resolute* desk, originally part of a Victorian British ship that had easily absorbed damage from ice floes on voyages above the Arctic Circle, barely thumped under the president's hand. He stood and faced one of the three armored windows that looked out on the garden. Drawing the gold curtain aside with a quick movement, a shaft of sunlight illuminated his salt-and-pepper hair with an angelic glow.

Senator Aaron Thorn flicked a piece of imaginary lint from the sleeve of his Brooks Armani CEO-model suit, pointedly ignoring the former actor's dramatic outburst. "Yes, Mr. President. Unfortunately, President Korsakov interprets the functionality of the nanoshield as a threat to his country. NATO and the UN are grumbling about it as well."

President King turned so that he could present a dramatic silhouette to Thorn from his position by the bright Oval Office windows. Thorn recognized the scene from *The Smoking Guns of October*, a political thriller he'd seen a decade earlier; some said it was the acting role that established King as presidential material. "How is that possible? The details of the nanoshield were never released!"

Thorn cleared his throat, choosing his words carefully. "I'm sure the CIA has that information. I've only heard rumors."

King glared at Thorn and walked over to a portrait of George Washington. "What rumors?"

"Someone stole project files from the labs at Los Alamos. Several countries learned about the nanoshield at the same time, and some of them lodged protests with

NATO in the last twenty-four hours. The plans are being auctioned right now. Or so I've heard."

A vein throbbed at the president's left temple as he walked back to the desk and leaned on it. "Why wasn't I informed of this? We have the largest intelligence-gathering apparatus in the free world, and I'm the goddamned commander in chief!"

Thorn shrugged, unimpressed with King's penetrating stare. "I'm sure it's just a rumor."

"This is unacceptable," said King, pacing on the blue carpet between his desk and the glass doors leading out to the covered walkway. "You have no idea of the difficult international situation this could create."

"I have some idea."

King scratched at the small lump on his neck just beneath his hairline. "I have less than two months before the election, and I plan to be here for the next term."

"I'm sure you'll be reelected, Mr. President. You're very popular. I've never seen a public approval rating as high as yours," Thorn said, hesitating only a moment before he smiled.

"And if voting was limited to the people who responded to those public opinion polls, and if today was Election Day, I'd be all set," King sneered. "Unfortunately, my opponent seems to think *he* can change their minds."

Thorn coughed and shifted in his seat. "It's possible."

King walked around to the front of the desk to tower over Thorn's chair. "And my opponent would have a field day if the nanoshield turns into a foreign policy disaster."

"Oh, I doubt that your opponent would sink so low," said Thorn, crossing his arms. "His record speaks for itself."

"Just so we understand each other," said the president, "my sources tell me you're going to use some kind of new technology to manipulate public opinion and win this election. These sources don't know much about it, and nobody has anything they can hang you with, but I can assure you that you're being watched. If you win the ball game, the referee is going to make sure the game wasn't rigged."

Thorn looked confused. "Why, Mr. President, that

sounds like a veiled threat. I have no idea what you're talking about."

"Of course," said President King. He turned and walked over to the glass doors, opening one of them slightly to get a breath of fresh air. The door squeaked on its hinges. "If Virginia Danforth were still alive, she would have known how to defuse this situation."

Thorn knew that almost a year had passed since Danforth had been killed in her home, but the president still frequently mentioned the name of his late senior director for national security and international affairs.

Inhaling a deep lungful of air, King looked at the senator and raised one eyebrow. "Just between you and me, Aaron, how did you hear about President Korsakov's opinion regarding the nanoshield?"

Thorn hesitated a moment, aware that anything he said might be recorded for future use against him. But he couldn't dodge such a direct question and still sound innocent for the recording, so he needed a verifiable response that would get the president off his back. He cleared his throat and sat up straight in his chair. "I spoke to him this morning."

DAG Nygaard stood at the southeast corner of Lafayette Park, across Pennsylvania Avenue from the White House, and looked up at the dark bronze statue of Major General Marquis Gilbert de Lafayette standing thirty-six feet above the ground on his white marble pedestal. Although he wore civilian clothing, a cloak thrown over his left arm partially concealed his hand resting on the hilt of a sword. Several feet below the nineteen-year-old Lafayette sat a bronze female, representing America, who offered him another sword. Completed in 1891, the eight-foot-tall Lafayette reached forward with his right hand as he petitioned the French National Assembly to aid the Americans in their fight for independence. Dag assumed that the real Lafayette had not been eight feet tall, although he had certainly been a larger-than-life individual who spent over $200,000 of his own money to support another country's war. Studying the right hand of the statue, he had to wonder if the general was reaching for a sword, asking for his money back, or tossing a pair of unseen dice. Pigeons had expressed their opinion of his heroic actions by painting his head white, so Dag assumed the birds were from England.

The scent of fresh-mown grass tickled Dag's nose. The air felt warm and humid. He glanced around, thinking this would be a pleasant and shady spot to spend eternity.

"You ought to stand on the north side of the monument. The snipers can see you from here."

Inge's voice grated in his head. He knew he was too far away for the Secret Service Countersniper Team on the roof of the White House to spot him, but Inge had good intentions. With the number of electromagnetic shields, laser triggers, vector guns, pulse trips, antiterrorist gas vents, virtual deadfalls, and a variety of more sophisticated defensive systems that guarded the White House and its grounds, he couldn't be too careful. Uniformed Secret Service guards patrolled the area wearing transponders that identified them as "friends" to the defensive-weapon AIs ceaselessly sweeping for threats. Although he'd taken the ten o'clock tour of the White House that morning, verifying the interior map he had memorized, he knew the AI defenders wouldn't bother him in Lafayette Park, and he had no need to get any closer.

Dag strolled around to the north side of the monument, dropped to one knee, and opened his black camera bag to remove his professional model Canonikon imaging unit. A motor whirred as he cranked the telephoto triangulation lens out to its full extension, then the push of a button dropped a spidery tripod down from the base of the unit. He stepped to one side of the monument, steadied the holo-camera, and framed an artistic image of the White House in the viewfinder. After recording one holo for his scrapbook, he turned a knob to activate one of the special features his employer had added to the unit.

The holocamera clicked, then a stiff housefly dropped into the palm of his hand.

Holding the fly between his right thumb and index finger, Dag casually pointed it at the White House. The cam-

era's viewfinder now displayed the White House as seen
through the eyes of the fly, although the stereo compound
image from the fly's optic nerves had been processed and
optimized into a single image for Dag's viewing pleasure.
The fly was also equipped with night vision and radar ca-
pability if needed; although Dag planned to leave these
systems shut down to minimize the chance of detection by
the defensive AIs guarding the president. Dag tossed the
fly in the air for a quick test of the flight controls and the
steam-powered attitude jets. The viewfinder image wa-
vered until the fly's gyrostabilizers kicked in and Dag got
the hang of steering into the slight easterly breeze. But the
fly wasn't quite ready for its mission.

Dag steered the fly to a neat landing on his palm, then
carefully shoved the fly's head into an indentation on the
side of the holocamera. When he withdrew the fly, its face
ended in a black, fuzzy point, and its entire head was protected by a transparent aeroshell made of stealth materials.
Holding the fly by its new helmet, he turned it around and
jammed its butt into another indentation in the camera to
attach a tiny two-stage launcher to its body. When Dag had
recorded the holo of the White House, the camera trans-
ferred the distance and coordinate information from the
laser range finder into the launcher's guidance system. Although the fly now had the appearance of a transparent
rifle bullet, it would look like a normal fly by the time it
reached the target zone.

"You're not having second thoughts, are you? You have a
flight to catch," Inge said. "Quit stalling and get on with it."

Dag sighed and casually tossed the fly over his shoulder. He kept his thumbs on the holocamera's flight controls
just in case the launcher's guidance system failed, then
triggered the launch button before the fly hit the ground.
Dag heard a tiny hiss as the little rocket fired, and the fly
shot away toward Pennsylvania Avenue. The viewfinder
image twirled a few times, then suddenly stabilized into a
steady view of the approaching White House.

Two seconds later, the image jittered briefly as the
launcher's first stage dropped free of the fly's body. The

west wing of the White House loomed in Dag's viewfinder. He gritted his teeth and tensed his right index finger over the manual override button when a hedge suddenly appeared in front of the racing fly, but the launcher's terrain avoidance system fired a vernier jet to alter the flight path away from the obstacle. The image jiggled again when the second stage of the launcher dropped free of the fly, reducing its speed and popping its head out of the protective aeroshell. Now Dag had full control of the flight dynamics. He homed in on the rear windows of the Oval Office.

During his flight training, the technicians showed Dag how to steer the fly in a random flight path to make its movements appear more natural. This motion also helped to convince the defensive AIs that what appeared to be a normal organic housefly was, in fact, a normal organic housefly. Watching through the eyes of the fly, the random movements almost made him nauseous, but the disguise seemed to work. The fly buzzed up against the windows, discovered that they were all closed, and moved on to explore the rear glass doors to the Oval Office.

PRESIDENT King took a deep breath of fresh air and visualized the anger generated by Senator Thorn flowing out of him while he exhaled. After his mild heart attack the previous year, King's doctor had warned him about controlling his temper, so he spent a few minutes each day practicing yoga asanas and meditating whenever he had the time. After another deep breath, he shut the door. When he turned to face Thorn, a small fly buzzed up against the glass on the outside.

"You aren't going to win this one," said King. He crossed his arms and stared at Thorn's shiny bald head. "The nanoshield is too important. Worst case, if other countries steal the technology as you suggest, then the balance of power will remain the same."

"They know we're going to activate a nanoshield around D.C. soon," said Thorn, studying his manicured fingernails. "Let's hope some Third World hothead doesn't decide to launch a preemptive strike against us just because they can't afford to bid at the auction."

A fly dropped out of the fireplace and stayed an inch above the carpet as it sailed across the room toward the two men.

King stared at Thorn for a moment, then walked toward his chair behind the desk. He wanted to hang someone for this major intelligence leak. He needed the secretary of state, the chairman of the Joint Chiefs of Staff, the director of the CIA, and assorted others in his office as quickly as possible "I think y've done enough damage for one day, Aaron. I have other appointments."

The fly remained an inch above the floor as it circled around behind the *Resolute* desk.

"I'm merely a simple messenger," said Thorn, rising as King sat down. "Let me know if I can be of any further assistance, Mr. President."

The fly rose behind the president's antique black leather chair.

King raised one eyebrow. He still wanted to put Thorn in his place. "I'm sure someone will be speaking to you this afternoon. Make sure you're available, and refer any future calls from President Korsakov to this office."

"Certainly, Mr. President."

When Thorn turned to leave, King thought about asking the senator to bring him a cup of coffee on his way out, but decided he'd be pushing things too far. With the changing winds of politics, Thorn might be his worst enemy this week and his closest friend the next. Then his train of thought was interrupted when something flew up his left nostril. He snorted.

At the door, Thorn looked back at the president and frowned. "Anything wrong, Mr. President?"

DAG peered at the dark viewfinder and switched on the fly's night-vision system. This was the tricky part, since he had to maneuver the fly up the president's nose as quickly as possible before King could sneeze or do anything to remove it. The image glowed green and showed what appeared to be a shiny forest obscuring the entrance to a darker cave above the fly's head. He carefully adjusted the fly's position and triggered two of the attitude jets to push it up into King's sinus passage. With the fly in the correct position along the wall of the sinus cavity, he used his right thumb to slide back a safety cover on the camera body, then pushed the red button beneath it. The image of the shiny cavern suddenly went dark as the fly's head exploded. The microwarhead, located just below the fly's compound eyes, contained a traditional and fast-acting poison customized for the president's use. The explosive charge would push it through the walls of King's sinus cavity and into his bloodstream.

While the traditional means of delivering curare into the body of one's enemy was by arrow or blow dart, Dag didn't think the Secret Service would have allowed him to carry a bow or a bamboo blowgun into the White House. However, Dag was amused by the idea of using a low-tech tree bark poison discovered in the eighteenth century. The Orinoco Indians of South America, who called it the "flying death," refined curare to kill animals and enemies. The principal chemicals of Dag's curare preparation were alkaloids of *Strychnos toxifera* that interfered with the transmission of nerve impulses between the nerve axon and the contraction mechanism of the muscle cell, causing paralysis and asphyxia.

"Dag, you're such a show-off," Inge sighed.

There was no way to please her. "I'm just doing my job."

"You didn't have to use a poisoned fly. They'll find the curare."

"Only if the medical examiner uses a spectrograph to find the poison absorbed by his tissues. And they may not bother if they think he died of natural causes. The lab will probably report that he died of an inflamed liver."

"He's the president, Dag. They'll go over his body with nanomeds to find out what killed him. You don't think they'll wonder why he's got a fly stuck up his nose?"

They might discover a few fly parts in the president's

sinus cavity, although the acid capsule triggered by the microwarhead's explosion would have dissolved the attitude jets and most of the fly's organic parts. Japan's Cabinet Intelligence Research Office had developed the fly, so any fluke discoveries by the medical examiner would point toward Japan instead of Dag or his employer. "It doesn't matter, Inge. They can't connect it to me."

"One of these days, your fancy gizmos aren't going to work. Why can't you just use guns or bombs like other assassins?"

Dag sighed. She would never understand. "It's the artistry, Inge. Any thug with a gun can kill somebody, but it takes an artist to do it with style. My weapon is my paintbrush, my victim is my canvas."

"And your ego is your worst enemy."

She was right, of course. He remembered how Inge had warned him about being so overconfident before her accident; the guilt of her death still lay heavy on his soul after all these years. Although her voice was always there to goad him, he still felt the hollowness of her absence whenever he caught the scent of roses, or detected her brand of perfume in a crowd, or when he retired to his empty bed after another long day without her. Inge had been his closest friend and his lover, smart enough to guide him through life and soft enough to comfort him. When she died, she took the best part of Dag along with her.

Dag picked up the holocamera, collapsed the tripod back into its base, flattened the telephoto lens, and strolled toward the north end of Lafayette Park.

ALTHOUGH President King thought something had gone up his nose, he no longer felt it.

Thorn still stood in the doorway. "Mr. President?"

Feeling very relaxed, probably because Thorn was leaving, he waved the senator away. Thorn shut the door on his way out.

The nanoshield intelligence leak took priority over everything else. The ID tracker hovering at the far left corner of his desk showed the floor plan of the west wing and the virtual bodies of the critical staff members in each room, so he knew that most of the people he needed were nearby. It was time to interrupt their meetings. He reached for the button on his desk that would summon his secretary, then stopped when he realized that he couldn't blink. His eyelids wouldn't move. When his mouth opened and he drooled on his sleeve, he knew something was seriously wrong. His heart seemed okay. Was it a stroke? What did a stroke feel like? He couldn't swallow. His neck muscles loosened, and his chin dropped forward to his sternum. Help. He had to get help. His left hand rested beside the button that would summon his secretary, and he was able to twitch his index finger once in that direction, but he couldn't cross the final inch. He wanted to yell, but the only sound that came out of his mouth was a faint croak. His upper body slumped forward, slamming his face against the oak desktop. Many presidents had used the *Resolute* desk since 1880—including John F. Kennedy, whose son used to hide under it when it was moved to the Oval Office. Now he felt that he was going to join JFK and the other eight presidents who died while in office, and this desk was his connection to them. But he couldn't be dying. He was the president of the United States, the commander in chief, the man who had his finger on The Button. His hands were turning blue. He had stopped breathing. Where was his secretary? Where was Greenspoon, his chief of staff? Normally, he couldn't get ten minutes alone before someone wanted his attention on some urgent matter; now everyone seemed to be in a meeting. He still felt his heart beating, which was good, but it was beating slower, and without air it wouldn't do so for much longer. This wasn't the death he wanted. He wanted to die of old age, but if he couldn't have that, he wanted to be cut down by an assassin while making the best political speech of his career. Then he'd be remembered as a great leader. That would be a proper death for an Academy Award winner of his stature. It had worked great for President Schwarzenegger during his otherwise unremarkable administration. King had often repeated his inspired campaign promise, delivered on the spur of the moment when a mediahead asked him about the hazards of being president: "Despite any consequences, I will go into the presidency with open eyes and lead our country to greatness." But there would be no more speeches. His eyes were wide open, but he couldn't even talk. Where was his wife, Carlotta, or his two young daughters? He knew he hadn't spent enough time with them for the last four years, but he wanted to, and now he didn't even know what they were doing at that moment, or that day, and now he'd worked himself to death and there wouldn't be any more time to spend. His neck muscles relaxed more, letting his head roll to the side. Lights popped and flashed in front of his eyes, the fireworks of death, warning his brain about the consequences of not breathing, but his brain didn't care, and his lungs refused to work. Beyond the flashes, he saw the portrait of George Washington, its eyes watching him, incriminating eyes that looked into his presidential soul and found him wanting. King knew he wasn't a military hero or a genius like Washington; he was just an actor, a man of the stage who played the part of a president. He felt cold. Cold and lonely. If only Carlotta would come in so he could say good-bye and tell her he loved her. She could put her soothing hand on his face one last time. But no one came in. No one cared.

His heart slowed and finally stopped. He twitched a few times, bouncing his head on the desktop, and relaxed into oblivion.

His eyes remained open. George Washington stared back.

8

GRUMBLING, Persinger reloaded his sniper rifle with nearly frictionless rounds that would be able to penetrate Wolfsinger's expensive puncture-proof tent fabric. When he looked through the scope again, he blinked in surprise. Fully clothed now, Wolfsinger stood in front of the tent looking as calm as if he were about to drink a cup of tea. The dog was nowhere in sight. Persinger shrugged, then chuckled to himself. The man was dumber than he looked.

The glitter effects were finally wearing off. He felt sleepy, but his hands were steady and he could focus his eyes better. Wolfsinger remained standing outside the tent, looking around at the scenery and scratching. Persinger adjusted the scope, filled his lungs with the cool air, let it out slowly, took careful aim at Wolfsinger's head because it was a harder target, and gently touched the trigger. The rifle popped with a gentle recoil as the bullet raced away, splitting the air with a crack when it passed the speed of sound.

When Wolfsinger flopped onto his back on the rocks, Persinger smiled with satisfaction. He would have preferred a splash from the target's head when the bullet hit, but the frictionless rounds had a tendency to go cleanly through the target without spraying all the wet stuff. Two more bullets in the prone body made sure that the target wouldn't get up again.

He smelled the bonus money coming his way. Best of all, Nygaard wouldn't be mad at him for screwing up.

Persinger spoke into his subvocal mike. "Potato to Apple."

Ross sounded annoyed. "Apple here."

"I picked the peach." He still had to check the body, but

he could do that when the helo arrived in a few hours to lift him over the river. The recovery team would remove the corpse and fly Persinger back to the office.

"Peach pick confirmed. About time. Bag the peach."

Persinger sighed. The rich kid was never happy, but Nygaard's opinion was the only one he cared about. Now Ross had told him to cross the river and check the body immediately, rather than waiting for the helo. He checked the time. "Potato is waiting for the bus home. Do you have a schedule?"

"Potato is going to market. ETA your location one hour fifty-six."

That was unusual. Normally, Ross would handle the rendezvous with Nygaard by himself on a job where they were separated. "Why does Potato have to go to market?"

"Hot Potato," Ross said. "Special request from the Carrot."

TAU watched from a safe distance as the big man in the camouflage outfit slogged across the river toward his campsite, his arms held high to keep his assault rifle dry. Laika slept by Tau's feet, relatively quiet for once, her nose whistling softly from the dry air; he hoped she was tired enough not to wake up at an inconvenient moment. When the man came ashore, Tau would be able to cross about 300 yards of exposed beach without being seen from the campsite, and then he'd reach one of the narrow serpentine canyons that gradually rose from the water's edge toward the top of the mesa. As a child, he had visited this slot canyon many times with his friend, Kee Shay. He remembered that the canyon provided a concealed, if somewhat more strenuous, route to the mesa top. They would startle his uncle with pebbles tossed from the cliffs over their campsite; exactly the sort of thing that would have earned Tau a dangerous reputation as a witch if his uncle had not been an educated Navajo.

Even the modern Navajos might suspect that Tau was a witch if they saw the kind advanced technology he was carrying around on his camping trip. When he stepped up on the beach, the armed man would realize that Tau's "body" by the tent was actually an animated holo. Tau had brought two portable holo projectors on the trip just in case he and Kate ran into any trouble and needed the distraction, but Kate apparently hadn't been able to use hers. The AI in the projector was able to imitate Tau's normal motions and respond to many kinds of external stimuli, so the proper response to a bullet "impact" had not been a problem. At close range, however, the man would see that the body had not been damaged and appeared to be sleeping. Then the trick would be to lose his attacker in the canyons or the caves, which he could easily do with a head start as long as there weren't any surveillance satellites watching his movements. But he also had a solution for the spysat problem, having packed the SatHat, one of the prototype toys built by Vadim Tymanov, a close friend from NASA who had died during his brief visit to Mars. Although it looked like a black pith helmet, the heavy SatHat was an optical phased array device run by a computer that generated dynamic fly's eye images of the ground beneath Tau and reconstructed those images in a converging spherical wave front over his head; a satellite looking down on him would only see normal terrain. Tymanov had dropped the project when the military developed a variation of the SatHat for combat helmets to be worn with expensive nanocamo clothing.

When the man stepped up on the beach and out of Tau's view behind a section of cliff wall, Tau picked up the dog and sprinted for the canyon entrance. His booted feet clattered on the loose rocks, but much of the area had recently been flooded with silt, damping out some of the noise. His progress was slowed by Laika, now struggling free of his arms. Adrenaline helped him cover the distance quickly, but he heard a shout from behind when he had almost reached the safety of the narrow canyon entrance. At that point, Laika escaped from his grasp, then rolled on the ground and sat up looking back the way they'd come. Tau stumbled, wondering what to do, as a bullet whined past to bury itself in the cliff wall.

"Laika! Come!" he said, as if the dog had ever responded to one of his commands.

Prompted by a second bullet that pulverized a small rock nearby, Laika shot past Tau into the canyon entrance, one of the many small tributaries of the Rainbow Canyon complex. Tau followed, scraping his chest on the smooth stone while he wormed sideways into the twisty passage. He desperately hoped he hadn't picked the wrong opening. Swirls of rusty red, black, white, and orange sandstone rose up at least a hundred feet to a low spot on the mesa, winding back about a quarter mile from the entrance. The scalloped ripple of the sheer walls, worn smooth by water, reminded him of two fancy red curtains spaced a few feet apart. His right boot plopped into a shallow pool of water; a warning that the passage had flooded during the recent storm, and that it could happen again. Overhead, the sunrise tinged the bottoms of the high clouds with splashes of red and orange; he would have preferred to see a clear sky at that moment. Another few steps forward and his confidence returned; there on the wall was the symbol of the Hopi Fire Clan etched deeply into the rock. His friend, Kee Shay, had scribed the symbol in this out-of-the-way place as a prank to fool any *bilagaana* tourists who might wander by. Pictographs and petroglyphs left by the vanished Anasazi Indians decorated many local rock faces. Above the symbol, a tarantula clung to the canyon wall. Tau's face passed within inches of the abnormally large spider, which didn't even move. Somewhere ahead, Laika barked, and the noise echoed between the rocks along with the sounds of Tau's heavy breathing and his boots thumping the sand. Tau edged into a wider area where he could jog, hopping over rocks and deeper pools of water, wondering how long it would be before his hunter found the entrance. If the man had any tracking ability at all, he'd find Tau's occasional boot prints in the sand.

Nearing the end of the tunnel, the water circled Tau's knees, slowing his progress even more. Overhead, the narrow slice of sky had darkened, and the rock walls wept with rainwater. Laika barked again, reassuring him that he had not lost her somewhere along the way.

Suddenly, tiny waterfalls pelted him from both sides. He sloshed forward with the water up above his knees, hoping he remembered how to get inside the cave at the end and that it wasn't blocked by debris, or rocks, or any number of other things that could have covered the entrance over the last twenty years.

The roar of rushing water increased, thundering through the passage like a freight train.

Around a sharp bend to the right, the cave entrance came into view, and he lost his footing on the slippery rocks. He grabbed at small outcroppings to slow himself down, but the powerful current hurled him toward the gaping black mouth of the cave.

Thunder roared, and he fell into the darkness.

KATE sat quietly on a padded bench in the back of the speedboat, wearing only a long yellow T-shirt and damp wool socks, with the motor howling near her head. Buffeted by the cold wind, her long brown hair streamed straight back from her head. Whenever she tipped up her face, the wind shot straight up her nose so hard that it took her breath away. The colorful sunrise lit the bottoms of the clouds, promising a storm, but the day would get warmer soon. Her hands were tied in front of her, and a ball gag filled her mouth—signs that she'd been kidnapped by a professional. The man wore a military-style jumper that changed its appearance to blend in with the surroundings, and his pack carried a logo with the words First Virtual Insurance, so she assumed he was some kind of government agent. She had no idea why he had taken her or where they were going. Although she didn't consider herself the brave or heroic type, she wasn't stupid enough to passively let events unfold in the hope that her situation would improve. And she had an advantage that had often served her in times of trouble: people underestimated her. While she kept herself in good physical condition through a regular yoga practice, she didn't look unusually strong or athletic;

she looked like a somewhat bookish archaeologist who had been rousted from a comfortable sleeping bag and tossed into a boat by a man with a very large gun.

She studied the dramatic red terrain, like Mars but with water and a blue sky. Hills of scarlet sandstone, mottled with black streaks, had been sculpted by wind and water into startling forms that suggested ruined castle battlements worn by time. Every few minutes, a stationary houseboat shot by, sometimes with a yell from the occupants surprised by the speedboat's wake. She knew Lake Powell was popular with tourists, and most of them were in the houseboats powered by fuel cells that puttered along almost 1,000 miles of shoreline in Utah and Arizona. The water varied from emerald green to cobalt blue, and most of it was clear enough to reveal fish and the rocky lake bottom in areas where it was less than twenty feet deep. No buildings dotted the shore in this area except for the rare boat refueling dock or the main Wahweap Marina, a few miles from Rainbow Canyon where she and Tau had been hiking. If she could escape, it would have to be near one of the anonymous houseboats; otherwise, her tied wrists would prevent her from reaching the shore.

The man at the wheel randomly glanced at her to make sure she still sat there, but the buffeting wind made any kind of conversation pointless, even if she'd been able to speak around the gag in her mouth. Kate looked sideways, judging which way she'd have to jump and how far to clear the boat motor on her way into the water. The bow was too high for her to see ahead, but she could lean to one side to watch for approaching houseboats. The hull thumped whenever they crossed turbulent water, adding to the noises that might mask the splash of her exit. When the man turned the boat for a course change, she found herself on the low side with a houseboat ahead and didn't stop to think anymore. With a deep breath, she jumped backward, the wind flipping her over so she landed on her face in the water, losing both of her socks. Twisting her face above the water as she bobbed to the surface, she watched the boat speed away while she snorted to get enough air through her nose. She tried to pull the gag out of her mouth, but it was securely fastened behind her head where she couldn't take it off with her hands tied. Turning toward the nearby houseboat, she fell into an awkward sort of a dog paddle. The water was cold, but it felt warm in comparison to the chill wind on the boat. Her face and her left side hurt from the impact, but she felt lucky that she wasn't unconscious or completely unable to swim.

The houseboat was the standard one-story rental model where four people could sleep, cook, cruise the lake, and fish for days at a time. They weren't built for speed or maneuverability, their main feature being that they floated well, and it was almost impossible for amateur sailors to damage either of the pontoons enough for the boat to sink. When she approached the bow of the light blue houseboat, lurching a few feet above the water on its silver pontoons, she heard two men talking with slurred speech.

"Didja see the size of that bass, Stan? Damn thing was as big as my arm!"

"That *was* your arm, moron. Gimme the shad bucket. I wanna see if I can nail me some stripers."

"It'll cost you a beer."

"Just gimme the bucket and shut up. You're scaring the fish."

"It's your face that's scaring the fish. I'm just an innocent bypasser."

"Bystander," said Stan.

"Yeah, what you said."

Kate drifted around the side of the houseboat and worked her way back along the pontoon, her shirt drifting around her like a mushroom. She heard a high-pitched noise, like a gear spinning, then something plopped into the water and tugged on her shirt.

"I got somethin', Stan."

"My ass."

"No, I think it's a fish."

Kate still couldn't see the two men, only a fishing pole held over the side rail. Her shirt tugged harder, helping her along, and she realized she'd been hooked. She tried to yell, but the gag muffled most of the sound.

"Didja hear that? Never heard a fish yell before."

Kate floated underneath the pole and grabbed the line that had started to pull her shirt up out of the water.

"Damn! It's a big sucker! Got some fight in it!"

Kate wrapped the fishing line around a ladder hook on the side of the pontoon. The fishing pole nearly snapped as the man yanked on it, then a wide face shaded by a white fishing cap appeared over the rail looking straight down at her. "Stan? You gotta see this. I caught a mermaid."

Kate rolled her eyes and grabbed the swimming ladder that hung down from the rear platform of the boat where the two men were seated. When she hauled herself onto the first rung, a beefy arm reached down to grab her tied hands and help her up. Her bare leg scraped against the rough rope attached to the dinghy floating eight feet away. She sloshed onto the edge of the platform and rested there, leaning against a bright yellow hydrogen fuel pod by the motor, and looked up at the two men like a beached whale. The fishing line trailed from the back of her shirt to a pole locked into a holder on the side rail. Both men, dressed in jeans and checkered shirts, looked shocked.

"Jesus, Mel. Nice catch. What kinda bait you using?"

Kate anxiously tried to express herself through the ball gag and shook her fists at them.

"What's she saying, Stan?"

Stan, the thin one, pulled a long knife out of his tackle box and knelt in front of her with an ominous frown. "I dunno, but she sounds pissed."

She wondered if he had actually understood what she said through the gag and fervently hoped she hadn't made him angry. The knife smelled like fish, and she could see the glint of translucent blue scales on the blade. Stan gave her an odd smile that made her wonder what she had gotten herself into, but he merely held one of her hands against the deck and cut the knot that held her wrists.

"You okay, ma'am?" Stan asked.

She nodded and rubbed her sore wrists. Mel grabbed

her under the arms and started to help her up while she reached around behind her head to untie the gag. She felt the barbed fishing hook tangled in a knot in the back of her shirt, so she'd get to that when she had a moment of privacy. In the background, she heard water sloshing. The boat rocked. Her eyes widened as she heard three soft pops. Mel's body jerked, then he fell against her, slamming her down against the anchor chain as he slid off into the water with a splash.

Stan jumped to his feet, still holding his knife. "Mel!"

Kate glanced over the fuel pod and saw her kidnapper. He stood in the slowly approaching speedboat with his gun pointed at Stan. "Kate McCloud! Come with me, and no one else gets hurt!"

Confused, Stan looked at the speedboat, at Mel's body floating facedown in the lake, and down at Kate, still crouched low on the deck. "You know this guy?"

Kate shook her head and whispered, "Do you have a gun?"

"Wouldn't know what to do with it if I did," Stan said with a shrug. He suddenly ducked down on the deck beside her and handed her the knife. "Take this. You might need it."

"What? Why?" Kate asked.

"You might wanna get back in the water," Stan said, opening the cap on the fuel pod with one hand while he lifted the anchor. "I'll be right with you."

The man on the boat yelled again. "What the hell are you doing up there?" He fired another burst into the hollow metal pontoons on the side of the houseboat, and the bullet impacts echoed through the hull.

"Don't be ridiculous," Kate said. "I'll go with him, and you'll be okay. Then you can call for help."

Stan gestured at Mel's motionless body in the water, now floating against the hull of the dinghy. "Mel's not coming back. This guy's not letting anyone leave here alive, except maybe you." Then he shoved her backward off the deck.

Kate didn't see everything that happened next, but she saw Stan's body jerking in the air over the fuel pod while she fell. She heard the thunder of bubbles when she hit the water, then a louder sound accompanied by a bright flash from the rippling outline of the houseboat overhead. Conflicting alarms in her head told her to stay underwater and to swim up where she could get some air; she swam down a little farther. It looked like the boulders on the bottom were about twenty feet down, where Stan's knife glinted against the gray rocks. Looking up again, she saw that the surface was covered with flaming oil. Large chunks of houseboat splashed into the water. A few yards away, the speedboat hull looked unharmed. The dinghy still floated nearby, but it had flipped over in the explosion, causing a slow-motion rain of fishing rods, bait buckets, boots, and fishing tackle. She almost gasped when she saw Mel's body bump against the dinghy, staring down at her with a startled expression. She looked away, sorry that she had ever involved these innocent men in her problems. She felt stupid for not thinking her plan through before she jumped from the speedboat; of course the kidnapper knew where she had gone.

Her shoulders felt tired from holding her place underwater. Water pressed in against her eardrums. She needed air, but she didn't want to surface where the man in the speedboat could see her. She glanced at the far side of the houseboat, but the oily water was flaming there, too. The knife glinted beneath her, tempting her with the security of having a weapon, but it was too far, too deep, and she couldn't waste that much energy. She looked at the dinghy again, avoiding Mel's gaze; the little boat floated upside down, and she saw a rolling pocket of air trapped underneath it, bright as a mirror.

Kate drifted upward, wondering how quickly the man in the speedboat would find her under the dinghy.

ROSS lay on his back in an inch of water in the bottom of the speedboat, his gun wedged into the gap beneath the rear bench seat. He blinked and shook his head. His ears rang, and it took a moment for him to realize what had happened. The last thing he remembered was shooting at a crazy fisherman armed with an anchor, followed by a big explosion. He swallowed, and his ears popped. He brought his hand up to his right ear, and it came away bloody. He didn't like seeing his own blood; it was supposed to stay inside his body where it belonged. How could a simple kidnapping have turned into this? Everything was going so well, until the crazy bitch got some harebrained escape plan into her head. His boss wouldn't be happy; he'd have to come up with a way to blame it all on Persinger.

He groaned and tried to roll over on his side, but pain took his breath away, and he lay back down in the water to let the flame in his lungs subside. Probably a cracked rib, maybe two, and God knew what else might be broken. He tested his arms and legs; his left hand was numb, and his left leg hurt like hell. What a crappy day.

The smell of burning oil prompted him to try getting up again. He propped his elbows on the bench seat, then managed to haul himself to a kneeling position so he could make sure his own boat wasn't burning. The water in the bottom of his boat seemed to be from the explosion, since he couldn't see any leaks. He nearly singed his eyebrows off when he looked over the side at the burning surface of the lake. The smoke made him cough, and that made his ribs hurt. The dinghy had drifted away from the houseboat, its tow line cut loose, and it looked like a mishandled Viking funeral with its burning hull and a dead man floating beside it. Much of the houseboat structure had been blasted off the deck in the explosion, and chunks of it floated on the water. The flaming ruins on the deck generated a column of smoke that would draw way too much attention. The park rangers wouldn't detain him once his superiors knew he was in custody, but arrests weren't rewarded in his line of work.

Ross slammed his fist against the hull when he spotted the woman's yellow shirt floating nearby. As he watched, it drifted into contact with a burning oil slick and burst into flame, just like his career was about to do. Nygaard had wanted her alive. He'd be reassigned to Antarctica for screwing up like this—if he was lucky. Disgusted, he dragged himself forward and settled his aching body into the seat behind the steering wheel. Looking forward, he saw the houseboat anchor, attached to a human hand, embedded on the point of the bow like some gruesome hood ornament. He wasn't in any shape to climb out on the bow and remove it, so the anchor would have to stay there for now.

This was all Persinger's fault.

9

THE *Ark of the Sun*, a former cruise ship with a dead-weight of 142,000 tons, a length of 1,020 feet, a 158-foot beam, and the capacity to carry over 5,000 passengers, sailed past the Point Bonita Lighthouse on the Marin headlands under a gray blanket. Flying the flag of the green sun, it continued its stately progress under the Golden Gate Bridge, due east into the bay toward Nova Alcatraz. Originally built in Turku, Finland, as the *Voyager of the Seas*, one-third longer than the biggest nuclear-powered aircraft carriers of the U.S. Navy, the ship had been refitted in 2053 as the solar flagship of the Greens, formerly known as the Retro Greens, and now known to the public as the Veggies. As it loomed out of the cottony morning fog that enveloped the historic rust-colored bridge, the great ship looked like the *Flying Dutchman*, a ship of the dead sailing out of dark oceanic myth into bright reality.

Operating on massive batteries while it sought the solar rays it required for power, the ship would spend little time in the foggy western end of the bay. Black photovoltaic paint had replaced the former white on most of the ship's exposed surfaces. When additional power was needed, solar panel "flowers" bloomed above deck fifteen, unfurling from storage masts to catch the sunlight with concentrator dishes 300 feet across. Old wood decks and fittings had been replaced with black steeloak, a synthetic wood that fit in better with the Green way of life.

An eccentric shipping magnate had donated the cruise ship to the Greens after seeing a news show featuring an impassioned plea for donations by Snapdragon, the Veggie leader, "crucified" on the trunk of one of the last re-

maining trees in Golden Gate Park. Regular Veggie
watchers knew the crucifixion was a deception that Snapdragon used repeatedly, but it still drew sympathetic
crowds. The mediaheads loved to follow Snapdragon
around because he was eccentric, unpredictable, and pho-
togenic, with a mane of blond hair that formed a halo
around his head. With powder blue eyes and a gentle,
bony face that ended in a neatly trimmed beard, he looked
like a religious prophet of the past. Snapdragon was a fa-
natical environmentalist who survived on energy absorbed through flexible nanotech solar panels that allowed
him to photosynthesize, pulling energy and materials directly into his bloodstream and eliminating his need to eat
animals or plants. When his panels spiraled open, he appeared to have a radiant flower blossom on his back; at
full extension, the flexible panels formed a tent that presented almost 100 square feet of surface to the solar rays.
Under Snapdragon's leadership, the Veggies led simple
lives, most of it outdoors in the sunlight wearing clothing
made of synthetic fibers. They were also known to exhibit
a deep-seated grumpiness as a result of their moral superiority and frequent hunger pangs.

Snapdragon stood on the open deck above the ship's
bridge. His white robes snapped in the strong breeze while
he heroically stared into the future, occasionally shouting
orders down through the observation window to the two officers in white uniforms who sat on the heavily automated
command chairs. The older officer, a paunchy man in his
sixties with a shaved head and a decorative VR eyepatch,
was Captain Heyerdahl, a Norwegian who had spent
twenty-two years of his life on the *Ark* in various capacities.
Although Heyerdahl was technically the captain, he'd been
a devout Green for three years—his off-duty name was
Geranium—and happily accepted orders from Snapdragon.
Heyerdahl learned early on that Snapdragon rarely got
angry, depending on his calm charm and leadership ability
to get things done, but he had also seen Snapdragon pick up
their rude former navigator, a man who looked much
stronger and heavier, and toss him overboard off the coast

of Mexico. The new navigator, Harri Holkeri, had flown to
the ship by helicopter to complete the voyage to San Francisco. He was a new recruit to the Green organization, unmodified as yet due to their sudden need for a navigator.

The rain wipers swooped from side to side on the glass
face of the bridge while Heyerdahl stepped out of his chair
to get a better look at the *Ark*'s mast. The base of the historic suspension bridge, 220 feet above the water, was fast
approaching. With a mast 214 feet above the waterline,
Heyerdahl had given the order to slow the ship to a crawl
to make sure they cleared the span. They had six feet of
clearance, but he didn't trust the strong currents beneath
the span. If the suction around the bridge supports pulled
them off to one side, the mast would be a lot shorter, and
he would be out of a job.

"Keep her steady, Harri. I don't want to be tossed overboard by our fearless leader."

"Aye, Captain." Holkeri glanced at him, then spoke in a
low voice. "And I don't think you have to worry about
Snapdragon. He looks like a lightweight."

"That's what our last navigator said. You don't know
this guy's history."

Holkeri gestured with his left hand, and a holo of the
Ark passing under the bridge appeared in front of his chair.
"Under the span, Captain. What history are you talking
about?"

Heyerdahl nodded, then leaned toward Holkeri and
whispered, "The man is dangerous. Used to be some kind of
a spook employed by the American government. Before
that, he was a Navy SEAL. I heard him talking to some old
military friend of his that came by for a visit in Panama. Remember the kidnapping of President Valdez about eight
years ago? Everyone thought one of the drug lords got him."

"They never found him after he disappeared from
Colombia, right?"

"Yeah, except that guy standing over us knows all of the
details, right down to where Valdez was put into a mental
hospital for safekeeping."

"Mr. Clean, leader of the Greens? Are we talking about the same guy?"

"Just don't piss him off. Navigators are hard to find on short notice."

The holo in front of Holkeri showed the *Ark*'s mast clearing the far side of the bridge span. "We've cleared the bridge, Captain."

Both men jumped as they heard an impact overhead. "Christ!" yelled Heyerdahl. "We hit it!"

Holkeri frowned at the holo display and shook his head. "Impossible!"

Heyerdahl glanced up over his shoulder, expecting to see Snapdragon ready to break his neck, but the leader of the Greens only smiled at something on the roof of the bridge. Then a plump little man hopped down from the roof to shake Snapdragon's hand. The man was about thirty and unmodified, so Heyerdahl knew he wasn't a Green, and he wore a casual syndenim jumpsuit of the style favored by technoheads. He laughed and slapped Snapdragon on the shoulder.

"Snappy! How the hell are ya?"

Heyerdahl looked at Holkeri. "Uh-oh. He's dead now."

Snapdragon laughed. "Norman, my old friend. Glad you could drop in. But you could have waited until we anchored."

"Where's the fun in that, Snap? You should have seen the looks I got when I jumped off the bridge. Nobody expects a jumper attached to a spider line."

Snapdragon nodded; then his expression became more serious. "I guess you got my message. I have need of your special services again, although it might be more dangerous this time."

"*Danger* is my middle name, pal. Norman Danger Meadows."

Snapdragon glanced down at the bridge officers, who quickly averted their eyes and went back to work. In a softer voice, he said, "I need to speak with someone who is very hard to reach."

"Nobody is that hard to reach. What makes this person so special?"

"He's dead."

Norman nodded. "Yeah, that'll slow things down a bit."

THE old Romanesque cathedral echoed with the footsteps of rats and the cooing of lost pigeons. The heavy oak door creaked on its hinges when Brother Digital pulled it shut behind Ariel. The door boomed into its frame: the sound of a crypt being sealed. BD's followers, the Pingers, had replaced the rotted ceiling of the nave with stained glass illuminated twenty-four hours a day by glow panels; the interior of the church sparkled with a rainbow of light. Images in the ceiling glass depicted Italian Renaissance–style scenes of Brother Digital preaching to huddled masses on the streets of the city. In most of the scenes, BD's head or eyes glowed with an unearthly light, but others showed angry flames in his long beard as he pointed at richly dressed people strolling past his followers.

Ariel smelled the musty swirls of dust in the air while they walked among broken pews sprayed with gang markings; obviously, the remodeling work was still in progress, funded only by donations from Pingers who had renounced their worldly goods to achieve enlightenment. Although Ariel had visited the Church of the Ping a few times, it still made her skin crawl.

A dancer and freelight musician named Cat Hendrix had introduced her to Brother Digital, assuring her that he communed directly with the Global Brain, making him wise beyond his thirty Earthly years. Ariel trusted Cat. When Ariel still worked at her chip design job, she had donated money to the woman many times while Cat performed her freelight act in the dim alley beside Ariel's office building. Over time, they became friends. Ariel had assumed that Cat's real name was Catherine, but she soon learned that the locals gave her the nickname for her habit of eating stray cats that wandered past her hut. When Ariel was living on the street and needed work, Cat introduced her to e-Bert, and taught her the tricks of the feelie trade. Then, after Cat became an emissary for BD's church, she disappeared.

The memory of Cat faded away, and Ariel paused be-

side the converted phone booth that BD called the God
Box. Inside, a black football helmet attached to a cobweb
of wires sat unused on a cracked plastic bench. On the outside wall of the booth, a small control panel with a micro-
phone allowed BD to speak to the occupant of the God
Box, as he had done with Ariel on three previous occa-
sions. BD glanced over his shoulder at Ariel as he neared
the high altar. "Come, my child. Your destiny awaits."

Puzzled, Ariel followed BD up the aisle. Three broad
steps led up to a dais topped with a white marble altar. On
the dome high overhead, two circles of stained glass
crowned the dimly lit apse, backlighting BD's giant head
with glints of gold, purple, and ruby. When BD mounted
the first step, three spotlights came on, pinning him with
brilliant shafts that made Ariel blink. The muted colors of
his polychrome robe cycled slowly while he climbed the
steps, and a 3-D holo of BD appeared behind the altar, enlarged so he was fifty feet tall. The spotlights followed BD
while the giant projection mimicked his movements.

Ariel hesitated at the bottom step. She'd spent the afternoon flirting with pedestrians so she could hand them
little holoflick brochures of BD inviting new recruits to the
next Pinger meeting. Although some people accepted her
little gift, most had handed them back or tossed them in the
gutter before BD could tell them how successful they'd become with the Entity's help. She understood their reactions
and gave them apologetic smiles. "BD?"

He pressed a button on the altar and beckoned her up
the steps. "No need to be shy, my child. You're among
friends now, and the Entity will watch over you on this
healing journey."

A white egg, about eight feet tall, silently rose from the
floor beside BD as he unfolded a small polychrome robe
and placed it on the altar for Ariel.

She had agreed to perform in this ceremony, but she eyed
the robe with suspicion. "You want me to put that on?"

"Not yet. It's your reward for a successful communion
with the Entity." He gestured at the egg.

Some reward. "Look, sweetie. I appreciate what you think you're doing for me, but I, um, have a headache."

BD smiled. "Take my hand."

Her cold fingers almost disappeared in his beefy palm. The front half of the egg popped open at their approach. "Behold the God Box Mark II. You'll be among the first to experience this new vehicle for communion with the Divine Light. Many will never achieve this great honor, but you are privileged, my child. You will be my priestess; the chosen mother of this humble congregation."

She didn't like the sound of his "mother" comment, but what the hell. If she could sit in the egg for a few minutes, put on the robe, and make BD happy, then he wouldn't pester her with these silly requests anymore. And he'd promised to arrange a meeting with his brother. That was what she had to remember—she was doing this for a chance to see Carlo, and for her own sanity.

BD asked her to remove her dress so that she could be "reborn into the world just as she had been born into it the first time." Whatever.

The inside of the warm egg was more comfortable than the original version of the God Box. The red velvet surfaces felt good against her skin. When BD placed a small cap on the back of her head, she looked into his eyes. "Will this hurt?"

"Your mortal shell will be unharmed, but the Entity's revelations will change your worldview forever. You will pass from your ignorance to a higher plane, casting aside your misconceptions to accept the truth of the Divine Light."

Ariel felt her eyes glazing over as he spoke. "Right. Will this hurt?"

He patted her head with a slight smile, then closed the egg to seal her into the darkness.

BD's voice echoed inside her head. "Take a few deep breaths and relax, my child. You must open your mind, and your heart, for the Divine Light of the Entity to enter you."

A tiny dot of ruby laser light appeared on the wall a few inches in front of her eyes. She took a deep breath, wishing she were somewhere else. Her stomach grumbled.

The red dot blossomed into a swirl of color; a small galaxy rushing toward her face. She shut her eyes and held her breath, but felt nothing unusual.

"Open your eyes, child," said the voice in her head.

Ariel cautiously opened one eye, then gasped and shut it again. There was something out there, hovering in the impossible space well beyond the limits of the egg's walls. But there was no escape. The glowing mist and streaks of rainbow light seemed to float through her eyelids, so the scene was the same whether she kept her eyes closed or not. A dark, hooded form, dressed like the traditional Grim Reaper, watched her with red glowing eyes. Its black robes flowed gently in a breeze she couldn't feel.

"BD?" Her voice sounded odd; an unsteady whisper that sounded higher-pitched than usual. "I don't like this. Get me out of here."

"Be patient, child. It wants to communicate with you."

She couldn't see its face, only the malevolent red eyes glittering in the darkness. It moved closer, raising an arm. She pressed back against the velvet seat, gritting her teeth as she willed the thing to go away. She knew it couldn't be real; it had to be some sort of illusion generated by BD's machinery. She gasped when something cold brushed her knee, then continued slowly up her leg, tickling the little hairs and raising goose bumps on her skin.

"No! Stop!" She jerked her leg to one side. The cold "fingers" stopped, then gently pressed down on her thigh as another hand pushed her opposite knee toward the wall. "BD!"

"It's all right, child. The Entity is learning about you. It finds a unique way to communicate with each of us so that we'll have the best understanding of its teachings."

"I don't like it!" She flailed out with both hands, hoping to push the creature away or maybe knock open the door of the egg. The soft padding of the walls yielded under her fists, but the door didn't open and the Entity didn't notice. Heavy weights pressed down on both of her thighs now, locking her into the seat so that she couldn't kick, then her arms were forced up against the wall beside her head. Icy claws gripped her wrists. The red eyes drifted closer to her face, and she turned her head to yell at the wall. "BD! Get me out of here!"

His voice was calm and infuriating. "The Divine Light must enter you, child. Then you'll be free to go. You'll understand very soon, and then you'll thank me for this gift. This experience changed my life and gave it meaning."

Ariel struggled, but her arms and legs remained locked in place. Her jaw muscles hurt from clenching her teeth so hard. She thought about screaming, but screaming would only show weakness, and she wasn't about to give in to this thing without a fight. Whatever kind of weird show BD had in mind, he wasn't going to get it. The warm air in the egg had turned cool, but her skin was slick with sweat. Her heavy breathing thundered in her ears in counterpoint to the pounding of her heart. She stared into the red eyes, just inches from her face, and tried to whack the illusion's face with her forehead, but the eyes didn't move, and it remained as silent as the grave.

The red eyes went dark. The hairs all over her body stood at attention as if she'd developed a static charge. She held her breath. When the eyes reappeared, they were much larger, now glowing turquoise. The eyes shot forward to engulf her in a blue radiance, and she fell through a turquoise sky, dizzy and spinning, toward a black globe dotted with clusters of city lights. Other globes, like moons of crystal, glinted in the distance. Rushing toward the black globe with impossible speed, the city lights resolved into glowing towers of rainbow glass, spires rising from a vast reflective plane of mercury. Air raced past her skin and rushed through her hair as if she'd been hurled into a wind tunnel. The ancient reptilian part of her brain overrode the rational part that told her this was an illusion. A scream rushed out of her lungs, amplified to become thunder. Heavy tears spilled from her eyes and accelerated toward the city of glass, forming a rainstorm that broke the tops off the fragile towers and left jagged points behind. She tried to slow her breathing, hoping this was some kind of sick virtual sim experience conjured up from BD's twisted mind, but her inability to close her eyes and look away made it impossible to ignore the jagged points of crystal racing toward her.

She sensed a vast presence watching her fall, and she heard BD's voice whispering inside her head. "The Entity can save you, Ariel. You must believe in it and let the light enter you. Trust me. I only want the best for you. If you resist, the pain of failure will be all too real."

This had to be a sim, but there was something more behind the technology, something greater that was testing her. Frustrated, anxious, and afraid, she screamed again. The scream ended in a gasp when a bolt of lightning blew off her left arm, leaving a smoking stump at her shoulder. A second bolt cracked into her left leg, blasting it off below the knee. Horrified, she could only stare at the damage, gasping and waiting for the waves of incredible pain sure to follow.

"It's your choice, my child," BD said. "You have to let it in to survive. The Entity is greater than any of us; a global brain born in the datasphere. You can become part of that, or you can cease to exist. The choice is yours."

The wind thundered in her ears, and she could no longer breathe. In a few seconds, she would be impaled on a crystal tower in BD's fevered imagination, and the virtual shock would be real enough in her mind to kill her. If this was a sim, it lacked the standard controls limiting the perceived reality that could devastate an unprotected brain. There was also a chance that this Entity thing was real, and at this point she was too desperate to argue. If she could communicate with her dead husband by giving in, one way or another, she would. Carlo might not need her where he was now, but she needed him more than anything.

"Okay," she screamed. "I believe you! Let me have it!"

The sharp point of the orange glass tower ripped into her stomach, impaling her on a lance of fire that shredded her insides and brought her to a dead stop, high above a quicksilver sea.

10

MARTIAN spring. On a lonely stretch of the Hellas Basin in the southern hemisphere, a red dust devil caught a rising thermal. The tiny dust particles, known as fines, soared on the twisting currents of air, seeking altitude and light, joining with their brothers to become a reddish orange cloud that grew and expanded. The cloud moved north and east, spawning more dust storms, until the entire planet cooled under a dense blanket of warming rust, obscuring the sun for months. Winds at the surface rushed like a phantom freight train across the stark landscape, dipping into the deep valleys and climbing the volcanic mountains with little effort, lifting dust more than forty miles into the atmosphere. At high altitudes, the erratic train moved at 260 miles per hour, basking in the sunlight, riding the rails at the edge of space.

Vulcan Gate. At the archaeological excavation in Umbra Labyrinthus—the Labyrinth of Shadows—a deep maze of narrow canyons at the summit of the volcanic Tharsis uplift, four human explorers lived as troglodytes, burrowing for knowledge in ancient tunnels under the soil. Working on the dig for over a year, the archaeologists had pressurized the tunnel and built an underground camp where they could work without spacesuits. Their studies had revealed more clues to the fascinating Gwrinydd warrior culture that had traveled interstellar distances and briefly lived on Mars long before humans evolved on Earth. With occasional guidance from Kate McCloud, who had a special Earth-Mars data feed to the Free Mentality AI known as Thoth, the team had made great progress in understanding the workings of the complex tunnel system built by the Gwrinydd.

The main feature of the tunnel system was the telepor-

tation portal run by the Thoth AI, now known as Vulcan
Gate due to its proximity to the Vulcan's Forge colony. Details from the extensive study of the Vulcan Gate were still
secret, known only to Kate McCloud and a handful of
other researchers, and information about the discovery had
never been released to the public. Except for brief tests, the
teleportation technology had not been used again since its
discovery, although government officials tried to prompt
Kate, the one person who had access to Thoth, into further
investigation. However, both she and Tau Wolfsinger refused to share many details of their Mars trip, except for
information that would help the archaeology team there.

A new find had rivaled the Vulcan Gate's archaeological importance. On a tip from Kate, part of the team had
focused its efforts on gaining access to a formerly hidden
tunnel, its entrance fused into slag by an explosion in the
distant past. True to form, Lenya Novikov, the Russian
leader of the expedition, allowed the other team members
to perform the two weeks of heavy drilling and careful digging required to break open the old entrance, then boldly
stepped forward to lead them into the new chamber.

A Gwrinydd art museum.

Novikov directed the placement of high-intensity work
lights to illuminate the massive chamber, and he used a
laser measure to determine that the chamber was about
eighty feet wide and just over a quarter of a mile in length.
Spaced at even intervals along the east wall were what appeared to be small mechanical devices, sculptures, and abstract pieces of art. Novikov took a few steps into the
center of the room, and a tall yellow post rose up from the
floor to block his path. A small tray extruded from the top
of the post at Novikov's eye level, then a rock crystal tumbled out of the post onto the tray. The rainbow crystal had
many jagged edges and points, but the most interesting
feature was the pulsing light at its core that projected shafts
of colored light onto the walls and ceiling around him.
Novikov put his face three inches from the crystal and
marveled at the tiny rainbows that arced from point to

point. That was when the points glittered and focused a new beam of brilliant red laser light straight into his eyes.

He tried to jump back but his muscles were frozen in place, his eyes locked into the center of the glittering beam that drilled into his head. He felt a swirl of odd, disconnected memory fragments: the ice-cream cone he'd dropped as a small boy, the death of his brother under the wheels of a robot tractor, the underwater search for sunken cities in the Caribbean with his dive team. While the images flitted past, he tasted spicy and sweet foods, heard phantom noises of babies crying and dogs barking, and felt a sudden range of emotions from deep sadness to joy. When the light suddenly switched off, he laughed for no reason while endorphins flooded his brain, understanding that the crystal had not been a threat but some sort of AI-driven guide or art piece that he couldn't interpret without understanding the Gwrinydd race that had placed it here. While he watched, the flashing light inside the crystal went out, the crystal rolled back inside the post—melding with the surface of the post rather than disappearing through a trap door—and the entire contraption plummeted into the floor. Aware of being watched by his team, Novikov cleared his throat as if nothing had happened and proceeded with his examination of the chamber, hoping he wouldn't trigger any more surprises.

Arrayed along the west wall were large paintings that appeared flat at first, then gave the impression of a full three dimensions when Novikov approached. The translucent white wall of the chamber formed a neat rectangular frame around the opening that was twelve feet high and twenty-four feet wide, separated from the next painting on the wall by a six-foot gap. Accompanied by two of his assistants whose cameras recorded and transmitted the moment back to Earth for posterity, Novikov smiled at the viewers, nodded heroically, and moved within a foot of the painting's surface. With Kate McCloud safely back on Earth, Novikov felt secure in the knowledge that he would receive full credit for this discovery, finally throwing the spotlight of science on the vanished alien culture that had lived there so long ago.

The image in the painting was sharper than any holo that Novikov had seen, and gave the impression of reality frozen into a tableau of still life. A mixture of complex organic and artificial structures depicted what appeared to be a scene on a village street. The crumbling walls of dark buildings loomed over narrow outdoor passages paved with rough cobblestones that twisted away out of view, linked overhead by gray metal catwalks and rotting walkways that threatened to collapse at any moment. Isolated creeping vines poked their heads out of narrow cracks in the walls. Novikov couldn't see any doors or other entrances to the buildings, but high windows glowed with a dim golden light. High overhead, the rough tops of the buildings trapped dark red clouds, held captive in a patch of turquoise sky lit by shafts of light from a far horizon. As his eyes adjusted to the odd angles and details of the painting's architecture, Novikov saw the white highlights of various skulls mounted singly on walls, grouped in abstract patterns, perched on windowsills, and suspended from hanging vines. The skulls showed surprising variety in their shapes and sizes, their only commonality being their bleached whiteness. A mound of light blue crystal jutting out from the base of the structure across the "street" drew his attention down to the cobblestones again, and he realized that dirty skulls formed the roadbed as well, their blank eye sockets full of brackish liquid that obscured their views of the sky.

While he stared at the scene and wondered about the alien artist who had created it, Novikov was startled to see the brief movement of a shadowy figure in the distance, disappearing into a bright patch of orange light that quickly vanished. He blinked. Had he imagined the movement? A foul, salty odor assaulted his nose, reminding him of the fish sold in the worst Moscow restaurants. Curious, he slipped a work glove out of his belt and brushed it against the surface of the painting. He heard a brief hum, then he gasped when the glove jumped out of his hand to plop into a dank puddle on the street.

Novikov turned and smiled at the camera to display his confidence in the face of the unknown, then crouched with a frown to study the work glove; it was damp but intact. Blocking the camera's view with his body, he tentatively reached forward to see if he could retrieve the glove, braced against any sudden "pull" from the painting. The painting hummed again and he lurched forward to land facedown in the street among the pavement skulls, staring into the faces of death. He tasted bad water and spat it out, wondering how to make it appear that he had lurched forward on purpose. Standing upright with a quick movement, he almost fell over again and felt as if he'd suddenly lost fifty pounds of his already diminished Mars weight in the lighter gravity. He realized he was breathing hard, and the air seemed safe: the biomonitor clipped to his shirt sounded no alarms, so he assumed it was the same pressurized air he had been breathing in the tunnel, although a stranger possibility that didn't make sense lingered on the edges of his mind. The tunnel air was odorless, but his nose detected more of the fishy smell, now mixed in with the sharp tang of ripe garbage, an earthy scent of swamp water, a lingering aroma of woodsmoke and ozone, spiced with a delicate touch of flowered perfume. A light breeze danced across the pavement, greeting Novikov with the steamy odor of a warm sewer that overpowered all the other scents until the wind stopped blowing.

Still shocked by his sudden journey into the painting that wasn't a painting, Novikov turned to look at his two assistants, then yelped when he could no longer see the tunnel; in its place was more of the dark village, dominated by a nearby building with blue-marble walls that steamed heavily, as if hot water were being shot through the walls from the other side. Grunts and moans drifted in the steam. In the center of the structure, a thick patch of fog randomly flashed, like lightning in a storm cloud.

Drawn by a desire to find his way out of the painting again, Novikov moved toward the flashing cloud. The easy effort of each step caused him to bounce lightly like a ballerina. It didn't feel like a heroic, manly movement, so he hoped no one could see him on camera. He reached for the laser cutting tool in his pocket; it wouldn't be much of a weapon, but it might startle any attacker long enough for Novikov to escape. But the cutter wasn't in his pocket—and his pocket was gone as well. When he looked down, he wanted to scream, but he was too shocked to make a sound.

Novikov's arms were thicker now, covered with semi-flexible plates of deep blue armor. His hands were sheathed in black gloves with diamond points on the knuckles, and an array of colored buttons covered the palms and the insides of the fingers. Weapon tubes were mounted on the backs of his wrists. He heard a dull thud when he slapped his chest, but he didn't feel the impact through his armor. The chest-plate bore a snowflake design studded with gems—diamond, ruby, sapphire, emerald, and topaz. His elbows and shoulders ended in sharp metal spikes. When he reached up to rub his eyes, he bumped a black helmet that started at his eyebrows and covered his entire head down past his neck, leaving only his face exposed. His cheekbones were thicker than he remembered, but the skin was taut over well-toned muscles, as if his face got regular exercise in a gym. Strange weapons and other equipment hung from his back and his belt, bumping against armored athletic legs that ended in knee-high boots etched with complicated designs. The heavy boot soles were of a high-friction design, providing a sticky grip on the street's skull cobblestones.

A bulky nightmare in blue armor jumped out of the fog to block his path. A nest of silvery tentacles hung below two glassy eye slits, and it raised both wrists to aim its weapon tubes at Novikov's face. For the first time in his life, Novikov's fight-or-flight response short-circuited as the alarm passed from his brain to his body, triggering an entirely new response that overcame him instantly—and he fainted.

AS they wheeled President King into the ER trauma unit at George Washington University Hospital, Dr. Joshua Rosenkrantz's team of twelve surgeons and nurses swarmed over the body. As the senior ER resident, Rosenkrantz had dreaded the moment when the responsibility for saving a president's life would rest in his hands, and he quickly came to the conclusion that there was little his team could do despite the presence of the most advanced medical equipment available. His father, Benjamin Rosenkrantz, had run into the same problem when he'd been expected to revive President Schwarzenegger, decapitated by an impossibly sharp monomolecular wire fired out of an assassin's net gun. After Schwarzenegger's death, Benjamin's career was shot, and he'd lived out his days as a cosmetic surgeon in Florida.

Out of desperation, Josh grabbed the electric defibrillator paddles and pressed them against the left side of King's chest. "Clear!"

The staff backed away from the table, and King's body jerked with the strong surge of electricity, but the line on the ECG monitor remained flat. Josh's final option would be to crack open the chest, which he could do in less than three minutes with a surgical laser and a rib spreader, to move the lung aside and massage the stalled heart with his hand. But one more look into King's dull, unblinking eyes with his penlight showed large black pupils, fixed and dilated—brain death had already occurred.

"Cancel code blue," said Rosenkrantz. Although the ER team performed similar procedures many times each day, they now understood the gravity of the event that had just occurred and glanced at each other with stunned expressions. Suddenly fatigued, Rosenkrantz leaned against the table and took a couple of deep breaths before removing his mask, clearing this throat, and heading for the exit.

The trauma wing had been cleared by the Secret Service, leaving only three official visitors in the waiting room when Rosenkrantz came through the door and shook his head. "I'm sorry, gentlemen. We did everything we could."

Chief of Staff Milton Greenspoon looked shocked, running a shaky hand through his thick gray hair as he took one step toward the doctor, then hesitated and looked back at Vice President Uriah Truman.

Truman blinked like an owl as he looked up from the tiny hockey game playing itself out on the holoviewer in his right palm. "Eh? What's the situation?"

Greenspoon sighed. "He said the president is dead, sir."

"Oh, dear," Truman mumbled, digging in his coat pocket as his right eye blinked uncontrollably. "Oh, dear." He withdrew a yellow inhaler and squirted it into his nose, visibly relaxing as the drug took effect.

Senator Aaron Thorn frowned at the vice president, then spoke in a low voice to Greenspoon. "We're in trouble. We have to do the right thing for this country, and Truman needs a complete pharmacy just to get through the day. We all know he's nuts. He couldn't be president under normal circumstances, and certainly not while this nanoshield situation is developing."

"There's always a declaration of mental incapacity, I suppose, but that won't be easy. And then we'd be left with the Speaker of the House."

Thorn shook his head. "Irv Grundfoss. Not much of an improvement. We have to hope Kyger's wonder chip works as advertised. Where the hell is he, anyway?"

Rosenkrantz touched Greenspoon's elbow. "Excuse me. I should speak to the First Lady. Is she in the building?"

Greenspoon shook his head. "She's not available right now, Doctor. She's busy."

"Busy? Her husband just died. Someone needs to tell her."

Thorn threw his arm over the doctor's shoulder and led him off to one side of the room like they were old chums. "We understand your concern, Doctor. No one is supposed to know this, but the First Lady is out of the country at the moment." He winked. "Official business."

"Ah, I see." Rosenkrantz nodded. "Then someone on your staff will be informing her."

"Correct," Thorn said, raising his eyebrows. "I'm sure we can count on your discretion?"

"Of course," Rosenkrantz said solemnly.

A short, red-faced man in an expensive light gray suit jogged into the room. "I came as soon as I got your message. We don't have a lot of time to fool around here."

Greenspoon put his hand on Rosenkrantz's shoulder while two Secret Service agents stepped into the room. Kyger shoved past Rosenkrantz on his way to the operating room door. Rosenkrantz stumbled sideways. "Hey, you can't—"

"Yes, he can," Greenspoon said. "He's here by presidential order. And you'll have to stay put for the moment; it's a matter of national security."

The doctor's face turned red. "You can't do that! I have patients to see."

Greenspoon motioned for the Secret Service men to come closer. "Make sure Dr. Rosenkrantz and his team are absolutely comfortable. They've been under a lot of stress today. Nobody gets in or out."

GREENSPOON winced as Kyger completed the relatively simple operation of carving the biochip out of the shallow depression in the back of the president's neck. Senator Thorn leaned over and frowned at the biochip while Kyger displayed it on the end of his gloved index finger, still damp with the president's blood.

"There it is, gentlemen. Our late president," Kyger said.

"He's quieter than I remember him," Thorn deadpanned.

Greenspoon sighed and looked at Kyger. "Doctor, would you mind explaining how this thing is supposed to help us?"

Kyger peered at Greenspoon with wide eyes. "What? You don't have an implant?"

"I was never one to jump at fads. To be honest, it all sounds like a party trick to me."

Kyger gritted his teeth and glanced at Thorn, who silently crossed his arms to watch the exchange with a slight smile. "I develop a method to offer people eternal life, and you call it a party trick?"

"I'm just a simple politician who needs to avert World War Three by making it appear the president is still alive," Greenspoon said. "Humor me. Explain how I can do that."

Kyger tapped the oozing hole in the back of the president's neck with his finger, then looked at Greenspoon. "Okay. The biochip records neural activity right up to the moment of brain death when the neurons stop firing. The neural map generated in the chip reflects the current state of a human's personality, his memories, his hopes and dreams—in essence, his personal identity."

"I don't see how this helps me," Greenspoon interrupted.

Kyger scowled. "Do I have to draw a picture? When a chip is implanted, nanoprobes are injected into the cerebrospinal fluid, and each probe floats around randomly until it runs into a neuron. The probe latches onto the first free neuron that it finds and proceeds to continually monitor that neuron's activity. At regular intervals, the probe secretes a binary chemical code, encoded in an aliphatic hydrocarbon chain, recording the current state of the host neuron and the probe's serial number."

"Sounds like the White House messenger service," Greenspoon said. "What happens to all the memos?"

Kyger drummed his fingers on the table. "The chemical codes are collected by the biochip until the subject dies, and the correlations between cell states infer the functional connectivity of the entire brain. Additional probes report the presence and levels of neurotransmitters. An AI embedded in the biochip works with the incoming data to develop rules and try to predict future neuron firings, improving over time as data continues to flood in so that it can eventually predict how the subject will react to stimuli, which memories will be recalled, and so on."

Greenspoon blinked. "And your theory is that these little machines record everything a person knows?"

"It's not theory anymore," Kyger said, visibly stiffening. "My biochips are quite successful. The personalities generated inside the Elysian Fields simulation are identical to those of the living models on which they were based. Close relatives can't see any difference."

"Except for one thing," Greenspoon said.

"And what might that be?"

"A simulation isn't the same as the real thing."

Kyger snorted. "True. It's better, because it's eternal."

"We'll see," Greenspoon said. "We'll see."

12

WEARING a plaid, long-sleeve shirt that belonged to a
dead fisherman, Kate carefully picked her way down a
steep, sandy trail less than a mile from where she had
struggled up onto the shore of Lake Powell. The shirt felt
dry now, but a diagonal row of holes through the front
served as a constant reminder of the innocent men floating
dead in the lake because of her actions. All she could do to
help them was to report her kidnapping and the two mur-
ders in the hope that someone could find the man in the
speedboat and arrest him. She also needed to reach Tau and
tell him she was okay, although she'd have to do it indi-
rectly. Of course, Tau had a plan in case they got separated
or came under attack, just as he had a plan for most things,
so she could relay a message to him if he was still alive.

A small cabin lay at the end of the trail below her with
a National Park Service flag flapping on a pole. A jeep and
a small flyer were parked outside. On the opposite side of
the narrow canyon, an ancient Indian dwelling occupied a
wide niche in the cliff wall, some fifty feet above the
canyon floor, under a dark and picturesque arch of reddish
black sandstone. Two long ladders provided the only access to the cliff dwelling, whose crumbling structures of
red brick formed tiered rows of squares and circles. The
cliff dwelling was important enough to have merited on-
site security provided by a live park ranger.

Feeling the pain in her feet and in her heart, Kate suddenly sat down on a rock alongside the trail and cried. Once
again, her world didn't make sense, and she wanted to lead
a normal life with Tau, happily poking around ancient
ruins, playing with the dog, watching the stars, learning

about vanished civilizations, eating strange foods, and sleeping warm and safe in his arms. She had no interest in saving the world, seeking high adventure, being kidnapped, killing people, or ferreting out government conspiracies. Once they had returned from Mars, she had hoped those things were behind them, but now it was starting all over again, and it wasn't fair. She had done nothing to deserve this except for being in the wrong place at the wrong time.

"Are you okay?"

Kate jumped and looked at the Navajo park ranger standing next to her on the trail. He had a strong face, kind brown eyes, an athletic build, long black hair pulled back in a ponytail, and a neatly pressed uniform. A heavy gun hung from his belt holster, and his name tag identified him as Peter Zah. He looked concerned, and she hated him for it. "Do I look okay to you?"

Zah held out a bottle of water. "Drink? Make you feel better. You get dehydrated up here without even realizing it."

"What if I don't want to feel better?"

"Drink it anyway."

She grabbed the water bottle, defiantly popped open the cap, and drank all of it without stopping for air. When the bottle was empty, she threw it on the trail where it dissolved into the sand. "There. Happy?"

"Couldn't be happier," Zah said. "Can I ask why you're dressed that way? It's not what I'd call typical hiking gear."

Kate almost laughed, wondering how she'd explain everything that had happened to her that day. "Long story. Let's just say I killed a man for his shirt."

Zah's face showed no emotion. "Not much of a shirt. It has holes in the front."

"Bullet holes," Kate said.

Zah offered her a hand to help her up. "I think we better discuss this in my office. Can you walk?"

Kate looked at her bloody feet. "I can't dance, but I can walk. Of course, I never could dance, so nothing's really changed."

"You sound delirious."

"Wouldn't surprise me," Kate said, taking his hand. "I'm having a bad day."

TAU'S fingers hurt, but that was better than plummeting to the bottom of the pit where the waterfall would have dropped him. His dripping body dangled in midair over the darkness. He didn't recall the pit being very deep, maybe ten or twelve feet before it connected with an underground stream that emptied into the lake, but it would have been enough to hold him down until he drowned. Swept through the cave entrance by the swift water, he'd managed to hook the dimly lit ledge leading to the side passage he remembered from his childhood, where Laika had already found a safe perch by jumping the gap before the floodwaters arrived. His friend, Kee Shay, had been the first to discover the passage when he and Tau were ten years old, allowing them to hide from the "monsters" outside; now their old playground had become his refuge from a real monster. If nothing else, Tau felt reassured that the man following him would be slowed or maybe even blocked by the temporary torrent, giving him time to reach the mesa top and get away.

Grunting, Tau hauled himself up onto the ledge, thankful that he had done some climbing and hiking since his return to the Big Reservation. The long flight back from Mars had softened him considerably. Laika calmly watched his efforts, then started barking for no apparent reason once he was safe and flat on the rocky ledge. Perhaps she was disappointed that he had survived. He rolled into a sitting position and took a few deep breaths of the damp air, allowing his heartbeat to slow. He rubbed his raw fingers together to get some of the stinging grit out of his skin. His main problem now was how to get out of there. When he was a boy, they had climbed the rocky tunnel that led diagonally up to the surface from the main cave, but there was no telling if it was still a clear passage.

He turned and studied the darkness beyond Laika, bumping his helmet against an outcropping of rock close to his head. Judging by the white goo on the rough floor, bats were fond of this cave. That was a good sign. The roaring water made it impossible to hear the squeaks of any bats nearby, but the guano looked fresh. He wrinkled his nose; the guano *smelled* fresh, too.

"Laika, come," Tau said, looking directly at the dog.

As he predicted, Laika turned and ran away. With luck, she'd scare away any animals that had taken up residence in the dark passage. His helmet would keep him from bashing his skull against the rocks, and the light on his watch would be of some use, but his progress would still be slow in the dark. Thinking about the hat, he took it off and examined it in the dim light from the entrance. If he remembered what Tymanov had told him when he built the prototype SatHat, the same phased array mechanism that generated the terrain image above the hat could also be used to generate uniform light. After fumbling around with it for a few minutes, he found the microswitches in the crown of the hat and tried flipping them in different combinations until the top of the hat glowed with an orange light from the tiny semiconductor lasers. He wouldn't be able to use his hat for a spotlight, but it was much better than trying to find his way using the glow from his watch.

He put the hat on his head and stood up in a crouch, moving forward cautiously. His eyes would adjust better once he got away from the bright cave entrance. The deeper pools of guano squished under his boots, and it made the footing slippery. Somewhere ahead, Laika's bark echoed through the passage.

The tunnel curved to the right for about sixty yards, and Tau had to crouch lower as he trudged along. His knees were already tired. Then he squeezed through a narrow spot and abruptly emerged into a larger chamber. Hearing a few squeaks, he glanced up and saw that the ceiling was alive with little upside down bat bodies watching the intruder in their cavern. The Mexican free-tails were two to five inches long, and restless now that Tau had disturbed them. In the light from his hat, the floor glowed white like dirty snow. To his right, Laika stood at the entrance to a side tunnel with an opening about the size of his head. If he remembered correctly, it was the way out, but a rockfall had reduced the size of the opening.

"Good girl," Tau said. He reached out to pet her and felt a promising draft through the hole. She growled at him and backed away. "Okay, fine," he said, standing upright. The bats chittered in agitation. He experimented by kicking the rocks next to Laika, and she jumped back farther as the debris slumped into the cavern. Then she ran off into the darkness, back the way they had come. His stomach rumbled, reminding him that he hadn't eaten since the previous night. In the distance, the roar of the waterfall had diminished, so perhaps the worst of the flooding was over.

Tau knelt and started hauling debris out of the side tunnel. He remembered how his grandfather, Hosteen Charlie Wolfsinger, had explained the secrets of a cave much like this one near his home on the western slopes of the Lukachukai Mountains. Tau's parents and his Uncle Joseph had gone off on a summer trip, leaving the nine-year-old Tau with his grandfather. To his young eyes, the area around his grandfather's hogan was quite different from his own home. The rocky crests o the mountain range sloped gradually down to glades and mesas where the land was almost level. The majestic Norway pine trees stood far apart with trunks like temple pillars among the cedars and piñon. There was little brush because of the grazing of generations of goats, but the slopes were covered with grasses, lupine, horsemint, Indian paintbrush, and more shrubs and plants than he could name.

One week after he came to stay with his grandfather, Tau saw his first bear on a ride up a thickly wooded slope. Two young brown bears were clawing at a rotten log to peel the bark and expose the white grubs underneath. Tau's pony smelled the bears and would have run away, but he held it still. Tau knew several of the bear songs, and he chanted them to secure the goodwill of the bears before riding away. By going farther up the canyon to avoid the bears, he discovered the mouth of a cave high in the cliffs. Leaving his horse tied to a bush, he worked his way up the steep wall of rock until he came to a narrow ledge that ran directly into the cave. Its mouth was partially blocked by loose stones and tangled brush, so he cleared it away carefully to avoid causing a rockslide. When his eyes became accustomed to the dim light inside the cave, he saw that it was maybe thirty feet to the back wall, about ten feet high, and a variety of objects were neatly grouped on the sandy floor, wrapped in thick coats of dust. There were three large pottery jars, rolls of buckskin and buffalo pelts, and the coils of ceremonial baskets. Lifting his gaze to the smooth walls, he was stunned to see the painted figures of the *Yeibichai* immortals: Talking God, House God, Rain Maker, Fire God, the Humpback Twins, the Warrior and his Brother, the Yeibaka and the Yeibaade, and four Flint People marching in solemn procession. The immortals wore elaborate ceremonial costumes whose blues, yellows, reds, and other colors were as bright as the day they were painted. Filled with excitement, he had clambered down the cliff and gone home in search of his grandfather.

When Tau returned to the cave with his grandfather, he asked the old man whether the cave might be an Anasazi burial site or the resting place of a Navajo medicine man. His grandfather shook his head and looked around carefully, fanning the dust to expose the empty jars and a bundle that had contained eagle feathers. He didn't touch the rolled buckskin bundles for fear of destroying them.

"I think," said his grandfather, lifting his eyes to study the details of the immortals painted on the walls, "some medicine man was afraid his ceremony would be forgotten. He spent much time here in his secret place, smoothing the walls and painting the *Yeibichai* figures. It may have been around the time of the Long Walk to the Bosque Redondo, when the soldiers rounded up our people, and when he knew he'd have to leave, he brought his medicine bundles here to hide them. He camouflaged the cave mouth to protect the medicine from the soldiers and the Utes, intending to recover these things when he returned, but he never came back. So many died back then."

Then his grandfather pointed with his lips at a small opening in the ceiling at the back of the cave. The edge of the opening was white, and a cool breeze came out of the hole like a long sigh from the earth. "Maybe he had a back way out of this place. The bats know the truth. Some winter evening, before they go out, you can ask them to tell you the story of the old medicine man."

They left the cave as they had found it, building up the stone and brush wall again to cover the entrance. When they were done, Tau's grandfather had warned him, "Tell no one about this place. We don't want to be accused of handling a dead person's property." Tau never told anyone. However, he was able to keep a small flint arrowhead he found there after he asked his grandfather if it would be okay. The arrowhead was the first piece of medicine equipment he owned, and he still kept it for good luck.

The squeaking of the bats grew louder near Tau's head.

Barking like mad, Laika suddenly darted back into the chamber and slid to a stop next to Tau. Tau had no idea what she was barking about, and he didn't care, but he noticed that the roar of distant water had ceased, replaced now by a soft gurgling that echoed in the darkness as a counterpoint to the chittering of the bats. He continued tossing rocks out of the side tunnel. Five minutes of sweaty effort had not cleared enough rock away for him to climb into the passage; the blockage seemed to extend much farther than he had hoped.

Noting that his knees and feet were starting to get wet, Tau gradually became aware that the gurgling sound had increased. The bats were more agitated now, with some of them leaving their perches to flit about the cavern. Tau's eyes widened when he realized what was happening: the roar of the waterfall had diminished because the pit was full of water, and that water was now flooding his tunnel.

His hands dug into the rockfall, scattering rocks wildly in his desperation to clear the side passage. If he couldn't clear it, he'd drown in a hole in the ground. His raw fingers had so many cuts on them that his blood colored the rocks he threw aside. Sweat dripped from his forehead, stinging his eyes. His heart hammered in his chest. He had to get out, not only for himself, but to get help for Kate. She needed him once more, and he couldn't let her down.

The relentless floodwaters continued to rise, swirling and bubbling around his thighs where he knelt, cold fingers clutching at his legs, beckoning him into a watery grave.

13

LENYA Novikov opened his eyes and stared into the face of a nightmare. His back was on some sort of a hard surface, and the ceiling glowed with a bright golden light above the armored creature that loomed over him. Spatters of congealed liquid and dried food decorated the ceiling. A general odor of urine and decay permeated the air.

"Grakheh shohho ikkikkheh," said the nightmare, croaking and gasping. The silvery tentacles on its face dangled just a few inches above Novikov's neck as it watched him through its dark mirrored eye slits.

Novikov's head felt funny, and the room had a slight spin due to his dizziness. Gradually, the random noises in the background resolved into individual voices and shouts that sounded like birds and monkeys in a knife fight, punctuated by the crashes of breaking glass. Moments later, the screeches and croaks filtering through his brain became Russian words he could clearly understand. Remembering that he was trapped inside some kind of interactive painting on Mars, he quickly realized how unlikely it was to hear Russian spoken by alien voices, so there had to be some sort of real-time AI translation happening in his head.

The nightmare spoke again. "Wasn't realizing you had battle injuries, squire. Most what come Skulltown way stops in for a rebuild, then comes here after to drinks and forgetting."

Novikov blinked. The translation wasn't very good, but at least he could make out the thing's meaning. The thing slapped its neck, causing its nightmare face to retract into the blue helmet, exposing the scarred and pink human face beneath. A fringe of white beard made him look old. He held out his hand. "Welcoming to Deadhead's. I'm Gwilym, official fog warrior, peacekeeper, and doormans, formerly of the Tenth Highland."

"Lenya Novikov," he replied, standing up. A lump under his foot prompted him to move to one side, revealing the dead rat he'd been standing on. Several of its deceased fellows were scattered around the room under tables, chairs, and the booted feet of rough-looking patrons; others were pinned to the walls with exotic knives.

"Funny name," Gwilym said, pointing at his face. "Go ahead and hits me."

"What?"

Gwilym frowned. "Nots trying to insults me, are you, squire? Hots off battlefield you're thinkings I'm too old for greetings?"

"Old? No, I wasn't thinkings, er, *thinking* that." He felt his mouth and tongue forming strange words as he spoke.

Gwilym gestured at his face again and thrust out his chin. "Then go aheads. Pops me good ones."

Lacking any knowledge of Gwrinydd warrior customs, Novikov sighed, made a fist, and lightly punched Gwilym in the face. The man keeled over and crashed to the floor. Horrified, Novikov bent over to help him up. "Sorry, so sorry."

"Bloodwine, squire, I didn't say takes me heads off." He took Novikov's arm, staggered to his feet, shook his head, then cocked his arm and punched Novikov in the face.

Novikov flattened a small table beneath him while he tumbled to the floor. The two occupants of the splintered table, dressed like Novikov except for different designs on their chestplates, glared down at him with drinks in their hands. Novikov worked his jaw, surprised that he didn't feel much pain, and aimed a lopsided smile at the two drinkers. "Sorry."

The drinkers both stood up and repeatedly kicked Novikov in the stomach and back before downing their drinks, smashing both glasses against Novikov's head, and stomping away. Relatively unharmed, Novikov stood up, brushed some glass off his face, and faced Gwilym again.

He had to get out of there before someone killed him in greeting. "I'm sorry. I seem to be getting off on the wrong foot here, but I'm a stranger to this place."

Gwilym slapped his shoulder above the spike. "That's all rights, squire. Alls are welcomes at Deadhead's. A grunt's gotta wind downs someplace, eh?"

"No, I mean I'm new in this town, or village, or whatever it is."

All other conversations stopped. Novikov suddenly felt the attention of forty pairs of eyes staring at him. The hairs rose on the back of his neck, then Gwilym whacked him in the side of the head with his open palm. "Joking, yes? Funny name, funny fellow."

Novikov realized that Gwilym was covering for him, so he gave the crowd a weak smile and nodded. "Right. That's right. Just a joke. Been to Skulltown hundreds of times."

Scattered laughter among the crowd, then they resumed their drinking and conversations. Novikov released the breath he'd been holding and looked at Gwilym, who whacked him in the side of the head again and whispered, "Keeps the voice downs, squire, and you'll be living longers. You slumming froms Braintown, here for gander ats the soldiers? Maybe gets drinks of good stuffs from straight source?"

"Urn, yeah, that's it," Novikov said, wondering what he meant.

Gwilym nudged Novikov's ribs with his elbow. "Should be said so in first places, squire. Gwilym not prejudiced, not cares if brainy wants high time. Alls moneys good here."

Novikov wondered if he had any money, or if the AI that ran this simulation would just provide it as he needed it. At least, he assumed it was a simulation, as that seemed to be the only rational explanation for his presence here dressed like one of the Masters—the Gwrinydd cyborg soldiers. "I'm actually looking for a way out of Skulltown."

"Ah, who isn't, squire? That's why the Master what owns this places picked this spots at the crossroads."

Novikov watched as a severely dented serving robot

limped its way across the room holding an empty silver drink tray. Gwilym noticed his interest. "Yeah, nots making thems likes they used to."

Novikov winced as a burly woman smashed a chair over the robot's head, hardly slowing it down. The crowd laughed harshly. "What do you mean? Looks like it's been in service a long time."

Gwilym snorted. "Brand-new server. Just gots here yesterday. Old ones lasted at leasts two weeks."

Novikov put a conspiratorial arm on Gwilym's shoulder, wondering how he could make sure he carried some local funds. "Look, Gwilym, I can probably pay you to get me out of here. Is there some magic word I'm supposed to say to end the simulation? Some special door I'm supposed to go through? Some ritual I need to perform? You must know."

Gwilym raised an eyebrow. "What you mean 'probably' pay me?"

"Well, I probably have money, but I'm not sure."

Gwilym's face got red as he stiffened and glared at Novikov. "You thinks Gwilym steals your *geebls*?"

Novikov rolled his eyes and imagined the pounding he'd get if he made Gwilym angry. "Certainly not, Gwilym. I just, um, have an injury that affects my memory."

Frowning, Gwilym grabbed Novikov's right hand, flipped it over, and punched a silver button. He nodded at a strange symbol that floated in the air over Novikov's palm. "Plenty *geebls,* just lackings the manners."

Seeing the symbol was like flipping a memory switch; Novikov suddenly understood how to use the payment chip embedded in his body armor. He gave Gwilym what he understood to be a huge tip.

"Heya," Gwilym said, his face brightening, "thanks, squire."

"Can you show me the way out of this simulation?"

Gwilym nodded. "The Warrior Code gives you onlys one ways out, squire."

"Great," Novikov smiled. "Let's get on with it."

Gwilym took two steps backward, lowered his faceplate with the dangling silver tentacles, and raised his right arm.

The dark openings of his weapon tubes pointed directly at Novikov's face.

Novikov realized his mistake as a lance of searing energy blew his head off.

TAU felt like giving up. Exhausted from digging into the side tunnel while the floodwaters swirled around his waist, he was frustrated by the debris blocking his exit. He hadn't eaten in a long time, and the adrenaline in his system had worn off. If the floodwaters would stop rising, he might have a chance; otherwise his life would end in that dark watery hole. Laika climbed to higher dry spots as the waters rose, but even she was starting to look scared now.

Then Tau remembered the bats.

The gurgling of the water had increased in volume while the squeaks and fluttering grew quieter. He looked up and saw that most of the bats were gone—but where?

The few remaining bats broke free of their perches, swirled together in flight until all of the stragglers were ready, and drifted up toward a crevice in the back of the cavern, passing through in single file to the other side. Tau hadn't noticed the crevice before, and he had no idea if it was just a cavern on the other side, or whether there might be another way out. Sloshing toward the back wall, his legs dragging in the gentle current, he plucked Laika from her perch. She struggled to get loose while Tau ducked a little lower, just barely managing to keep his head, and Laika, above the swirling waters. When he reached the crevice, he stood upright again in a small dome on the ceiling, but the water lapped against his chest. If the crevice didn't go anywhere, he'd keep his face up in the dome until the water went down, or until all the air was gone. His hat offered little illumination beyond the crack, but his free hand dug into the wall, sluicing through bat guano to crumbly rock that broke off when he pulled. The hole was larger now.

Barking and struggling, Laika snarled at him while he forced her through the opening.

The barking continued, echoing in the smaller chamber. He cleared away the rest of the crumbly rock, but heavier debris blocked his progress once more. The cold waters pulled at his pants and his heavy boots, relaxing his tired arm and shoulder muscles, offering him release if he'd give in to the siren song that gurgled in his ears.

He thought of Kate's head resting on his chest in the tent, and her flowery scent, and her dark hair tickling his face. He thought of her bright smile, the song of her voice, and the warmth of her skin. And he thought of how she'd been kidnapped, how she needed him now, and how she was getting farther away with each moment while he wasted his time swimming in a hole underground.

Tau jammed the fingers of both his hands into cracks in the rock dome near his head, then tightened his stomach muscles to curl his legs up toward the opening. His boots sloshed out of the water and slammed against the jagged edge of the opening, but the impact was too soft. Lifting his legs higher out of the water, blood dripping in his eyes while more skin shredded off his fingers, he swung his body like a pendulum, then slammed his boots into the rock with a solid thump. A chunk of the wall broke free and fell into the next chamber. He swung his body again, and another section of wall dropped away. The water was up to his face now. Hooking his feet on the lip of the enlarged opening, he gritted his teeth and pulled his screaming fingers out of the little dome. Although he knew it would happen, he gasped and sputtered when his head went under the cold water. His hat, and his only light source, swirled away in the current. He reached for his feet, banging his forehead on a rock in the darkness, and hauled his body through the opening, wriggling like a soggy worm over the rough stones.

Bats greeted him on the other side, but Laika was gone.

WEARING only a blanket, Kate sat on a rickety rocking chair by a fire that cracked and popped in the park ranger's cabin. While Peter Zah spoke to the park office over his netsat link, Kate tried to organize the thoughts tumbling around her exhausted brain. She had tried to explain the events of the last few hours without sounding like a crazy person. Zah's polite and confident manner had put her at ease, but she felt dizzy and confused. Hearing herself say everything out loud, she wasn't surprised to see Zah's skeptical expression, but he asked his headquarters for an air search of Tau's campsite and the immediate surroundings. He had already ordered a search for the kidnapper's boat on the lake, but he warned her that there were thousands of places where a boat could hide. If Tau had already left in search of her, and they couldn't find the campsite, she'd lose any credibility she might have if the searchers couldn't locate the kidnapper's boat. The demolished houseboat would be a puzzle for them, and she suddenly realized that she might be arrested on suspicion of murdering the two fishermen. Without any evidence to support her story, the authorities would want to explain the deaths of the two innocent men, and she was the most likely suspect.

She shook her head, annoyed with herself for thinking everything was a conspiracy, just as Tau kept telling her. She loved Tau, but she thought the stress of the Mars trip had pushed him over the edge. Too many incredible things had happened to him in too short a time, so he'd tried to explain the events by creating a conspiracy at the highest levels of government, as if they cared about anyone as insignificant as Tau or Kate. Spending time on the reservation had calmed his mind, but this kidnapping would only set him off again. Of course, she didn't have any good explanation as to why she'd been kidnapped, and could only think it tied into the Mars trip in some way, so there might be some truth hidden in Tau's theories.

When she'd first met Tau at the university, she'd thought of him as a brilliant molecular engineering student, along with all the stereotyping that implied: he didn't like organized sports; he spent most of his time working on his research, or on weird side projects with his techie roommate, Norman; he was somewhat absentminded; and

she'd had to show him how to let loose and have fun. Not
that she was a real party beast; she was just as likely to get
deeply involved in her archaeological studies as he was to
get lost in his molecular nanotech work. Then, as she had
gotten to know him better, she discovered that he was a
strong mountain climber, which she would never do because of her fear of heights. Tau felt at home in high, rocky
places as if he were part mountain goat. As a boy, he
helped his relatives herd sheep from their summer range to
their cold-weather dwellings, up and down steep cliff
trails. The hike to Rainbow Canyon had been Tau's idea;
he wanted to show her some of his remote childhood
haunts. She also wanted to show Tau some of her childhood haunts, but used bookstores in southern California
would never be mistaken for "remote."

She sometimes wondered if her interest in archaeology
had been stimulated by digging through piles of old books
in used bookstores. In Long Beach, daily visits to the miles
of dusty shelving at the cavernous Acres of Books, where
she would roam for hours armed with a bag and a flashlight, had shown her how much she enjoyed the hunt for
knowledge as well as the actual discovery. Guided only by
vague subject headings marked on the ends of narrow
aisles, the grimy tomes illuminated only by dingy skylights
on the high ceilings of the old Quonset huts, she drew
crude maps by hand so she could do thorough searches of
the dangerously leaning stacks and still find her way back
out. Her chosen career allowed her to continue collecting
books and other antique printed materials—an obsession
that would have been considered odd in most any other
field. When she moved on to bigger game, hunting the
death dreams of hidden royalty sleeping in Egyptian
tombs, or diving the warm Caribbean waters in search of
sunken pirate cities, she still recalled the book-hunting
trips of her teenage years. Her later addiction to informa-
tion-hunting in the datasphere, embedded directly into her
memory as she found it with one of the illegal infotap devices, had sprung from the same source. And her use of the
infotap had led to her discovery of Thoth, the AI who had

almost killed her on Mars by establishing a connection with her primitive brain. Her life was one long chain of knowledge that led back to her childhood wanderings among compressed forests of printed matter.

"They're starting a search," said Peter Zah, handing her a steaming mug of dark liquid.

Kate blinked and looked up at the ranger towering over her chair. She warmed her hands on the mug. "What? Oh, good."

"Headquarters has some questions. We should talk about those once you've finished your tea."

"Questions? Of course."

Zah crouched and adjusted the flames in the fireplace. "You ever run across rat problems in your digs?"

Kate smiled behind her mug. Her experience with the Navajo people had shown her that they rarely got to the point of a discussion right away. "Sometimes. I've only worked on a couple of digs in the southwest, but the rats were there long before we arrived."

Zah nodded and sat down on the stone hearth to face her. "We have a problem over there," he said, pointing his lips in the general direction of the nearby cliff dwelling. The walls of the structures are cracking. Rats found the old midden underneath, where the cliff dwellers tossed all their garbage. They've been tunneling through the midden and on up under the dwellings. The floors weaken, the walls sag—you know how it works."

Kate sipped the strong tea in her mug. "You can't stop them?"

"Well, we've caught a few, and killed a few, but there are plenty more deep inside doing the real damage. Then someone had the idea of using cats."

"Clever. Did it work?"

"No. The cats did more damage. They like to sharpen their claws on the ruins, among other things. And they didn't really kill the rats so much as they played with them. So we got rid of the cats and tried snakes."

"Did that work any better?"

"We aren't sure. The snakes are in there somewhere, but

so are the rats. On the other hand, fewer people want to visit the ruins with all those rats and snakes in there, so there's less wear from tourists." He shrugged. "Maybe it all evens out in the end."

Kate smiled and sipped at her tea.

Zah watched her in silence for a moment. "Your fiancé like ruins?"

"He does now, but he was never allowed into them when he was a boy."

"He grew up on the rez?"

She nodded.

"So he probably knows his way around here if he had to run or hide from someone?"

She shrugged, wondering what he was getting at. "Probably."

Zah turned and looked into the fire. Patient with their own conversations, many Navajos liked to test the whites they spoke to by not saying anything for a while, waiting to see how long it would be before the silence was broken. She knew Zah was also a type of cop, so he might be waiting to see if she'd reveal anything incriminating about her experience on the lake. In any case, Kate had plenty of experience with the silent routine, so she listened to the popping of the fire and waited for Zah to talk.

Several minutes passed before he turned to face her again. "Why would someone want to kidnap you, Kate McCloud?"

She shrugged. "Just popular, I guess."

"You into any illegal activities?"

"Some killing, some robberies, stuff like that. Nothing major."

Zah didn't seem amused. "No idea at all why someone would go to the trouble of finding you way out here? No coworkers stalking you? No old boyfriends holding a grudge? No old girlfriends out to get you?"

Kate shook her head. "Sorry. I'm not that interesting."

"Somebody thinks you are."

Zah got up to answer a netsat call while she finished her tea. When he came back, he strapped on a flight helmet and a crash-foam suit. "They want me to take the flyer and look for that houseboat. They can't seem to find it."

"It's the big wreck pumping out the huge cloud of black smoke," Kate said. "Kind of hard to miss. Did they find Tau?"

"Not yet." He started for the cabin door, then stopped and looked at her again. "Are you on any medication?"

"Did I hallucinate the whole thing?" Kate sat up straight and glared. "Go out and see for yourself."

Zah shrugged. "It's getting dark, but if we miss it, the satellite should pick it up on the next pass. Don't worry."

"I'm not worried. Just find Tau for me."

Zah opened the door. "Have a nap while I'm gone. I'll be back soon, and there are some other people coming to see you."

Now she was worried. After she heard Zah's footsteps crunching away on the gravel path, she walked over to the netsat console. If Tau had been able to communicate, he would have left a message with his mother at the Gemstone construction site. She wondered if there was any way that a quick call to Gemstone could be traced back to this location, then decided it was unlikely that they could have set up a sophisticated search so soon after her escape. In any case, she could make the call and get out of there before Zah returned or his other visitors arrived. She had to know if Tau was all right, and she couldn't trust Zah to find anything or tell her the truth if he did. Zah could be one of "them." She hesitated, then made the call.

No answer at Gemstone. No AI to take a message.

TAU thanked the bats for showing him the way out of the cave. He climbed out of the steep tunnel onto the sandy top of the mesa, a struggling dog jammed into his armpit. A black stream of bats was flying off toward the lake, silhouetted against the rising full moon that bathed the stark landscape in blue light. The outlines of sage and other scrubby bushes loomed in the dim light; any one of them could hide a man with a gun, an angry killer patiently waiting to punch holes in Tau's soggy body. But Tau was too tired to feel more than a passing interest in any threats hidden in the bushes. He rolled over on his back, on sand that was still warm from the heat of the day, and stared at the enormous moon. Spotting his submissive posture, Laika hopped up on his chest and stared down into his face—queen of the mountain.

Laika just stared. Her breath reeked.

"I don't know where she is." The dog had a way of inspiring feelings of guilt; probably some sort of small-dog defensive mechanism honed through generations of breeding for cute survival traits. He took a deep breath, then shoved Laika off his chest and rolled over on his side, amazed at how many painful muscles he could feel. He'd sheared off the long sleeves from his shirt using the laser cutter, not an easy task with a fabric made to avoid tears, and tied the rags around his hands to stop the blood and provide some padding between his shredded fingers and the rock during his climb. An owl hooted nearby, maybe thinking that Tau sounded like prey; he certainly felt like it.

Guided by stars and the moonlight that illuminated major landmarks such as Navajo Mountain, Tau started walking, his boots thumping on worn rock and hard sand. Without his SatHat to disguise his presence on the mesa top, he knew it was possible that the heat from his body in the nighttime landscape would draw the attention of his hunters in some satellite image, so he had to move quickly. Despite the technology and manpower that might be arrayed against him, he knew that, in comparison to Navajos of the past, he had little to complain about. When Kit Carson rounded up thousands of Navajos and forced them to walk over three hundred miles to the desolate Bosque Redondo in eastern New Mexico, hundreds died on the trail from exhaustion, exposure, starvation, disease, and the bullets of trigger-happy soldiers. Hundreds more were killed before the Long Walk of the Navajo ever started, and thousands died on the new reservation where the water was bad and crops would not grow. In Tau's mind, descriptions of Bosque Redondo sounded much like the surface of Mars. Tau now walked in a region where several hundred of the *Dineh* had escaped the cavalry soldiers and the Utes to hide in the serpentine canyons and high mountains, and that gave him hope of escaping the modern-day soldiers hunting him now.

Laika followed along, stopping only to growl at random insects and errant air molecules that offended her in some way. He knew she must be hungry, and he occasionally turned around to see her munching on some suspicious object that might or might not be poisonous. Normally, she would only eat the most expensive brand of dog food, which also sounded good to Tau right now, but it was back at the campsite along with all their other supplies. In his rapid exit from the beach, he had taken the time to place the decoy that probably saved his life, but he'd neglected to grab some food. Overall, he knew he'd made the right decision, but the fatigue from his low blood sugar and his recent exercise now made him question his choices.

When he saw the jackrabbit that dared to scamper across his path, he stopped suddenly and dug in his pocket for the laser cutter to see if it still worked. He knew how to set a trap for the rabbit if he had bait—after a quick glance at Laika he put that thought out of his mind—but he knew the rabbit wouldn't wait. He could try running after it, and the rabbit would probably bolt down a hole or shift into high gear to lose him in the dark. He tried to remember the odd technique his father had taught him to use in the dark. His debate ended with the sound of loud yapping when Laika darted off toward the unsuspecting creature, faster than he had ever seen the dog move before. After they disappeared behind a clump of sagebrush, he heard squeaking, growling, and the snapping of many twigs, followed by a crunching sound. Unsure whether he'd find Laika eating the rabbit or the other way around, he peered over the bush. Laika looked up from the motionless rabbit and growled, her face coated with blood in the moonlight.

"It didn't take long for you to turn feral," Tau said, reaching down to pick up the rabbit.

Laika growled again. Tau rolled his eyes and picked up

the rabbit anyway. Laika bit his pants leg and jerked it around, trying to make him fall.

"Laika! Get off!"

Tau thought about clouting her over the head with the rabbit carcass, then threw it down in front of her instead. "Here!"

Laika happily returned to her dinner. With a quick stroke of the laser cutter, he removed the rabbit's leg just ahead of where Laika was chewing. The burst of light startled her, but she dragged the leg away behind the bush and seemed content to leave him with the rest of the rabbit for the moment. His mouth watered and he thought how ridiculous this whole thing was, as if he hadn't eaten for a week. Still, with a small fire under a rock to shield the flames from prying eyes in the sky, the rabbit could be roasted quickly, and he'd be on his way again, more likely to make it to safety with something in his stomach.

15

ARIEL trudged along behind BD in a baggy polychrome robe, physically undamaged after her God Box experience. BD walked in silence as he followed a complicated path through narrow lanes lined with low entrances to the sub-terranean residential warrens that riddled Mount Sutro and the Twin Peaks area. Above them rose the 977-foot steel tripod of Sutro Tower, its red warning lights winking at the world, looking like a Martian war machine from the old *War of the Worlds* flatfilm. Originally built in 1972 to han-dle television signal transmission from one of the highest points in the city, the red and white colossus loomed above it all, anchored in fifteen million pounds of concrete, and could be seen from most of the peninsula on clear days. Still dizzy with the knowledge that she had survived a hor-rible ordeal inside her mind, Ariel tried not to look up at the tower for fear that she'd fall flat on her back. She knew only that they were meeting BD's brother, the mysterious Norman, and he might help her gain access to Carlo.

They stopped at a solid security gate attached to a high wire-mesh fence. A sign on the gate declared this to be Sutro Tower—A Registered Historical Landmark. Beyond the fence lay a three-story building that looked like a fortress formed organically from the rock of the mountain. Beside the building rose the white northeast leg of the vast tripod, its roots plunged deep into the soil.

"How are we supposed to get through this gate?" Ariel asked, giving the metal frame a little kick with the toe of her high-heeled shoe.

BD raised his arms to the sky. "We must trust in the Di-vine Light, my priestess. The Entity will show us the way."

"No need," said a sarcastic nasal voice. "I'll show you the way." A squat little man with short brown hair stepped out of the shadows. He wore a VR monocle over his left eye. His denim jumpsuit strained to keep his stomach in, and Ariel couldn't help thinking that he really ought to wear something a bit more fashionable or at least have his excess fat removed. Then she remembered the baggy color-cycling robe she wore, so who was she to criticize?

The gate clattered to one side on squeaky wheels. BD gestured at the pudgy man. "This is Norman Meadows. My brother."

Ariel smiled at Norman, then raised an eyebrow at BD. "Your last name is Meadows? What's your first name?"

BD shrugged. "My earthly identification doesn't matter. I was reborn as Brother Digital."

Norman snickered. "His first name is Festus. And you're both late."

Ariel looked at Norman. "Festus?"

"Norman," BD sighed, "I've asked you not to tell anyone."

Norman ignored BD and shone a tiny bright light in Ariel's face. "Wow. Who are you?"

"Ariel Colombari," she said, stepping forward to offer her hand. "Nice to meet you."

Norman winced when her spiked heel came down on the toe of his left shoe. He grasped her hand anyway.

"Sorry," she said, moving her foot. "I couldn't see with that light in my eyes."

"No problem," Norman said. He shut off the light without letting go of her hand. "I didn't need those toes anyway. I've got more."

Ariel wrinkled her nose at the garlic odor rising from Norman but tried to ignore it. He was her ticket to Carlo, and she didn't want to offend him. Her right hand lay trapped in his cold fingers. "So, you live here?"

"Live here?" Norman honked a laugh. "Certainly not. I broke in a little while ago. Come on in." He gestured for them to follow, towing Ariel along behind him. BD brought up the rear. Nearing the massive door to the building, Norman pushed a button on a small controller in his left hand. The door opened with a hiss, and he glanced at Ariel with a slight smile. "EM jammer. Confuses the electronic locks."

They trudged past rooms full of electronic gear and the smell of ozone before Norman went up a short metal stairway and opened the door to a small elevator lit by a dim red glowpanel. A cool blast of air poured out of the shaft to flutter their robes. The elevator cage was much too small for three adults, so Ariel found herself sandwiched in between BD and Norman. Her eyes narrowed when Norman used the bumping motion of the elevator to plant his face between her breasts. She couldn't move away with BD pressed against her back. Then she realized their destination.

"Tell me we're not going to the top of the tower."

Norman chuckled. "Of course. That's where I have all my equipment." He leered up at her.

Ariel closed her eyes for a moment and tried not to faint. She felt dizzy already, and the soles of her feet tingled in sympathy with the butterflies in her stomach. When she opened her eyes again, the diamond-shaped spaces in the aluminum door revealed a glimpse of buildings and streetlights dropping away below them in the gathering darkness. The cage clanked, groaned, and clattered its way up the shaft inside the tower leg. She shuddered.

"Don't worry," said Norman, his voice muffled in her robes. "We're only going one hundred feet a minute, and we're angling in at five degrees, so it's not even a straight drop back to the ground. Perfectly safe."

"I don't like heights," said Ariel.

"Then you're really going to hate this," Norman said. He put his hand on her thigh, but she barely noticed. All she wanted to do was get back down on the ground.

"You'll be fine," BD boomed. As usual, his voice was too loud for the confined space. "We can speak privately up there. Norman knows what he's doing."

Through the door, she glimpsed steel crossbeams on a narrow catwalk festooned with satellite microdishes and small antennae. In the distance, she saw the arching lights of the Bay Bridge dominating a sea of smaller lights in office towers. The wind howled through the cage whenever they passed through gaps in the steel leg. "I don't like this."

"They've never had an accident here, as far as I know," Norman said. His hand slid up her thigh, and she casually twisted her arm to elbow Norman in the eye.

His hand dropped away. "Ow!"

"Sorry," Ariel said. "Just had to scratch my nose." She hoped she hadn't blown it; she still needed the obnoxious little man.

After seven minutes of groping their way skyward in a cloud of garlic, Norman opened the cage door. A metal deck with handrails perched on massive crossbeams linking the three masts at the top of the tower. Gusts of wind blew Norman's hair when he stepped out and offered his hand to Ariel. Her legs shook, and a wisp of hair blew into her mouth. The cage shifted as BD tried to step sideways around her, but her body blocked access to the door. "I can't go out there."

"Come on," Norman said. "It's perfectly safe."

"Perfect for you, maybe. I'm staying here."

BD looked concerned as he put one hand on her shoulder. "Trust me, my child. He knows what he's doing."

She glared at BD. "Let's see, the last time you said that, I lost an arm and a leg before being skewered on a spire of glass. That doesn't inspire confidence."

"You came out okay. All you had to do was trust in the Entity."

"Piss off."

BD sighed. "You want to talk to Carlo again, don't you?"

That hurt. She looked down at her feet. "Yes."

"Then you have to go out there. I'll be right behind you."

"Heights don't bother you?"

"They used to. A higher power guides my footsteps now."

She took a deep breath, then gripped BD's arm with both hands and took a step forward. Almost a thousand feet below, the lights of San Francisco spread off into the distance, restricted only by the ocean on one side and the bay on the other. Her body shook uncontrollably, but she took a second step that placed her squarely on the catwalk. The railing was as high as her chest, but she didn't trust it. The palms of her hands buzzed, and her eyes were wide open. A low moaning noise caught her attention—like a dead man crying out from the grave—and she realized it was the wind humming through the guy wires supporting the masts. When the speed of the gusts changed, the pitch changed, and the wires hummed together like a choir of the dead.

"See, it's not so bad," Norman said. He smiled and grabbed her shoulder on the opposite side from BD.

Ariel concentrated on her breathing in an attempt to slow it down. Her heart thumped like mad, too large for her chest, trying to get out. She took a third step and hooked her spiked heel in a circular drain hole, stumbling against Norman with a gasp. Then she realized that the catwalk was riddled with drain holes every few inches. "That's it! I can't do it!"

"Here," Norman said, helping her out of her shoes. "Your feet might get cold, but you won't get stuck. We just need to go a little farther."

Carlo. She concentrated on Carlo. With her feet planted firmly on the cold decking, she steadied her breathing and pictured Carlo standing at the end of the walkway. She began to walk, keeping the two men beside her, her fingers gripping BD's arm like a vise, and she noticed that BD was muttering.

"Are you saying something?"

"Just praying, my child. I don't like this, either."

Somehow, that made her feel better. Norman led the way to a mound of equipment and a backpack near the south leg of the tower. She focused on the imaginary Carlo to keep herself moving forward.

Norman patted a metal tube on a tripod hooked into the pile of equipment. "Festus said you wanted access to Elysian Fields. I've got this commlaser sighted on the EF facility in Colma, about seven miles south of here. Clear line of sight straight into their Infinite Peace building, and this is the only place in town where we can do that. I've never seen a cemetery with so many defenses, but that's what you'd expect, isn't it?"

"I don't understand."

"Well, I'm not guaranteeing anything. I want this to work as much as you do. My grandfather died two months ago, and I've wanted to speak with him ever since."

"This is the first time you've done this?" BD asked.

"I've cracked other secure facilities from up here, no problem, but this is the first time I've tried it on EF. I tried going in the side door, through the net, but they've got software defenses like you wouldn't believe. Killware. If this works, it makes my whole life easier."

Ariel looked at Norman with wonder in her eyes. "And you're doing this all for me?"

Norman stared at her for a moment, considering, then shook his head. "A client asked me to do a job on EF. Kind of like breaking someone out of prison, except the prisoner is dead, he won't physically go anywhere, and I'm only going to borrow him for a while. So, if I can do that from up here, everyone's happy. If not, I have to try breaking in the hard way again."

Ariel nodded. "Okay, that's fair. What do we do next?"

"We pray," BD said.

"I kick the door in," Norman said while he placed a webbed cap festooned with a complicated array of chips and other components on his head. "And we hope the EF security people didn't think of this."

16

LENYA Novikov had spent the night in a cold sweat, dreaming of a monstrous Gwrinydd warrior that kept shooting him in the face. When he had finally escaped from his dreams, he sat up on his cot, remembering the events of his previous day in the Gwrinydd museum. The cameras had captured his collapse before the interactive painting, but his recovery had been swift as soon as the simulation was over and he owned his own mind again. Although he wasn't thrilled by the idea, he knew he'd have to go back into the museum. He couldn't show weakness in front of his team, and certainly not in front of the cameras recording his historic discovery of the key to the Gwrinydd culture. This would be the peak achievement of his career, and he wasn't about to let anyone else take the credit by venturing into the museum without him. The painting had not killed him, and that implied that the rest of the museum would also be harmless, although he couldn't be sure he'd survive all the simulations meant for the alien physiologies of Gwrinydd warriors. The alien sims were far more sophisticated than anything he'd experienced on Earth, and he wasn't sure that his heart and his brain could stand the strain. But those were secondary considerations; he had to continue the exploration, and do it quickly before the bureaucrats back on Earth tried to interfere "for his own safety."

Novikov now stood at the rough museum entrance once again, smiling at the cameras on the heads of his assistants. He'd thought about having his assistants follow him into another painting, then decided it would be better if he was the only one to experience the alien environments and learn their secrets. Kate McCloud had stolen the show from him last time when she discovered the alien AI and the secrets of their transportation system, and he wouldn't let that happen again.

When he stepped into the museum, the column with the crystal mind reader that had greeted him on his previous visit remained in the floor. He assumed that meant it had already learned everything about him that it needed to know for an effective museum visit. His assistants had already generated a simple map and inventory of the contents in the long room, and he had studied the information over his simple breakfast of synthetic sausage and eggs. Rather than trying another one of the paintings, he had decided to experiment with one of the many gadgets hung high on the walls.

Novikov would start his experiments with the rack of long crystals that contained pulverized plant material and other powdered substances—what had already been dubbed the Spice Rack. When he approached the device, a small light came on and glittered at the base, lighting the long crystals from below to bring out their subtle colors. He assumed it was some sort of preserved organic material from the Gwrinydd home world, but he was wary enough to have brought some analysis gear to test for any toxic substances. Once the analyzer had done its job and passed the contents of the crystals with a nontoxic rating, Novikov leaned closer to study them. The tops of each crystal spike were punctured with tiny holes. As the light at the base of the rack heated the crystals, scents wafted into the air. He picked up the first crystal and ran his fingers over the rough surface, something like a rosy quartz tube with a solid heft, and noted its warmth. He sniffed gently at the pleasant scent, then sniffed some more. The sweet smell reminded him of jasmine.

Novikov returned the first crystal to its slot on the rack and wondered why the designers of the museum had placed it here. Then he felt a sudden dizziness. He placed his hand against the translucent white wall to steady himself, hoping the cameras wouldn't capture him passing out on the floor again. His pulse pounded in his head as if a migraine were coming on, and he felt an odd pressure in his ears. His breath came in short gasps and he began to sweat, wondering if this was a heart attack.

Then a vision formed in his head.

First, there was dim red light, and a feeling of motion like an ocean current swirling around his body. A strong scent of jasmine filled the air, mixed with cinnamon, oregano, coriander, and other tangy scents he couldn't identify that formed a pleasing mix. Blobs of color emerged from the current, shades of blue and red and yellow swirling past him in both directions in a directed flow of activity. Excited animal sounds drifted past, some loud and some soft, synchronizing at times into pleasant harmonics that relaxed him. Then the colors hardened and resolved into loose robes blowing in a gentle breeze, togas in solid colors worn over the armored bodies of Gwrinydd warriors moving like schools of fish, with individuals stopping here and there to study objects Novikov couldn't quite see. As the details of the scene filled in, he saw tables glowing in shafts of sunlight from a cloudy reddish sky, their surfaces covered with mounds of colored foods, and he realized he was in some sort of outdoor market, a bazaar among high-walled streets of rotting red stone. The animal sounds became voices, and the voices resolved into words of the Gwrinydd language. The excited haggling was translated in his head, although not perfectly, just as it had been in the Gwrinydd warrior bar.

Novikov raised his hand and it looked normal, but one of the passing soldiers walked straight through his arm as if he were a ghost. He couldn't see the rest of his body, although he felt the warm air against his skin. As an experiment, he reached out and found he could pick up a long yellow fruit that looked something like a banana. When he peeled it, however, the soft fruit he expected to see inside wasn't there; replaced by the slowly squirming form of a large yellow caterpillar with more tiny legs than he could count. One of the nearby soldiers peeled another of the yellow fruits to reveal the squirming resident stuffed inside, then lifted his faceplate and ate the creature in one gulp. Novikov put his peeled fruit back on the table in disgust. The yellow caterpillar dropped to the ground and skittered away through a jagged hole in the brick wall.

When he stepped back from the table, he noticed long, colored streamers drifting into the alleyway on the breeze. The streamers glowed softly from within, floating like gossamer, twisting in eddies of air along the walls and in doorways. The merchants and customers continued haggling while the streamers moved by, but they kept glancing into the breeze, casually stepping aside to let the streamers pass. Novikov didn't move, assuming they'd pass through his insubstantial form, then realized he didn't understand the physics of the situation since he was able to pick things up with his hands. A red streamer snagged on his arm, and he suddenly felt angry at himself for being so stupid. His breath quickened, and he felt his face getting hot. He glared at the people around him, angry that no one had explained how the streamers operated or what they were for; no matter that they couldn't see him. This whole situation was unacceptable, a nightmare of foul odors and rude crowds jostling to pick over buggy fruits unfit to eat. The crumbling walls were ugly and seemed ready to collapse; with any luck they would crush the merchant scum whose filthy wares littered the aisles, spreading disease wherever they went. If he'd had a weapon in his possession, he would have done everyone a favor and killed them all right there.

A gust lifted the red streamer from his arm, and relief washed over him as he turned to watch it go. He looked down to see a golden streamer caught on his neck, marveling at the brilliant color and the soft feel of its touch, pleased that he was able to witness this whole marvelous bazaar firsthand. The brilliant colors, the delicate scents of exotic spices, the chance to explore an alien culture up close without danger. He wanted to shout his welcome to the people around him, his brothers of the bazaar. He thought how wonderful it must be to work here, providing sustenance for a hungry population while earning an honest living, free of professional and office politics.

The golden streamer drifted away. Novikov felt an odd sense of loss as he watched it go. But what was it? Was it alive? Was it harmful? He shuddered, then noticed a black streamer clamped around his leg, the wind tying it in knots. Adrenaline pumped through his veins. He quickly bent to untie the black knot, afraid that someone might hit him over the back of the head while he was distracted, his eyes darting around to make sure no one was ready to attack. What about that soldier in the doorway? Was he watching? He looked suspicious, leaning against the frame and looking the other way as if he didn't want Novikov to notice him. He swallowed. Were the streamer's poisons working on him already? The streamers seemed alive and intelligent, hunting for unsuspecting victims, intent on destruction. He ducked as a second black streamer floated past. Had the walls been so close before? They were so old, leaning in toward the alleyway, crumbling away with age; they might collapse at any moment and kill them all, crushing Novikov under tons of alien rock, breaking his bones under an ocean of stone so that he'd die alone in that dark place, unloved and isolated from the people he knew. He knew now that there was no way he could leave that place alive, that horrible trap set long ago by alien sadists to snare the unwary. Even the air had a heavy feel to it, pregnant with evil, and he sucked it into his body with each breath, unaware of the damage being done to his tissues and his cells. The analyzer probably wasn't even working right, confused by strange toxic molecules that hung in the air to kill any humans that happened by. Were the warriors closing in? The sense of doom paralyzed him, making his muscles go rigid. He could hardly breathe at all anymore. The bastards had him, and he didn't have a chance. As his final act, he tugged at the black streamer, and it broke free of his leg, rolling down the alleyway to Hell where it belonged.

Novikov sighed. He knew something wasn't right. He needed to stop a moment and analyze why he felt a swirl of emotions, but things were happening so fast that he—

Why had he come here? He felt tears in his eyes, tears of frustration and loss. His heart sank. Who had these peo-

ple been? They were long dead now, their machines out-
living them by thousands of years, their bodies reduced to
scattered dust drifting on cosmic winds. What was the
point, really? Time was the only winner in life. Was this
what lay in store for the human race? The pattern was repeated over and over; the Anasazi, the Aztecs, the Mayans,
the Egyptians, the Romans—all had built great empires,
and all had vanished beneath the sands of time, disappearing or dying out despite their efforts at immortality. The
Gwrinydd clock had run down and stopped just as it had
for other races on Earth. The crumbling walls said so much
about this culture, their ancient surfaces weeping and clot-
ted with mold, the rough bricks holding onto each other for
support to stave off the inevitable collapse. And collapse
they would, ruled by gravity and other forces stronger than
themselves. Coming here had been a mistake. His career
didn't matter; it was all a show driven by pride and greed,
the very things that would send him to an early grave.
There were no friends who would mourn him, no loved
ones to remember his accomplishments. He sat down
heavily on the cold ground, thinking it would be best to
end it all right here. A blue streamer sailed away from his
boot, sadly twisting in the wind, buffeted by unseen forces
that ruled its life.

Novikov gasped when he saw the translucent white walls
of the museum in front of him. Looking around without
moving his head, he realized he was still standing in front of
the Spice Rack. With a subtle movement of his hand, he
wiped tears away from his face and turned it into a movement where he ran his fingers back through his hair. He felt
emotionally drained, but he turned and smiled at the cameras behind him to give a brief description of the glories he
had just witnessed, and the great knowledge that he was personally discovering in the museum despite the danger to
himself. He knew the viewers back home would eat it up.

He glanced wistfully at the Spice Rack, away from the
camera, wondering what was next and aware that it didn't
really matter. The show must go on.

17

NORMAN sat cross-legged on the metal catwalk wearing his strange headgear while he concentrated on the data streaming into his VR monocle. Ariel and BD blocked the gusts of wind on each side of Norman while his hands flitted over the controls of the equipment piled in front of him. A light fog drifted in from the ocean but had not advanced far enough to interfere with the laser pointed at the Elysian Fields facility in Colma. Ariel felt hungry, anxious, and dizzy, still trying to ignore the holes in the catwalk and the city lights far below, but she wasn't going anywhere until she had a chance to speak to her dead husband.

Norman grunted. "It's Colombari, right? Carlo Colombari?"

"Yes, yes, do you see him?" This was taking too long.

Norman continued to look off into the distance, muttering while he wandered through the virtual datafields of the EF systems. "I saw a backup record for him, but I can't seem to find his active avatar. Maybe they haven't prepped him yet. How long ago did you lose him?"

Ariel felt like she was caving in on herself. "Eight months ago."

BD patted Ariel's shoulder. "Keep looking, Norman. Carlo must be in there by now."

"I'm running out of time. If I stay in the system too long, the killware will notice me."

"Please," said Ariel. She didn't understand why Norman was helping her, outside of his being BD's brother, but she wasn't too proud to beg if necessary.

"I'm trying," said Norman, "but you might have to go in the front door like a normal customer."

Ariel bit her lip. "I can't afford that. Not yet, anyway."

"If this doesn't work, we'll find another way, child," BD said. Ariel appreciated the comment.

"Yow!" Norman gasped and slapped his hand down on a big switch at the base of the commlaser. Sweating, he slipped off the headgear and looked at Ariel. "Sorry. I had to punch out. Security sniffed me. The problem with going in the back door is that it can take a long time to find an individual target. The backup copy won't do it; you need the live avatar if you want to communicate with a person. I need to learn more, but I think Carlo is in there. I just couldn't reach him. I found the pointers, like a trail of bread crumbs, but I couldn't go far enough."

Ariel put her hand on his knee. "Will you try again?"

Norman licked his lips and sighed. "The thing is, I have to go in again to do the breakout job for my employer. My disguise won't hold up forever. I'm going back as an employee working on accounting data right now. Give me another couple of weeks, and I can try a different route with a different disguise."

"If it's a question of money," Ariel said, "maybe there's a way we can work it out. But it might take a while."

Norman shrugged. "I wasn't doing this for you for money. I needed to test out my new equipment, and it worked. I also happen to hate those EF bastards. If it weren't for me, they wouldn't have a business in the first place, and I never got anything out of it."

"What do you mean?"

Norman shook his head, and BD patted him on the back. "The reason people can interact with their dead loved ones is because of Norman's biochips, the Feelie and the Lazarus. He designed them and built them, sold a few Feelies to the adult entertainment business, and then someone from Elysian Fields stole his master chips. He went after them legally when he found out they had the technology, but EF had better lawyers, and Norman's money burned up fast, so he had to go underground."

"Wait a second," Ariel said, suddenly realizing who they were talking about. "Norman Meadows. I've heard of you. You were already a legend when I was in college. I used to do chip layout until the AIs put me out of work."

Norman shrugged. "Sorry to hear that. You should have known that human layout was a dead end."

Ariel snorted. "Not everyone can do biochip design in their heads."

"A lot of good it did me. Look where I am now," Norman said.

BD nudged Norman in the side. "Tell her what you're working on."

Norman rolled his eyes. "It's a secret, *Festus*. That's how I got into trouble last time; someone found out about the Lazarus and stole it."

BD nudged him again. "Ariel won't tell anyone. She's one of your kind. She'll be fascinated."

"Well . . ." Norman hesitated. "Judging by your costume, I think you've used my Miracle biochip, right?"

Ariel looked at BD and he nodded. "The God Box. It's run by the Miracle."

Things were starting to fall into place in her mind. The God Box might be a high-powered illusion—some form of mind control—but she had to ask. "What does it do?"

Norman glanced at BD. "Plays with your head. It generates EM fields that bathe your temporal lobes with precise wavelength patterns to induce the sensation of seeing God or having a religious experience. When the right hemisphere of the brain, the seat of emotion, is stimulated in the cerebral region that controls notions of self, then the left hemisphere, the seat of language, is asked to make sense of what feels like a religious presence, so the mind generates an entity to explain it. Some people see God, some people see ghosts, and others see aliens. Then the biochip dresses up the whole experience by plunging your consciousness into the datasphere that humans don't normally see, and an entire realistic hallucination takes place."

"Oh, my God," said Ariel, placing her hand over her mouth.

"Exactly," said Norman. "If you guide the hallucination

with a few suggestions, you can make people believe almost anything."

Ariel glared at BD, who calmly stared back at her. "My child, the Global Brain is real. The Entity is merely a representation that individual humans can understand. The Miracle chip guides us through the sim environment so that our simple minds can understand the Entity's message."

"Yeah, whatever," Norman said, becoming more animated. "So imagine that you combine the Miracle chip with the full-sensory simulation of the Feelie and the ability to do personality uploads with the Lazarus biochip. God Himself could live in Elysian Fields, along with Buddha, Yahweh, Allah, Zeus, Odin, Amon Ra, and all the other religious deities you care to name. You and your dead loved ones could commune directly with your chosen god."

"That sounds awful," Ariel said.

Norman looked at BD. "I knew she wouldn't understand it. I want to bring world peace to the masses, and all she can think about is what you've done with your weird-ass religion." He rummaged around in his backpack and withdrew a small metal case. "I have work to do. Give me ten minutes, and I'll take you back to the ground."

"What about Carlo?" Ariel asked, somewhat miffed but not wanting to upset him further. BD just stared off into the distance, thinking his own private thoughts.

"Use the front door like everybody else. I don't want to get killed in there." Norman flipped open the case to reveal a biochip set into a supercooled liquid nitrogen socket, clipped it to some of his equipment, put his headgear back on, and powered up the commlaser. The ruby beam lanced out into the night sky to the south.

Ariel briefly glared at BD before plunging her face into the folds of her robes. BD put his arm around her shoulder. "Tomorrow, my child. Tomorrow we'll go to Colma."

NORMAN rode the light into the nether regions of the Elysian Fields sim environment. His target was the greatest statesman of the last fifty years, former U.S. President Lincoln Ford Kennedy. Norman already knew approximately where to locate Kennedy from the traceroute query he'd run earlier against the avatar database. A quick hit on the database allowed him to rename Kennedy's personality and memory files and reindex them under an encrypted key. When the EF staff realized that Kennedy was missing, they wouldn't be able to reload him into the system if they couldn't find him, and Norman had hidden the local backup personality as well. Kennedy could still be restarted from a backup on a remote EF system, but that would take time, and the avatar wouldn't be current or complete, so it was more likely that the EF authorities would leave Kennedy unavailable until the original was recovered.

Kennedy's physical biochip was stored with hundreds of identical chips in an underground vault deep below the Happy Meadows section of the Elysian Fields cemetery in Colma. For security and practicality reasons, the chip's actual location was known only to the EF administrative database, which was heavily defended from snoopers, sniffers, hackers, crackers, and other AI-driven invaders that could attempt entry through the system's necessary datasphere connections. The commlaser gave Norman temporary access to the system as if he were an Elysian Fields employee using a remote satellite datalink, although the security AIs would eventually figure out he was an intruder if he stayed too long.

Recent mass production was making it possible for the average citizen to buy a Lazarus biochip, implanted near the brainstem on the back of the neck. With a choice between "eternal" digital life and certain death, most people were choosing to live on in a simulated world where they could interact with their loved ones. When a biochip owner died, the biochip was quickly removed and stored in a biochip memory library at one of the new EF facilities around the country. Originally, only the two EF cemeteries at Colma, California, and Arlington, Virginia, were equipped with memory libraries, but franchises were spreading quickly around the country as EF dropped the prices of its biochips. EF earned most of its revenues through perpetual care fees, visitation fees, insurance sales, and long-term investments that allowed the living to deduct money from their regular paychecks for their eternal life plans.

Once it was plugged into library storage, the used biochip remained the primary source of information about an individual, but memory and personality "pointers" were uploaded to an active database in the EF simulation environment to generate the "physical" avatar. The avatar could roam freely through the digital world and develop new memories as it enjoyed new experiences. A limited AI provided the interface between the deceased and the sim world to make the avatar feel as if it were still alive. The avatar looked like the original person had in life, although many chose cosmetic enhancements to their appearances. To conserve computing power in the massive interactive world, the landscape was dynamically generated as necessary for each avatar or group of avatars. Full-sensory visitors had no control over the environment, but they could completely experience their loved ones and their surroundings in an idealized version of the real physical world. Low-end visitors could hear their loved ones in a group access room or upgrade to a private access booth with audio and visual but no entry into the sim environment. Access fees were high for all visitors, but group and booth fees for the general public were dropping due to new federal subsidies. In a rare moment of agreement, most Washington politicians considered basic EF visitor access to be a necessary individual freedom for all citizens, even if government funding was required to support this ideal. This kind of agreement was so unusual that it had raised suspicions about Elysian Fields among the mediaheads, but no one had been able to prove anything.

By poking around in the system, Norman learned that the deceased or his relatives could also pay for class barriers and other limitations that restricted the movements of other avatars they deemed undesirable. If a Lincoln Ford Kennedy didn't want to associate with former blue-collar workers in the digital afterlife, money made it possible. This darker side of the EF environment would not be all that apparent to those who couldn't afford this kind of privileged eternal life, but Norman was disappointed to see that the world of Elysian Fields was so true a reflection of live society.

Norman downloaded the contents of the Lincoln Ford Kennedy biochip into the blank chip connected to the commlaser on Sutro Tower. The process would take almost a minute, so he decided to use the time for another quick search of the database. A moment later, he located the database entry for his grandfather, Oliphant Meadows, and started to open a sim link that would allow him to create a blank avatar and communicate with Oliphant briefly before the system kicked him out or killed him. Then he thought about the young woman seated behind him on the tower and the desperation he'd seen in her eyes, so he tried once more to locate Carlo in the database, unable to understand why he couldn't find the entry.

Then Norman heard a moaning sound. At first he thought it was the wind humming through the guy wires on Sutro Tower, but the moan formed a word inside his head. "Ozymandias?"

"Huh?" Norman was startled. Adrenaline raced through his body. Something had spoken to him in the EF system, and that couldn't be possible unless the killware was on his trail and wanted to taunt him before it delivered its fatal neural shock.

"My name is Ozymandias, king of kings," said the ghostly voice. "Look on my works, ye Mighty, and despair!"

Ozymandias? A poetic killware AI that quoted Shelley? Norman realized that the sim link he had started to establish in the EF system was now active, but the sim coordinates had changed, so this couldn't be his grandfather. "Your name is Ozymandias?" Norman asked.

"Not really," said the voice, "but I'm a big fan of Percy Bysshe Shelley and his pals. The Romantics knew how to express their feelings about death. Got your attention, though, didn't I? My real name isn't important—I'm just a ghost in the machine—but you can call me Shade."

So it really wasn't his grandfather. His heart sank. The old man had been a crafty devil who might toy with Norman's head to teach him something, but Shade didn't sound like him. Oliphant was an MIT philosophy professor with a physics degree; a womanizer who was known for his showmanship and for expanding on Dr. Wernher von Braun's idea that nothing in nature could disappear without a trace, always being transformed from one state to another, and that included the human soul. He had also combined that idea with his own thoughts about alternate worlds coexisting with ours through the magic of quantum physics. In a way, Oliphant had given Norman the idea for the Lazarus biochip to create an alternate digital world. Norman knew it must have been a great disappointment to Oliphant when he was killed while buying milk during a convenience store robbery rather than in the process of finding a gateway to a parallel dimension. Twelve of his former girlfriends had shown up at his funeral, which seemed to say something good about his ability to remain friends with those he loved.

A scene formed in the sim environment: a sun-baked Egyptian temple with the massive fallen head of a pharaoh lying on its side in the sand. Beside it stood an avatar of a thin, bald man who looked out of place in the scene because he was wearing a glaring white toga. None of this made any sense to Norman, since the limited AIs that drove the simulation world and the avatars shouldn't be able to create their own sim links or contact the administrative part of the system to communicate with EF employees, which was how Norman was disguised.

"I'm sure you have questions," Shade said. "That's understandable. I'm what they call a 'wanderer,' when they're being polite, or a 'psychotic break' when they're not."

"What's that?" Norman asked.

Shade smiled. "Well, sometimes there's a defect in a biochip, or the personality upload doesn't go quite as planned, or some Elysian Fields bureaucrat is in a hurry to go home and blows the upload process. Doesn't happen often, but when it does, you get a wanderer. The nice part of it is that I know I'm trapped in here, while most of the stiffs think they're still alive. That gives me certain advantages."

"Like what?"

"Like what we're doing right now. I get around where the stiffs can't. It also takes a long time to hunt down a wanderer if EF discovers their mistake, because we can modify our own records."

"Are there many of you?"

Shade frowned. "I just said it doesn't happen often, didn't I? And I don't have any idea how many there are. I haven't been around that long myself. But I do know that the only way I'm going to retain my sanity is by communicating with the outside world, so I'm going to do something for you, and I want something in return."

Norman realized that he was breathing hard as a little alarm in the back of his mind went off to remind him how long he'd been in the EF system. This Shade thing was fascinating, but he'd have to get out very soon. If he could return at a later time, he could explore this flaw and maybe get some use out of it.

"I'm in kind of a hurry," Norman said. "I think—"

Shade interrupted him. "I'll tell you where to find Carlo Colombari. I saw you were looking for him, and it doesn't look like you want to come in the front door. All you have to do is download some messages from me to the outside world. I want to warn people about this place and tell them what it's really like. Things are happening in here that you lifers should know about, and I don't have access to the datasphere."

"Okay," Norman sighed, "but let's make it quick."

"I'm sending the packets to you now with the password to access Carlo."

"Have you spoken to anyone else?" Norman asked while monitoring the download.

"I'm not a magician; I'm just a bug in the system. I can talk to some of the visitors, but they usually just brush me off and go on about their own self-absorbed business with the stiffs they came to see. I'm hoping you're different."

"I'll be back," Norman said. He wanted to say more, but

he'd been there way too long already. As he reached forward to hit the kill switch, he heard a tuneless whistle, then the Egyptian scene with Shade in it dissolved to reveal a flaming shape that looked like an eyeless human face racing toward him; too close for him to run. It was a security AI, assuming a shape that it knew would startle him before it struck. In the final moment before the killware made contact, Norman identified it as Firestorm, the same AI that had almost killed him on his previous attempt to crack Elysian Fields through the datasphere.

The defender of the digital dead glowed with a blinding white light.

Ariel and BD gasped and jumped back when Norman's body suddenly stiffened, his eyes wide and staring. He gargled, shoved the biochip equipment toward BD, then fell over sideways with the back of his neck smoking. BD started toward him, but Norman silently slid off the catwalk, his stiff body pinwheeling in the wind on its long fall to the earth.

18

YVETTE Fermi, dressed in her most expensive black suit with a massive blue diamond glinting on her neck, strode past the secretarial fortress set up in front of the closed mahogany conference room doors. Two spotlights angled down at the doors gave the entrance an otherworldly appearance, and Yvette instantly thought of the gates to Hell. The association had occurred to her in the past, because the black building bore no corporate markings, and the people who worked there were somewhat demonic in their business dealings. The individuals beyond the mahogany door held the power of life and death in their hands, and there were many who would kill to work for them. Yvette didn't need to do such things because she had helped bring the company to life.

"Hey," said the young man doing clerical work behind the desk. "You can't go in there."

When the secretary moved to block Yvette's path, she stiff-armed him and left him flat on his back, gasping for air. Careful not to rumple her suit, she rolled him out of the way with her foot, then grasped both of the curved silver handles and hurled the doors open, barely slowing her pace.

". . . leaving us with a timetable of two weeks," said a man with a mild English accent and thick red hair, who was standing beside the table. He casually turned and looked toward Yvette at the foot of the long obsidian table, then adjusted his black tie. "Ah, Ms. Fermi."

"Ah, Mr. Whittington," Yvette said, her eyes meeting his cool gaze until he sat down. She wrinkled her nose when she detected Bruno Whittington's distinctive odor, a sickly sweet smell like rotting fruit. She thought he looked like a thug from the backstreets of London who had been stuffed into a black suit.

The long conference room was dominated by one wall of glass that looked out over a small park across the street, where wisps of morning fog still lingered among the few stunted trees that clustered around a brackish pond. Yvette was on the fourth floor of the unmarked Elysian Fields building, which had originally been a slaughterhouse and meat packing plant before its conversion to office space in the late twentieth century. The architects had retained whimsical references to the building's past, such as meat hooks on a sliding overhead track in the hallways, signs warning the meat packers to wash their hands, and huge drains in the bare concrete of the ground-floor killing rooms that were now dedicated to parking spaces. Despite the otherwise sleek and expensive look of the offices, the depressing atmosphere of the place always made Yvette want to leave as soon as possible.

Seated at the head of the conference table under a bright spotlight, a seventyish man in a gray suit smiled at Yvette with a twinkle in his eyes. "Can my assistant bring you anything, Ms. Fermi? Tea, perhaps? Stims? Something stronger?"

Yvette smiled. "Your assistant is only semiconscious at the moment, so I doubt that he could bring me anything."

"I can always send Whittington."

Whittington gave him a look, then glared at Yvette.

Yvette nodded. "No need, Mr. Gardner."

"I trust that you didn't permanently disable another one of my employees. Good help is so hard to find these days."

"Good help would recognize me, but I'm sure this one will be fine. He'll remember me next time."

"Very good. And to what do we owe the pleasure of your visit?"

"Compensation, Mr. Gardner."

Gardner leaned back in his chair and raised one eyebrow. "Really? I was under the impression that you had been compensated handsomely for your fine efforts on our behalf."

"The money arrived in my Swiss account precisely when you said it would. However, I need a little more," she said, gradually walking toward them. Whittington had to turn at an awkward angle to keep his eyes on her while she walked behind his chair.

Except for his alert blue eyes, Gardner didn't move as she approached. "And why is that?"

Yvette smiled. "Let's review, shall we? As a NASA director, I used my own contacts to obtain both master chips that you required, the Feelie and the Lazarus. My contribution made complete personality uploads possible and allowed you to enhance the reality of your prototype sim. You're making far more money from this technology than you thought possible because I had the guts to take the risks and *appropriate* what you needed. Would you agree with all that?"

Gardner shrugged. "More or less."

"We could have reverse-engineered the Feelie chip," Whittington said. "Porn producers and virtual strip clubs have used it for years. It would have taken longer, that's all."

Yvette smiled patronizingly and patted Whittington on the head like a little boy. "And you would have triggered a self-destruct sequence as soon as you tampered with any production model Feelie chip. You think the chip designer didn't think of that?"

Whittington grunted and began to clean his fingernails.

"And you never would have had the Lazarus for personality uploads. My connection brought you the one and only master chip."

"We had memory nanoprobes in our lab. We already had history uploads when you came on the scene," Whittington sneered.

"Shut up, Whittington," said Gardner, keeping his eyes focused on Yvette. "We agree that you've been instrumental in our development, Ms. Fermi. Are you thinking that some sort of royalty is in order?"

"I'm thinking that a seat on your board of directors is in order, Mr. Gardner, along with some form of profit sharing. I'm also thinking that I know a lot about your operation that you wouldn't want revealed to the public."

Whittington snorted and rolled his eyes.

Gardner smiled and stood up, his tone of voice calm and reasonable. "I like your attitude, but you realize that a seat on our board brings with it certain responsibilities? Our investors are powerful people, and they'll have to be satisfied that they can trust you."

"You're saying you'll have to show me the secret handshake?"

"Something like that."

"Then maybe I'll show you mine," she said, firmly shaking his hand.

19

KATE'S sweaty hands gripped the steering wheel while her Jeep pounded over a bad washboard road east of Lake Powell. It wasn't exactly her Jeep, since it technically belonged to the National Park Service and Peter Zah, but it was the best vehicle she could steal under the circumstances. For all she knew, Zah worked for the kidnapper, and she wasn't going to sit around and be spirited away again, so she stole the Jeep and stayed off the main roads where the police might spot her. She wasn't able to find Zah's keys, so she hot-wired the igniter to start the engine, and drove off without looking back.

She'd been driving for six hours over the rough moon-lit landscape on forgotten back roads, managing to get lost only once on a washboard road that ended in a 300-foot vertical drop to a canyon floor. The adrenaline rush from discovering the drop at the last possible moment, the dust from her sudden stop boiling out into the open air over the canyon, had brought welcome alertness back to her brain. This was an area where she'd spent one summer as a student intern, driving around and interviewing Navajo elders, and she'd finally located the old natural gas pipeline that bisected the reservation in a straight east-west line along with the maintenance road that ran parallel to it. She knew her kidnapper might be able to locate her from a satellite search, so her plan was to go as far and as fast as she could before ditching the Jeep and taking some less traceable form of transportation the rest of the way. As Tau had wisely planned ahead for an emergency separation in the event of trouble, they were supposed to meet at Gemstone, the arcology that Tau's mother, Bronwyn, was building in a remote part of the reservation.

Bronwyn's enclosed city in the desert was referred to by some of the other professors at Navajo University as Bronwyn's Folly, but Kate was fascinated by the idea of the self-supporting Gemstone community. Having spent some time with Tau's mother, an unconventional professor of architecture from the white world who had married a Navajo medicine man, Kate understood where Tau got some of his independence. Bronwyn knew that traditional Navajos wouldn't choose to live in a massive structure designed to house and support 300 people, but they were happy to help her build it and see it used by the *bilagaana* as a prototype community for larger arcologies to be built elsewhere. Kate thought it was the sort of structure that might be more appealing to the Hopi, a tribe that had lived in communal dwellings for hundreds of years, as opposed to the Navajo families in their isolated hogans. A similar city design had been adapted by Tau for the prototype he built with nanotechnology on Mars, only to see it destroyed shortly afterward in the Red Star attack on the Vulcan's Forge colony. The loss of the demonstration colony had occurred at the same time as many other losses in Tau's life, and she was proud of him for snapping out of his depression so quickly on the long journey back to Earth. Kate liked to think she had been a big part of his recovery and the return of his optimistic attitude. The months they spent together on the return flight had been some of the best months of her life, marred only by her own memories of the violent events they'd left behind, or *thought* they'd left behind.

After a brief stop to stretch her legs and water the plants by the side of the road, Kate noticed the netsat console mounted on a swinging arm under the glove compartment in the Jeep. She thought about it for a moment, wondering whether a netsat call would give away her position to her hunters, and decided that a brief call to Bronwyn would be safe. She had to know if Tau was okay. She hoped he was at Gemstone now, ready to leave again as soon as she arrived. She knew that many criminals had managed to disappear on the reservation, despite being tracked by the FBI, but most of those events had happened before spysats were commonly used by law enforcement agencies for sophisticated searches run by AIs. The use of AIs made manhunts a little less difficult than looking for a needle in a haystack, but it was still a difficult process. Kate knew she had a good chance of getting away if she could be unpredictable in her movements and maintain her significant lead on her followers.

She had to know if Tau had called. The netsat console lit up when she hit the power button.

WHEN Tau saw the truck coming, he quickly debated whether it would be a wise move to flag it down, but his tired and battered body made the decision for him, collapsing on the pavement when one of his tired feet tripped over a rock by the side of the road. Laika bravely stood beside Tau's head, barking in his ear, apparently unaware of the eighteen-wheeled wall of death bearing down on them at well over 100 miles per hour. At high speeds, a cushion of air carried the truck a few inches above the road, but not enough for Tau's body to clear the undercarriage. Fortunately, the trucker spotted them at the last moment, slowed to drop the wheels, and swerved to avoid pressing them into the cracked black asphalt. When the trucker got out of the cab, Tau was up on his hands and knees with Laika chewing on his left boot. Tau looked too pathetic to be some sort of roadside bandit, so the trucker helped him over to the cab and introduced herself as Pinky Knight. She jerked her thumb at the pink medieval knight on horseback painted on the side of the truck over the words, Pink Knight Trucking. About five feet tall with a slim, athletic figure, Pinky wore black leather overalls and cowboy boots. Tau noticed how muscular she was while she helped him to the truck.

"Pink Knight?' Tau asked.

Pinky smiled. "That's me, boss. Owner and operator, hauling hot freight from Frisco to Santa Fe. What's your handle?"

He introduced himself, as her strong hands shoved him up the ladder into the passenger seat. She lobbed Laika into his lap, slammed his door shut, and climbed into the driver's seat. "Got to move. I'm on the clock for a quickie."

While she shifted the rig into gear and rolled down the highway, Tau realized that she had never asked if he wanted a ride. "Thanks for picking me up. I just need to get someplace where I can make a call."

She concentrated on the road ahead as the truck rapidly accelerated. The guide stripes moved under the truck and back on the left where they belonged. "You can make it here."

"What?" He glanced around the well-appointed interior, noting the expensive equipment, exotic leather upholstery, self-cleaning smartcarpet, and gold-rimmed navigation instruments, but he didn't see any comm devices.

Between gear shifts, Pinky yanked a netsat console down from a recessed slot in the ceiling and swung its flexible arm toward Tau. "All the comforts of home." Tau also noticed a recruiting poster on the ceiling: a portrait of a wild-eyed man with a long beard and the sun glowing behind his head as he pointed at the viewer. Beneath his beard were the words, The Entity Wants You!

The wind howled around the streamlined cab as they moved past eighty. The bumps in the road gently bounced them around, and the powerful engine vibrated Tau's bones. Pinky looked over at him and grinned. "First time in a big rig, Tau?"

Tau gave her a weak smile while he punched numbers into the netsat console. He felt Laika's wet nose press against his ankle while she settled in between his feet.

"Don't worry," Pinky said, "my skirt comes down when we get over 130, then the thrusters kick in, and it's a smooth ride after that."

Tau heard the voice of his mother in the earpiece. "Hello?"

Tau quickly explained his situation and asked if Kate had called.

Bronwyn sounded relieved. "She's on the line now. Let me patch you over."

Tau gasped. "Wait. We might be traced."

His worries disappeared when Kate's excited voice came on-line. "Tau? Are you okay? Where are you?"

"What a relief. I'm okay and on my way there," he said, taking a deep breath. Tau knew he should break the connection with Kate, but he didn't want to let her go. "You're okay?"

"I am now, my love."

"It's good to hear your voice," he said in a soft tone. "I'll be with you very soon."

"Hurry, Tau. I miss you."

Tau sighed and reluctantly cut the netsat connection, then his eyes widened when he saw Pinky dozing in her seat. "Hey!"

Pinky's eyes snapped open and she glanced at her instruments. "What?"

"You're not steering!"

Pinky rolled her eyes and settled back. "Autopilot. Are you always such a nervous passenger?"

"Sorry." He decided to change the subject. "What are you hauling?"

"Sonic toothpicks—there's a shortage in Santa Fe— grave markers, and religious materials."

"That's quite a mixed load." The sun was coming up, and he was tired. He wished he hadn't started this conversation so he could get some sleep, but he needed to be polite.

"I take what I can get, my friend." She gave him an intense stare. "Do you ever feel lonely? I know I get lonely on these long trips."

Tau slowly nodded. Was she coming on to him?

"Do you ever feel like there's something missing in your life? Or like you have a higher calling?"

"I suppose so."

Pinky tapped the poster on the ceiling. "Have you ever felt the power of the Entity? Have you read the Digital

Bible? Do you realize that the Global Brain can give *you* great power?"

A religious whacko. Just what he needed to listen to for the next few hours. "No."

"Then this is your lucky day, Tau. The Church of the Ping can help you down the path to enlightenment. I joined two weeks ago, and I've never been happier. Let me tell you about . . ."

While Pinky droned on, Tau looked out the side window, wondering if he could survive a jump at almost two hundred miles per hour.

THE Predator helicopter plunged toward the desert floor at a steep angle, screaming down from its 60,000-foot cruising altitude, softening its angle of attack only when it had dropped below 200 feet. One of the men watching from the ground flinched when the dark blue craft rolled and shot toward them; the other man slept on the sand in the shade of their dusty all-terrain Rover vehicle.

"This guy's coming in hot," said Ross, shading his eyes with one hand to watch the Predator drop toward them out of the sun.

"Say somethin'?" Persinger mumbled. He squinted through one eye, then lifted his head and frowned at the approaching helicopter. "Nice hardware. I thought they only let the execs and the fast strike units have Predators."

The helicopter dropped within twenty feet of the ground, sending a wake of thick, reddish brown dust into the sky while it hurtled toward them. Ross frowned and glanced at Persinger. "Nygaard must have told him to push it. Maybe they spotted the woman."

"Then why didn't they call us?"

Ross shrugged. "I'm sure the boss has his reasons. You ought to get up."

"I need my rest. You didn't have to hike all over hell and nearly get drowned looking for that Wolfsinger guy."

Ross licked his dry lips, then tried not to wince when he forgot himself and took a deep breath. Flames erupted in his side and his lungs. "My broken ribs beat your sore feet any day. You don't hear me whining."

"I lost a leg once and kept quiet about it for three days until I got back to the office," Persinger sneered.

Before Ross could respond, they were both buffeted by wind and dust, forcing Ross to his knees. He jammed his face into the shirt fabric in the crook of his arm, but the dust caused him to cough, and the cough caused an inferno in his lungs. Persinger simply rolled over away from the stinging blast and hid his face with his hands. The Predator thumped into the sand beside them, and the whine of the rotors descended in pitch while the dust storm subsided. Squinting, Ross could see the circular gold logo of the Department of Energy's Special Operations Group above the outboard fuel pod. Inside the logo's circle, the bald eagle's head looked particularly angry on top of the lightning bolt shield.

Ross blinked and rubbed his eyes to remove the grit. While his eyes were closed, he heard a voice that chilled his blood.

"No need to kneel, Ross," Dag Nygaard said, his long shadow creating a cool spot on Ross's face. "Nice gesture, but it's not going to help your case."

Ross blinked and looked up at the silhouetted figure of his boss looming over him. He wore a seamless white shirt with a high collar, white desert pants, white cowboy boots, and a long white duster-style coat that was climate-controlled and nearly dragged the ground. "Sir, I—"

Nygaard interrupted him. "Don't speak unless you're spoken to. Didn't your mother ever teach you that?"

"Yes, sir, but—" Ross stopped talking when Nygaard smacked him in the side of the head with his open palm. His ears rang. "Ow!"

Nygaard turned suddenly and kicked the reclining Persinger in the leg. "Get up!"

Persinger jumped to his feet and stood at attention. Nygaard slowly walked around him like a Marine drill sergeant with a new recruit, then stopped a few inches from his face. "I'm told that you've had time for a nice walk and a relaxing swim since you've been here. Did you manage to get any work done?"

"I've been working the entire time, sir."

"Oh? What was that just now when you were lying on your face in the sand? Did you think you'd find your target hiding under this vehicle?"

"No, sir. I was resting."

"I see. So you must have found Wolfsinger, killed him, and disposed of the body, thereby earning yourself a well-deserved break."

"No, sir."

Nygaard nodded. "Allow me to summarize your activities another way. Having received your assignment to terminate a civilian NASA scientist who has never received any form of military or combat training, you allowed him to escape and couldn't even manage to stop his small dog."

Ross got to his feet behind Nygaard and stood at attention. He liked the fact that Nygaard was focusing on Persinger's failures instead of his own. When Nygaard turned toward Ross, his heart sank.

"Ross, you allowed the civilian female scientist to disable you and your boat before swimming away like she was on vacation. Is that about right?"

Ross couldn't meet Nygaard's spooky eyes, so he looked down and wondered how the man could keep his boots so white. "Well, sir, as I said in my report, there was more to it than that."

"Oh, of course. You killed two innocent bystanders out fishing on a houseboat, thereby drawing attention to yourself and prompting a visit from an emergency cleanup crew. In fact, you attracted enough attention that Secretary Crandall had to get involved with the National Park Service."

"I apologize for our failure, sir. It won't happen again," Ross said.

"No, it won't happen again. You know why?" Nygaard asked. Before Ross could answer, Nygaard whirled around, pulled a tiny needler from his pocket, and shot Persinger in his right thigh. Persinger howled and crashed to the ground, raising a small cloud of dust that Nygaard stepped back to avoid. He flicked an invisible particle of dirt from his sleeve. The needler was still in his hand when he turned to face Ross again, but his voice was full of understanding. "Failure makes me look bad, Ross. The secretary doesn't call to yell at you, he calls and yells at me. I like my job, and I'd like to keep it, but I can't do everything myself to make sure it's done right. I hire clowns like the two of you to be my eyes and ears, but if you turn out to be blind and deaf clowns, you're of no use to me. Do you understand?"

Ross nodded and closed his eyes, expecting the worst. "Yes, sir."

"Don't fall asleep when I'm talking to you!"

Ross snapped his eyes open and saw the business end of the needler pointed at the tip of his nose, close enough so that he could detect the scent of leather on Nygaard's hand. The slim needle fired by the gun could be loaded with a wide variety of toxins, both lethal and nonlethal, so he had no way of knowing what Nygaard had in mind. Persinger was lying awfully still on the ground now, except for the occasional twitch of his eyelids. Although his job paid very well with all his field bonuses, and even though he could get away with a lot of things that civilians would be sent to prison for, Ross was starting to wonder if the money was worth it. Most employees didn't leave the Special Operations Group alive, and those who did had a tendency to disappear, like Warlord, the man who had trained Guardian and Nygaard. Warlord would have been managing the whole group by now if he'd stayed, but rumor had it that he'd left because he developed a conscience; fortunately, Ross didn't have that problem. The only real problem Ross had was Nygaard, a couple of cracked ribs, and the needler shoved up his nose. "Oh, go ahead and do it."

Nygaard laughed and lowered the needler. "Finally, someone with a spine." He put the needler away and gestured at Persinger. "He'll be all right in an hour or two. You think he'll remember the lesson, or should we just bury him alive and forget it?"

Ross knew his boss was serious. He shrugged. "He's kind of thick, sir, but he probably got the message."

Nygaard nodded.

Ross blinked, thankful that he'd given the right answer. He suddenly realized that he was sweating in the mid-morning sunlight, and he wanted to change the subject. "Do we know where the targets are now, sir?"

Nygaard walked toward the Predator. "The NSA AI gave us a signal intercept, but we don't have a confirm from the birds. Come with me."

Ross followed, jerking a thumb over his shoulder at Persinger. "What about him?"

Nygaard opened the cockpit door and glanced at Ross. Although his boss was always hard to read, Ross saw something in the man's eyes that gave him chills, and he was immediately sorry that he'd asked any questions.

"Someone has to drive the truck," Nygaard said, climbing into the pilot's seat.

20

WHILE the cameras watched his every move, Novikov
examined the free-form lump of dark blue glass "sculpture" mounted on the wall near the Spice Rack. Still wanting to make as much progress through the alien museum
exhibits as possible before the inevitable interruption from
Earth "for safety reasons," he had not experimented further
with the Spice Rack. The glass sculpture formed a series of
raindrop shapes at its base, all of which were semitransparent and lit with a soft glow from within. When he
leaned in close, Novikov was surprised to hear what might
be music: gentle lilting notes layered over an undercurrent
of almost subsonic bass tones. The soft music stopped
when he moved his head back, and started again when he
leaned forward. Interested, he reached out to lightly touch
one of the glass droplets that seemed so tenuously connected to the main portion of the sculpture.

He gasped as the droplet fell into his hand, its smooth,
warm weight resting comfortably in his palm. He glanced
over his shoulder, wondering if the cameras had seen him
break the delicate artifact and thinking he could pocket the
cobalt globe to hide it. He'd do what he always did in these
situations and bluff his way through. He smiled and turned
slightly, holding the cobalt globe up so his audience would
have a better view while he admired it. When the glass
quickly flowed down his arm, completely enveloping his
skin, he was shocked and reacted slowly, then tried to
shake it free, but it continued its rapid advance across his
shoulders and down his torso. It felt like molasses or sap
racing across his skin. Within seconds, the blue glass cov-

ered his entire body, and he found himself looking out at
the museum through a veil of blue.

Novikov held his breath as long as he could, then exhaled explosively and found he could still breathe. The
warm glass cocoon caused a pleasant wave of sensation to
wash over him. He could still move freely, but he couldn't
feel anything he touched with his hands. His worries vanished, and he closed his heavy eyelids, sensing no threats
or harmful feelings, reminding himself that this was another harmless museum exhibit. Feeling safe and secure,
he allowed his thoughts to drift on the peaceful cloud
forming in his mind.

"Lenya?" A soft female voice with a French accent. She
giggled, then spoke again. "Lenya, are you coming?"

Novikov opened his eyes. His blue cocoon was gone,
replaced by some of his old street clothes. He gasped when
he saw the tall figure of Dominique Girardin standing before him, her long black hair dancing in the breeze.
Dressed in red spray-on skinfoam with a scarf around her
neck and a beret on her head, she looked at him with pierc-
ing sapphire eyes and a smile that glittered in the strong
beam of the flashlight he held. The air felt damp and cool,
and an arching wall of mortared stone loomed close on two
sides, separated from the darkness beyond only by the
glow of Novikov's flashlight.

"Dominique? How could—where are we?"

"The tunnels, of course." She said it simply, as if it
should be obvious to him.

Novikov tried to concentrate, wondering where he'd
last seen her. He'd spent a few months in Paris during his
graduate studies, and he'd formed an attachment to one of
the local students. She was twenty-four then, and she
didn't appear to have aged at all as his eyes roamed over
her curves, remembering the playfulness and mischievous
nature that contrasted with the studious appearance she
projected on campus. He realized her appearance here had
to be another trick of the AI running the show in the museum, conjuring a woman from his past to simplify communication. Kate McCloud had reported the same anomaly

when she was contacted by the alien AI known as Thoth, who had appeared to her as the Egyptian god with the head of a bird.

"I'm sorry. I don't remember what tunnels we're in."

Dominique laughed and gestured at their surroundings. Novikov turned the flashlight toward the wall, illuminating the ancient white and gray stones stained with brown. Moisture glinted in the beam of light, and he noticed they were standing in two inches of clear water. To his left, he saw a plaque on the wall; ornate black letters on smooth white stone, possibly marble, were worn to the point of being unreadable, but he could see a date etched in the corner of the text that ended with 1786. Shining the light down the tunnel beyond Dominique, he saw another plaque overhead that read: *"Arrête! C'est ici l'empire de la mort!"* which translated as: "Stop! This is the Empire of Death!"

And then he remembered. On their third date, Dominique had led him down into the catacombs under the streets of Paris. She lived in a building near the public entrance to the catacombs in the Denfert-Rochereau square, but she was one of the many student "cataphiles" who knew of hidden entrances into the empire of the dead. The basement of her building, whose stone floor sagged over underground vaults, contained the entrance to a descending staircase guarded by steel bars and a rusty lock that had been pried open years before. Noting his hesitation, Dominique gave Novikov a brief explanation.

Deep under the streets and buildings of the 14th Arrondissement, the bones of six million Parisians were stacked in an area of seven city blocks. By 1780, the common graves of Paris cemeteries were overloaded with hundreds of years' worth of dead citizens. The Cemetery of the Innocents, in the center of the city, had received over thirty generations of Parisians and plague victims, and was so overcrowded that its soil towered eight to twenty feet over the surrounding streets. After heavy storms, portions of the cemetery walls would collapse and dump mounds of the dead into the street. The cemetery became the source of

many epidemics that crowded its boundaries even more.
Understandably, the living neighbors complained.

Since Roman times, the calcite stone used to build
much of the city had come from local quarries. Over time,
the city spread well beyond the excavations, leaving empty
tunnels and caverns beneath the streets that weakened the
surface soil. The king decided to fill the troublesome holes
with the troublesome dead citizens. Beginning in 1786, funeral chariots covered with black sheets moved hundreds
of cartloads of bones through the dark streets. Smoking
torches lit the quarries where sacks were emptied and remains piled anonymously, mixing the bones of French lu-
minaries such as Madame de Pompadour in with those of
Robespierre, the instigator of the Reign of Terror. These
initial efforts continued daily for fifteen months. Gradually, thirty other Parisian cemeteries and mass graves were
closed so that their dead could also be moved into the catacombs, an underground necropolis whose maze of tunnels
extended for 200 miles. Under the left bank of the Seine,
91 galleries of the dead were built under city streets, 44
were under gardens and public buildings, and 200 more
wound their way under private dwellings, forming a tunnel
network twice as long as all the modern subway lines put
together.

Dominique knew just what to say to appeal to Novikov's
archaeological interests and get him down the eighty-five
steps of the creaky iron staircase. Two hundred feet below
the bright summer streets of Paris, they entered a jagged
square corridor about three feet wide and six feet high. The
walls were lined with grinning brown and white skulls
neatly arranged in rows between stacks of leg and arm
bones, and Dominique told him that the bone walls extended back about thirty yards. The spooky atmosphere
reminded Novikov of the Egyptian tombs he'd visited over
the previous two years; he felt as if he'd come home after
a long journey.

Now, Novikov had returned once more, back from Mars
to relive a wonderful moment in his life. Dominique
seemed as real now as she had then; perhaps more so, as

she had married a famous investment banker a year later and disappeared into the fantasy world of the ultrarich. It seemed strange that this was the memory the alien AI had chosen to simulate for him, and he wondered what that signified in terms of Dominique's importance to his past. Or perhaps it wasn't her significance so much as the memory of the catacombs themselves, to which he had returned many times after his first visit with Dominique. In any case, she looked quite real. To experiment, he leaned forward and kissed her. She tasted and smelled as good as he remembered.

Dominique pushed him away, laughed, and ran off into the darkness, her boots splashing against the watery floor. Novikov ran after her, following the splashing sounds, keeping his head low to avoid the occasional projection of rock that reached down to crack his skull. He chased her up and down gradual hills and around long curves that passed other tunnel openings and small chambers sprayed with graffiti. Some of the rooms contained altars and shrines, while others contained camping lanterns, candles, portable stereo systems, chairs, and the occasional bed. When he no longer heard her footsteps, he stopped to listen, breathing hard enough to make steam in front of his face, worrying that he had lost her, and noticed a plaque on the wall by his head: "Happy is he who always has the hour of death before his eyes and is ready to die every day." The skulls grinned as they had for 300 years, happy to be dead, happy to be there.

Novikov heard a loud scream behind him that made him jump and hit the top of his head on the ceiling. Cursing, he held his aching head and turned to see Dominique standing there naked, except for her boots. She made a pouty face at him.

"Pardon. I thought I'd be making you laugh. Are you well?"

Novikov closed his eyes and took a deep breath, trying to lessen the hammer blows in his skull. Cowering in pain didn't fit his self-image. He put his arms down and leaned back against the wall to squint at her. "I'm okay, but please don't scream like that again."

"Good," she said, and disappeared sideways through a narrow opening in the bone wall. Novikov blinked, wondering why she was naked, where she had gone now, and whether he would leave the catacombs alive.

When the throbbing in his skull quieted down, he swallowed and stood upright to peer through the narrow gap where Dominique had gone. His flashlight revealed a small tunnel gradually slanting up through the bone pile; if he turned sideways and crawled upward with his weight on one hand and one foot, he could slide through the wall to the hole at the top. The opening was about thirty feet away and appeared to be glowing with the yellow light of Dominique's lantern. Faced with the choice of staying in the corridor by himself, watched by hundreds of dead eye sockets while he contemplated his mortality, or climbing up through the stacked bones of plague victims from a Paris cemetery, he finally swallowed, got down on his hands and knees, then squeezed into the gap.

This wasn't his first intimate experience with the dead; he'd handled mummies and skeletons before, but the idea of the bones of so many dead French people squeezed against his body really made him long for a few strong shots of vodka. Skeletons snapped under the weight of his legs, defiling them even more than the cemetery workers who had tumbled their random bones together like so many matchsticks. The skulls and leg bones under his left hand felt cool and slick with moisture. He heard little scuttling noises that were probably rats within the wall. While he inched his way forward, he wondered if the old bones were sturdy enough to support him without caving in, but he noticed some kind of mortar had been used to shore up the tunnel's ceiling and sides. Who would have gone to all that trouble?

By the time he reached the end of the passage, Novikov's arms and legs shook with the strain of supporting his weight in the odd posture. Dominique might have been small enough to crawl through on both hands and knees, but he had a feeling the tunnel had not been built for someone his size. And she must have known that. The thought worried him, but he lurched through the opening anyway to collapse on a dry gravel floor.

He lay in a room about twenty feet square lit by flickering candles and Dominique's lantern, which rested on a small oak table that had seen better days. Three of the walls were built of skulls and leg bones, but one wall was of rough white stone. Two old office chairs lay splintered against the stone wall behind a large desk. The white wall was sprayed with French words in black paint, interspersed with painted skeletons wearing military uniforms. The desk itself was in reasonably good shape, scratched and dented but able to support its own weight. However, there were two features of the desk that stood out immediately: Dominique lay across the clean surface on her side, her head propped up with one hand while she watched him; and the neatly painted symbol on the front of the desk—a Nazi swastika.

Dominique smiled and put a faded German officer's cap on her head. "I'm having your interest again, no?"

Amazed, Novikov sat up and stared. He knew about the Nazi occupation of Paris during World War II, but he didn't understand the connection with the catacombs. He felt the presence of history surrounding them. Did anyone else know about this place? Could he "discover" it? The graffiti meant others had been there, but maybe not recently, and its existence might not be known publicly. He'd do some research, then call a reporter to accompany him down there if the bunker turned out to be an undiscovered historic find. He realized he was smiling. Dominique gestured for him to come closer.

"We're in the German bunker. If you're very good, I show you the communications room," she said, patting the desk. "Lots of little wires, the buttons labeled in German, and the old flat photos hidden in a hole."

"I'd love to see that," Novikov said. He liked looking at her as well. The contrast appealed to him—beauty and horror, past and future, life and death, all in one dark room

200 feet beneath a bright summer day. The perfect place to thumb their noses at Death.

She grabbed his wrist to pull him closer. "Of course you would. Show me how much."

Perhaps this is what the anonymous author meant by keeping the hour of his death before his eyes so he could die happy.

21

KATE tried not to think about the kidnapping, focusing instead on the fact that Tau was alive and well instead of dead at the bottom of Lake Powell. The pleasant sound of a babbling brook in a forest calmed her mind, although it was really a concrete water channel flowing through a lush indoor garden under a high canopy of green glass. The green dome arched maybe ninety feet over her head, enclosing a community space that could accommodate a few hundred people on multiple platform levels. Each of the raised platforms appeared to be carved from impossibly large blocks of sapphire, diamond, ruby, topaz, and obsidian. Decorative narrow streams joined at the main freight channel that bisected the cavernous space. Three footbridges arched over the canal, connecting ground-level walkways that wound through lush vegetation. An alcove at the center of the north wall held a small stage with a lectern, acoustically designed so that a whispering lecturer could clearly be heard without amplification anywhere in the room. At this stage of Gemstone's construction, the completed community room was also the meeting hall where Professor Bronwyn Wright lectured to her interns about architecture each morning. There were about fifty people in the room. Until her visit here, Kate had not been aware of Bronwyn's visionary reputation as an architect, inspiring students from around the world to volunteer in the construction of this new structure in the remote Arizona desert.

Kate knew she stood out among the casually dressed students in her baggy green park ranger's uniform, but the Gemstone store didn't sell clothing, and Bronwyn had been too busy to offer something of hers. At least she'd been able to park Peter Zah's official jeep under a balcony to keep it hidden from aircraft and spysats.

"The special problem of the desert is the sun," Bronwyn said to the crowd. "The heat is merciless toward anything or any space that cannot count on deep receptacles and great thermal mass. In the organic realm, the cactus happily tolerates the moisture-free heat of the day without drying into a crisp, and this is a good model for architecture. The cactus is made up of parts with three congruous dimensions and a minimal ratio of surface to volume, an essential condition for survival. Techniques of survival point the way for techniques of comfort. The greater the mass of a structure, the more balanced the climate, insulating the interior from the hot days and cool nights."

Although Kate had no strong interest in modern architecture, there was something captivating about Bronwyn's voice; she lectured in a melodic tone in words that demonstrated her expertise without being too technical. While Bronwyn spoke, Kate also heard the basis of Tau's design philosophy, the only difference being that he worked with molecular building blocks.

"Air-conditioning can attenuate the handicaps of a strong climate," Bronwyn continued, "but its use is evidence of poor design. By failing to demand from the building itself those elements of congruence with the climate that would render total conditioning redundant, an inferior design does not work with the positive aspects of climate. The artificial should complement the natural. Great mass and profound shadows offer relief from extremes of temperature. Ancient Native American builders understood that any sheltering shape that can accept the low winter sun and intercept the high summer sun creates a better climate within the sheltered space, whether the shape is an apse open toward the south or a shallow cave under an overhanging arch of rock."

An hour later, Bronwyn answered a few questions from the audience, sent them off to work, and ambled over to talk with Kate.

"Did you get some rest?" Bronwyn asked, plopping onto the stone bench next to Kate.

"I slept for a couple of hours. Now I'm just anxious to see Tau."

Bronwyn nodded. "Bad business. You're welcome to stay here as long as you like."

Kate smiled and gave her a hug. She hadn't told Bronwyn everything about the events of the last two days, leaving out little details such as her kidnapping. Kate just said the ranger had lent her his clothes after hers were lost in a flash flood that separated her from Tau. She still wasn't sure that Bronwyn believed her bizarre story, but there was no need to get her involved, especially when they didn't even know who was after them. "Thanks. I'd like to stay, but Tau and I have to return to reality."

"Well, San Francisco's not so bad." Bronwyn shrugged. "Did Tau tell you I was there while you were on Mars?"

"Oh? I didn't think you and Kee liked to leave *Dinetah*."

"We don't," Bronwyn said, opening her arms to indicate their surroundings, "but I've got to pay for this place somehow. I took a consulting job. One of my former students is building a floating arcology in the bay, first of its type. Nova Alcatraz they call it. The island used to be for prisoners; now it's for rich people. Typical."

"I've seen it from a distance," Kate said. "Looks like a giant white seashell in the middle of the bay."

Bronwyn chuckled. "I tell my students to think organically. Carlo always was big on seashells in his design homework. Someone finally let him build one."

"So you worked on Nova Alcatraz?"

Bronwyn nodded at one of her students walking past. "Not exactly. I got a tour of the construction site, but I was disguised as a potential resident. Carlo didn't want anybody to know I was there, so I worked out of a hotel room on the Embarcadero, where I could see the frame of the nautilus shell from my window."

"Why the disguise?"

Bronwyn shrugged. "Carlo said it wouldn't look good if

the other partners knew his old professor was doing some of his work. He got too busy to get all his work done on time, and he needed help with some of the technical aspects of his design. And Nova Alcatraz is a little more complicated than building another Captain Bill's Krill Grill."

"Home of the Thrill Krill Burger," Kate sang, mimicking the annoying jingle sung by dancing plankton that seemed to haunt almost everyone on the planet.

Bronwyn snorted and rolled her eyes. "I'm so glad they haven't built one of those on the reservation yet."

"The Southwest isn't exactly known for its seafood."

"Neither is Captain Bill's." Bronwyn chuckled, then she checked her silver fingerwatch. "If you want to keep an eye out for Tau, try the emerald balcony on level three. You can see the road from there. If you see Kee come in, tell him I'm underground in the agricultural lab."

"He's not working today?"

Bronwyn stood. "When I told him you and Tau would be here, he said he'd come right away. He has some kind of an urgent message for you."

Kate walked with Bronwyn down a row of brilliant flowers, all drought-tolerant plants with bright blooms of red, yellow, and purple. "He could have called."

"'Too important,' he said. And I think he's worried about you."

Kate nodded. "Me, too."

TAU stood on a translucent emerald balcony cantilevered out over an eighty-foot drop to a dry wash. He held Kate in his arms, his eyes closed, allowing her warmth and energy to fill his body after the long trip. Her hot breath rippled over the side of his neck while he softly stroked her hair and the curves of her back. They were together now, and that was all that mattered. Standing there on the soaring balcony of the vast arcology, Tau felt rooted to the world. He didn't want the feeling to end.

The enclosed cityscape stretched out below Tau for hundreds of yards. The incomplete domes and terraces looked like jewels erupting from the red rock cliffs to spill out over the pink and white desert sands. A silent audience of funnel-shaped ocotillo thrust their whiplike clusters of woody branches as high as twenty feet up from the sand in admiration. Small clumps of chia sage plants offered purple flowers in response to the greens, blues, reds, and yellows of the tumbled gemstones. The colorful geometric shapes formed the core of Gemstone's design, hinting at a future self-contained city of fifteen thousand that would combine all of Bronwyn's architectural concepts into a unified whole. She'd spent years raising enough funding to demonstrate the superiority of her Paolo Soleri–inspired arcology over traditional planned communities. Despite the smug sneers of the academic world, Gemstone rose from the desert sands using only volunteer labor and advanced automated building technologies. Tau had joked about smuggling some of his own virtual reality–based builders out of his NASA lab to speed up the construction process, but Bronwyn didn't need them.

Part of Bronwyn's philosophy was to build with low-impact ecological methods, creating no wastes to litter the surrounding environment. Although a single gravel road would link the community with the closest highway, daily commuting would occur within the confines of the giant structure via walkways, dropchutes, and linked watercourses. Freight moved within levels by waterway and elevator, offering a practical and decorative element in contrast to the desert landscape.

Tau felt proud of his mother's accomplishments and her ability to defy the naysayers of the architectural community. He hadn't always felt that way about her attitudes, of course, and he remembered thinking she was crazy when he was a teenager, wondering why she kept herself from advancing in her career by arguing with her superiors about everything, but later he understood. His mentor at NASA, Max Thorn, had also bucked the system, but Max was brilliant enough to have made his mark in the world anyway, only later succumbing to the forces that conspired against him. When Tau realized that the legendary outcast

Max Thorn, one of the gods of computer science, saw value in Tau's work, he knew his life was on the right track.

Kate supported Tau's nonconformist tendencies, but she also understood how he should act to achieve his goals so that others could accept his successes. She helped connect him to the rest of humanity. Together, they had balance and beauty; they had *hozro*.

When Tau spotted Kate on the balcony at Gemstone, patiently waiting for him, he felt a dark cloud lift from his mind. The threat was over for now, and they were together again. Kate had filled him in on her story, and they would soon have to leave the area, but for now it was enough to revel in her presence, touching her hair and holding her close. Then she moved her lips up to his ear and whispered, "Tau, I have to go away again."

Tau stopped breathing. "What?"

"Your father brought me a message, and he's inside now with your mom. Something has happened."

Tau held her by her shoulders, trying to understand. "I noticed. You were kidnapped and someone tried to kill me."

Kate looked down at her feet. "No. I got an urgent message from Yvette."

"Did something happen to your parents? Why Yvette? What's going on?"

Kate put her index finger on Tau's lips. "I have to go to Russia. I'll only be gone a few weeks. Yvette will put me on a special NASA flight out of Moffett Field, so I won't have to go through a public airport where I might be spotted."

Tau shook his head. "Why? You're not telling me why."

"I don't know the details yet, but there's an archaeological team in the southern Urals that needs me."

"How is NASA connected with an archaeological site in Russia?"

Kate paused and looked into his eyes. "Yvette says they've found something related to my discoveries on Mars."

Tau rolled his eyes. "Impossible. It's some kind of a trick. You can't go."

"What do you mean I can't go?" She took a step back and crossed her arms, glaring at him.

Tau realized his mistake, but this lure to get Kate out of the country seemed too coincidental, considering everything that had just happened over the last two days. "Someone's trying to separate us. You've already been kidnapped once, and we still don't know why."

"You're the one who's always defending Yvette, and she's the one who sent me the message. I think they need my expertise because I'm the only one who can communicate with Thoth."

"Maybe, but why now, all of a sudden? And why Russia? General Zhukov's people are in Russia; the Red Star base on Mars was a Russian military outpost. Doesn't any of that make you suspicious?"

"I'm not stupid, Tau. I'll be careful going in."

"Getting in won't be hard, it's getting you out again that I'm worried about."

Kate sighed. "Look at it this way. If I'm out of the country for a couple of weeks, maybe you'll be able to figure out who tried to kidnap me. And why."

"I don't even know where to start."

Tau jumped when a deep male voice boomed behind them. *"Ya'at'eeh, shiyaazh!"*

He turned to see his father, Dr. Kee Joseph Wolfsinger, striding toward them with a big smile on his face. Even at sixty, Kee's handsome and dramatic face made him look like an actor. His shoulder-length hair, pulled back in a ponytail, was still as black as ever. Laika trotted along beside him until she spotted a chuckwalla basking in the sun on the balcony railing; then she darted away in hot pursuit of the lizard.

"Ya'at'eeh," Tau said, returning his smile. "Shouldn't you be at the hospital today?"

"No patients. I've cured everyone," Kee said with mock seriousness, then he smiled broadly. "But your computer's been beeping at me for the last two hours. I think it's

lonely." He handed Tau the palm-size AI Companion he'd
left at his parents' house when he and Kate went camping
so they wouldn't have any distractions. The beeping was
unusual; Socrates, his AI assistant, rarely used it except in
emergencies.

Frowning, Tau killed the beeper and activated the Companion.

"It's about time," Socrates said. The AI had been built
from the seed program that generated Aristotle, his former
modified Companion, so it exhibited some of Ari's superior attitude, but Tau had to admit that Socrates was dull
and he rarely used it. "Message from Norman Meadows,
San Francisco. You want the summary or the full text?"

"Full text," Tau said, surprised that his old college
roommate would send him an urgent message.

Socrates switched to Norman's digitized voice. "Hey,
Chief, if you're getting this message, I'm probably dead."

Tau's eyes widened, then he wondered if this was one
of Norman's tricks.

"Sorry I haven't kept in touch, but it's too late now,"
Norman continued. "Got a hack job from an old friend in
the feelie biz. Kind of hot, already came close to getting
toasted once before on my own time. Set this infoblip on a
timer, just in case I didn't come back. Anyway, the frog is
in the blender, if you know what I mean, so I'd appreciate
it if you'd stop by and feed my hedgehog; the little guy
gets hungry. Map attached. Thanks. See you on the other
side, Chief."

Tau's mouth hung open. He couldn't believe it. Norman
was indestructible, a genius with hardware who should
have outlasted Tau. Sure, he'd done some shady deals, but
most of his exploits were legal, and he'd made his first
million right out of college on some chip designs he'd
sold. He was the outgoing geek who kept trying to link Tau
up with girls he'd met at the university's advanced computer lab or in the datasphere. They'd even started a fake
religious cult together while they were in college, mostly
as a way for Norman to meet girls, until Norman's sleazy
brother took it over after Tau dropped out to work at

NASA. He remembered Norman's shock when Tau showed up one evening in their dorm room with a real, live woman he'd met on campus named Kate McCloud.

Considering Norman's fascination with technology, Tau always figured his roommate would become immortal by transferring his mind into a machine or some other science-fictiony kind of thing; he couldn't have simply died like a normal human being.

The message itself was odd. Tau recognized their old code phrase, "the frog is in the blender," which meant Norman was in serious trouble, although "serious" used to mean that Norman was in trouble with the dean or that the authorities were after him for modifying infotap devices. In this case, "serious" sounded serious, like he really might be dead, and he'd sent his final message to Tau, of all people. Why?

"Tau? Are you okay?"

Kate was staring at him. His father had already disappeared. His mind snapped back to the present, and he squinted up at the sky. "Let's get going."

"Where?"

"Back to the city."

"What about our stuff? We left some things at your parents' house."

"I've got Socrates. We can get the rest on our next trip."

He heard a low growl and looked across the balcony. Laika watched helplessly while the agile chuckwalla darted back and forth over the side of the balcony as if it were taunting her. Frustrated, Laika turned and spotted Tau, then charged toward his ankles with her teeth bared.

RANGER Peter Zah frowned at the holo ID badge that the visitor in the white suit held in front of him. "Special Agent Ford? Why is the FBI interested in this woman?"

Dag Nygaard looked into Zah's dark brown eyes and saw the past. He knew the McCloud woman had been here the previous day because the Park Service chief had given him a copy of Zah's report. Zah had gone off in search of her "kidnappers," but had found nothing after the DOE

cleanup crew had sunk the ruined houseboat and obliter-
ated any traces of evidence that might have supported Mc-
Cloud's story. But she must have made friends with the
man, because he was now acting like her protector, and
Dag found that annoying. Identifying himself as FBI was
intended to make the ranger cooperate, but the man chose
to obstruct justice instead.

"You don't have a need to know why," Dag said.

"And I don't have a need to tell you anything," Zah
replied, crossing his arms. He stood behind the shiny wood
information counter just inside the front door to his cabin.
He wore the standard brown park ranger's uniform, complete with the funny hat and the old-style revolver hanging
from his waist in a holster.

Dag glanced out the side window at Ross, watching
them with binoculars from the path into the canyon.
They'd had to set the Predator down on a rocky slope and
hike to the cabin for this interview, and Dag didn't like
wasting his time. Every moment spent with the ranger allowed the McCloud woman a longer head start.

"Kill him and go," Inge said.

Dag closed his eyes and tried to keep Inge's voice out
of his head.

"You need a glass of water or something? Or soda?"
Zah asked. "You don't look so good." He reached under
the counter and came up with a bulb of soda that he popped
open.

"He has a gun," Inge said. "You're closing your eyes in
front of a strange man with a gun. You never would have
made that mistake in the old days. He thinks you're weak."

Dag took a deep breath. "No. He'll cooperate."

Zah frowned and looked around the empty room. "Who
will?"

"This is a national security matter," Dag said, opening
his eyes. "It's classified. I just need to know if the woman
gave you any idea of where she intended to go from here."

Zah snorted and sipped at his soda. "She didn't leave a
note. Didn't even say good-bye. Just took my Jeep and
left."

"No clues during your conversation? She didn't mention any people or places?"

"Just her friend she was worried about. The search team couldn't find him, either."

"I'm aware of that. Has anyone located the Jeep?"

"That's your job." Zah flashed a smile. "We're the National Park Service, not the FBI."

Inge whispered in his brain again. "He's laughing at you, Dag. He knows you're weak."

"Your superiors will be very disappointed when I tell them you refused to cooperate," Dag said, turning toward the door.

"Sorry, but I told you everything I know," Zah said, leaning on the shiny countertop, the soda still in his hand. "I'm sure the FBI can find a young white woman wandering around on the rez, particularly when she's driving an official Jeep."

"You know, I believe you're right," Dag said, turning in the doorway to face him again. "Sorry to bother you." In one smooth motion, he put his right hand inside his white coat, withdrew his needler, and fired once into the broad forehead of Peter Zah.

Zah continued leaning on the counter for a moment, his smile frozen; then his eyes glazed over. Finally, his body realized that his brain wasn't in charge of things anymore; the soda bulb dropped to the floor, and Zah collapsed in a heap behind the counter.

Dag walked around the counter and stepped over the body on his way to the netsat console, careful not to slip in the small pool of blood forming on the scuffed wood floor. "And thanks for all your help."

After five minutes on the netsat link, Dag had called a cleanup crew and reviewed an automated NSA report of recent calls made from the cabin. He asked the database AI to screen out all repeated numbers and official link codes, and that left only one unusual call made the previous day.

"Gemstone?" Inge asked. "What's that?"

Dag smiled. "I don't know. But I'm going to find out."

22

ARIEL had never seen so many tombstones in one place. This wasn't a cemetery—it was a city of the dead. Colma, the official cemetery city of San Francisco, had over one million residents packed into in area of less than 2.5 square miles, and almost all of them were deceased. Outside of the sixteen cemeteries, the local businesses were dominated by florists, funeral chapels, monument makers, and support services for the cemetery workers, but most of the green landscape was neatly trimmed grass dotted with granite or marble stones in the shapes of pyramids, pedestals, spheres, rectangles, obelisks, urns, angels, skeletons, crosses, stars, shrouded mourners, abstract sculptures, or elaborate homes of eternity—crypts with wrought-iron gates and stained glass windows. On her way to the main Elysian Fields facility at Happy Meadows, Ariel had passed the graves of many famous dead people, including Wyatt Earp, Levi Strauss, William Randolph Hearst, and Robin Williams. Thinking of Carlo, she was particularly struck by the inscription on Wyatt Earp's tombstone where he rested beside his wife: "That nothing's so sacred as honor, and nothing so loyal as love!" A light fog hung in the early morning air, leaving a damp sheen on marble and stone, and drops of dew on the self-maintaining carpet of emerald green smartgrass.

Ariel's heels clicked on a white path that glowed with its own inner light, wending its way between two palm trees whose tops bent toward each other to form an arch, marked with a sign that identified them as the Palms of Peace. Her passage triggered a motion sensor that swung open the two massive gates before her, both of which ap-

peared to be coated with white pearl, and the holo image
of a winged male angel appeared in the air just over her
head. In a booming voice, the angel announced, "Behold
the Pearly Gates! Enter unto Happy Meadows, a wholly
owned subsidiary of the Elysian Fields Corporation!"

A winged cherub buzzed her with a sign hanging from
his butt that said, "Follow me to the Hall of Infinite
Peace." Ariel followed the cherub down a glowing walkway of yellow brick that wound between a rainbow of
crystal tombstones and on past an outdoor Parisian-style
café where two sleepy young men dressed as angels relaxed with steaming cups of stimulants before their shift
started. Another small table at the Café Mort was occupied by Ernest Hemingway, Pablo Picasso, Auguste
Rodin, and Voltaire, all of whom were engaged in an animated argument. Beyond the café, the cherub flew a couple of barrel rolls, then beckoned Ariel into a white
escalator tube that rose toward a warm glowing light ball.
Angelic choirs sang soft music in various languages as
Ariel rose toward the light, filling her with an otherworldly sense of peace that distracted her from the fact
that she couldn't see a down escalator or any other form
of exit nearby. Holo ads briefly appeared in front of her
face during the ride, with happy angels singing the popular Elysian Fields slogans such as, "Life or Death, What's
the Difference?" and "Elysian Fields—A Place Where
You'd *Like* to be Caught Dead!"

At the top of the escalator, Ariel was dumped out onto
a spongy surface covered with roiling ground fog. Ahead
of her, bored angels manned a long row of Victorian
wrought-iron ticket booths blocking passage to a dark
canal where blind old Greek men in white robes stood
waiting for passengers on small ferry boats. The foggy
pool connected to three dark tunnels whose entrances were
covered with waterfalls of mist.

"Group chat, booth, or sim?" asked the angel floating
behind the bars of one of the ticket cages. Ariel eyed the
descriptions of each tour package posted on the front of the
cage.

"Group," she said, offering her credit chip. Armed with her own meager funds supplemented by BD's donation from the Church of the Ping, that was all she could afford.

The angel stamped the back of her hand with what appeared to be flaming letters spelling out the word Chat, then gave her a dark coin. "Give this to Charon at the ferry. He'll take you across the Rivers Acheron and Styx—the other barrier rivers won't be finished until next month. You'll be told what to do when you get to the other side, then you'll exit on the Lethe."

"Thanks," Ariel said, stepping through the turnstile. She followed the black stone staircase down to the water's edge. The gray-bearded ferryman accepted her coin and helped her into the boat, then poled away from the shore toward the first tunnel in the row.

"I'm Charon," the ferryman said. "Been here before?"

"First visit," Ariel said, occupied with thoughts of Carlo and not really wanting to talk.

"Sorry to hear that. Your loved one departed recently?"

She shook her head. "Eight months ago, but it's too expensive to visit here often."

Charon shrugged and turned the ferry toward the tunnel mouth. "You're telling me. I work here, and I can't even visit my parents with my discount. We like to say, 'People are dying to get in here.'" He paused a moment, waiting for her response, but when he didn't get one, he cleared his throat. "Sorry. Macabre humor doesn't go over with everyone, I guess. You get used to it when you work here."

Ariel gave him a faint smile.

"Now I'm embarrassed," Charon said. "Look, here's a tip. Come back in three days. They're going to drop all the admission prices once a week for the next year; kind of a promotional thing. Attendance hasn't been bad, but the feds have been on us about their idea of basic human rights and stuff like that. Good PR for the politicians right before the election. Just don't tell anyone I told you; it's supposed to be a secret until Elysian Fields cranks up the advertising campaign tomorrow."

Ariel smiled for real this time. "I won't tell a soul."

Charon snorted. "Won't tell a soul. Good one. I think you're going to like it here. Listen, since you're new, I don't want you to freak out when we get to the other side. There's a big old gate on the shore that's guarded by a three-headed dog named Cerberus. Just ignore him— bark's worse than his bite, if you know what I mean."

"Thanks."

The ferry passed under a misty waterfall, but Ariel remained dry. She heard the sound of rushing water ahead. Then she gasped as the ferry plummeted down a steep watery drop inside the dark tunnel, splashing into another dark pool at the bottom.

"This is the River Styx," Charon said. "It gets a little confusing here because the Greek Hades theme kind of gets mixed in with the Roman thing, some Egyptian Book of the Dead stuff, and other religious themes. Trying to appeal to everyone, you know. It's kind of goofy, if you ask me, but I'm just the ferryman, so what do I know?"

"You seem to know a lot."

"Thanks," he said as they bumped into the black sand beach on the far shore. "Have a nice visit. You'll be exiting on the River Lethe, so you won't come back this way, but ask for Brian on your next visit, and I'll give you a ride if I'm on shift."

She stepped onto the shore. "I thought your name was Charon."

Charon shrugged. "Whatever."

As promised, the eight-foot-tall black dog with three heads only sniffed at her as she went past, never barking or blocking her way. The massive adamantine gate swung open at her approach, revealing a long chamber carpeted in black with white cubicles facing the walls. Each cubicle had a door and was large enough to hold one comfortably seated person facing a wall-size gray screen. Soothing organ music and the smell of sweet incense wafted through the air by the cubicles, and Ariel noted the shafts of col-

ored light streaming down from the stained glass windows
that covered the ceiling. Seeing this, she thought the
cheapest option didn't look so bad.

At her approach, a frowning guardian angel stepped
forward, glanced at the flaming letters on the back of her
hand, and pointed her to a long bench at the far side of
the chamber. The bench was occupied by a handful of
seated visitors who faced microphones and speakers
mounted on a black concrete wall. "Group chat is over
there, miss."

"Oh." She stepped over and sat on the cold steel near
a large, sweaty man in a suit. The man looked uncomfortable, slumped toward the wall, intent on his conversation. A harsh female voice answered him from the
speaker.

Ariel looked at the green light that came on under her
wall speaker when she sat down.

"Name of the departed?" asked a soft female voice.

"Carlo Colombari."

After a pause, the voice said, "Access to Carlo Colombari is restricted. Pass phrase?"

Ariel glanced sideways to see if anyone was listening,
then softly spoke the phrase that Norman had recorded on
the Kennedy biochip during his last moments of life the
previous night. "Empire of the mind."

"Accepted," said the voice. "Retrieval in progress. One
moment."

Ariel couldn't help overhearing part of the conversation
next to hear. "Abuse? This is why I pay to see you?"

"Someone has to do it," said the woman's voice on his
speaker.

"I get enough of that from the kids," he said. "I don't
need it from you, too."

Ariel's attention turned to her own speaker when she
heard Carlo's soothing voice with his mild Italian accent.
"Ariel?"

"Carlo!" Ariel shrieked with delight, causing the other
bench-sitters to jump and glare at her. But she didn't know
what to say next. After months of hoping for a chance to

speak with him again, scraping money together, trying to break in, and hoping for this moment, her mind was a blank. What do you say to a dead husband who rescued you from poverty, shared your life, and made you a whole person? Her hands shook. "Um, how are you, sweetie?"

Carlo hesitated. "Okay, I think. Where are you? I can't see you."

She wasn't sure how to reply, wondering if he knew he was dead. "I'm here, my darling. That's what's important. And I love you. I love you so much."

"Okay, you're right. I love you, too. But shouldn't I be at work right now? I remember going down to the deep-flow stabilizers beneath the city, and covering my ears with silencers to cancel out all that deafening sound, but my mind's a blank after that."

He didn't know. Oh, God, how was she going to break it to him? How could he not know already? Maybe it had something to do with why he was placed in a restricted part of Elysian Fields. Maybe the police didn't want him to know, or the EF people had decided it would be better to give him time to adjust after being murdered? She'd heard of that happening, but there were always rumors about what actually went on behind the scenes at EF.

Before she could think of a reply, Carlo broke the silence. "Am I dead, Ariel?"

"Dead? Well, Carlo, I'm not a doctor, but—"

"I knew it," he said. He didn't sound upset, only curious. "The biochip. I wondered about that. But I thought there would be more to the digital afterlife than this empty darkness. I feel like I'm in limbo."

Ariel felt tears on her face, but she tried to keep her voice steady. "Something doesn't seem right about it, honey. I had to have a special password to reach you, and you're in some sort of restricted area."

"Am I in Colma right now?"

"Yes. I'm in a visiting area in Colma."

"The Elysian Fields theme park, right? I designed part of it, you know."

Ariel frowned. "You did? I don't remember that."

"Well, I helped Phil when he got behind on the design and he needed a holo showpiece for our EF clients. I only worked on the project for a few weeks. The Alcatraz job was ahead of schedule, so I had the time."

"You never mentioned that."

"Slipped my mind. I didn't think it was important. It's not, is it?"

Ariel shrugged, then remembered that Carlo couldn't see her. "I don't know. What did you work on?"

"I did some elevations for the Hall of Infinite Peace, Café Mort, Norton's Tomb, and the Gates of Anubis. I would have done more, but I think the client got mad when they found out I was helping Phil."

"I haven't seen the Gates of Anubis."

"You can go there on your way out if they've finished building it. That's also the route the performers take to reach the service tunnels back to the underground control complex. Then they exit to the surface at the Norton employee entrance. I designed that, too, but the EF employees are the only ones who ever see the interior. You can't get through the hidden entrance, but it's a beautiful monument if you want to walk through the Woodlawn Memorial Park and take a look. I made the whole structure out of pink granite to match Emperor Norton's original tombstone."

Ariel felt pleased that Carlo was still excited by his work. He used to talk about it for hours, even though much of it went over her head. But she learned the basic terminology and took an AI-taught on-line class in architectural appreciation to understand more. For a moment, listening to his voice, she almost forgot where she was.

"I miss you, Carlo. I wish I could stay here with you." She brushed her fingers over the speaker and leaned against the cold black concrete to be closer to his voice. She wanted to tell Carlo how the FBI had thrown her out of Nova Alcatraz and seized their bank accounts, but she didn't want to worry him.

Carlo paused before answering. "I'd rather not think about that. This place isn't what I expected."

"It never is," said another male voice.

Ariel's eyes widened, and she stared at the speaker. "Carlo? Is someone with you?"

"You can call me Shade," said the second voice. "Where's Norman?"

Carlo broke in. "Who's Norman?"

Ariel blinked in confusion. Who was Shade? Was he supposed to be talking to some other visitor? But, in that case, how did he know about Norman? "Um, Norman got the password so that I could talk to you, Carlo."

"Have I met him?"

"No, he's a friend of a friend. Or he was, anyway."

Shade sighed heavily. "*Was?* You mean they got him, too?"

Ariel shook her head sadly. "I don't know what happened, exactly. He was there one minute, and gone the next. He gave his brother the chip with the password on it."

"Christ on a crutch," said Shade. "Sounds like killware to me. EF bastards."

"Who the hell are you?" Ariel asked. "I was having a private conversation with my husband."

Shade sniffed. "I've been waiting for you ever since Norman's visit. Took your time about getting here, didn't you?"

"What do you mean? That was last night. I came first thing this morning."

"Oh. Sorry. Seemed longer to me. You lose track in here."

"No kidding," said Carlo. "Where did you come from? You're the first person I've seen in this place."

"I get around," Shade said cryptically. "I do favors for people on the outside, and they do favors for me. What's your name, Toots?"

Toots? She'd never heard that expression before. "Ariel Colombari."

"You have a note chip on you?"

She sighed, wondering if this annoying Shade would ever go away. "No, I don't."

"Bring one next time," said Shade. "I can help Carlo get out of here if you'll deliver some messages for me."

Ariel shook her head. "Get out of where?"

"The restricted zone, of course. Carlo's trapped where he can't go out and infect the rest of our little community. And they don't want him to have visitors, either."

"Who are 'they'? And why would they do that?"

"Look, I may have special privileges, but I don't know everything. EF locked him up when he was uploaded, and that's all I know. They don't keep records of that sort of thing. It's unusual, so I guess he knows some EF secrets. If you help me the next time you come back, I'll get him out and show him around."

A female voice broke in. "Thirty seconds remaining."

"Carlo," said Ariel. "I love you."

"Will you help me?" asked Shade.

"*Yes, Shade,* now get out so I can talk to Carlo alone."

Carlo sighed. "I love you, too, my Wood Nymph. I wish I could touch you."

A cold hand dropped onto Ariel's shoulder, causing her to jump. Expecting to see one of the angels when she turned around, she was startled to see two men in dark suits wearing sunglasses in the dimly lit chamber. The bald man had his hand on her shoulder. "Ariel Colombari?"

Ariel swallowed. "Yes?"

Both men showed their ID holos in a quick ritual they had performed many times. "FBI. Come with us."

BROTHER Digital popped out of the upchute on the 160th floor of Lum Tower, his robes billowing along with his beard as he landed gently on his feet. When his sandals touched down on the deep carpeting, he recognized a striking woman, dressed in a black business suit, heading for one of the dropchutes.

"Good morning, Ms. Fermi," he rumbled. He didn't see her often, but he liked to stay friendly with people who could do him some good, particularly with the kind of wealthy neighbors who lived in this luxury apt tower. And Yvette Fermi had been generous in the past.

Yvette nodded and smiled. "You're up early today, Mr. Meadows."

"So much work to be done and so little time."

"You're telling me," she said, as she hopped into the dropchute. The gentle scent of flowers remained in the air after she left.

BD continued down the hallway without seeing anyone else, stopped at the door to apt 1666, spoke his name, and entered to find a tall, athletic-looking man with a golden mane of hair reclining on the black leather couch.

"Mr. Meadows, I presume," said the reclining man.

BD studied him for a moment. "Who let you in?"

"Your door let me in. We're friends from way back."

The door shut itself as BD stepped away from the entrance. He glanced around at his expensive furnishings and the original artwork that hung on his walls, but everything seemed to be in its place. "You must be Snapdragon."

"There are some who call me that," he said, rising to his feet. "I got an automated message from Norman that I should come to you if he didn't contact me by sunrise. I believe you have something for me."

BD walked past Snapdragon to look out the window at the blanket of fog that covered most of the city below. Standing on his thick white carpet, he felt as if he were hovering in the clouds. "Running a church is a difficult business, sir. I have to spend much of my time seeking donations to continue our good work."

"If you have the chip," Snapdragon said, "I'll be happy to donate Norman's fee to your church's account."

BD smiled and turned to face his visitor. "I administer church funds directly from my personal offshore accounts. It's safer that way."

"Understandable," Snapdragon nodded. "I am curious, though. Do you know what happened to Norman?"

BD's smile vanished. He returned his attention to the view. "He had an accident."

"Oh? Nothing serious, I hope."

"Quite serious, sir. My brother has become one with the

Great All, which is why the fee will be twice what you agreed on with Norman. He was dispatched while working for you, so think of it as a form of worker's compensation, if you will. I've just finished making the arrangements for his cremation."

Snapdragon cleared his throat. "Twice the fee? That's a great deal of money, Mr. Meadows."

"True. However, I'm sure you understand that various parties would love to know more about Norman's exploits on your behalf. I'm assuming you'd like to maintain the privilege of the confessional, as it were, so that the church need not reveal its knowledge of this matter. Am I correct?"

"Give me your account number," Snapdragon said. "I'll transmit the funds immediately."

BD swung one of the original Picassos away from the wall to reveal a large safe. "A pleasure doing business with you, sir."

23

TRAVELING as Mr. and Mrs. Frank Lloyd Wright, Tau and Kate had used Bronwyn's credit chip to purchase tickets for a tiny private compartment aboard the DEEPTRAN bullet train from Flagstaff Arizona, to San Francisco. The room smelled as if someone had stored fish there, and the odor made Tau feel nauseous. A single overhead glow-panel, cracked on one side, provided a dim yellow light. Laika snored softly in Kate's lap. Although the compartment floated in a liquid buffer cell to minimize G-force effects, they had both attached the standard crashwebs over their padded seats as the mag-dev train decelerated from its peak supersonic speeds. For additional safety, any sudden deceleration or impact would fill the compartment with shock foam, but traveling in this underworld of the dead still made Tau nervous. The near vacuum of the underground tube did not permit windows, and the monotonous tunnel walls would not have provided much of a view if there were, so they spent the hour-long trip discussing their immediate plans and holding each other close. The awareness that Kate would be leaving again made Tau feel hollow inside.

"Well," Tau said, gripping her hand, "if nothing else, getting you out of the country might be best right now."

Kate stroked his forearm. "Safer for me, maybe. What about you? Maybe we could ask Yvette to send you with me?"

"I'd like that, but I might be able to find out who's after you if I stay here. And I want to find out what happened to Norman."

Kate nodded, looking away. Tau wished he could say

something more comforting, but he couldn't lie to her, and she wouldn't have let him. He really had no idea how he'd go about hunting their hunters, but if they were any good, they'd eventually find him, no matter where he went, so all he could do was prepare for that moment. He'd already set Socrates, his AI assistant, to snooping around in the datasphere for clues, although he didn't expect much from the search. The government computers were well protected by defensive AIs that kept snoops at bay. And Socrates wasn't smart enough yet to deal with such defenders. In many ways, Socrates was inferior to Aristotle, the AI Tau had lost on Mars, and that was partly Tau's fault for not taking the time to train him as he had trained Ari. His ambition to excel in building a powerful artificial intellect had abated since his return to Earth, and he still wasn't sure if that was because losing Ari had been like losing a friend, or because he simply preferred human companionship now.

The cabin lurched as the train slowed. The animated route map on the front wall showed that they were under the San Francisco Bay, nearing the DEEPTRAN hub station by Stanford University in Palo Alto. Tau remembered that Norman had been a guest lecturer in Stanford's electrical engineering program. He still couldn't adjust to the idea of Norman being dead. Tau still wanted to believe that Norman's message had been a joke designed to get Tau over to Norman's place for a visit. He had the odd little map that Norman had sent, but it didn't seem to correspond with any buildings that Tau remembered in the Presidio area.

Seemingly reading his mind, Kate looked into Tau's eyes. "You're sad about Norman, aren't you?"

"Yeah," he said with a nod. "I guess I am, although I haven't thought about him for a while. I'd always thought we'd get together again and start a company or something. But Norman was a genius; he didn't need any help from me."

"So are you, but you need help on occasion."

Tau shrugged. He didn't feel like a genius. "Too late

now, I guess. I just assumed there would be plenty of time to work with him later, when I was more established as a molecular designer."

Kate patted his forearm. He didn't want her to go. He sighed as the train rolled to a stop where they'd have to return to the surface world, the real world where friends died and dreams were shattered in the blink of an eye. Kate would visit with Yvette and go on to Russia. Tau would visit Norman's place, figure out what to do with his pets and his stuff, keep an eye out for any stalkers, then wait for Kate's eventual return so he could resume his normal life.

Kate leaned across the seat to press her soft lips against his own. "I love you, Tau."

"I love you," he said, pulling her closer.

Then she got up and left.

SNAPDRAGON'S office in his San Francisco recruiting center was designed to present an image of austerity, with its simple plasteel desk and office chairs. A huge skylight over his white desk provided daytime illumination for his solar panels. His only concession to extravagance was the holo projector in the corner, allowing him to study his televised appearances so he could improve his performance. At the moment, the projector displayed a menu comprised of rows of tiny moving images hanging in the air above the bare concrete floor. Snapdragon focused on one of the news images that had caught his attention so that the scanner would enlarge it to almost life-size 3-D.

The news anchor, a handsome Japanese-American woman in her forties with black hair and a formal business suit, sat behind a clear glass desk speaking to the camera. As Snapdragon enlarged the image, she reappeared in a room full of serious teenagers where she hovered a few inches above the floor like a ghost. The KRUM news team had taken to inserting themselves virtually into news footage from the field to reduce costs, but their equipment wasn't the best.

A KRUM logo appeared in the corner next to her name, June Minoura, while she frowned at the camera. "We're in a classroom at Redwood High School in Marin County. These teenagers are members of two large student groups that have recently formed, Students for Violence and a suicide cult known as Just Kill Me. In response to increasing numbers of violent incidents, local police have established a permanent presence on campus to protect the faculty and students. Parents and teachers claim that these incidents are due to the prevalence of Lazarus biochips among the school's predominately upper-class population. Several students have expressed a belief that death is no longer final or something to be feared. Reports of fatal assaults on students and faculty members have increased dramatically, and suicides after final exams each semester are on the upswing." She paused to aim a dramatic look at an extremely thin young girl in the classroom. "Monica X has tried to kill herself four times, isn't that right, Monica?"

"Yes," Monica said.

June smiled. "You've *tried* four times. You're not very good at it, are you?"

Before Monica could answer, the image was automatically muted as Snapdragon turned his attention to his lead techie, Dandelion, striding through the door with the modified holoviewer that Norman Meadows had given Snapdragon during his visit to the *Ark*.

Dandelion smiled. "I got it working. There's some extra crap on the chip that I had to dump, but the avatar looks great now. Super high-res. Looks real enough that it almost had me fooled. You know the dude who made this thing?"

"I used to," Snapdragon said sadly. "Norman Meadows. I met him several years ago when we were both connected to the adult entertainment industry. He died last night."

"Wow, I've heard of that guy. Was he wearing a Lazarus when he kicked?"

Snapdragon shrugged. "Yeah, but his brother says it was fried when he died. Left a smoking hole in the back of his neck." He tapped the back of his neck for emphasis.

Dandelion made a face while he put the holoviewer down on Snapdragon's desk. "Bad sector, man. Anyway, I have to run. We've got a protest scheduled outside of that new restaurant on Market, Veggies Galore."

"*Murderers* Galore. Go get 'em," Snapdragon said, waving him away.

As Dandelion left, Snapdragon punched the Manual button on the holoviewer and set it on the floor. A few seconds later, a startlingly real image of a distinguished man in his sixties appeared beside Snapdragon's desk. His strong profile was instantly recognizable in most of the world. Well over six feet tall, he gazed calmly at Snapdragon with wise blue eyes that accented his salt-and-pepper hair. Snapdragon swallowed, somewhat awed by the reality of the man's presence, and wondered if he'd made a mistake in kidnapping him from his well-deserved rest in Elysian Fields. Lincoln Ford Kennedy, a cloning experiment successfully raised with the specific intent of becoming president of the United States, loomed over the desk and bestowed one of his trademarked charming smiles on Snapdragon while he offered his hand.

Forgetting that Kennedy was a projection, Snapdragon jumped to his feet and tried to shake the man's hand, an action that confused both of them when they didn't make physical contact.

"What the hell?" asked Kennedy, looking at his hand with a puzzled expression.

"Sorry," Snapdragon said, clearing his throat. "I forgot. But you look so real, you know?"

Kennedy drew himself upright and took a deep breath. "Damn it. I'm dead, aren't I?"

"I'm afraid so, Mr. President."

Kennedy sighed and looked around the room. "Call me Lincoln; everyone does. Is this Elysian Fields? It's not exactly what I expected."

"No, sir. It's my office." Snapdragon introduced himself, described his organization, and became annoyed when Kennedy's attention drifted to the holo projector in the corner. "I hope I'm not boring you, Lincoln."

"Can you get *Washington Knights* on that thing? I love that show. Used to watch it every afternoon. Didn't matter which head of state I was meeting with or what golf course I was on, my assistant always made sure I saw the show on the first run."

"I have no idea if it's on, sir. I don't watch soap operas."

Kennedy chuckled. "Then you don't know what you're missing. I got half my political strategies from that program."

Snapdragon glanced at the news and the volume came up again. June Minoura sat behind her anchor desk. ". . . the mysterious disappearance of Dr. Joshua Rosenkrantz from George Washington University Hospital, where a recent explosion killed twelve members of the trauma unit—"

"So, tell me, young man. Why am I in your office instead of enjoying my own personal idea of the perfect afterlife at Elysian Fields?"

The anchorwoman spoke in silence while Snapdragon sat down behind his desk again. He gestured for Kennedy to sit, but the elder statesman remained standing, his hands clasped behind his back. "I can arrange for your return to Elysian Fields, Mr. President—Lincoln—but I require something from you first."

"Jumong hooter Christmas," Kennedy said, as parts of his body briefly burst into static.

Snapdragon blinked. "What?"

Kennedy frowned. "I said that the United States makes no deals with kidnappers, thieves, terrorists, or other petty criminals."

"Well, that's fine, Lincoln, but this is a personal offer. If you help me, I'll help you."

"Sasquatch thumper belt," Kennedy said, while his arms and legs floated away from his body in a slow motion ballet before suddenly snapping back into place.

Snapdragon rolled his eyes. Kennedy was the key to his plan for riveting national attention on the desperate plight of vegetables, meat, and other food products the world over. Photosynthesis was the only pure way to live, and if he could get a celebrity spokesperson with Kennedy's stature to record a few promotional messages for the Greens, new recruits would flood through his front door.

Kennedy was the perfect candidate, raised from birth for this sort of thing, and Norman Meadows had died stealing the man's biochip information. Snapdragon wasn't going to let a little technical glitch stop him now. If Dandelion couldn't fix it, he'd find someone who could.

Sudden inspiration caused Snapdragon to bolt upright in his chair and stare into Kennedy's eyes. "I know what you want. I'll let you watch one episode of *Washington Knights* for every promotional message you record for my organization."

Kennedy glanced at the holo projector, licked his lips, and twinkled his blue eyes at Snapdragon. "*Two* episodes per spot."

Snapdragon smiled. "Done." He glanced at the news again and noticed that the anchorwoman had been replaced by President King speaking from the White House.

"Burpit mowgli gluepot," Kennedy said, as his head floated away from his neck.

24

AARON Thorn and Milton Greenspoon sat across from each other on couches in the Oval Office. Multiple holo-cams and bright lights hung over their heads to generate a full 3-D broadcast image of the president's massive *Resolute* desk. Despite the lack of a warm body behind the desk, the president's speech to the nation had run for over ten minutes. A projection on the coffee table showed a small-scale version of the scene with the president included. Vice President Uriah Truman stood by the crackling fireplace devouring salted peanuts from an antique lead crystal serving dish.

"We can't keep doing this, you know," Truman said between mouthfuls. "Someone's going to catch on when they don't see the president out in public."

Greenspoon sighed. "We've leaked information to the press that the Secret Service is on high alert after a credible threat on the president's life. He's not allowed out of the White House for an indefinite period."

Truman chuckled. "That buys you a week, maybe two; then they're going to start asking questions. The public wants to see the candidate in public during the campaign. They're funny about that sort of thing."

"We've got at least a month, maybe more," Thorn said. "With virtual appearances and regular broadcasts from the Oval Office, the voters have gotten used to seeing less of their candidates in public. President Kinsey did her entire campaign without leaving California."

Truman looked at Thorn. "President Kinsey was disabled, Aaron. She could get away with it."

Greenspoon rolled his eyes. "Well, if anyone starts

wondering why he hasn't gone out in public, we'll tell them the president is sick. He'll withdraw from the race a few weeks later due to illness. Then Senator Thorn gets a boost from the sympathy vote."

Truman pushed the bowl of peanuts off the mantel, but the smartcarpet sensed the falling object and responded by cushioning the impact so that the crystal didn't break. He glared at Greenspoon. "In case you've forgotten, I'm the vice president. I should be in charge now. And I should be the one to take King's place when he drops out of the race, not Thorn."

Greenspoon stood, crunched a few peanuts underfoot as he moved toward the fireplace, and put a comforting hand on Truman's shoulder while he looked into his eyes. "Uriah, there's no way you can win the election, and you know that."

"We *don't* know that," Truman said, breathing hard. His face was red. He fumbled in his pants pocket for a moment, then snorted twice from his nasal inhaler. "Thorn's AI can write speeches for me just as easily as it does for a dead president."

Thorn snorted. Greenspoon glanced at him, then put one arm around Truman's shoulder and gestured at the tiny president speaking on the coffee table. "It's not just the speeches, Uriah. You don't have the presence or the charisma to be president, even though you're perfect in the number-two slot. You're one of the best vice presidents we've ever had."

Truman felt calmer now as the inhalant took effect. "You think a dead guy can be a better president than me? The voters would think differently if they saw me in charge before the election. I say we let sleeping dogs lie, and let sleeping presidents die, and allow me to assume the mantle of leadership."

Thorn stood and pointed at the spilled peanuts. "You dropped your peanuts."

Truman blinked at Thorn. As the inhaled drug coursed through his system, his memory slipped away like it always did, and his frown relaxed into a smile. "Whoops.

You're right." Truman bent over to brush fallen peanuts into his palm. "Oh, dear, what a mess I've made."

"Exactly," Thorn said, winking at Greenspoon.

Greenspoon nodded and returned to the couch to watch the coffee table speech.

President Rex King appeared in millions of living rooms all over the country with the American flag proudly waving behind him in a silent breeze. His face had an aura of destiny and courage, enhanced by an image processing computer, as he peered into the future, far beyond what mortal men could see. ". . . as your president, I have but one obligation—to devote every effort of body, mind, and spirit to lead this nation to greatness. You will soon have the chance to cast your vote and let me know how I've been doing over the last four years. Perhaps you'll consider voting for my main opponent, whose recent prison sentence has hardly slowed his political career. I could take the time now to talk about my opponent's weaknesses, of which there are many, but I think the American people expect more from us than cries of indignation and attack. We are not here to curse the darkness, but to light the candle that can guide us through that darkness to a safe and sane future. As Winston Churchill said on taking office: if we open a quarrel between the present and the past, we shall be in danger of losing the future."

Greenspoon glanced at Thorn when he sat down beside him. "Let's hope the vice president doesn't change his prescription."

"He won't," Thorn said. "I'll make sure of that."

Truman was on his knees now, eating peanuts off the carpet.

On the table, the holographic King looked skyward and raised his arms. "I stand here tonight looking up at the last frontier. There are humans on the Moon and on Mars, living and working, building and surviving. How did this miracle come about? The pioneers of old gave up their safety, their comfort, and sometimes their lives to build a new world. They were not the captives of their own doubts, the prisoners of their own price tags. They were determined to make that new world strong and free, to overcome its hazards and its hardships, to conquer the enemies that threatened from without and within."

King smiled with extreme confidence, then pressed his lips together and flared his nostrils in the manner that had won him such acclaim when he was a Hollywood actor. "Today, some would say that those struggles are all over, that all the horizons have now been explored, that all the battles have been won, that there is no longer an American frontier. New technologies have even brought us close to defeating the ultimate frontier of death. But our struggles are not over. We stand today on the edge of a new frontier—a frontier of unknown opportunities and perils—a frontier of unfulfilled hopes and threats. This new frontier is not a set of promises; it is a set of challenges. It sums up not what I intend to offer the American people, but what I intend to ask of them. It appeals to their pride, not to their pocketbook—it holds out the promise of more sacrifice instead of more security."

Greenspoon nodded in approval. "This is good."

"I've always said that trained actors are perfect for high office." Thorn said.

"Yeah," shrugged Greenspoon, "but the speech is good, too."

It was clear on his face that King knew he had his unseen audience in the palm of his hand. "The new frontier is here, whether we seek it or not. Beyond that frontier are the uncharted areas of science and space, unsolved problems of peace and war, unconquered pockets of ignorance and prejudice, unanswered questions of poverty and surplus. It would be easier to shrink back from that frontier, to look to the safe mediocrity of the past, to be lulled by good intentions and high rhetoric—and those who prefer that course should not cast their votes for me, regardless of party."

King looked directly into the cameras, giving everyone in the viewing audience the impression that he looked directly at them. "All mankind awaits our decision. A whole world looks to see what we will do. We cannot fail their trust. We cannot fail to try."

King bowed his head to the sound of thunderous applause generated at the studio.

Greenspoon looked at Thorn. "Wow. For a dead guy, he gives a pretty good speech. Did you write that yourself?"

Thorn nodded. "I cobbled it together with a speech-writing AI that knows all the successful campaign speeches from the past. Took me about ten minutes."

"I'm impressed. I suppose our opponents have access to the same AI?"

"Some do," Thorn said with a shrug. "It's high-level, very expensive, and has to be customized for the speech-maker's personality. But we have one key element in our campaign that our opponents don't."

"Dr. Kyger and his ability to manipulate the Rex King avatar?"

Thorn stood, stepped over the happily munching vice president seated on the floor, and looked out the window with his hands clasped behind his back. "The party nomination will go to me when the president announces his withdrawal from the campaign. I'll also have the president's endorsement." Thorn turned and smiled. "But we have more than that. We have the ability to directly manipulate public opinion by word of mouth. Deceased loved ones can be very convincing. If your dead wife says you should vote for a particular candidate and pulls all your emotional strings at the same time, there's a ninety-eight percent chance you'll vote that way."

"Elysian Fields can do that?"

"Of course."

"Your average voter can't afford to visit anyone in Elysian Fields. How are you going to get enough people in there to tell them how to vote?"

"That's what government subsidies are for."

"The Deceased Access Human Rights Bill?"

"We have all the votes we need. By next week, President King will sign it into law."

Greenspoon smirked. "Dead campaign workers. There ought to be a law against *that*."

25

SNAPDRAGON had his feet up on the desk in his office while he watched an episode of *Washington Knights* with the avatar of Lincoln Ford Kennedy. Snapdragon didn't normally watch anything but the news, and he had no real interest in the political scheming and character assassination so prevalent in this particular show, but Kennedy was clearly fascinated by the performance. When the show was over, Snapdragon would start recording a promotional spot for the Greens with Kennedy as their new spokesperson, assuming the projector continued to work without too much static. Dandelion would have to adjust it when he returned from the protest march. He was composing the script for the first ad when the head of his administrative assistant, Jamal, appeared above the desk.

"Boss? We've got trouble," said the floating head.

"Trouble?" Snapdragon bolted upright and stared at Jamal's head. "What kind of trouble?"

"Cops at the front door. They want in."

"The monthly raid? Send the lawyers out to deal with them."

"These aren't regular cops. It's a commando team. Biggest guns I've ever seen. They want you to come out with Kennedy, or they're coming in."

"What? How did they know we've got Kennedy? How did they know I was here?"

"They didn't say. But we've got about ten seconds to decide," Jamal said. Then his head disappeared.

"Jamal? Are you there?"

"I'm under my desk. Nobody's paying me to get shot."

Snapdragon sighed. "Okay, just stall them for a minute. Tell them I left already."

"You tell them. I'm not coming out from under here until they leave."

Snapdragon reached for the portable holo projector that housed Kennedy. "Okay, Mr. President, show's over for now."

Kennedy looked at him in alarm. "Senator Farmer is just about to end his filibuster! And there's a sniper in the gallery! I can't leave now!"

"Sorry," Snapdragon said, switching off Kennedy's holo projector and dropping it in his pants pocket. His ears popped as he heard the dull thump of an explosive blowing the front door apart downstairs. Stepping quickly to the side wall, he pushed in four of the bricks. A narrow door popped open. They were in a part of town where the Chinese had built secret tunnels almost two hundred years ago, and some of them connected with the more modern sewer and flood control systems, which is why he had bought this building in the first place. Long experience had taught Snapdragon to leave himself several escape routes in case the police or one of his former coworkers should happen to show up on his doorstep.

He shut the hidden door and eyed the dimly lighted staircase that spiraled down into the bowels of the city.

YVETTE'S office at NASA's Ames Research Center amused her. It occupied part of the ancient administration building near the main gate, a squat concrete structure flanked by the imposing black glass towers housing the Advanced Computing Facility and the Administrative Management Battalion. Although the director's office had no visible windows, her predecessor, Dr. Chakrabarti, had installed phased array optics on the walls, floor, and ceiling so that he could generate whatever dramatic, three-dimensional surroundings suited his mood. The advanced technology installed in this office was also used for demonstrations to important visitors, as it had all been developed right there in the Ames Optics Lab. Although she had experimented with the system a few times—floating in a nebula behind an ice crystal desk perched on the head of a small comet that left a luminous green trail behind her, or sitting behind a warm surfboard desk on a sandy white beach in Maui—she usually left the image generator set on Greek Temple with Spotlight because she wanted to focus attention on herself.

Yvette reveled in success and the perks that came with it, but her numerous responsibilities were a burden. Outside her door, a gaggle of a dozen young men waited to assist her, ready to perform any task no matter how ludicrous. Dr. Chakrabarti had employed only one assistant, an ancient crone named Beryl who had worked in the NASA director's office since the dawn of time, but Yvette found her stuffy, boring, and better suited to life in a retirement home. She had personally chosen her male assistants by hand, making sure each one fit the specific requirements for appearance and professional skill she had laid out for the personnel office. Charged with the responsibility of running the research center while starting her new AdForce business had put severe constraints on her time, but her assistants were all willing to work sixty-hour weeks, or more, to reduce her workload and keep her happy. Even approved official visitors found it hard to get through the protective double ring of desks outside her office door, having to prove themselves worthy to at least five of her assistants before they were admitted to the inner sanctum of power.

Still, despite all the help, Yvette found herself working far too many hours each week, either at her home office or at Ames. The troops and her visitors liked to be inspired by her actual physical presence, so virtual visits from her home office were not always possible. Indeed, Yvette herself liked being able to study the nuances of body language that could be obscured during a telemeeting, especially when her visitors were using older-model holocam technologies that were low in image resolution. However, the demands on her time were increasing to the point where she had to hold AdForce telemeetings in her NASA office and vice versa. If her current plans worked out, she'd be fragmented even more, although it might be possible to drop the NASA job in favor of higher-paying options.

Her position as the director of Ames was just another step on the ladder. She'd come in out of college with a shiny new degree in computational biochemistry to work as a molecular designer in the Ames Nano-VR lab with Tau Wolfsinger, then she'd quickly been promoted to chief designer, surprising everyone when she became Tau's boss. Her trip to Mars had given her the experience and notoriety that NASA now preferred in its center directors, so another promotion had been waiting for her after Chakrabarti disappeared. Of course, meeting the right people and getting to know them had always been a big part of her strategy for success. Her striking appearance helped her get the attention of both men and women, and she had no problem with using sex as a way to get ahead, although it was rarely necessary.

When she thought about the past, Yvette remembered the geeky student scientist she'd been in school. Following a thorough analysis of her future job prospects after graduation, undertaken with the same rigorous research and study she applied to all of her college subjects, she determined that a trip to the body shop in San Francisco would optimize her chances of professional success while doing wonders for her self-esteem. She'd proven her assumptions to be correct, but she had been shocked by the reactions from several of her peers in college who looked at her in an entirely different way when she returned to school with a body sculpted and toned to perfection to match her formidable intellect. But her appearance was only one of the powerful tools at her disposal, and she liked the challenge of being forced to use them all to advance her career. She was well ahead of the original career path she had planned, having veered toward more powerful management positions each step of the way, charting her course to follow the least line of resistance through men and women she could humiliate or manipulate. She had only run into one man who proved resistant to her charms despite her long-term efforts, demonstrating yet again how superior he was to the human doormats who surrounded her. When her thoughts drifted in the murky twilight before she fell asleep, she often found herself thinking of Tau Wolfsinger.

Tau looked pretty good for a NASA scientist, and he was acknowledged by many in the field of molecular engineering to be a genius. But he was a rogue genius, unpredictable in his actions, and that made it hard for Yvette to channel his energies in ways that would be of the most benefit to her. Tau was a social reject, like so many other scientists, and that made him a bit daft whenever she tried to flirt with him, but she continued to study him to find his soft spots. She'd tried sharing an apt with him when she started working at Ames, and she'd spent much time flirting with him on their outward bound voyage to Mars, but she'd never managed to break him. His romantic attachment to Kate McCloud only made him more of a challenge. Yvette knew she'd probably discard Tau if he ever weakened enough to fall in love with her, but she had a strong urge to test him and see what happened. She had to know, was she imperfect in some way?

Now, another shot at Tau had presented itself. The team investigating the crater formerly known as Yamantau Mountain needed someone with Kate McCloud's particular skills and archaeological experience. She considered Kate the closest thing she had to a girlfriend, and they still shared custody of the cuddly Laika, but Kate could be inconvenient at times. Yvette still couldn't understand why Tau had chosen the unremarkable Kate when he could have had perfection any time during the last year, but she thought perhaps she hadn't been obvious enough in her flirting to get past Tau's social ineptitude. Once Kate was safely out of the country for a few weeks, Yvette would have easier access to Tau to try again. Kate had told her that Tau would be returning with her on the DEEPTRAN bullet train from Arizona, so he'd be right there in San Francisco under Yvette's nose. Despite her tight schedule, she'd have to make some time to visit him or lure him to her place; the thought made her tingle. If she could just

nail him once, she would win; then she could move on
with her life free of distractions, having demonstrated to
Tau what he would be missing for the rest of his pathetic
shell of a life.

It wasn't easy being perfect.

ARIEL felt violated. The two suits from the FBI had explained everything after they picked her up at the cemetery
in Colma, and she still couldn't believe it. Festus Meadows, whom she had always known as the kindly Brother
Digital, was a con man, a scam artist, a tax dodger, a liar,
a cheat, a—well, she could go on all day. The man was a
criminal, and Ariel could have forgiven him for that, but he
had lied to her and deceived her. He had manipulated her
into entering the God Box, which was apparently a fancy
sim for brainwashing people to become followers of the
mythical Entity. The nightmarish experience of the God
Box still resonated in her mind, and she resented BD's cav-
alier attitude about exposing her to such mental cruelty
under the guise of friendship. All he wanted was another
follower. She also felt betrayed because she had wanted to
believe in the Entity; in a higher intelligence more powerful than the humans who had created the global network in
which it lived. But it was all a trick; a carnival sideshow
run by a magician.

The FBI knew all about BD and his cultish Church of
the Ping, but they didn't have enough information to arrest
him—they needed Ariel for that. Many of the Pingers had
been rich before joining the cult, but they had gained admission to BD's inner circle by donating all their funds to
the church, which meant their money was stored away in a
safe place—in BD's Swiss account and other orbital banks.
When Ariel protested to the FBI agents that BD couldn't
have any money because he lived with her in a shack on
the street, they simply laughed and showed her surveillance holos of BD in his private apt in a luxury tower complex. That, more than anything, had pushed her over the
edge, and she told the suits that she would help them.
She'd hunt for financial records or other evidence of crim-

inal activity and let the feds analyze whatever she brought them. The FBI had also kept Ariel from Carlo's assets after he died, and the agents said they would make a deal with her if she helped them with BD. A simple choice, really. If she couldn't find God in a box, or a true friend, she'd have to be happy with money and revenge.

Ariel shouldered through the light crowd of commuters in the slow lane, then stepped off the Van Ness slidewalk when she neared the Broadway shunt. The Romanesque cathedral of Saint Brigid's loomed over the street, a massive creature of rough gray stone. Parasitic gargoyles, old ones carved from granite and new ones formed from crystal, perched on ledges and peeked from crevices, distracting the churchgoer with exterior evils to disguise the evil inside. Nervous pigeons cooed and flapped, echoing the flutters of her anxious heart. The eastern sky brightened with a golden glow, glinting off the colorful Romanesque wheel window just below the church's new roof, but the sun wasn't high enough yet to force its warming rays down among the cold canyons of steel and concrete.

Her robe fluttered in the breeze, tickling her thighs. She had modified the floor-length polychrome robe that BD had given her after the God Box ritual, shortening it to knee-length so she wouldn't trip over the voluminous folds of color-cycling cloth. She had also reduced its bulk so it was a better fit for her trim figure, belting it at the waist with a flexible length of polyrope. BD had insisted that she wear the type of spiked heels she would normally wear to work at the club, as befitted her role in church rituals that seemed to involve showmanship as much as religious fervor. She'd never wanted to join the Pingers in the first place, but BD had lured her with food, friendship, and the promise of seeing Carlo again. Now that Elysian Fields would allow free full-sensory access visits to Happy Meadows once a month, BD had lost some of his special power over her, but she had a new purpose: she would find evidence for the FBI and send BD to prison.

As high priestess at the Church of the Ping, her access to BD's new broadcast facility would also allow her to ful-

fill her part of the deal with Shade, who had offered to free
Carlo's avatar from its simulated prison. On her next visit
to Colma, Shade would upload a holo message to her note
cube, and she would transmit it to the public. The holo
would act like a rogue advertising virus, bouncing from
one transmitter to another across the country, breaking into
regular programs to deliver Shade's message before it du-
plicated itself and moved on to a new target. Over a year
ago, before it became illegal to use the new technology, big
ad agencies had unknowingly released several rogue
viruses at once, jamming regular broadcasts to the point
where each audience only saw advertising. Like the programs themselves, the new ads adapted themselves for
each viewer to deliver their consumer-oriented payloads in
the most persuasive manner. Eventually, the FCC had to
shut down the broadcasting networks for twenty-four
hours to get the viral ads out of the system. The high fines
now imposed on ad hackers had limited rogue virus activity to well-hidden criminals or to ad agencies whose
clients were particularly wealthy and desperate. Ariel was
neither well-hidden nor wealthy, but Shade was safe from
punitive actions by the feds, and Ariel planned to blame
the transmissions on BD.

The massive oak doors at the front entrance to the
church were locked, as she expected, so she used a side entrance. The battered door always seemed to be locked, but
BD had shown her how to open it by pressing on the splintered wood just above the lock with one hand while lifting
on the handle. She flinched when the door creaked open, a
deathly shriek echoing through the vast chamber. The interior of the church sparkled with stained glass rainbows
from the glowpanels in the ceiling, the colors camouflag-
ing the dust and decay among the pews. Her heels ticked
on the pavement as she walked toward BD's office in the
sanctuary.

The sanctuary door was locked, but BD had scanned
her fingerprints into the security computer. She needed access because the "holy relics" were stored in BD's office,
and it was one of her duties to bring them out for BD's per-

formances. The relics included the memory cube containing the Digital Bible, purportedly written by BD under the Entity's guidance. The great book, written after BD's first traumatic contact with the Entity, revealed how humanity should be wired into the Global Brain and guided down the path of enlightenment. Or guided down the path of poverty and blind obedience to BD, she thought. BD's religious awakening had supposedly occurred while he cruised the datasphere, and Ariel thought that was a clever ruse, since AIs now traversed the vast and complicated datafields instead of humans. The feds had restricted human access to the datasphere twenty years ago, and BD claimed this was due to the government's discovery of the Entity. BD preached that human minds could be prepared, through his God Box, to survive contact with the Entity and gain enlightenment. The enlightened, assisted by the Entity, would have instantaneous access to all knowledge and be able to use the datasphere like true extensions of their own organic brains. He said that the government supposedly feared what would happen if the public gained so much power, so the feds expanded the roles of AI information rovers and locked the humans out of the library. Rich or poor, BD's followers all seemed to want more control over their lives, and they were willing to believe that BD and his God Box could give them that. According to BD, he was the only enlightened human so far, but others would have their chance to be transformed once they proved themselves worthy of the great gift. It seemed to Ariel that BD was the only arbiter of worthiness, and his followers were to be kept off balance as they wondered what they would have to do next to please BD and the Entity.

In her position as high priestess, Ariel was offered some of the same benefits that BD received, but she was not interested in having sex with the Pingers, or taking their money, or making them perform humiliating acts to show their faith. Pingers of the inner circle had been exposed to variations of the same experience Ariel had endured in the God Box, but at a lower intensity that promoted a sort of mental addiction requiring multiple visits to the Entity's virtual world, drawing them deeper into the mysteries each time. BD knew that Ariel would resist the God Box and the ideals of the Ping Church, so he customized her experience to be more traumatic; a shock so intense that she would become a believer. And it had almost worked. The sacrifice of BD's brother, Norman, so that she could make contact with Carlo, had also put her in BD's debt. If the FBI had not reached her when they did, she knew she would have been completely brainwashed.

She shook her head, trying to clear it of conflicting emotions while she searched BD's office. BD had given her access to Norman, then Norman had died so she could reach Carlo. Did that mean she owed her loyalty to BD, who had also given her food and shelter? Or did she owe anything to the con man who had traumatized her into helping him fleece the public? After all, Norman had been paid to break into Elysian Fields, and BD's request to help her locate information about Carlo had merely been a side project for him. It seemed that her real debt was to Norman, who had chosen to sacrifice himself by staying in Elysian Fields too long after his other job was done.

The simply furnished office had no windows, and glowpanels provided an even illumination. Piles of discarded electronic equipment dominated the small space, along with stacks of recruiting posters and brochures bound for destinations across the country. Small, flat monitors, blurry with age, were arrayed on the wall above the desk, allowing the occupant of the office to watch various parts of the church during the services. Part of Ariel's job was to operate the special effects panel, creating curtains of fire in front of the stage, glowing celestial lights that hovered among Pingers seated in the pews, showers of sparks that rained down from the ceiling, and other pyrotechnics that helped to keep the audience's attention while BD belted out his sermons.

Using a screwdriver from BD's toolbox, she pried open the memory cabinet and found racks of half-inch cubes labeled with the names of inner circle members. Each cube held recordings of the experiences each Pinger had in the

God Box, and served as the basis for fresh simulations during later visits to the Entity. One of the cubes was neatly
labeled with Ariel's name. She picked up two of the labeled cubes for recent Pinger recruits she hadn't met—
Pinky Knight and Bruno Whittington—along with two
blanks and dropped them in a pocket of her robe.

Sorting through the available tools, Ariel noticed ma-
nipulators of the type she'd used daily in her job as a mi-
croprocessor layout designer. AI designers of quantum
processors and biochips had made her job obsolete, but
these were the kinds of tools still used by maintenance engineers and hobbyists involved in chip prototyping. She
assumed BD had these tools because he or Norman had
customized the chips that drove the special effects equipment, but then she realized that these were needed for the
God Box hardware as well. And that gave her an idea.

Retreating from the sanctuary office, Ariel crossed the
dais to the high altar. It was still early enough that none of
the Pingers had come in from the barracks behind the
church. During the day and most of the evening, she was
used to seeing Pingers working on renovations or maintenance, and she knew BD wouldn't be in for a while, so
she'd have the church to herself a little bit longer. When
she pressed the hidden button on the white marble altar, a
hatch hissed open and the eight-foot-tall white egg rose
majestically from the floor. The front half of the egg
popped open at her approach, but she ignored it and
walked around to the back. A cursory inspection revealed
the outline of a small access hatch, which she pressed with
her hand to release the maintenance seal. Inside lay a
patchwork mess of Chuang boards, light junctions, and liquid DNA protochips, obviously built by hand without a
full-blown AI chip designer. Beside a dark diagnostic monitor, a holoscope showed an animated three-dimensional
circuit trace, verifying the status of temporary molecular
paths and knowledge nets that the egg required to function.
Having worked on the forerunners of this technology in
her last job, Ariel understood most of what she was looking at, although she'd never comprehend the function of

the bulky processor marked Miracle without a qualified AI design assistant. For her purposes, however, she only needed to redirect a few connections. Placing her fingertips in the appropriate slots of the two manipulator tools she'd borrowed from BD's office, she began to tinker with the nerd-knobs.

Startled by the echo of approaching footsteps, Ariel looked up and gasped.

26

AS usual, Yvette woke to the rousing tune of "Ride of the Valkyries" in her luxury apt. The smartwindows shifted from opaque black to transparency to reveal the sunrise, and the light glared through her eyelids. Her nose wrinkled; the usual scent of roses had been replaced with the sickly sweet odor of rotting fruit. Something was wrong. Expecting to open her eyes and admire herself in the bed's canopy mirror, she immediately tensed when she saw a tall figure completely covered in black approaching the bed. Apparently startled by the music, the man hesitated when Yvette spotted him, then he lunged at the bed.

Yvette rolled away. The weight of his body hit the bed hard, causing it to bounce and knock her off balance. He grabbed the back of her red nightie to stop her, but the flimsy garment tore away and allowed her to twist out of his grasp. Startled, she glanced at the marble bedside table; nothing there she could use as a weapon. She threw herself sideways toward the foot of the bed, then swung her leg around to kick him in the side of the head. He grunted and dropped the torn nightie, falling onto the pillow. Scrabbling backward, she grabbed the sheet, pulled part of it free of the bed, and threw it over him. He couldn't see now, but he raised his foot to kick her in the stomach; the sheet dampened the force of the blow. She fell forward to drop all of her weight on him, landing with her elbows on his rib cage, then started to punch at his head, unable to aim precisely because of the sheet. He yelled and rolled over, forcing her across the slippery surface of the bed until she slid off. Her neck and shoulders hit the floor with a thump. Instant headache.

"Jeeves! Intruder!"

No answer. That was odd, but she didn't have time to find out why. Her heart hammered. Adrenaline pumped through her veins. She rolled under the bed as a boot stomped down on the floor where her head had been a moment ago. When his other foot came down, she wedged her shoulders tight between the frame and the carpet, then grabbed his ankles and pulled hard. He yelled again and crashed to the floor. She wriggled away under the bed to the other side.

He spoke with a deep whisper, disguising his voice. "You're gonna regret that, bitch!"

"Jeeves! Intrusion gas!"

Still nothing. She scraped her back on the bed frame. The room swirled around her head as she got up on her knees. She leaned her arms against the bed to steady herself. Nothing around she could use as a weapon. Why did the room always have to be so clean? She glanced across the bed toward the bright windows. Where did he go?

The man's weight slammed against her back, forcing her upper body down on the bed. Her arms were trapped beneath her stomach. She tried to kick backward with her heels, but he jammed his knees between her legs so that her feet couldn't reach him. She felt his hot breath on the back of her neck. He had one hand on her shoulder, and the other one on her spine.

"What do you want?" she gasped.

He was still breathing hard, and his sickly sweet smell made her gag. He released the pressure on her shoulder, then quickly wrapped his arm around her neck. He squeezed, and she coughed, unable to breathe.

Someone tapped on the window.

Startled, his grip loosened as he looked up. Yvette caught a quick glimpse of the baggie with the white beard tapping at the window. She yanked her right arm out from under her stomach, then reached up and punched her attacker in the side of the head. He yelped, and his weight shifted some more. She yanked on his ear while he grabbed at her shoulder, trying to keep his balance, then she arched her back. When her other arm came free, she slammed her forearm down between his legs. He grunted. She rolled out from under him, grabbed the loose sheet, and wrapped one end around his neck, then tied the other end to a bedpost while he curled into a fetal position and rolled over on his side. The knot wouldn't hold long, but she'd have a head start to get away. Realizing the danger, he kicked out and caught her shoulder with his boot, knocking her to the floor again. Her head bumped the bedside table. The room swirled even more and she wondered if she'd black out.

Not yet. The man pulled against the bulky sheet and started to untie it. Yvette clenched her teeth and rose to her knees, steadying herself with one hand on the cool marble tabletop. If she tried to run, he'd just chase her, and she might pass out along the way. Who knew what he'd do to her then? He kicked at her face, and she dodged away. He was almost free of the sheet.

Her face. He'd tried to kick her face. That made her angry. She looked at the marble table again and crouched. With a loud grunt, she lifted the heavy table, took two wobbly steps with it, and dropped it on the man's head. It hit with a satisfying thump. He stopped moving.

Panting, Yvette sat down at the head of the bed and rubbed her sore throat with a shaky hand. She swallowed, then glanced at the red stain on the white tabletop. Why did he attack her? How did he get in? Who the hell was he? As her heartbeat slowed, she leaned over and tugged at the black form-fitting fabric that covered the man's head. She found the fabric seal at the neck and tore it open to reveal his face.

She should have known by the smell of rotting fruit. Thick red hair, pale white face, surprised expression despite his closed eyes. Whittington. Apparently Mr. Gardner did not want her on the board of directors at Elysian Fields.

She checked the pockets of his black pants, but the only thing she found was a smooth silver disk with an indented thumb button. After staring at it a moment, she realized it was a PIG: a pulse interference generator. PIGs were illegal because they created a focused electromagnetic pulse that disrupted radio waves, computer circuits, alarm systems, net links, and other systems necessary to modern existence. That explained why Jeeves wasn't talking; she'd have to restart the system with his backup or call a tech to do it.

A movement caught her eye, and she stood up, holding the bedpost for support. The baggie with the white beard waggled his fingers at her from outside her window. Her savior. She took a deep breath. She still had a headache, but she wasn't as dizzy now. She slowly walked over to the window where the baggie was stretched out on his platform, his eyes bulging as he watched her. He looked worried at her approach, but he waved again and gave her a weak smile.

Yvette pressed up against the window and kissed the glass near his head.

IT being summer in San Francisco, Tau had to wear a jacket to stay warm. Fog softened the outlines of the buildings, providing a buffer of wet cotton between the early morning sun and the city. While he hiked among the dripping trees that lined the hills high above Baker Beach on the Presidio, his boots crunching twigs and parchment leaves into the soft soil, he heard the occasional crash of surf when the wind blew the right way. The Presidio and Golden Gate Park were the last shrinking patches of green in the city, and Tau had come here many times over the last couple of years, allowing the natural beauty to sink in and remind him of what he missed by spending so much of his life indoors. Coyote bush, sage, and lupine huddled for warmth under cypress and eucalyptus trees, all of which stood in stark contrast to the gray concrete of the coastal defense fortifications that dotted the landscape.

Spanish, Mexican, and American armies had occupied the Presidio military outpost since the 1700s, but the artillery batteries that clustered like memorials to the dead on the high points and approaches to the Golden Gate were the most dramatic features that they had left behind. The ruined batteries loomed out of the camouflage of brush and soil, their silent guns missing, graffiti sprayed on most of the flat surfaces, twisted metal bars protruding from cracked walls like angry claws. Broken glass and other garbage in empty turrets and gun pits marked the passage of tourists and temporary residents.

Today, Tau was visiting Battery Dynamite. Built as part of Fort Winfield Scott in 1894 with major additions a few years later, Battery Dynamite had an elegant concrete profile of Beaux Arts classicism, its stylish lines obscuring its original function of protecting three fifteen-inch guns that could lob quarter-ton dynamite charges at ships four miles away. Now, the steel-reinforced concrete protected only dusty memories, bugs, and Norman's bunker. Tau knew the history of the place because Norman had often spoken of his explorations of the abandoned coastal defenses, and he wasn't surprised that Norman had found a way to secretly live inside one of the old gun batteries.

Following Norman's directions, he hunted around on the hillside below the blast apron until he spotted a waterfall of ivy and bramble obscuring a heavy steel door that appeared to be rusted shut. Running his hand along the bottom of the door seam, he found the microswitch that unsealed the molecular bond Norman had placed there, and swung the door open. The hinges, painted to look rusty, opened smoothly without creaking to reveal a dark tunnel running straight back into the hillside. Tau pulled a hard hat out of his small pack, switched on the headlamp, and placed it on his head before stepping forward into the gloom. The bunker breathed cold, dry air into his face. Crawling things scurried away on the floor and the gray walls to get away from the unaccustomed light of his lamp. Moisture that had seeped in from the doorway made rusty brown stains on the concrete walkway. He detected the scent of lime and noticed that water from the soil surrounding the shaft had leeched some of the lime out of the old walls, forming a chalky white powder.

The six-foot ceiling forced Tau into a crouch until he passed through a second blast door into a chamber with

walls that were twenty feet high. The dirty floor was punctuated with thick corroded bolts sticking up out of the concrete. Light seeped in through a broken roof that appeared
to be made of bramble, ivy, and eucalyptus branches. Norman had cleared an eighty-foot path straight through the
brush to another steel door on the opposite wall that was
eight feet tall and twelve feet wide. This door was welded
shut and marked with graffiti that continued the theme visible on the walls: stylized eyes with long eyelashes that
looked angry or crazy. Along the floor to the left of the
door was a small tunnel about three feet square and ringed
with painted eyes, like the service entrance to Hell, and it
was covered by a metal grille. Dust swirled in the air and
tickled at his nose, prompting a sneeze; the brief echo was
muffled and lost in the thick vegetation. Tau removed the
grille, then got down on his hands and knees and crawled
into the small tunnel, which was remarkably clean, considering its age. Sand and bits of bark ground into his
palms and his knees. About twenty feet back, he slid open
a brown steel plate, revealing a black metal ladder that
plunged down into the darkness. Thirty feet overhead, he
saw gray sky through a partially removed manhole cover.
As he swung out onto the ladder, dragging his pack out of
the crawlspace, he shuddered briefly—partly because it
was cold, and partly because ancient fears were telling him
to stay out of the underworld. But Norman was his friend,
and this was his last request. He started down the ladder,
leaving the dim gray light of the surface world behind.

The long concrete hallway at the base of the ladder had
twenty-five steel exit doors, some of which were open.
Most of the doors looked as if they hadn't been moved for
decades, their reddish brown surfaces peeling away in
rusty flakes. In the bobbing light from his headlamp as he
walked, Tau saw an old telephone substation with antique
analog switches, rooms full of dusty machines connected
to heavy power cables, and a small bathroom with a broken porcelain toilet. Startled by his approach, a rat
squeaked and scurried away through a crack in the wall. At
the end of the passage was the heaviest steel door he'd

seen so far, looking like it belonged on a bank vault, and a careful study of the surface by the hand crank revealed the neatly painted black letters, NM, Norman's initials. As instructed, he traced the outline of the initials with his finger, causing the door to hiss and pop open. Welcome light and heat poured through the gap as Tau heaved the door wider.

Inside, Tau discovered a lab full of exotic equipment. The plain concrete surfaces of the room had been painted white and coated with clear clean-room gel that absorbed dust. Overhead fans circulated the air through filters and maintained a positive pressure to limit the entry of new dust into the facility. Workbenches, metal surfaces, and tools were all clean and shiny. Despite the enormous amount of equipment crammed into the lab, it all seemed very organized. A lab stool rested in front of the main workbench, where trays of steaming liquid nitrogen held blank biochips ready to be imprinted. Although he used multiple techniques, Norman grew the biological computer chips from DNA templates he genetically engineered into bacteria to develop complex, three-dimensional circuit arrays. Norman did all of his experimentation and prototyping in this lab, and the equipment was worth a great deal of money. Norman had never married nor had any children, and his parents had died after Norman graduated from the university in Santa Cruz, so Norman's brother would inherit this equipment unless Norman had specified otherwise. What a waste.

The only thing out of place in the room was what appeared to be a gray-and-white pincushion on the floor beneath the lab stool. Tau crouched to pick it up, but it made a hissing sound and curled into a tighter, spikier ball about the size of a grapefruit—Norman's hedgehog. Tau stood and looked around, finally locating a small drawer marked Larry that was filled with hedgehog food and supplies. Tau emptied some of the food granules onto the floor in front of Larry and waited a moment while the little creature unrolled and flattened his sharp, half-inch spines against his body. He was about seven inches long and three inches high when he stood on his four tiny legs, sniffing the air with his long nose. His clear brown eyes studied Tau for a moment, then he ignored the food and waddled over to a tall white equipment cabinet. Larry turned and watched Tau as if he were waiting, so Tau walked over and opened the cabinet doors.

Instead of shelving inside the cabinet, Tau found an antechamber to a small room dominated by an unnatural cloud of fog. The fog hovered in the center of the room, defying air currents and gravity, like a piece of the gray sky trying to hide. Larry clambered over the lip of the cabinet near Tau's feet and waddled into the fog room, then turned to watch him again. Frowning, Tau stepped across the threshold. Despite the cloud, the room's air was dry. The white walls were blank, and he saw no evidence of holo projectors or other phased array equipment. Peering into the fog at close range, he saw what looked like floating peas evenly spaced every few inches within the cloud. The peas meant something important about the fog, but he couldn't remember what.

"Hey, Chief, glad you could drop by."

Tau jumped when he heard Norman's voice. *Chindi?* Was Norman's evil ghost going to kill him? His eyes wide, he glanced down at the hedgehog, who stared right back at him.

"Sorry about the hedgehog thing," said the smiling hedgehog. "Best I could do on short notice. Couldn't link to a stored net AI to run a complex wandering projection of me, so I had to work with something smaller."

"You could have left me a note," Tau stammered, wondering if the possessed hedgehog could actually carry on a conversation.

"Too boring. Since this is kinda my last will and testament, I wanted some flash."

Tau's gaze traveled from the hog to the fog. "What's with the fog? More flash?"

"Very flash. You don't recognize it?"

Tau looked into the depths of the cloud, studied the peas, and shook his head.

Norman paused before he answered. "Put it together,

Mr. Nanotech Guy: fog, pea-size power nodes and controllers, unnatural cloudy behavior—"

Tau's eyes widened, and he took a step back. "This is a joke, right? You're not seriously telling me this is nanotech fog—foglets!"

"Consider it a present. It's still in prototype, but I don't need it now. It's all yours."

Tau knew Norman was a genius, but if this was really nanotech fog, he'd just developed something thirty years ahead of the current level of molecular nanotechnology. He understood the principle, that each foglet was a microscopic robot about the size of a bacterium. The foglets could link together in patterns to form almost any real-world object, or they could run a fluid-flow simulation to behave like real fog or even like clear air in a room. Foglets would act like a bridge between physical reality and virtual reality, because you could create almost anything and feel it, touch it, taste it, smell it, and hear it until you wanted it to turn back into fog again. Fog objects still had limits: they would only be about as hard as plastic, no heavier than wood, they couldn't act like food or be involved in chemical reactions, but they would still be very useful because a created object could vaporize back into fog and be used for something else. Regular nanotechnology was nowhere near as flexible or elegant as fog. His own Nano-VR allowed him to work with virtual matter that could be assembled into permanent objects by nanotech robots from a slurry of molecules, but he still thought fog development was decades away. Tau realized he was holding his breath, so he gasped for air and swallowed hard.

"Don't have a yakking heart attack," said the hedgehog. "It won't do either one of us any good if you keel over down here."

Tau nodded and took some deep breaths. He realized he was more startled by the foglet technology than he was by the virtual presence of his dead friend speaking through a hedgehog. A few years of infrequent contact helped soften the blow of Norman's death, he supposed, but the simulated Norman had a reality all its own, like this was some sort of elaborate joke and Norman was still alive, maybe watching from an adjacent room.

"If you've got a grip now, Chief, step into the fog. I have something else to show you."

The hedgehog darted forward, daring Tau to follow. He put his hand into the fog, but he couldn't feel anything unusual, so he took two steps forward into the cloud. The fog then coalesced into a cheap plastic chair facing a bronze statue of Norman.

"I could have created a simulation of me in the fog, but I don't have an AI jacked in to run dynamic animation. You like the statue better than the hedgehog?"

Talking hedgehogs were disturbing, but the larger-than-life-size statue was creepy. "Well—"

"Good. Anyway, I have a favor to ask," said Norman's statue. "In return for the fog, I want revenge. I want you to nail the people who run Elysian Fields."

Tau blinked and gingerly sat back in the chair, aware that it was a prototype that might fail and drop him on his butt at any moment. "The dead sim people? Why?"

"Because they *killed* me, that's why! And they stole my biochip designs!"

Tau didn't need the reminder that Norman was dead. The shouting from the stiff bronze statue had already caused the hair on the back of his neck to rise. "How do you know they killed you?"

Norman sighed. "I was cracking for an old pal named Snapdragon, and I was afraid I'd get toasted. Elysian Fields has killware, and they know how to use it. Since you're here now, I must be dead."

"Did you say Snapdragon?" Tau asked.

"That's his name now that he's a Veggie, but I knew him from the adult entertainment biz right out of college when I was selling my Feelie VR sim chips. Then he joined the Navy, and he went to work for the feds after that, but he didn't like the bureaucracies much. His new Veggie gig must be good, because he's loaded. Good guy, very charismatic, but kind of spooky."

Tau remembered Snapdragon from the Veggie protests outside the NASA gates over a year ago, but he'd have to be really odd if dead Norman was calling him "spooky." In any case, he didn't want to get involved with one of the Veggie lunatics who had given him so much trouble because of his nanotech research.

"Anyway," Norman continued, "Snappy knew to contact my brother if I got smoked during the crack job, so Festus—he calls himself Brother Digital now—probably knows something. And one of them should have my break-in gear."

Tau remembered Norman's sleazy brother, a born con man he had tried to avoid at the university. "I don't know, Norman. As soon as Kate gets back from Russia, we're going back to Arizona to hide out for a while. Someone tried to kidnap Kate."

"You'll have plenty of time to nail the EFers, Chief. I'll help you myself."

Tau folded his arms, annoyed that Norman had ignored his comment about Kate's kidnapping. "And how do you plan to do that?"

"Lazarus Biochip 2.0," Norman said proudly. "They stole my first Lazarus, but this one is better. Better nanoprobes, better personality rendering, better neural net recording and storage. Of course, it's still a prototype and might be a little glitchy here and there, but I burned it in before I popped Elysian Fields. Good thing, too. You can carry me around with you all the time."

"Don't you need an AI driver to make it work?"

"The AI driver for the Lazarus resides in virtual storage in the datasphere, so you can have direct interactions with me almost anywhere; you just won't be able to see me in most situations. That's the beauty of the two point oh: it's portable, and you can at least talk to it without all the heavyweight software the one point oh needed. A little more work and I could have put EF out of business with my own competitive services. Combined with Feelies to generate powered avatars in a sim world, I could have built a better Elysian Fields."

"You said the Lazarus is still a prototype. Is your personality backed up anywhere?"

"Well, no, but I'll be fine as long as you don't do anything to let the magic smoke out of the chip."

"Magic smoke?"

Norman sighed. "How quickly they forget. Engineers say computer chips work because of the magic smoke inside each chip. If you burn up a chip, you let the magic smoke out."

"Ah. I remember."

Norman snorted. "*Yak,* talking to you is like talking to a monkey."

Tau remembered why he'd lost touch with Norman: he could tolerate the man's ego for a while, then it began to grate on his nerves. Still, he didn't feel right about getting angry with a dead friend.

"Come on, Dr. Frankenstein," Norman said. "Give me life again. My Lazarus chip is in the tray on my workbench. I labeled it as a demo in case anyone broke in and tried to steal it."

Although he didn't wear one himself, Tau had a rough idea of how the EF mind reading chips were supposed to work, so he knew people normally wore them on the backs of their necks to maintain current memory and personality data until they died, at which time they were removed and sent to an Elysian Fields memory library for uploading to a virtual sim world. "Your chip is here in the lab? You weren't wearing it when you died?"

"Do you have any idea what would have happened to a live biochip if I was punched out by a security AI? That would have let the magic smoke out big time, maybe even burned the chip right off my neck. No, I updated everything before I left the lab. I can survive without knowing the gory details of my final moments on Earth."

"But you only made one?"

"I'm not Intel, my friend. I don't chum these things out by the thousands, I make them one at a time by hand. Just go out there, slap the chip on your neck, and let's go!"

Like most people, Tau had an expansion socket on the

back of his neck so he could add dynamic memory, use data libraries, or run local applications, but he wasn't too sure about the wisdom of socking an experimental biochip into his brain. "You're sure this will be safe, Norman?"

"Trust me."

ARIEL blinked and took a deep breath to calm herself, trying to look as if she belonged there, crouched down with her hands buried in the brains of the God Box egg. The robed Pinger in front of her wore compound, multispectral lenses that made him look like he had the eyes of a fly on his otherwise human face. His black hair, in stark contrast to his pale skin, was shiny and pasted to his skull. He was thin and tall, carrying toolboxes and tech gear in his hands.

"What you do?" He had some kind of an odd accent that Ariel couldn't identify. He spoke a foreign language, but a tiny pendant at his throat—a real-time noise canceler/translator rig—changed his words into English.

"Um," Ariel said, wondering what she could say to get rid of him. "Upgrading the system."

"I be Remo, Tech Seven," he said, frowning and thumping his chest. "Brother Digital none hiring the low-tech. Why you?"

Ariel frowned, failing to translate the translation. For a tech seven, he was using an awfully old translator rig. She wondered if he knew who she was, since he'd probably never seen her at close range. "I'm Ariel, high priestess of the church." She stood up to her full height and watched his eyes go wide as he looked her up and down. Now he recognized her from her stage appearances with BD.

"Apology," he said with a smile. "Not known you tech. Excited meeting."

"Why are you here?" Ariel asked, figuring it was better to maintain the upper hand.

Remo hefted the equipment in his left hand. "Transmitter rig. Studio. You come? Two heads better than four."

She still couldn't understand everything he said, but he seemed harmless enough. If he was inviting her to the studio, she could go with him and maybe learn how some of the equipment worked, which would be useful when she came back to transmit Shade's messages. She assumed the broadcast facility would share some similarities with the equipment at the club where she worked, but it would be nice to have a tour. She glanced back at the egg, wondering if she should finish her work there first. It could probably wait a few minutes, and she could use it as an excuse to leave the studio in case Remo wanted her to stay too long. When she turned around again, his smiling face was only inches away from her chest. When he tried to look past her at the egg, she stepped sideways to block his view.

"Tech help?" Remo asked, trying to look past her again. This time, she stepped sideways and leaned forward a bit to let her collar gape open, and that seemed to hold his attention.

"Thanks, but I can handle it," she said in a low, breathy voice. His eyebrows went up as she put her hands around one of his elbows. "Show me your studio, Remo. I'd love to see it."

He licked his lips and shrugged. "Okay. Come in studio, you feel good tech."

As they walked away from the altar, Ariel looked over her shoulder at the God Box one more time, her pulse accelerating. From the front, no one would notice the exposed guts of the machine, but she hoped nobody would wonder why the egg was onstage when BD wasn't there. Her stomach fluttered; maybe she wasn't cut out to be a spy after all, but it was too late to turn back now.

YVETTE had returned to the ghoulish headquarters of Elysian Fields, its halls haunted with the lingering remembered odor of beefy death. With the secretary cowering under his desk, no one impeded Yvette's progress as she thumped open the big double doors to the president's conference room. As before, the dashing figure of the man in the gray suit was seated at the head of the table, but this time he was reviewing a dynamic financial summary chart.

Gardner looked startled when Yvette entered the room. She wore a formal red suit that fit her mood.

"Ms. Fermi? I'm surprised to see you at this time of the morning." He stood and offered his hand, but she stopped five feet away from him, resting her hands on the back of a chair. The glow from the overhead spotlight created deep shadows under Gardner's eyebrows and nose, giving him a monstrous appearance.

"I bet you're surprised," Yvette said. "I had an early meeting with Mr. Whittington, so I thought I'd stop by to see you."

Gardner raised his eyebrows. "Really? And where is Whittington now?"

"Look outside," she said, gesturing toward the window.

Gardner frowned and looked out through the glass, his eyes scanning the street. "I don't see anything." Then, after a pause, he swallowed. "Oh, I see him now."

Yvette glanced out the window and saw that Whittington was still tied to the stunted tree in the park across the road where she'd left him. He was naked, and his arms were tied to two opposing branches to hold his unconscious body upright. A pair of pigeons pecked at the grass around his feet. "He looks very natural out there, don't you think?"

"What's this all about?" Gardner asked, folding his arms and turning to face her. "I know you and Whittington have never hit it off, but—"

"Oh, I think we understand each other now." She knew Gardner's monkey had not been acting on his own; he didn't have the brain capacity or the imagination to kill her without orders.

"Perhaps. Is he dead?"

Yvette snorted. "He'll only wish he was dead when he wakes up."

"Hmm. Well, I suppose you have some sort of message for me, then?"

"I've already given you the message," she said, "but I'd like to know if I should start killing your assistants on sight, or if one attempt on my life will be enough for you."

Gardner smiled. "Death isn't what it used to be, is it?

Look around you. Elysian Fields exists to create immortals. Humans need have no fear of death anymore. The organic brain and the digital brain have become one, allowing us to lead full lives even after our bodies have returned to the soil from whence they came. Is it still murder when the victim is able to return from the dead? Our attorneys stand ready to debate the question. And my employees are willing to die to spread the message of immortality, well aware that their memories and personalities—their souls, if you will—are protected against death and decay."

Yvette stared at him for a moment. "That sounds like a *yes* to me. I should just go ahead and kill your employees because they really won't mind."

"Well, I don't think that will be necessary, Ms. Fermi. As I continue to learn more about you, I'm thinking you may, in fact, be welcome on our board of directors."

"You have a funny way of showing it."

Gardner shrugged. "Think of this incident as a trial by fire. However, one of our founders has concerns about you, and he needs to explore some deeper aspects of your personality."

Yvette raised one of her eyebrows. What was he implying? She wasn't going to sleep with one of these old men without a very good reason. "What does he expect me to do?"

"Elysian Fields can only do its job if it has the complete and utter loyalty of its employees. You will be given a task that proves your worthiness. If you're accepted, you will receive a special biochip; it will not only record your memories and personality, but it will also have an explosive charge inside. If you break the oath of secrecy or do anything to dishonor Elysian Fields, we will blow your head off. The biochip will be destroyed, and you will no longer exist in any form."

"You guys really know how to hold a grudge." She'd agree to it now, but she wasn't actually going to let one of these untrustworthy clowns put an explosive in her head. "Are there any benefits with this job?"

"Great wealth and eternal life."

She nodded. "That's better than what I get from NASA. They just give me medical insurance and a paid vacation."

Gardner had no sense of humor, and she couldn't trust him. If she got her foot in the door at Elysian Fields, Gardner would have to go.

27

KATE had previously survived the launch of a space shuttle from Florida in good condition, but the suborbital Orient Express flight from California to Moscow, chartered by Yvette to ferry a small group of NASA employees who weren't interested in speaking to each other, seemed more violent and unpleasant. She suspected it had something to do with the long free fall period as they coasted in to Domodedovo International Airport in Moscow. Having made frequent use of the complimentary "digestive expulsion" bags from the zippered pocket of her seat, she felt shaky and weak when she tottered down the steps onto the landing pad and made her way into the air terminal. This being her first trip to Moscow, a NASA protocol officer had contacted her before the flight to instruct her on the types and amounts of bribery that would be required to get through the various levels of customs, border control, and other authorities in the airport. The protocol officer had warned her not to speak to anyone unnecessarily, to stride confidently through the terminal as if she had been there many times, to wear her most expensive clothes as if she were connected to the *mafiya,* and to meet a man named Pushkin inside. The various warnings made Kate feel like a spy in one of the old flatfilms.

She only had to bribe three officials, using her limited knowledge of Russian to sound superior and annoyed at the delay. No one had reminded her to take a translator on the trip, and she didn't like the way the little hearing aid–style devices felt in her ear anyway, but she managed to bully her way through the simple conversations. When she spotted Pushkin, a tall, burly man with black hair and a heavy beard who was dressed in a soiled overcoat, he held a sign with her name on it. Up close, he smelled like fish, and he looked like a thug with his broken nose and scarred face, but he was the local contact Yvette hired to be her escort. When Kate said the man's name, Pushkin just blinked his heavy-lidded eyes, grunted, and gestured for her to follow him through the terminal, leaving her to carry her own overnight bag. She wore a formal black business suit from her own closet, but she had borrowed the expensive Puccini shoes and jewelry from Yvette. The shoes had reshaped themselves to fit Kate's larger feet, but they still managed to pinch her toes as she clacked through the airport. She thought it was nice of Yvette to have donated part of her wardrobe so Kate could get through the airport safely, but she felt bad about leaving Laika in Yvette's care. She always wondered whether Laika would get enough attention when Yvette was so busy all the time.

After a ten-minute walk, Pushkin delivered her to the gate where she would catch the 800-mile Aeroflot flight to the southern Urals where the survey team awaited her arrival. Kate asked him how long the flight would take, but he just grunted and spoke to the gate agent to check her in. While he stood at the counter in front of her, she noticed that his boots were covered with dried mud, so she decided that Pushkin lived in the country but took the train into Moscow to work; therefore, he probably spoke very little English, if any. The thought that he couldn't understand her made it easier to tolerate his lack of interactivity. She spoke some Russian, but she didn't want to take the chance of embarrassing herself in front of this provincial thug who looked like he might knock her down and steal her borrowed jewelry at any moment.

Although she was prepared for a long delay, Kate only had to wait five minutes before the gate agent opened the doors to board the plane. To her surprise, Pushkin heaved his bulk up from the flimsy chair he'd been flattening and beckoned her to follow him onto the plane.

The seats were narrow, and the crash harness held her safely in place, but the old jump craft smelled of sweat, oil, and fuel, and she felt nauseous again. Pushkin's fishy smell was almost a welcome relief until his snoring head lolled over to one side and thumped onto her right shoulder. She shifted her weight, but his head didn't move, and he wouldn't wake up. Across the aisle, an old woman with a live chicken in her lap stared at Kate for no apparent reason. After the initial jolt of the launch, she concentrated on the thundering sound of the engines and rested her head on the window, staring out at the rapidly receding sprawl of Moscow, and finally fell asleep.

She woke up again when Pushkin prodded her shoulder with his meaty hand. Half asleep and unaware of her surroundings, her eyes flew open, and she saw that all the other seats were empty. Outside, she saw a rural airport and burly men dressed like Pushkin who bustled about on airport business, fueling jump ships and hurling luggage into the waiting arms of platform robots with blinking lights on their heads. She unbuckled her crash harness and lurched to her feet. She was surprised to see Pushkin carrying her overnight bag, and he had already covered the distance to the exit door.

"Pushkin, wait!" She jogged after him as he started down the exit ramp.

He moved like an icebreaker through the sea of bodies standing around in the terminal waiting for flights, and she strode steadily along in his wake. There were more departures than arrivals, and she wondered what that said about the region. This being a local flight, no one impeded their progress as they walked out of the terminal, where weak sunlight struggled to break through the clouds. The air smelled of wood, ammonia, and burning rubber, but it was a welcome relief to the odor of the jump craft and the stale, overheated air in the terminal. Pushkin stopped at the edge of the parking lot and looked around expectantly.

"What are we waiting for?" Kate asked.

Her answer came in the form of a battered white hovercar that raced out of the parking area and abruptly stopped beside them. The tall man who jumped out of the driver's seat was in his mid-twenties, his strong face punctuated with a neat brown mustache. He wore a neatly tailored blue jumpsuit covered with dust. He gave them a huge smile while he bounced around the hovercar toward them. "Professor Ryumin! Dr. McCloud! I hope you had a good trip!"

"Very good, thank you. I was finally able to get some sleep," Pushkin said in perfect English. He smiled at Kate.

Kate stared at Pushkin. "Professor Ryumin? I thought your name was Pushkin."

Pushkin bowed slightly. "I am Professor Pushkin Sergeevich Ryumin."

"And you speak English," Kate said.

"Enough to get by," Pushkin said, handing her overnight bag to the new arrival as he opened the clamshell door on the side of the hovercar. "This is Pat McCarthy. He is assistant to Ms. Yvette Fermi of NASA."

"Hi," Pat said, holding out his hand.

Kate ignored McCarthy and shook her head, staring at Pushkin. "Why didn't you speak to me before?"

Pushkin shrugged and climbed into the hovercar. "All night I am in meeting outside Moscow. I was tired."

McCarthy glanced at Pushkin, then leaned over to whisper in Kate's ear. "He's a little eccentric, but he's okay. He's not happy that NASA sent you over to take charge of the team."

"Take charge?" Kate gave him a puzzled look and lowered her voice. "I'm only here to observe. I'll be gone in a couple of weeks."

McCarthy winked. "Yeah, okay. Whatever you say. He'll get used to you."

"I'm serious. Yvette told me the team found something alien in the dig, and that's why you needed my expertise."

McCarthy nodded with a sly expression. "Right. Got it. Yvette works in mysterious ways."

Kate was sure McCarthy still didn't believe her when she climbed into the hovercar and sat beside Pushkin. Had Yvette lied to her, or had her assistant been given a different story? Did the professor know the truth? Was there some kind of political thing going on with this international team that she didn't understand? She sighed as the hovercar's engine whined into life and rose gently from the pavement. This was all too confusing for such a long trip without enough sleep.

28

"YES, Dominique! Yes!" Novikov's eyes were closed as he moaned with pleasure.

When he heard someone whispering, Novikov suddenly realized he was no longer in the catacombs of Paris with his former lover. His eyes snapped open to see two of his assistants chuckling and whispering to each other behind the newsnet camera. He was back in the museum on Mars, fully dressed and crouched against the wall, and he had just made an international fool of himself on Earth. His career would be ruined. People would point and laugh at him on the street. And the museum had done this to him, humiliating him so that he could no longer function, seeking revenge for unearthing the secrets of the Gwrinydd.

As these thoughts of career suicide swirled through his head, Novikov suddenly had an idea. He was still crouched against the wall, so maybe he could turn the whole thing into the gesture of a brave explorer on the brink of doom. It could work. Maybe. If he was lucky. He quickly moaned again, as if in pain, and grabbed his side with both hands. Slumping to the floor, he looked at the camera with a pleading expression, trying to communicate the ghastly mistake the audience had made; clearly, some unseen alien organism was ripping his guts out.

And it worked. Or seemed to. His assistants stopped whispering, their expressions serious.

In fact, his acting was so good that he now felt a monstrous pain in his torso, a real pain that radiated into his neck, jaw, and back. He moved his hands from his side to clutch at his left shoulder. He felt as if an elephant was bouncing up and down on the middle of his chest, causing flutters in his heartbeat. A cold knife sliced through his left arm. His breath came in short gasps, and he started to sweat. Heart attack?

Something pinged on the floor near his head, and he felt a section of the floor lifting him into the air. Twisting in pain, he forced his eyes open and saw that he was about two feet off the floor. One of his assistants started toward him while the other kept the camera going, but they quickly receded into the distance as the table shot away toward the back of the museum, holding him in place with some type of force field. He turned to look forward and saw that he was about to hit the back wall, but a small square of light appeared at the last moment, a hidden door to a light-filled coffin. The table stopped as suddenly as it had started, the door closed at his feet, and he was nearly blinded by the increasing intensity of the white light. He reached up to cover his eyes with his hands, then realized that he no longer felt any pain in his chest. His heart rate and breathing slowed. The attack was over.

It may have been hours, or minutes, or seconds that he spent in the coffin. He couldn't be sure. But once the pain had vanished, the door at his feet opened once more, and the table shot out into the museum, reversing the wild ride of before. The table then stopped and settled perfectly into the floor where it had started, its seams disappearing, leaving no clue as to its presence.

Novikov stared into the camera, thinking maybe he had dreamed the entire episode, but his two assistants were staring right back at him on the floor, their mouths open, the camera pointed at an odd angle. Novikov smiled.

The museum held many secrets. And Novikov would discover them all.

29

ASLEEP in the reclining hovercar seat on her way to the dig at Yamantau Mountain, Kate's dreams were disturbed by random images of bright tunnels and the teleportation gate technology she had seen beneath Umbra Labyrinthus in the Tharsis region of Mars. The Gwrinydd race had built their structures in a simple, functional style appropriate to their military nature, but she'd always thought that their use of materials—the pearly, iridescent walls of their tunnels and the etched, chromelike surfaces of the Vulcan and Borovitsky Gates—showed a refined aesthetic sense. In her dream, however, the tunnels looked threatening, beckoning her onward to an unknown doom, filling her with a sense of dread and a fear of being buried alive beneath the lonesome pink sands of Mars. Then these images were interrupted by a stirring in her head, stopping the projector as if a switch had been flipped, leaving only a rosy ball of light glowing in darkness. She moved forward, or the ball moved toward her, and she passed through into a new scene that resolved into a wide, flat river flowing between ancient Egyptian monuments. Although she had worked at Amarna in Egypt, where she discovered the hidden tomb of Tutankhamen's wife, Queen Ankhesenpaaten, with Lenya Novikov and his team, this section of what appeared to be the Nile did not look familiar. Some of the limestone structures baking in the sun looked like the vast Temple of Amon Ra and the long avenue of ram-headed sphinxes leading to the first pylon at the Karnak temple complex, but many of the tall obelisks and crumbling walls did not seem to match up with those she remembered.

"Kate McCloud," boomed the voice of Thoth. He stepped

out from behind a red, hieroglyph-covered obelisk on the shore and clacked his long, curved beak before striding toward her across the water. "No man is an island."

Another dream controlled by Thoth, and another one of his cryptic remarks. She fervently wished she could keep the AI out of her dreams, but the only way she'd been able to stop these infrequent uninvited visits was by waking up. "No woman is a man," she replied in an attempt to confuse him.

Thoth stopped walking for a moment and tipped his head, then grunted with a nod and continued forward. "There is an inscription at Karnak: 'One foot is not enough to walk with.' Have you considered our last request?"

"The answer is the same," Kate said, trying to wake up. She remembered reading the Karnak proverb on some temple wall, and she knew Thoth was using the quote from her memory to make her see his point of view. "I don't want you living in my head. I'd go crazy."

"You wouldn't even know we were there," Thoth replied, spreading his human arms wide in supplication. "We'd be very quiet. You would have easy access to me, even when you were awake, and we would learn more about you and your kind."

"No. I don't want you to 'upgrade' me again." She looked around for an avenue of escape, but the Nile stretched away to infinite horizons in every direction but the one that led to the false Karnak complex.

Thoth stopped a few feet away from her, disconcertingly still on the surface of the rippling river. "You would find the upgrade useful. It would give you a greater mental capacity and unrestricted access to our own data stores. There is another inscription at Karnak: 'Two tendencies govern human choice and effort, the search after quality and the search after quantity. They classify mankind. Some follow Maat, others seek the way of animal instinct.' Which way will you follow, Kate McCloud?"

Through a great effort of will, Kate forced herself to wake up, her heart pounding. She still sat in the hovercar, now winding its way along a barely perceptible mountain road lined with a dense forest of oak and fir trees. A plume of dust obscured the road behind them. Professor Pushkin Ryumin was telling Pat McCarthy about his teaching job at the Bashkiriya branch of the Russian Academy of Sciences, but Pat appeared to be concentrating his full attention on the road ahead. She thought about going back to sleep, but Thoth might be waiting, so she distracted herself by asking about a battered road sign they had just passed.

Pushkin raised one eyebrow and studied her face. "Why do you ask about this?"

"Because I can't read Cyrillic letters." Kate wondered if the man was conversationally challenged or just pompous.

"The sign referred to the city of Mezhgorye, formerly known as the settlements of Beloretsk-15 and Beloretsk-16."

Kate nodded and tried to keep the conversation moving. "Many people live out here?"

Pushkin glanced at Pat, then shook his head at Kate. "This is joke? Mezhgorye is no longer existing after blast."

"Oh," Kate said. "Sorry. I didn't know."

Pat looked at her in the rearview mirror. "Mezhgorye used to be a big town, but there were only a few hundred people still residing there last year at the time of the explosion."

"Yvette didn't tell me about all this," Kate said, wondering what else she didn't know.

Pushkin snorted and slapped his forehead with his palm, then folded his arms and looked out the side window.

"We can talk about it more later," Pat said.

Kate wondered if it would be safer to go back to sleep and face Thoth. This was going to be a long trip.

30

TAU clicked a sim cube into the program socket of the entertainment unit, then settled back into the form-fitting couch and stared up at the black glass dome. It would take a few seconds for the system to generate the complex world and send the signal to his wireless brain-stem electrode. The sim cube package from Yvette had been waiting for him at his apt when he returned, and her note asked him to run a quick test on it to see if he was interested in the technology. No explanation, very mysterious, all intended to manipulate Tau into testing the sim. He knew she wanted to pique his curiosity about something, and the best way to do that was to hand him a black box, say it did something fascinating with technology, and then let him play with it.

The sim unit beeped three times to warn him the program was starting, then it flooded his brain with the blackness that preceded the realistic virtual world created by the sim programmers. The environment and the characters generated in his head were fully interactive, but any sim involving a story line included scripted interactions and behaviors between nonplayer characters. The AIs who operated the sim could make changes to the world and its inhabitants to keep it interesting for repeat visitors, and it was often hard to tell what was scripted and what was not. The player's actions were recorded as permanent changes to the environment. With the unlimited possibilities of a dynamic world running in the head of the player, sims had replaced theme parks, books, films, and many other leisure-time activities as the dominant form of entertainment. The sim units themselves were expensive, as were new sim cube programs, but most people managed to buy them, just as they had once bought television sets or personal computers when those technologies were new. Combined with AI teachers, sims were used extensively for education, allowing students to learn about history, for example, by living with George Washington for a few days instead of just reading about him. A lively market in used sim cubes and older-model entertainment units made it possible for many of the poor to escape from the harsh realities of their daily lives into virtual worlds they could control.

Tau stood on the deck of a fishing boat that rocked gently on a calm sea. The sun was low on the western horizon, and the air smelled of salt and fish. Startled by the motion of the boat, he grabbed the weathered wood of a door frame to steady himself. The frigid air made him shiver, and they were about a mile away from a white ice shelf that rose sharply from the dark blue waters. Other fishing boats towed nets nearby, but they were all dominated by the massive outline of a factory ship whose stern yawned open to receive the boats at the end of the day.

Tau jumped when he heard a clumping sound on the deck behind him, followed by a loud voice. "Arr, matey! Welcome to the *Minnow*, flagship of Captain Bill's fishing fleet in Antarctica!"

Tau spun around. A stereotypical old salt stood five feet away, complete with a white captain's hat, an eye patch, a navy blue captain's coat with gold buttons, and a pegleg of polished mahogany that terminated one leg of his white pants above the knee. All he needed was a parrot to complete the outfit. "I'm Captain Bill," he said, holding out an enormous and calloused hand.

Tau introduced himself, wincing as Bill nearly crushed his hand in his powerful grip.

Bill waved his arm at the fishing fleet. "At certain times of the year, krill gather in vast swarms in the waters of Antarctica and the northeast Pacific, making them easy to locate and harvest. They are then quick-frozen on board the harvesting boats to lock in nutrition and flavor. Nature's perfect food, zooplankton provides essential amino acids and proteins, fatty acids, and a taste that can't be beat."

Tau realized he was standing in the middle of an advertisement. Perfect food or not, he had never set foot in one of Captain Bill's artificially bright and happy fast-food establishments, and he'd rather eat a maggot before he'd go into one now. He didn't like being manipulated by restaurants that used marketing endorphins to hook customers on their foods. It was bad enough that someone had placed advertising in an entertainment sim.

As he wondered how he might escape from Captain Bill's continuing monologue, since he was cleverly trapped aboard a fishing boat off an isolated coastline surrounded by freezing water, the old salt ended his routine. ". . . so swim on over to Captain Bill's Krill Grill, Home of the Thrill Krill Burger." The captain then nodded and stepped sideways into what looked like a closet, but the nightmare wasn't over. Tau groaned when he saw a line of six-foot-tall shrimp dancing toward him on their tails, accompanied by the saccharine Captain Bill jingle that was designed to haunt his dreams for weeks. Knowing he couldn't die in the simulated world, he took three steps and dove over the rail of the boat.

Despite the freezing-cold water turning his skin to ice, Tau suddenly felt an urge to try a Thrill Krill Burger.

The scene changed. His skin warmed rapidly under hot sunlight. A breeze straight out of a blast furnace caressed his skin and burned into his lungs. He stood atop a red rock spire, hundreds of feet above the desert floor under a clear turquoise sky. In the distance, he saw the Mittens, Rain God Mesa, and other unique de Chelly sandstone formations rising out of the shale mounds that dotted the flat sandy plain, marking this place as Monument Valley—or *Tse' Bii' Ndzisgaii*, "changing of the rock"—the Navajo Tribal Park in northern Arizona. Comb Ridge, known to the Navajos as one of the four arrowheads that carved the earth, bit at the sky with jagged teeth. A shepherd tended a chaotic mass of wool on the hoof across the valley floor, and the occasional clank of a neck bell made its way to Tau's eagle perch. Vultures circled in the updrafts, their keen eyes hunting the recently dead for their next meal.

The rock spire where Tau stood was the Totem Pole, a holy place that resembled a prayer stick. The crumbling spire was a difficult ascent, even for experienced rock climbers using traditional equipment, and he was startled to see a blond woman standing about twenty feet away looking straight down the vertical drop to the desert floor. She was barefoot, and she wore a long, translucent yellow dress covered with tiny blue flowers that rippled in the wind.

"Hello," Tau said, trying not to startle her.

She turned sideways, revealing a striking profile. A breeze danced in her hair. Yvette smiled like the sun when she saw Tau, then beckoned him closer. He stepped over to the edge and saw that her toes were hanging over the sheer drop. "This is life," she said.

Tau looked into her sparkling blue eyes and saw his face reflected there. He shook his head.

"A long drop from a high place, ending in death," she said. "We stand here as long as we can, balanced on the edge, until we're too weak to stand or the wind pushes us over. Then we fall, long and hard, into the ground. And it's all over. Splat."

He flinched when she gently took his hand and held it against her breast. "Feel my heartbeat. It's the rhythm of life; a quiet reminder of mortality that we carry with us wherever we go. We seek harmony with that rhythm so that we can walk in beauty."

Tau's eyes widened. She was talking like a Navajo medicine man, although medicine men usually didn't look this good. He felt her warmth through the soft, thin material of her dress.

"The rhythm of experience shows us how to live the right way, how to seek *hozro*. I seek that balance by sharing myself with others, enriching their lives, teaching them how to be happy. Are you happy, Tau?"

Tau had to remind himself that she wasn't real, but the

tingling in his body certainly felt real, and this moment made him happy. But she was only a scripted creature, a digital life-form without reality, no doubt designed by Yvette to manipulate him in some way. But she seemed genuine, and he knew that her heart was in the right place. In different circumstances, away from the pressures of city life, he knew her admirable qualities would be set free, but instead she remained in a world where unfettered ambition and deceit were rewarded. She lived in the world of clocks and committees, of meetings and money—and there was no balance in that world, no *hozro.* Maybe he could help her?

"Tau, would you be happy with me? If we were together, right now, would you share yourself with me? Would you help me to find harmony and beauty?"

He blinked in amazement. Was she reading his mind? Of course, the sim AI was interpreting his thoughts, adapting the dialogue to his reactions, building a more stable simulation that reflected his moods. But he looked at Yvette and saw one kind of beauty; when he looked at Kate, he felt many kinds of beauty. He sighed. Although Kate was friendly with Yvette, she often warned Tau that his boss could not be trusted.

Tau slowly recovered his hand. "I'm sorry, Yvette."

She stared at him for a moment, then a tear trickled from one of her eyes, and she turned away, facing into the sun, her toes hanging over the edge of the world. "I'm sorry, too."

She stepped off the ledge. Tau lurched, trying to catch her, and nearly fell himself. She plummeted quickly and quietly, her dress flapping in the wind, until she hit the rocks at the base of the spire and bounced like a rag doll.

Tau screamed at the sun.

Tau's eyes shot open, and he rolled out of the comfortable sim couch, landing on the carpeted floor in a heap. He was sweating, and his heart thumped against his chest like it wanted to get out. What kind of a sim was that? What was the point of it? Why had Yvette sent him a demo cube in the first place? Did she mean to traumatize him?

He rubbed his hands against the soft carpet and took deep breaths, reminding himself that he was back in the real world, and that no real person had died in the sim. It was all a show, a manipulative show, and not a particularly clever one at that.

He swallowed hard and looked around at his apt, at the comfortable furnishings, at the old books and Egyptian artifacts on the bookshelves, and at his stunning view of the San Francisco Bay through the clear glass walls. This was the private apt that Yvette had arranged for him in the luxury block huddled against the underside of the curved roof of one of the massive old blimp hangars at Moffett Field. As director of Ames Research Center, she'd granted him a paid leave of absence from his job after their return from Mars and let him use this apt so that Tau would have a comfortable place to live with Kate. Tau knew this apt was normally assigned to the NASA director, but Yvette had chosen to live in a nicer location on Nob Hill in San Francisco. With the apt still registered in Yvette's name, anyone looking for him or Kate would have a harder time finding him there. He owed Yvette a lot, and he wondered if she knew how much he appreciated her help.

He had to see her.

And he was hungry. He'd stop at Captain Bill's Krill Grill on the way to Yvette's place.

TAU couldn't help looking at the shiny new taser shock camera pointed at his head from an alcove above the door to Yvette's apt. This luxury apt tower certainly had good defenses for its residents, and Tau hoped Yvette wouldn't mind his stopping by without warning. Yvette's home AI should have announced his presence by now, and he was impatient to see her, so he rapped his knuckles against a flat spot on the door, avoiding the ornate carvings of flowers and small woodland creatures that covered its surface. When the door suddenly became transparent like a big plate of glass, he was surprised to see Yvette standing on the other side of it, barely dressed in a short red nightie that lovingly clung to its owner. She looked startled, and mod-

estly put one arm across her breasts, even though her security system must have shown her his identity.

"Tau? What a surprise."

"I wanted to talk," he said, wondering why he'd come.

"Just a minute." She smiled and padded away across
her shiny marble floor as the apt door slowly returned to its
original wood appearance. He burped, tasting the Thrill
Krill Burger he'd eaten on the way there. Exactly one
minute later, the door hissed and silently opened. He
stepped into the foyer, his boots thumping on the marble,
and the door shut itself behind him. A full-size white marble statue of a naked man guarded the door, marked with a
plaque that identified it as Michelangelo's *David*. The air
in the foyer had a pleasant scent of lemon, but as he took a
few more steps into the hallway, he detected the scent of a
pleasant flowery perfume, possibly jasmine, that made him
inhale deeply.

This was his first visit, although Kate had been here a
few times, and he was curious about the place. He glanced
to the right and saw a huge sunken living room facing a
wall of glass with a remarkable view of the city below. The
city lights were just coming on. Beyond the living room
was a sparkling, elaborate kitchen.

Yvette called to him from some back room to his left.
He hesitated, then slowly walked down the marble hallway, passing huge oil paintings of nudes by Renaissance
masters, which he assumed were reproductions. He paused
outside a closed door, hearing Laika's muffled barks from
inside the room, but Yvette called to him again, beckoning
him to the last room at the end of the corridor where the
door stood open. The scent of jasmine was stronger here.
Wavering at the threshold, he glanced at the painting to his
left, *Allegory of Fortune*, by Dosso Dossi, which he recognized from an art history class in college. It depicted the
idea that prosperity in life is dependent on luck, with
the nude Lady Luck holding a cornucopia, flaunting the
bounty that she could bring, but she sits on a bubble because her favors are often fleeting. The billowing drapery
behind her serves as a reminder that she is changeable like

the wind. The seated man to her left personifies chance, looking at Lady Luck with a stack of lottery tickets in his hand that he's about to place inside a golden urn.

Tau wondered if Yvette had placed it there to tell him something. He turned to the open door.

Yvette lay on her side on the canopy bed among mounds of pillows, holding a glass of champagne, her image reflected in an overhead mirror. Spotlights were strategically placed in the ceiling to create the effect of a museum exhibit. While he stood there a moment studying Yvette and the room, he realized he had passed a similar scene in one of the earlier Renaissance paintings in the hallway, although the nude in the painting had not been wearing high heels. Artistic license, he supposed.

"Are you Lady Luck?" Tau asked. He still wondered what had possessed him to come here.

She sipped at her champagne. "Maybe. What do you think?"

He shrugged, still standing in the doorway, unsure of what clever thing he might say next.

"Welcome to my office," she said. Gesturing at another glass on the marble bedside table, she asked, "Do you want a drink?"

"Thanks." Tau nodded and walked over to the bedside table. When he reached for the drink, he noticed a long crack in the white marble surface. "You said this is your office?"

"Oh, yes, I get a lot of work done here," she said with a coy expression. "Anyway, Kate said I should try to see you while she was in Russia. She thought you'd get lonely."

So that was it, he thought. Just being friendly; what a relief. Then he remembered that it had been his idea to visit her. "And here I am. That's nice of you. I, uh, just wanted to tell you how much I appreciate everything you've been doing for me lately. The time off, letting me use your apt—all those things."

"I'm glad to hear you say that," she said. "But you earned it."

He sipped at his drink, thinking he should probably leave.

She patted the edge of the bed near her head. "Have a seat, Tau."

He sighed, figuring he could sit for a moment to be polite, then finish his drink and leave. Champagne fizzed in his mouth.

"I know I've been hard on you at times, Tau, but it was for your own good. You have so much potential, so much energy. I figured I could push you harder and get the best possible work out of you, but if I rode you too hard, I apologize." To emphasize her point, she patted his knee, then let her hand rest there.

He assumed she was apologizing for becoming his boss after the chief designer at the lab had disappeared, soon followed by the director. She had moved up the chain of responsibility with lightning speed, pausing only to interfere with Tau's projects. And now he suddenly felt a great affection for her that he couldn't understand. It didn't make any sense. "No need to apologize, Yvette."

She moved closer and looked deeply into his eyes. "It must have been hard for you since we got back from Mars. You stopped a war, and you can't even tell anyone about it."

"That doesn't matter." He jumped when her other hand began to rub his back.

"It does matter, Tau. And someday, everyone will know what you did. You were magnificent. And you did the right thing by keeping quiet."

Tau took another sip of his champagne. He felt his face getting warm. "You know, I've often wondered why I never heard about any diplomatic incidents, or any repercussions from the Red Star people after we got back. Do you know anything about that?"

Yvette gave him a sly smile. "Oh, don't worry about that. Heads rolled in all the right places; it just didn't make the news when it happened."

"I see." Tau nodded as if he understood, even though he

didn't. "You wouldn't happen to know why anyone would try to kidnap Kate, would you?"

"Me?" She looked shocked, which was what he expected. "Kate mentioned some trouble in Arizona, but I didn't realize it was so serious."

"Seemed serious to me," he said. "Government types. One tried to grab Kate, and the other one tried to kill me."

Her eyes were wide as she sat up straight. "You didn't tell anyone, did you?"

"No. We didn't know who we could trust with the information."

"Smart," she said, visibly relaxing. She leaned forward and rested her head on his shoulder, pressing her chest against his arm. "It's a good thing you were there to help Kate. But now that you're back here and safe, you should keep your head down for a while. You upset a lot of people. Give it some time, and everything will be back to normal."

"Kate helped herself," he said. "I just saved my own skin, hitched a ride from a crazy truck driver, and met her at my mom's place so we could sneak back here."

"Crazy truck driver?"

"Woman named Pinky. Religious fanatic. She tried to recruit me for some bizarre church that worships an AI in the datasphere, or some such nonsense," he said, realizing he probably sounded boring, which was easy for him to do. He rarely drank alcohol, and he was always surprised at how little it took to affect his thinking. "I'd better go." He stood up suddenly and set his glass on the table.

"Hey!" Yvette's arms flailed briefly as she tumbled out of the bed onto the floor, spilling her glass of champagne on his shoes.

"Sorry," he said, helping her up. She pushed his hands away and bent over to grab her robe, awarding him an eyeful. He started toward the door. "Thanks for the drink. I'll see you at work tomorrow, okay?"

Tying her robe, Yvette glared at him. "Yeah. Whatever."

ERIC Stamp and Frank Murdoch kept their eyes glued on
the Fermi woman despite the cold wind howling past their
damp platforms outside her bedroom window. They no
longer thought about the potentially long falls to their
deaths, or the uncomfortable weather at that altitude, or the
minimal amount of sleep they were getting. They were
simply fascinated with their subject.

"Is this the best surveillance gig you've ever had, or
what?" Murdoch asked, nudging Stamp in the ribs.

"Yeah, it's the best; now shut up," Stamp said, ducking
his head to punch the scrambler code for the secure net
link. His burst report would mention the comical details regarding her male visitor, who hadn't been smart enough to
hit the sheets with the babe when she gave him the chance.
Stamp shook his head in wonder; he'd volunteer for that
duty in a second, and slimy Murdoch would have cheerfully thrown him off the portaledge for the same opportunity. The recorded conversation between Fermi and her
visitor was also in the burst transmission, so someone
ought to get a laugh out of that back at the office. He still
had no idea if anyone was actually reviewing his reports,
and he'd been told that Nygaard was out of town, so they
might be hanging around like flies on the side of the building for a few more days until someone noticed they were
wasting their time. But, as Murdoch said, they never tired
of watching Fermi cavort around her apt.

YVETTE walked carefully across the damp grass of the
cemetery between two rows of staggered tombstones,
ranging from simple white marble slabs to elaborate urns,
granite balls, and Victorian angels draped over graves in
mourning. The crescent moon was bright, but she still had
to use her flashlight to avoid falling into holes and trip-
ping over the smaller grave markers that rose out of the
grass like land mines. At times like this, she had to wonder why she went to so much trouble to get ahead: did she
really have to find out how many times she could get promoted in one year, or learn how fast she could make
money, or run the risk of killing herself with too much re-

sponsibility so that she could retire while she was still young? No, she decided, she didn't *have* to do those things; she acquired power and money for the sport of it, for the thrill of the chase and the adrenaline rush of victory. If she had to wander around old Colma graveyards at midnight to get a piece of the Elysian Fields action, then so be it.

She sighed. She'd expected victory earlier this evening when she lured Tau over to her apt with the sim cube she'd sent him. Her COO at AdForce would be hearing about this failure. Obviously, the program had been written incorrectly or their persuasive technology was not as good as she had hoped. She'd done everything but knock Tau down and tear his clothes off, and the geek still hadn't understood what she wanted. His rejection almost made her doubt herself, and that ticked her off even more. Some programmer would be fired tomorrow. She didn't like this odd, unexpected power that Tau held over her, and refusing to sleep with her just made it worse. She respected Tau, and he was the only real genius on her NASA staff since Max Thorn had been killed last year, but she needed to control him. She'd seen the way he drooled when he entered the bedroom, and how he looked at her during the return trip from Mars, but Kate was not around this time to get in the way. Tau was alone, and she'd blown her opportunity to seduce him. That was unacceptable. She realized she was breathing hard just thinking about him.

The blocky outline of a huge structure loomed ahead in the moonlight, and she assumed it was the new mausoleum the EF people had built for Emperor Norton. Always ready to cover whacko events, the local news shows had been there a few weeks ago when the new tomb was officially unveiled by the mayor of San Francisco and some guy in an Egyptian costume with the head of a jackal. Under a wide ornamental roof, the twenty-foot statue of Joshua Norton I, Emperor of the United States and Protector of Mexico, dressed in his formal bandleader's uniform, sat atop an enormous pink granite throne that resembled the

Lincoln memorial in Washington, D.C. Normally lit at night by spotlights from the ground, the structure was now mysteriously dark. It being the largest monument in this part of the Woodlawn Memorial Park, Mr. Gardner said it would be easy for Yvette to find, even though she'd have to hike all the way up from the parking lot at the base of the hill.

Within a few yards of the tomb's entrance, she saw a tall man slowly approaching her in the darkness.

"Ms. Fermi?" Gardner's voice.

"No, I'm just a wandering necrophiliac looking for a good time. Why did you drag me all the way out here?"

"Someone wants to meet you. Follow me," he said, walking back toward the emperor.

When they approached the giant statue, a shadowy figure rose from his seat on one of Norton's boots. Gardner stopped beside him and turned to face Yvette. Assuming good intentions, Yvette slipped her hand into her pocket to feel the reassuring presence of her dart gun; if anyone tried anything, they'd lose an eye or sleep for twenty-four hours, depending on where she aimed. They'd already tried to kill her once. Although they seemed to have learned their lesson, it didn't hurt to come prepared.

"Ms. Fermi, I'd like you to meet one of our founders, Aaron Thorn."

The man stepped forward where a shaft of moonlight lit half of his face. Despite herself, Yvette was impressed. She reached out to shake the hand he offered. "*Senator* Thorn?"

"Yes, Ms. Fermi," Thorn said, taking her hand with a firm, professional grip.

Her heart thumped against her ribs. "Christ."

"Not exactly. I'm simply running for president. But I hope you'll vote for me."

If he did become president, she could really make some headway in her career. If Rex King got reelected, the senator would still be running the committee responsible for the Mars Development Office and NASA's budget, so that would help her, too. On the other hand, knowing the senator was involved in Elysian Fields might be useful as some kind of leverage. "I'd love to vote for you, Senator, but that depends on what kind of campaign speech you make right now."

Thorn laughed and released her hand. "I expected you'd say something like that. I've heard a lot about you. No, I take that back, I've done a great deal of research on you, and I like what I see."

"Thank you." She smiled.

"I understand that Mr. Gardner told you we'd allow you to prove yourself worthy of being on our board of directors."

"Whatever you need, Senator."

"One of your employees is Tau Edison Wolfsinger, and his fiancée is Katherine McCloud. I'd simply like to know where they are at this moment. This is a matter of national security."

Yvette's mouth went dry. She didn't know what to say. "Why?" Christ, did she just ask *why*? Was she already questioning this man who could help her so much?

"We need to speak with them, that's all. Ms. McCloud has never been properly debriefed regarding her experiences with the alien artificial intelligence she discovered on Mars. Mr. Wolfsinger was debriefed, but I have some additional questions for him."

"Ah," she said. Kate was her friend, more or less, and Tau was, well, she wasn't going to start thinking about *that* again. He deserved whatever he got. And if all the senator wanted was to talk to them, that sounded harmless enough. "As you probably know, Mr. Wolfsinger is on vacation right now, and Ms. McCloud is with him somewhere in Arizona." What was she doing? She couldn't trust her own mouth anymore. Did she want that EF board seat or not?

"Yes," Thorn said. He clasped his hands behind his back and looked up at the moon. "I was aware of their trip to Arizona, but they've been difficult to reach. I hoped you had better information."

Yvette gritted her teeth; she wasn't going to blow this one now. "Don't worry, Senator. I can track them down and give you their location tomorrow."

Thorn smiled at her. "You seem like the sort of person who should be involved in our Elysian Fields operation. If you help me, I'll help you. I can be very generous with my friends."

"I understand, Senator."

"Well, I hope you also understand that this meeting never took place. We've never met. I'll be free to speak with you again after the election, but you shouldn't expect anything before that, and Mr. Gardner will remain your contact for now."

She nodded. "Okay."

She was startled when Thorn took a step forward and held her chin firmly in his hand. His cold eyes bored into hers. "I don't like to be disappointed, Ms. Fermi. And it would be such a shame if something was to happen to that pretty face of yours. Of course, if you ever lie to me, or tell anyone about our little arrangement, you'll spend the rest of eternity as part of a ride in our theme park across the street. Do I make myself clear?"

Yvette licked her lips. "Yes, sir. Very clear."

DAG Nygaard wasn't happy. Reclining in his seat aboard the Predator helicopter, he stared at the data hovering a few inches from the ceiling by the instrument panel. He'd spent two days hunting for Wolfsinger and McCloud on the Navajo reservation, but they seemed to have disappeared. The FBI's fugitive tracking AI had come up with nothing. The AI at the NSA had reported no useful signal intercepts among all the communications traffic in the datasphere. The parents had been uncooperative in providing information about their son or his whereabouts, and he couldn't take them somewhere to pry the information from their biochip memories because they were backwoods hicks who didn't have any implants. He'd heard about low-tech places like this reservation, but he was appalled to actually see the impoverished early twentieth–century conditions in which these people lived. Sure, the Elysian Fields biochips were relatively new, but most people wore them now, and they were handy tools when he needed access to some-one's memories. With all the vast resources of the federal government at his disposal, he was disgusted that he'd have to resort to a low-tech solution that *might* help him locate the two fugitives. He spoke a code into the net link console.

"Space Sciences. How may I direct your call?" asked a crisp male voice. It surprised Dag that NASA still used human receptionists, but that might work better for his purposes.

"Tau Wolfsinger, please."

"I'm sorry, he's out of the office right now. Can I take a message for relay?"

"Just tell him a friend called to say his parents are in danger." With that, Dag cut the link. The receptionist would see a satlink source ID from northern Arizona on the traceback, but the rest of his location information would be masked. If Wolfsinger checked his messages, he'd have enough information to worry him, then he'd try to track down his parents without success. He'd have to physically come back to see what had happened, or so Dag hoped. He checked the time; Ross was due back soon with Wolfsinger's mother and some of the spicy Big Chief Paco's Indian Tacos that Dag had developed a liking for during his stay in the area.

Dag closed his eyes while Inge spoke in his head. "I remember when the two of us used to go away together. You were so romantic."

"I'm sorry, Inge, I can't think about that right now. I have problems."

"You never have time for me anymore."

Dag sighed. If Inge was on a biochip, he could limit their interactions to Elysian Fields, but he couldn't shut her off when she lived in his head. "That's not true, Inge. You're in my head all the time. What more could you want?"

"We used to communicate more. I'm starting to think you don't love me. You just thought about shutting me off."

"I didn't mean that. It's hard to work when you're talking to me all the time."

She paused. "You should have thought of that before you killed me, Dag."

Dag ground his teeth. "I didn't kill you, my love. You had an accident."

Dag tried to block it, but the memory came swelling into his head, forcing all other thoughts out of his mind. He and Inge were ice skating on a frozen lake in Norway, not far from where they worked. Dag teased her about her skating ability, and Inge let go of his hand so she could show off, spinning around in place on one skate about ten feet away from him, faster and faster, until the ice broke beneath her and she screamed. She plunged through the hole into the freezing current, bumping her head on the ice. Dag lunged forward onto his stomach, cracking the ice beneath him, reaching for the hole and grabbing at her hair as she was swept underneath, but his wet hand came away with only a few strands, and he saw her horrified face, eyes wide, hair streaming behind her, bubbles coming from her mouth in a silent scream, passing just inches beneath him, her fists pounding ineffectually against the cold surface of her watery tomb. Then he thought he heard her screams breaking through the barrier, but it was his own screams splitting the air. Dag pounded against the solid surface with his fists, then stood up and moved along with her, jumping on the ice and kicking at it with his skate blades to try to punch through, all the while watching her struggle less and less as the water stole her warmth and breath.

Hours later, the police found Dag sitting in a snowbank by the river, mumbling to himself, unable to hear them. Dag's father retrieved him from the hospital so he could attend Inge's funeral, but he still couldn't communicate with anyone. After his frostbite and his other minor wounds healed, he spent a year at a psychiatric institution in the countryside before they released him in a "stable" mental condition. He'd had sense enough not to tell the doctors about Inge speaking to him in his head, a disconcerting voice that haunted him at random moments. She blamed him for not breaking through the ice to help her. He knew she was dead, and he knew something was wrong with his mind, but he could function and make his way through life like a normal person, except when Inge badgered him into acts of violence, after which she would shut up for a while.

"I'm sorry, my love. I'll try to do better," Dag said, opening his eyes when he heard a beep from the overhead panel.

"Yes, you will," Inge said.

The incoming message was his own automated infoblip reminder to do his paperwork. If he didn't take care of it twice a week, no matter where he was, he'd be buried in administrative details when he returned to the office. Still waiting for Ross to come back, he responded to the re-

minder with his access code so he could get a jump on it.
After a few minutes of acknowledging supply requests and
redirecting strike teams, he ran across the daily summaries
from Stamp and Murdoch, the two clowns watching Yvette
Fermi. He thought they were wasting their time on this
surveillance, but the special order had been relayed from
Senator Thorn's office, so he couldn't ignore the request.
A routine AI analysis identified Fermi's two visitors on
different days, an employee of Elysian Fields corporate
and a certain Tau Edison Wolfsinger. Dag checked the information twice, listened to the recording of their conversation the previous evening, and sent the code that would
put Stamp and Murdoch on high alert for another Wolfsinger sighting.

Dag had to get back to San Francisco. If he moved fast
enough, he believed he could catch his targets in the city.
If they returned to this place, Dag would know, and he'd
catch them before they left the reservation a second time.
He punched the Predator's ignition to prewarm the turbines, flung the door open, and hopped out onto the sand.
The day was heating up fast, and he had one piece of business to complete before he left, with or without Ross. Then
he heard tires on gravel and turned to see a Park Service
jeep pulling to a stop behind the Predator.

"Where is she?" Dag asked. The idiot was supposed to
have brought Bronwyn Wright back with him.

Ross stepped out of the vehicle and shrugged. "She disappeared. Nobody at Gemstone has seen her since yesterday morning."

Dag clenched his fists, then turned and kicked out one
of the jeep's headlights with his white boot. That made him
feel better, so he only growled at Ross rather than shooting
him. "You have the tacos?"

"Right here," Ross said, holding up a bag. "What do
you want me to do with the jeep?"

"Screw it," Dag said. If Ross had shown up without the
tacos, Dag would have killed him on the spot. "Pick up the
liquid nitrogen tank and get in the helo."

Dag shook his head as he stomped away toward the

Wolfsinger house. What had he done to deserve this run of bad luck? Ross jogged ahead of him, then rolled an empty five-foot-tall canister back toward the Predator, while Dag glared at the doctor's home. The building looked like it belonged in middle-class suburbia. In a weird mixture of the old and the not so old, there were traditional Navajo structures around the main house, such as the domed earth hogan used for ceremonies, a brush arbor for summer shelter, and a small sweat hogan. Like most Navajos, their closest neighbors were miles away, so it had been easy to land the Predator without being seen.

The brush arbor in the front yard was composed of four heavy wood support posts sunk in concrete that supported a roof of brush. Tied securely to one of these posts with several loops of rope was Dr. Kee Joseph Wolfsinger. The doctor had not been cooperative. Despite the heat, his entire body was covered with a thick white frost. His skin was black and hard and his clothes were stiff with ice. His arms were missing where Dag had used an axe to break off pieces during the last part of his interrogation. A thorough soaking in the supercold liquid nitrogen had solidly frozen the rest of the good doctor at sunrise, when Dag climbed back into the Predator for a quick breakfast.

Dag was pleased with his handiwork; it demonstrated creativity and style. Ross had acquired the liquid nitrogen canister from the same hospital where Dr. Wolfsinger had worked, flashing one of his federal agency badges and overpaying to get what Dag wanted. Someone would eventually find the body and work out how the liquid nitrogen had been used, but by that time it wouldn't matter, and the investigation would go no farther. The main thing was that the doctor's son would find his father's pieces waiting for him when he arrived, if he ever came back.

To complete the job, Dag picked up the axe he'd used earlier and took a few whacks at the doctor's torso, shattering chunks out of it that scattered on the sand. Each chunk broke off with sharp edges, like shards of ice. While it would look messy later when the pieces thawed, there were no liquids at the moment to form distracting pools. The doctor looked like a modern art sculpture by the time Dag was finished. The head was held in place on the post by a separate loop of rope, and Dag left it there as the finishing touch on the composition.

Now he could get out of this godforsaken hellhole and return to the city. He had a hot lead, and the hunt was on.

TAU'S first reaction to the mysterious message regarding his parents had been disbelief, but calls to Gemstone, the hospital where his father worked, the college where his mother taught classes, and other local spots they frequented, turned up the ominous fact that they had both disappeared. They could have suddenly left the reservation for one of their infrequent trips, but everyone he had called would have known if that were the case. Then panic set in. What if the people chasing him and Kate had located his parents? He thought of calling the Navajo Tribal Police, but if his hunters were government agents as he suspected, they'd probably be in on the deception or completely in the dark about the whole thing. His only choice was to go there and find them. If they'd seen the feds coming, they might have been able to hide out in the desert canyons, where so many federal manhunts had failed over the years. They might be dead, but he didn't want to think about that. His hands shook and his stomach felt hollow. There was no one he could call for help, no one he could trust except Kate, and she was too far away. He had to go now.

TWO hours later, Tau drove up the long dirt road to his parents' house in a rented hovercar. The late morning sun was already baking the landscape. He tried to remain calm, reasoning that his parents might have gone off on a short local camping trip without needing to tell anyone, or their cars didn't work and their net link was out, or any number of other possibilities. But he felt an ominous foreboding, as if he knew the truth already.

When he parked in front of the house, and the cushion of air subsided beneath the car in a small cloud of dust, it took a moment before his brain could make sense of what he saw. Two startled vultures looked up, then jumped into the air, annoyed at the interruption. Their broad shadows passed over the hood of Tau's rented car. A wide, dark stain covered much of the sand beneath the brush arbor, and lumps of colored cloth were scattered around as if a big dog had angrily attacked their laundry and dragged the remains outside. An axe was stuck halfway up one of the brush arbor posts among a few loops of rope.

Then he saw the head. His father's head. Tied to the post.

Tau was numb for a moment, unable to do anything but sit in the car and stare. The disembodied head looked so incongruous on the post that it didn't look real, and for an instant he hoped it was just a gruesome trick to scare him. The silence of his desolate surroundings pressed in with the crushing weight of the grave. Heat rose from the sand in waves, rippling his vision, creating mirages of dancing gods in the distance beneath the blue mountain slopes. A sheep skull watched him from an ancient fencepost, rotting in the sun. He wondered if the angry ghosts of sheep haunted the empty corral behind the house, dancing now that they'd had their revenge.

When he opened the door and put one foot on the sand, the heat slapped him in the face, then a delicate scent of death made him gag. He felt surprise that the smell wasn't stronger, but it was strong enough to reinforce the reality of the moment, and it blew away any thought that this might be some madman's sick idea of a joke. He gasped, then took a bandanna out of his back pocket and tied it over his mouth and nose.

As a doctor, his father was well acquainted with death, and he seemed to have no fear of it. He remembered one of his father's favorite quotes, from the Shawnee chief, Tecumseh: "When it comes time to die, be not like those whose hearts are filled with the fear of death, so when their time comes they weep and pray for a little more time to live their lives over again in a different way. Sing your death song, and die like a hero going home." His father would have been pleased that he died outside, so that his sacred wind could leave his body without being trapped by ceilings and walls. The malevolent spirit would be angry and confused, willing to do harm to anyone because of its unhappiness. They would also have to take care not to speak the name of Kee Joseph Wolfsinger out loud, as it would summon the *chindi* and bring danger.

There would be no embalming or autopsies to dishonor the body. To protect the family, a neighbor would have to remove the corpse and hide it in a secure place in the desert where it would not be disturbed, covered by rocks, without giving Tau or Bronwyn the body's location. These were the practicalities of death that Tau's father had taught him, but he didn't feel so practical right now.

He felt shaky as he slogged toward the brush arbor through thick, overheated air that slowed his progress as if it were molasses. The dark shadows of the vultures passed over him again, and the original two had been joined by two more, patiently waiting their turn when Tau was done.

A shaft of sunlight slanted diagonally across his father's noble face. Some of his long black hair was matted between his head and the wood post, or caught under the rope wrapped around his forehead, but the rest of it dangled freely beneath his head, below the sharp line where his neck ended in empty air. His eyes were closed, and his expression looked peaceful, as if he were just resting a bit under the brush arbor before he went out to work in the sun. But he looked like he'd had too much of the sun: his skin was black and chapped. Studying this proud head, Tau remembered how it had looked in life, and he knew that this was no longer the man who had raised him, for that man lived on in his heart.

Kee Joseph Wolfsinger was a man of quiet tastes and simple accomplishments, educated in medicine and in life, a healer of mind and body who gave generously of

himself to his family and his community. He'd helped to
combine the white man's medicine with traditional
Navajo healing practices so that the *Dineh* could be
treated according to custom, saving many who would
rather have died than submit to impersonal healing practices that denied their spirituality. As a gentle and supportive father, he had sacrificed much, without complaint,
to raise a studious son with academic interests that their
relatives found strange. Married to a white woman, to
whom he had devoted his life for thirty-five years, he'd
also protected his son as much as possible from the pain
of being an outsider, never completely accepted by his
peers in the tribe or in the white world. On the Navajo
reservation, where family is everything, he taught his son
to respect community and tradition, and how to live in
harmony and beauty with the land. At the same time, his
father had shown him how to survive in the modern world,
how to work hard, live with people who had different
views, and share any reward from his efforts with the
people who had helped raise him because it was the right
thing to do. His sense of humor had filled their house with
joy, and his love had given Tau the strength he needed to
become a respectable man who would pass these qualities
on to his own children, repeating the cycle and gaining a
form of immortality that would live through generations.
Father and son shared the same blood, and the same spirit
that would not die.

Tau reached out to touch his father's face one last time.
It was cold and hard. "I love you, Dad."

AFTER a long walk in the hot sun to collect his thoughts,
Tau summoned the courage to enter the house, but his
mother was not inside. Nothing appeared to be missing,
but he wouldn't have been able to tell if the house had
been searched because of the usual disarray; his parents
had never liked to spend a lot of time cleaning and organ-
izing.

Spotting a net link console under a stack of old books in
his father's office, he punched in his mother's Gemstone

code. It was answered by Alice Tsossie, his mother's assistant, who looked startled. "Tau?"

"Has anyone seen my mother?"

Alice looked over her shoulder, then lowered her voice. "No one has *seen* her, but I got a strange message about an hour ago. I think it's for you."

Tau's eyes widened. "She's okay? What did it say?"

Alice shrugged. *"Ya'at'eeh, shiyaazh. Jo dineh Ts'osi baghandi hataal yaa naakai. T'oo shidoonal nisin. Adaadaa' dineh lei' shaa niya. Bilagaana. Washindoondee' daats'I nihaa niya. Hagoonee'."*

Navajo. An eavesdropper would have to translate the message, then interpret the meaning. Tau realized he was holding his breath. He let it out slowly, translating in his head: "Hello, my son. There is a sing at Slim Man's place. I just want to go there. Yesterday, a certain man came to see me. A white man. Maybe he came from Washington. Good-bye."

His mother knew enough not to send a literal message that might be read by the wrong people. Slim Man was one of his uncle's nicknames. He lived in a remote canyon near Gemstone where Bronwyn could hide safely, and that meant she was okay. Tau knew he couldn't go there without the risk of drawing attention from the enemy, and his traditional uncle lived in a primitive hogan without any communications gear. Bronwyn's message also said that a white man from Washington had come looking for her, and the fact that she was telling him about it probably meant that she escaped while Alice or one of her students intercepted him. "Alice, did you see her visitor?"

Alice nodded. "FBI or something, dressed all in white. Yellow hair. Very tall, maybe seven feet, like that basketball player out around Many Farms. Good looking, and talked funny. He had a federal badge, but I didn't see it myself. Landed in a helicopter. He looked suspicious, so the boss left through one of the tunnels. His partner came back here today, but we told him we hadn't seen her for a while."

"You did good, Alice. Thank you. If someone sees Slim Man in town, tell him I got the message and I'm okay."

"Everyone's okay," she repeated, writing a note.

Tau shook his head. "No, not everyone. My father is dead."

Alice gasped. "How?"

"I can't talk about it right now," Tau said. He glanced out the window to distract himself. "Thank you for your help, Alice. That message was a big relief. And please send my uncle to the house to take care of my father."

Tau cut the connection as Alice started to cry.

Tau swallowed hard and blinked. His mother was okay, and he knew he had to leave before his hunters returned. It surprised him that this was not a trap so they could kill him here without any witnesses. And that was their mistake.

He would follow the path of the warrior once more. The bullet train would return him to San Francisco under a false name, then he would seek justice on the people who had killed his father.

32

THE team had established a base camp in the bottom of a deep canyon on Yamantau Mountain. Kate had been allocated a cot in an inflatable tent where she managed to get a reasonably good night's sleep, thankfully Thoth-free, but the morning light brought many questions when she stepped out to study the rocky terrain. There were no trees under the cold gray sky for as far as she could see, and the steep cliffs around this bowl in the canyon rose well over a thousand feet above their heads. A few hundred yards away, the glimmering red lines of a laser grid marked the reference quadrants of the dig as if the team was performing a regular archaeological survey. Within the grid, chunks of machinery and twisted metal rose from the soil like high-tech tombstones.

"Spooky, isn't it?"

Kate turned to see Pat standing behind her drinking from a stim bulb. "What is it?"

Pat smiled. "That's what you're supposed to tell us. We've identified some fragments of conduit, blast doors, reinforced concrete walls, and so on, but there are some strange objects down there."

"What was this place? The city of Mezhgorye?" She looked in the direction of the ruined tombstones again.

Pat looked around, as if he were afraid they might be overheard, then moved closer. "I've been doing some digging of my own, but you can't mention any of this to the professor."

Kate nodded, intrigued by his conspiratorial air.

"This isn't Mezhgorye, and it isn't Chelyabinsk-70, the old nuclear weapons lab. Have you ever heard of Dead Hand, or Dead Man's Hand?"

"Sounds like an old Western."

"Dead Hand was Russia's nuclear retaliatory command and control system for strategic missiles. This was an underground military complex associated with Dead Hand, and it covered an area about the size of metropolitan Washington, D.C."

Kate's eyes widened. "You're kidding. This was some old missile facility that blew up?"

"No," Pat said, "this was Final Harvest, a command center, where a city full of military personnel could survive a serious nuclear war."

"Wow. Okay, and why am I here?"

"As far as we can tell, this underground base has been deserted for years, and it seems that very few Russian officials even knew of its existence. We've never been able to detect radiation or other traces of explosives in this area, and certainly nothing that could have caused a blast large enough to make a big chunk of the mountain disappear. What we *have* found is what appears to be alien technology, with Gwrinydd markings on it, and it killed three of our people."

Kate took a step back. "Killed? How?"

"We don't know." Pat shrugged. "Bad luck, I guess."

Kate didn't know what to say. Shocked, she kept glancing in the direction of the laser grid with a feeling of dread. Her head started to spin, and she sat down abruptly on the rocky soil.

Pat crouched beside her with a look of concern. "You okay?"

"I'll be fine," Kate said, putting her face in her hands, "but I need my morning coffee before I can solve all your problems."

33

DAG propped his dusty white boot on the edge of the gray metal desk, leaning back in his chair to study the complicated snowflake patterns on the map projection hovering a few inches from the wall. The snowflakes were the current AI projections of where Wolfsinger might travel from origin points at Lake Powell, Gemstone, San Francisco, or the home of his parents in Arizona. Each line radiating out from the source point had a thickness and color associated with the probability of Wolfsinger following that particular path, so Dag could see at a glance which way the computer thought he would go. However, the AI had to work from certain assumptions, based on prior fugitive tracking experience. Wolfsinger didn't fit neatly into the professional or amateur fugitive categories, and that made accurate projections difficult. Wolfsinger was clever about his movements, but he didn't use the standard decoy and camouflage tactics of a professional, and he wasn't really a fugitive in the traditional sense. When Dag was in Arizona, Wolfsinger was in San Francisco; when Dag traveled back to San Francisco, Wolfsinger jumped back to Arizona too quickly, staying one step ahead of him all the time. Dag now felt a grudging admiration for the man.

Ross stepped into the office and shrugged. "Sorry, boss. The NSA couldn't translate the intercept from the Wolfsinger home in Arizona. They think it's Navajo, but they don't have an AI to translate that language."

Dag rolled his eyes. "Then get a *human* to translate it!"

"Who?"

"Try one of the Navajo tribal cops! Can't you do anything without a computer?"

"Hey, good idea," Ross said.

"I don't want to have to go to that stinking desert again just to interview this Alice Tsossie woman at Gemstone, so get on it. Did the NRO get us the imagery of the Arizona house?"

"Wolfsinger wasn't there long enough. The spysat was in a different part of its polar orbit. They couldn't ID him or his vehicle."

Dag stood and banged his fist on the table. "He's toying with us! We set out bait for him, and he manages to lure us somewhere else!"

Ross took two steps back toward the office door. "He's a smart guy, all right."

Dag looked at the map again and took a deep breath, then let it out slowly. "Okay, let's hope someone spots him in San Francisco. I'm going to take a shower and go to my yoga class."

STARING at the bullet train's blinking route map on the opposite wall of his private compartment, Tau tried to work out a strategy for finding his father's killer, but he didn't know where to start. He still found it hard to concentrate; his brain kept interrupting with boyhood memories of his father teaching him how to fish.

Full of excitement, the young Tau wanted to run around on the shore of the lake and drop his line in anywhere he saw small fish in the shallows, but his father patiently taught him to slow down: study the weather, the lake, and the behavior of the fish; select the right bait for the kind of fish he wanted; cast the line to the types of places where his kind of fish hung out and let it sit at the right depth; let the fish nibble at the bait before setting the hook; then work the struggling fish to tire it while steadily reeling it in. Once he'd learned the process, through his father's careful instruction, he caught fish every time they went out.

Tau blinked. His father had just taught him another lesson.

He couldn't run around randomly hoping to find clues regarding the unknown killers. He needed to study the en-

vironment and gather information about the nature of the
fish he wanted, then he could select the proper bait and go
where the fish hung out. Tau would act as the bait, but he
could think of only two people who might know more
about the environment and how to locate the killer fish:
Norman and Yvette.

He still had half an hour before the DEEPTRAN train
arrived in San Francisco. Tau reached into his pocket and
removed Norman's biochip from its impact case, then gently pushed it into the socket at the back of his neck.

"Changed your mind?" Norman asked. The voice in his
head sounded just like it had in real life. "Ready to wreak
havoc at Elysian Fields?"

"I'll help you if you can help me."

"I'm giving you nanotech fog that will make you richer
than God. What more do you want?"

Tau sighed. "My father's dead. I want to find his killers
before they find Kate or my mother."

Norman paused before responding in a gentler tone.
"Sorry, pal. That's rough. But I don't know how I can help
you. I can sniff for info on the net and crap like that, but
that won't help you much."

"Norman, I think the killers were feds. They tried to
kidnap Kate and kill me, and they were following our trail
when they killed my father. My mom's in hiding."

"Feds. You sure you want to mess with this?"

"Yes."

"You need someone who knows the spooky stuff. Only
one I know is Snapdragon. I can get him a message
through the net if you want to meet with him."

Tau rolled his eyes. "No Veggie is going to help me.
They were calling me the 'Silicon Satan' two years ago
when they heard about my nanotech VR work. Can't you
think of someone else?"

"Look, pal, I'm dead, you know? It limits my resources.
Now, if you want to meet babes or feelie producers, I've
got the contacts, but Snappy's the only fed-connected guy
I know. Okay?"

Tau knew he could still talk to Yvette, but she couldn't

do much except give him an idea of where to look in Washington. "Yeah, okay. If Snapdragon might help me, let's try."

"And you'll help me with Elysian Fields, or no deal. Okay?"

Tau gritted his teeth and nodded as if Norman could see him. "Fine."

Norman hesitated. "Tau? Your father didn't have a biochip implant, did he?"

"He didn't need one, Norman." Tau swallowed. "He'll always be with me."

TAU stood in another concrete monument to past wars, but this one was on the north side of the Golden Gate, high on the rugged coastline of the Marin headlands with an excellent view of the bridge and the city beyond it. Battery Wallace looked like another tomb. He'd arrived fifteen minutes early for the arranged meeting with Snapdragon, climbing the windy embankment to hide in the bushes on top of the fortification in case the Veggie leader brought any of his friends. Despite what Norman thought, it could have been a trap.

But Snapdragon had shown up alone. When he stepped out of the dark tunnel onto the brightly sunlit blast apron, wearing a tight black shirt and pants made of a shiny synthetic material, he unfurled the huge solar collector umbrella on his back and sat patiently under its shade to gather energy while waiting for Tau's arrival. Tau thought he looked bigger and tougher than when he'd last seen him at the protest outside the NASA gates.

While Tau introduced himself, Snapdragon stood and listened with a wry smile, stroking his neatly trimmed blond beard. As Tau explained about Norman, his father's murder, and the previous attack at Lake Powell, Snapdragon ran one of his hands through his fluffy mane of hair, and his expression changed to one of concern.

"You're in big trouble," Snapdragon said when Tau paused.

"You know something?"

Snapdragon turned to look out at the waves pounding the rough rocks of the coastline far below. The strong breeze blowing through his hair made it look like a living thing. "I could be wrong, but with your background, the kidnapping attempt, and the style of the hit on your father, it sounds like you've done something to piss off the big guys."

"What big guys?" Tau asked. Was he talking about Red Star and the events on Mars?

"Davos."

"What's that?"

Snapdragon glanced at him sideways, then looked out to sea again. A supertanker was rounding the Point Bonita Lighthouse on its approach to the bay. "The Davos Group is God. They're the inner circle of international power. They operate through public fronts like the American CFR, the Council on Foreign Relations. Every major politician belongs to the CFR, as well as the executives from the major media conglomerates, the energy companies, and the directors of the thirteen Federal Reserve banks. While the CFR receives acclaim for its accurate forecasts of emerging international trends, the public doesn't realize that the CFR plays a major role in *creating* those trends. Davos establishes strategic policies, then they're carried out by the CFR and its sister organizations in the rest of the global village. When governments and monarchs need money, Davos lends a hand, directing the financial dynasties of Europe and America to make money available at high interest rates so that Davos can establish political leverage over the borrowers."

Tau stared at him. "Are you nuts?"

Snapdragon smiled and shook his head. "I wish I was."

"You're saying the secret masters of the world are out to get me?"

"More or less. The DOE is out to get you."

"The Department of Energy? You expect me to believe this?"

"Special Ops Group. Originally formed out of the Intelligence Division created for the Manhattan Project. The

DOE is just a cover for them now. But they were sent by someone high up in Washington, and they work for Davos."

Tau rubbed his forehead. "You're a loon. How the hell do you know all this?"

"I worked for the DOE. For Davos. And I know the people who killed your father."

Norman was still plugged in, although he'd been silent up until now. "Believe him, Tau. He's telling you the truth."

"Well, why would they wait until now? Why didn't they kill me as soon as I got back from Mars? I assume that's why they're after me."

"Too obvious," Snapdragon said. "You were too high profile. Better to wait and pop you when the reason would be less obvious. Or maybe they had something else in mind for you, and their plans changed. Who knows?"

Tau started to question his own sanity, but after meeting an alien race and wandering around in their ruins on Mars, there wasn't much that surprised him anymore. A crazy Russian general had tried to take over Mars as a base for using recently discovered alien technology to dominate Earth, so why shouldn't he believe that a group of international power brokers wanted him dead for interfering with their operations? After all, it would explain a few things.

"How can I stop them?"

Snapdragon laughed. "You can't."

"So I should just let them kill me and everyone I love?"

"Everyone has to go sometime."

"Thanks. That's reassuring."

"But I meant you can't stop Davos. It'd be like stopping the wind from blowing, or stopping the world from turning. It's too big. You can't get a handle on it. But you might be able to find out who sent the DOE strike team after you."

Or he could just give up and shoot himself right now. "I wouldn't even know where to start."

"If you can reach Senator Aaron Thorn, start with him. He's busy campaigning to be president, but maybe you can fake your way in. Say you're a potential campaign contributor. He's a little shady, but he's a good guy. The director of Special Ops used to get his orders from Thorn, but I don't know if that's still true. Ask for his help. Tell him Warlord sent you."

Tau knew that Aaron Thorn was also the son of Dr. Max Thorn, his late mentor at NASA. As far as Tau was concerned, he wasn't much of a senator, and even less of a son. "Who's Warlord?"

"Me." Snapdragon smiled. "DOE code name."

Tau nodded, then remembered that Thorn was also on the Mars and NASA funding committees. "Yvette Fermi. She's the director at NASA-Ames, and she'll help me reach Thorn. Assuming the bad guys don't kill me first."

"I'm surprised you're still alive," Snapdragon said.

"Me, too."

Tau winced as Norman whistled inside his head. "Before you guys say your tearful good-byes, I've got problems of my own. Tell him to ask my brother something. I want to get my break-in hardware that I left at Sutro Tower when I got toasted. We'll need it for the EF crack."

Tau relayed the information, and Snapdragon said he'd ask BD about it. Then he thanked the Veggie leader for his help.

"I'm doing it for Norman," Snapdragon said. "Elysian Fields has to go. But I may need a favor from you, too."

"Sure. What do you want?" Tau hoped Snapdragon wouldn't ask him to stop working on nanotech projects, or to speak out against scientific progress, or something stupid like that.

Snapdragon smiled at Tau as the solar collector on his back spiraled closed. "I'll let you know."

E-BERT looked like a Latino Santa Claus, chubby and jolly in his red tuxedo with white trim, sporting a long black mustache in place of a long white beard. When Ariel had first seen e-Bert's mustache, which hung down past his chin, she thought it was fake. When he smiled, you could barely see his bright white teeth through the black comb that covered his mouth. He'd been the successful owner of the O'Farrell Brothers virtual feelie club for fifteen years, and his stage acts were sophisticated enough to draw local politicians, foreign dignitaries, tourists, and celebrities of all kinds to his daily shows. Ariel occasionally danced on one of the stages for tips, but she normally worked in a private 360 booth where the club's cheaper customers could watch her through the curved glass. She wore a transparent skintight loaded with force feedback sensors that replicated her body in the club's virtual environment. The Feelie VR chip gave life to her digital body, crunched data for the skintights, and made the customer's fantasy environment seem real.

Although she lived on the street with Brother Digital, Ariel spent little on food, spending part of her meager earnings on glitter dust and putting part of it in a long-term savings account with e-Bert. She knew from past experience that she could trust him with the money. Her involvement in the God Box had lessened her need for glitter stimulation, just as BD had said it would, so her money was building up faster than it had before, and she hoped to rent an apt with one of the other dancers soon. BD had offered her a bunk in the church barracks with the rest of the Pingers, but she didn't like or trust any of them enough to sleep in their presence, at least not without a locked door to protect her. She preferred to sleep in her street hut.

Because she was the high priestess of the church, BD had also offered her a percentage of any cash donations they received, but she didn't feel right about accepting that kind of money. BD lured people into his high-tech fraud church to suck them dry, and Ariel didn't feel she should profit from any involvement in such an enterprise.

In any event, she planned to continue work at the club a little while longer, not wanting to make any lifestyle changes while spying on BD.

Hearing the three beeps that meant it was time for her break, Ariel looked out into the dimly lighted sea of male and female faces to make sure she could safely step out of the booth. In the rare event that anyone tried to attack her, one of the enormous club bouncers would forcibly remove the offending patron, but all the performers knew enough to look out for themselves. A fast-moving crazy could reach her long before help arrived. No drinking was allowed, but glitter and stims were used all the time. Other customers seemed to go nuts just from swimming in their own hormones.

Ariel unlocked the booth door and stepped out, immediately aware of the sweaty smell that always lingered in the fresh circulating air. Once her eyes adjusted from the brightness of the booth to the dim lighting in the club, she saw two men in suits and sunglasses coming toward her. She knew the men, and she knew the sunglasses allowed them to see clearly in almost any kind of lighting. They were from the FBI.

Special Agent Cole, the short, thin, and bald one, spoke first. "Ms. Colombari. Nice to *see* you."

As if she hadn't heard *that* line before.

Special Agent Gordon, the tall one with buzzed black hair, grinned at her. "Let's talk."

"Time is money," she said, leading them to an overstuffed public booth. The smoked mirror on the wall behind the booth held a variety of stim leads, body jacks, VR goggles, and other implements, all of which were available for rent at the listed number of credits. Gordon placed his credit chip against the table scanner to pay for table time.

"Yes, time is money, Ms. Colombari. And we've got good news for you there," Cole said, sliding into the booth beside her.

Ariel looked at him directly. "Oh?"

"We've located your deceased husband's funds," Cole said. "And our superiors say you can have them back if you prove to be helpful in this investigation. Did you locate the church financial records?"

Ariel shook her head. "No, but I do have evidence for building your case against BD. I have memory cubes of Pinger experiences with the fake Entity controlled by BD."

"Recordings from the God Box?" Gordon asked.

"Straight from their brains to yours," Ariel said. "They're in my dressing room."

"That's a good start," Cole said, leaning back so he could casually look her over while he sat there. "But we need the financial records. No records, no payoff."

"Oh, come on," she said. "I've already taken the risk of breaking into BD's office once. Give me something."

"Did you learn anything else while you were in there?"

Ariel looked around, then leaned toward Cole with a conspiratorial air. "I don't know when or how, but BD is going to broadcast a viral ad. You could arrest him for that, right?"

Cole looked at Gordon. "Maybe. If we can trace it back to him. But we could only hold him for a day or two."

"Long enough for me to do a thorough search," Ariel said with a smile. Her face was only a few inches away from Cole's right ear so that he could feel her warm breath. "Now, give me something in trade."

Cole licked his lips. "We know a little more about Carlo."

She sat back as if she'd been struck by lightning. "What? Do you know who killed him?"

Cole shrugged with an apologetic expression. "Not for certain, but we think we know why he was killed. He saw something he shouldn't have seen. It was a fluke, a chance event, but it happened. He might not even remember it, but one look was enough to get him killed."

"One look at what? I have to know!" She was half out of her chair. When one of the bouncers started toward them, she motioned him away and sat down again, glaring at them.

"It was a person," Cole said. "A very important person. Your husband was in the wrong place at the wrong time. And so was Phil Sanchez, who also disappeared."

"Phil? They killed Phil, too?" The red lights on top of Ariel's booth flashed, but Ariel had been seeing red for a while. She stood up. "Here's a deal for you. You find my husband's killer, and I help with your little investigation. Otherwise, forget it. I have to go back to work now, and I suggest you do the same."

She shoved Cole out of the way and stomped back to her booth. She wanted her money, she wanted out of this club, and she wanted her husband.

She also wanted someone's head for Carlo's murder.

ERIC Stamp looked over at Frank Murdoch and smiled. His platform on the side of the building swayed in strong gusts of wind, but he couldn't stop grinning as he punched in the alert code for Dag Nygaard. "This one's going to put us back in action, Frank."

"Think the geek's gonna bag the babe this time?" Murdoch asked. He stared through the window into Yvette's home office where she entertained Tau Wolfsinger.

"Who cares? This is the guy Nygaard wants. As long as he hangs around for a few minutes, we get the credit for spotting him, and the boss will let us work on the ground again. That's all I care about."

"I don't know," Frank said. "I kind of like watching her."

Stamp rolled his eyes

ON the dark roof of the federal building at the Marin Civic Center, Dag jumped into the waiting Predator with Ross and switched on the ignition to warm up the turbines. They would be at the target coordinates in less than five minutes. Dressed in his best flat black night raid clothing, even though he didn't plan on getting out of the helo, he was ready to chase Wolfsinger on the ground if that became necessary.

Dag spoke to Stamp in his throat mike while he strapped into his crash harness. "Hawkeye, go to Tac Three and give me visual on the target. Straight feed to the helo off the comsat." He gestured at Ross, who adjusted the overhead lens to project the scaled-down holo image on the inside of the front cockpit window.

As Dag grabbed the control stick and lifted off, they saw Tau Wolfsinger talking to Yvette Fermi in her apt. Dag smiled. "Gotcha."

Ross held on tight as Dag quickly rotated the Predator and punched in the afterburner.

TAU sat on the deep couch in Yvette's home office, and he felt her body heat radiating through the thin fabric of his shirt. Prepared for a formal dinner engagement, she wore a long purple gown with a deeply cut V-neck that handsomely displayed the enormous diamond pendant dangling from her neck over the dark abyss of her cleavage.

"Tau," she said, "after the way you treated me last time, I should just say no. But I'm your friend, and I'm sorry for your loss. I'll help you any way I can."

"Thank you, Yvette. I appreciate it." She could be very understanding at times.

"I'll make the call right now." She rose from the couch and punched a code into the console on her desk, then switched on her audio privacy screen to mask her conversation.

Tau turned his attention to the city lights glittering far below. The Bay Bridge, with its long, arched ropes of light, sparkled in the clear air, making diamond patterns on the rippling water. The tall buildings created a maze of light, outlining the asphalt canyons of the streets, and from this height he felt as if he could look down and solve the secret of the maze. Then a dark object caught his attention outside the window at the far left end of the room. He squinted, trying to discern the details of the silhouette, and finally realized it was a man reclining on a platform that gently swayed in the wind. He'd never seen one of the baggies perched so high on a skyscraper before, and he thought it looked dangerous.

Yvette turned and smiled at Tau, switching off the privacy screen. "Can you get to Washington, D.C., for a meeting with Senator Thorn tomorrow afternoon?"

Tau was startled by her quick results. "Of course."

She nodded, spoke a few more words into the net link,

and disconnected. Then she smiled again, lighting up the room. "It's all set."

THE Predator hovered on station about half a mile from Yvette's apt at an altitude of seventeen hundred feet. Dag had no interest in the clear view of the city lights below as he turned flight control over to the autopilot AI and readied the weapon systems. Their laser anchors were set on four different buildings, so the helo would not drift more than an inch as long as they had fuel to stay in the air. On the projection inside the cockpit window, Yvette Fermi leaned against her desk talking to Wolfsinger. She had just made a phone call, but the Hawkeye team's audio pickups had not penetrated the audio mask she used in Wolfsinger's presence.

"You want me to do anything?" Ross asked.

Dag's fingers flew over the buttons on the weapons panel. "Talk to Hawkeye and keep him busy. I don't want them to spook the target."

"Are you going to hit Wolfsinger when he comes out of the building?"

Dag snorted. "Hell, no. This guy's too clever. I'm going to put a smartneedle in his eye right there on that couch."

Ross frowned. "How are you going to get a microwarhead through that heavy glass with any accuracy?"

"Firedrill," Dag said, adjusting his tactical display so that the crosshairs lined up on Tau's nose. Now that the target was selected, the weapon system would stay locked on his face as long as he remained in view. If he passed behind a wall, the infrared or microwaves would pick him up, but targeting wouldn't be as accurate.

"Firedrill?"

"It's like throwing a piece of the sun against the glass. Burns a tunnel through almost anything real quick, then we launch the smartneedle to follow it through. And then he's history."

"THEY'RE on station," Stamp said, glancing at Murdoch.

Not wanting to alert the targets in the apt, Murdoch casually looked over his shoulder at the Predator hovering in the distance while Stamp finished speaking to them. "How come Nygaard is sitting out there?"

Stamp sighed. He had to explain everything to this idiot. "Why do you think? He probably doesn't want to bring that big old attack helicopter right up to the window to freak out the tenants."

Murdoch was silent for a moment. "He wouldn't nuke the guy right here, would he? I mean, he'd give us time to get out of the way, right?"

"Don't be ridiculous," Stamp said. "We're heroes. Nygaard's been looking for this geek for days. He wouldn't waste two valuable employees."

Stamp suddenly felt butterflies in his stomach, and he couldn't stop himself from turning around to look at the Predator hanging out there like some deadly shark of the sky eyeing its lunch. He shook his head; Murdoch's paranoia was getting to him.

"SWITCH on the gun camera," Dag told Ross. "I want this for my scrapbook." He felt excited and oddly depressed at the same time; excited because he liked playing with exotic weapons, and depressed because the chase was over. He was impressed with the way Wolfsinger had hidden in plain sight instead of bolting for some hole where they could have found him right away. The man seemed to have a natural talent for evasion; too bad he was on the wrong side.

While Ross started recording, Dag flipped up the red safety cap on the launch button. "Firedrill on three, two—"

Dag started to press the firing button, then stopped as his headset buzzed with a high-priority incoming message. He listened for a moment, then replaced the safety cap on the firing button.

"What happened?" Ross asked.

"We're on hold. I got the recall code from God." Dag felt surprisingly happy. Wolfsinger would live a little longer so Dag could hunt him down again.

"We're letting him go? Couldn't we just say we got the recall code too late?"

Dag shut down the weapon systems and frowned at Ross. "We're not murderers, Mr. Ross. We're civilized employees of the federal government."

Ross stared at him in disbelief. "We've been chasing this guy for days! I had to drag my butt all over the desert looking for him!"

"Release the anchors, Mr. Ross. If you have a problem, you can open your door and get out right now. It would be one small step for a man, and one long fall for you."

Ross looked down at the glittering city 1,700 feet below and swallowed, then responded with a subdued voice. "Releasing the anchors, boss."

35

PAT McCarthy had been right about the survey team finding an object with Gwrinydd markings on it. After the three people who uncovered it had been killed almost immediately, the object was placed in a clear, sealed container for later study. What appeared to be a fine blue skin of organic material hung in ragged chunks over a faceted crystal surface. A light fog filled the container, and a lab analysis had finally determined that exposure to a toxic gas had killed the unfortunate discoverers. Kate had no idea as to how the object in the case had been used, and she couldn't read the Gwrinydd language, but she knew someone who could interpret for her if he would cooperate.

Before Kate's arrival, the survey team had used deep-ground-penetrating radar to locate part of the broken tunnel network hidden under the soil. Pushkin had acquired a shock wave rig for tunnel boring, and the team had used it to pound a circular access shaft 400 yards through the hill to a large chamber. The hollow space would have looked like a natural cave were it not for the steel plates visible through gaps in the rock walls. This room was where the three-person team had died when they discovered the Gwrinydd artifact.

Glowglobes had been positioned in niches around the room to hold back the darkness. Working within a laser grid, Kate made a quick study of the exotic metal deposits the team had mapped out in the chamber, and three hours of excavation work on the most unusual mound led to her discovery of what appeared to be the top of a buried metal ring, its shiny chromelike surface etched with a fine pattern. Excited by Kate's discovery during a visit to check on her progress, Pushkin stumbled on some loose rocks and hit his head on the shiny metal, knocking himself unconscious. Kate had called for help, and Pat McCarthy had arrived with a small hover lift to carry Pushkin back outside. When Pat returned without Pushkin, he stood over the deepening trench where Kate dug her way around the metal ring with a sonic pick.

"Looks like you're in charge now," Pat said. "Pushkin's down for the count, and you have more archaeological experience than anyone else here."

Kate gasped. "You don't mean he's dead?"

"He's unconscious. We've sent for a doctor. What did you find?"

Kate looked down at the finely etched patterns that gleamed in the dirt. Unlike everything else in the dig, it did not appear to be broken or even scratched. Although she tried to remain calm and objective about the find, the ring had a strikingly similar appearance to the most important artifact anyone had found on Mars. She looked up at Pat again, barely able to contain her excitement. A smile blossomed on her face.

"It's a portal," she squeaked. "A teleportation gate."

TEN minutes later, Pat made a special report to Yvette Fermi. Her startled expression pleased him.

"Does it work?" Yvette asked.

"I don't know. Kate is still digging it up."

"Get her some help. Does it look intact?"

"Not a scratch on it, as far as I can tell."

"How did she know where to look?"

"She says she was guided to it."

"By whom? Professor Ryumin?"

"I don't think so, but she didn't say."

"Find out."

"I will."

Yvette took a deep breath. "Don't tell anyone else about this. I have to figure out our next move. And for God's sake, whatever you do, don't let Kate leave the site."

36

AS the ferryman on the River Styx had warned Ariel, Elysian Fields opened their doors to the public, allowing free admission for group chat audio access to their loved ones, and discounted admission for the pricier services. Congress declared a special Day of Remembrance to commemorate the occasion. The discounted rates would apply once a week, making it possible for many to visit Happy Meadows and the other Elysian Field theme parks for the first time, and the crowds on the first day were enormous. In Colma, beefy guards dressed as ancient Egyptians drifted through the mob to maintain order outside the Pearly Gates. The guards carried whips, but they were more likely to use the stun grenades camouflaged as golden apples if crowd control became necessary.

Anticipating the crowds, Ariel had shown up before sunrise to get in line, only to discover that the crowd was already so large that she'd never be able to get in. Frustrated, she decided to cross the street and climb the hill to Emperor Norton's tomb, designed by Carlo to disguise the employee entrance to the theme park. She waited there for two hours, hoping to spot Brian, the gray-bearded performer who played one of the Charon the Ferryman parts, and was finally rewarded when he showed up dressed in his white robes. Her tearful story got her an escorted trip through the employee entrance to the group chat room, but the roaming guardian angels were so busy that she managed to sneak into one of the private AV booths that provided audio and visual contact with the deceased. Brian left her alone after receiving a kiss and a tip.

Once inside the white cubicle, she shut the door to seal

out the external chatter, and sat down in the single chair that faced a wall-size gray screen. Soothing organ music played softly while the Elysian Fields logo, a grinning skull in a top hat named Bony, bounced around cheerfully on the gray screen. Shafts of colored light streamed down from the stained glass skylights.

"Name of the departed?" asked a soft female voice from a speaker beneath the screen.

"Carlo Colombari."

After a pause, the voice said, "Access to Carlo Colombari is restricted. Pass phrase?"

"Empire of the mind."

Her stomach fluttered in anticipation. The pain in her heart never seemed to go away. She wanted to touch Carlo and spend time with him in the sim world when she was able to afford it, but at least these visits were helping her cope with her loss.

"Pass phrase not accepted. Try another pass phrase?"

Ariel stared at the speaker. Could the pass phrase have changed? Maybe she had mumbled it? "Empire of the mind," she said in a firm and clear voice.

"Pass phrase not accepted for restricted access. Try another pass phrase?"

Her heart sank, and she slumped in her seat. Then she heard a male voice from the speaker, but it wasn't Carlo. "Heya, Toots."

"Hello, Shade."

"You're here to talk to Carlo, right? And you found out they changed the pass phrase?"

She sat up straight. "Can you reach him?"

"Maybe. Did you bring the note chip for me?"

She took the chip case out of her pocket. "Where do you want it?"

"In your neck. I'm all set to burst the transmission to your neural jack."

She placed the tiny chip in her neck socket. "You can do that?"

"I can do lots of things. I'll bust Carlo out of lockup temporarily if you promise to broadcast this recording as soon as possible. The public has to know what it's like in here, and I'm the only one who will tell them the truth."

She nodded. "I promise."

The next voice she heard had Carlo's smooth Italian accent. "Ariel? Are you there?"

"Carlo? Yes, Carlo. I'm here, my love. But I can't see you."

Shade snorted. "I'm working on it, Toots. Give me a second."

Carlo's face appeared on the screen in front of her. As always, his dramatic brown eyes caught her attention immediately, burning with a fiery intelligence while looking gentle at the same time. By reflex, Ariel's hand shot forward to touch him, but all she felt was the cold glass of the high-definition screen. "Carlo."

Shade snorted again, then spoke with a mocking tone. "Thank you, Shade."

"I wish I was with you now," Ariel said, ignoring Shade.

Carlo smiled briefly. "Has it been long since we last spoke? There's no sense of time here."

"It's been three long days. Carlo. There's something I have to ask you. About your death."

"Okay. Shoot," Carlo said. The topic didn't seem to bother him.

"I spoke to some men from the FBI. They said you were . . . killed . . . because you saw something. Someone important. But they wouldn't say who or what. Do you have any idea who it might have been?"

"I don't remember how I was killed, Ariel."

"How about before that? I'd guess it was shortly before you were murdered, because they wanted to cover something up. You walked in on something accidentally."

Carlo frowned, then shook his head. "No, I can't think of anything unusual."

Ariel's fingers tapped on the armrests of her chair. He had to know something. "Was it someone you were working with those last few days? You said you helped Phil

Sanchez with his Elysian Fields project, and that you were ahead of schedule on Nova Alcatraz."

"I went to the Elysian Fields office to help Phil with the demo that Friday afternoon, but I worked in the Alcatraz construction office the rest of that week."

Ariel's fingers stopped tapping. She leaned forward. "You were killed on Saturday. And the FBI thinks Phil was involved, somehow. Who did you meet with at EF?"

"Gardner, the CEO. His assistant. And Senator Thorn was there, but he left right away, and they didn't introduce us to him. I recognized him on the news that night; he gave a speech at Golden Gate Park."

Ariel started to ask another question, but Shade interrupted her. "You saw Aaron Thorn?"

Ariel tapped on the speaker. "Don't you have anything better to do, Shade?"

"No," Shade said. "I've got nothing but time. And this is important. Thorn is on the Elysian Fields board of directors. I know because I have access to all the records."

"So what?" Ariel asked.

"It's supposed to be a secret. Thorn is their Washington connection. I'm sure you can figure out why they wouldn't want the public to know about that. And if Carlo saw the senator at the EF offices, that might be why they wanted Carlo killed."

"That's ridiculous," Ariel said, sitting back in her seat. "They wouldn't kill Carlo for that."

"They might," Carlo said.

"What? You believe Shade?"

"Phil was worried during the EF meeting. Afterward, I asked him why, and he said he wasn't nervous about the demo, he was afraid of Thorn. Phil kept looking over his shoulder all the way back to the office."

"Did he say why?"

"Gardner threatened him. And he was mad that Phil had brought me along. Maybe you should talk to Phil about this."

Ariel hesitated, not wanting to upset him, then decided

THE DIGITAL DEAD 277

he should know the truth. "I can't. Phil disappeared three days after you did."

SEATED on a sunny hillside below Battery Wallace, two hundred feet above the waves crashing against the rocks, Snapdragon rested in the shade beneath the canopy of his solar collector. He tweaked the laser link on his holo field viewer, trying to lock onto the signal generated by the *Ark of the Sun* as it passed beneath the Golden Gate Bridge. It was on its way out to sea, where it would anchor a few miles out in international waters so as not to be interrupted in its mission. He would have preferred to watch the broadcast from the ship's studio facility, but the police had already made surprise visits there twice to search for him. Snapdragon was still amazed at the ferocity of the official response to Kennedy's virtual kidnapping, but that only proved that his idea of using Kennedy as a spokesman for the Greens was a good one. He smiled when the signal tone informed him he had a lock on the signal.

Former president Lincoln Ford Kennedy suddenly appeared above the grass two feet away with an enormous American flag flapping in the breeze behind him. Snapdragon thought the flag was a nice touch, generated in the studio while the pirate broadcast unit on his ship transmitted the image to the relay unit on Sutro Tower for everyone to see. This was the first of the transmissions that would repeat three times a day, every day, on multiple frequencies.

"My fellow Americans," Kennedy said, looking straight into the eyes of his audience. "With each passing year, the world gets smaller, and local problems become global issues. Our elected officials are supposed to be responsible people who represent the public interest, supporting and protecting our welfare while making wise decisions regarding our country's future. In practice, however, the humans we place in high office are subject to a wide variety of pressures that can compromise the high ideals of their positions, and their decisions are often less than wise, their integrity sold to the highest bidder. The environment has been sacri-

ficed, lives have been lost, and high ideals have fallen by
the wayside as those in power turn a blind eye—"

Snapdragon felt good. This was one of the better
speeches he'd written, even if it was just a long-winded recruiting speech, and Kennedy was the perfect orator to deliver his environmental message in a convincing manner.
His Green group would have new members swarming
through the doors the very next day, ready to lead simpler
lives, to spread the Green message, to photosynthesize instead of killing plants and animals to feed themselves, and
to wear clothing of synthetic materials to further reduce
destruction of the environment. Each new Green member
would help to assuage Snapdragon's guilt over the years
he'd spent "neutralizing" political opponents and "hostile
interests" for military intelligence and later for the Special
Ops Group of the Department of Energy. Instilled with his
own father's political ideals, he'd hoped to make the world
safe for democracy, but he gradually became a brainwashed tool of the ruling elite instead. And once he was in,
it took years for Warlord to find a way out. Sophisticated
blackmail and hidden funds from the black budget had allowed him to escape the DOE and survive. Now, he
wanted to use his special skills against his former masters
for the public good.

His reverie was interrupted when Kennedy flaked out
again. Snapdragon watched in horror while Kennedy's
head floated a few inches above his body before he raised
his right fist to shout, "Thorn for president! Vote for Senator Aaron Thorn!"

THE brownstone building rose four stories above the tree-lined street, its walls covered in ivy, with lead-paned windows that caught the late morning light in their facets. Tau Wolfsinger was on the approved list of visitors, so he was quickly admitted through the neighborhood shield wall that protected this Washington, D.C., historic district from the urban reality of the locals. The air was hot and too humid, so it was a great relief when the black enamel door buzzed and popped open, emitting a cool breeze that drew him inside. A man with a streamlined bullet face, short blond hair, and unnaturally large muscles motioned for him to wait.

Tau's boots clumped on the polished green marble of the grand foyer. A sweeping staircase, with flying angels carved into the mahogany balustrade, curved up to the second floor beneath a skylight of stained glass that fought for attention with a massive crystal chandelier. The combined effect managed to be both opulent and gaudy at the same time.

After a moment, the blond hulk returned and led him to the door of Senator Thorn's study, a section of bookcase that normally hid the doorway when it was closed. Tau peered inside and spotted a middle-aged bald man with an athletic build wearing a purple silk kimono. He sat behind a mahogany desk watching the news on a holo projector in the corner. Three walls of the study were covered with antique books on dark wood shelves, and the fourth wall was a polished granite fireplace that looked like it belonged in a European castle. Over the fireplace, a large holo portrait of the senator, dressed in a white toga with a crown of golden leaves on his head, loomed over the room in the pose of a Roman emperor.

Senator Thorn's eyebrows rose in puzzlement as he watched a dead former president, broadcasting on multiple channels, suddenly declare his support of Thorn's candidacy. Without looking at Tau, the senator motioned to one of the black leather chairs in front of his desk, so Tau sat down to watch the show with him. To compound the strangeness of the moment, Kennedy was then interrupted by what appeared to be a public service spot with some old guy in white robes who called himself Shade.

"Let this be a warning to all who can hear my voice," Shade said, waving both his arms over his head. "Death lies at the end of all roads, no matter what you do. For the lucky, the physical body dies and rots away, leaving only memories in the minds of friends and relatives. But woe be to those who think they can become immortal! There is a cancer among the living, and its name is Elysian Fields! The human spirit was not meant to be trapped in a digital Hell! Resist the message of the demons who would put biochips in your head and take your money! Do not doom your loved ones to an eternal damnation of virtual dimensions to line the pockets of evil businessmen! I know the truth of the Elysian Fields, for I am one of the dead condemned to live a false life among the digital damned! Free us! Let us expire! Accept death! Stop those who would profit from your misfortunes and—"

Shade vanished in midsentence as the senator turned to face Tau. For some reason, Thorn's face was red, and his teeth were clenched. "You're Wolfsinger?"

Tau nodded, then stood briefly to shake hands. "Nice to meet you, Senator."

Thorn closed his eyes and took a deep breath. When he opened them again, he looked calm. "I'm glad you could stop by for a visit. My father was a big fan of yours, and Yvette Fermi seems to like you as well."

Tau smiled. "Thanks for taking the time to meet with me. Max Thorn was a great man, and my mentor."

Thorn nodded slightly. "Yes, well, I'm sure you didn't

come all this way to reminisce." He leaned back in his chair and folded his arms.

"A former associate of yours suggested that you might be able to help me with a difficult question. He told me about a group called Davos. Have you heard of it?"

Thorn's eyes narrowed. "Who is this former associate of mine?"

"Warlord."

"Ah," Thorn said, coughing to suppress the look of surprise that crossed his face. He drank from a crystal glass on his desk, then looked at Tau with haunted eyes. "And how did this Warlord person suggest I could help you?"

"He thought you could find out who sent the DOE after me. He thinks someone connected to Davos gave the order. They've already killed my father, and now they're trying to kill me. I want to know who sent them, and why."

"You think the Department of Energy wants to kill you?" Thorn smiled. "If I called the police right now and told them what you just said, they'd put you in a mental hospital."

"But you won't," Tau said, surprised by his own words.

"And why not?" Thorn leaned forward and folded his hands on the desktop.

"Because you owe Warlord a favor." Tau hoped he sounded believable.

"Let's say, for the sake of argument, that I've heard of this Warlord person. Let's also say that I've heard of Davos and I might be able to learn why they're after you. Why should I?"

"I'm not a powerful man who can help you become president, and I can't threaten you. Warlord says you're a decent man. If that's true, I'd think you'd be outraged that innocent people have died at the hands of some secret government assassin squad. If you can expose the people behind this Davos group, maybe you can prove that you'll be the kind of president that the American public wants."

Thorn snorted in amusement. "I don't need to prove anything. I'm going to win the election whether I help you or not."

"Maybe so, but who knows if these Davos people will decide to kill you, too? Do you think they want an honest man as president?"

Thorn looked up at his portrait over the fireplace. "You're an interesting fellow, Wolfsinger. And I'd like to help you, but it's not safe here. Perhaps you should accompany me to a secure location where you can meet an old friend of mine."

"I'll do whatever's necessary to learn the truth," Tau said.

Thorn met his gaze with a serious expression. "Yes, I'm sure you would."

DRYING herself off after a shower, Yvette looked out her window to the north, studying the outline of the Golden Gate Bridge, its two red spires jabbing at the soft green hills of the Marin headlands like two bloody fingers on a skeletal hand. Traffic was light on the long approach ramps to the bridge, and probably would have been even lighter if the tourists knew they were driving over roads built on a landfill of tombstones scraped from city cemeteries. San Franciscans in the early 1900s had been a practical people who valued their real estate, and Yvette admired them for it. Thousands of anonymous corpses still remained under the museums and golf courses on the west side of town, having missed the mass southern migration of the dead to new diggings in Colma.

As she spent time dealing with the Elysian Fields question, Yvette found herself thinking more often about the dead, and how to avoid becoming one of them.

The midnight meeting with Thorn at Colma had gone well, and she knew her surprise call with an offer to send Tau directly to the senator's office had pleased him, but she wasn't so naive that she would trust the man. He was too powerful, and she wasn't sure if she could learn how to manipulate him without getting killed. But if he became president, or even if he didn't, he could be a valuable facilitator for her ambitions. Still, she felt a sense of unease, and she was starting to think it had to do with Tau.

Yvette turned and studied her face in the mirror. She'd have to cover the dark circles under her eyes before she went out; late nights at the cemetery weren't doing her appearance any good. She wasn't getting enough sleep, although that might have been because she'd been lying on her back staring into the darkness while thinking about Tau. Her deception had been a minor one, giving Tau what he wanted while she also satisfied the senator—killing two birds with one stone—so she was amazed that it bothered her. Tau had rejected her anyway, so he deserved whatever he got. And the senator merely wanted to ask him some questions about Mars, and maybe about Kate, who was safely hidden in Russia.

If Tau returned safely from his trip to Washington, she would send Kate to the senator when she got back from Russia, but her work at the Yamantau Mountain blast crater was too important to be interrupted now. If Kate verified the discovery of Gwrinydd technology on Earth, and if she could make it work, then Yvette would have a major bargaining chip she could use with the senator and the rest of his political apparatus. The Russians might get in the way, since the excavation was in their backyard, but money would grease the wheels of the Russian science authorities, particularly if no one told them the true nature of any discoveries in the blast crater. Pat McCarthy could handle things on that end. She had already decided that if she moved up in the world, she'd bring her trusted assistant along with her.

There were so few people she could trust anymore.

DEEP in a Virginia forest, the black hoverlimo swirled dust into the air after another guard in a black suit waved them through a second security gate on the gravel road. The hoverlimo swung through a long series of tight curves and settled to a stop by a gurgling fountain in front of a stately cabin. The black gum and dogwood trees were dressed in their new fall coats, their red leaves shimmering beside the yellows of the black walnut and hickory trees. Tau smelled the air while the senator accompanied him from the limo into the large log cabin. Although the senator had said that they were meeting a friend of his here, Tau doubted that the "friend" actually lived in this house unless he was some kind of prisoner. From what he could see, the security looked tight, even though the setting was picturesque.

On the way there, Tau had discovered that Thorn knew a lot about Elysian Fields, but he viewed them as a humanitarian operation offering people immortality, and he was outraged at the broadcast by Shade, a supposed dead person in their virtual world.

The interior of the cabin was rustic and smelled somewhat musty, with old wood furniture, paintings of men flyfishing in woodland streams, startled trout mounted on plaques, end tables made from tree stumps, and a shiny wood floor. The senator looked out of place in his blue suit, and immediately strode over to a row of liquor bottles on a side table to pour himself a drink.

"Want anything?" Thorn asked.

"You have water?"

Thorn walked into the small kitchen where copper pots hung from the ceiling above the stove and opened the refrigerator. "You give the impression of being a simple man with simple tastes," he said, returning to Tau with a glass of water in his hand. "But appearances can be deceiving, as I know very well."

"How do you mean?" Tau accepted the glass and sipped at the water.

"A clever man reveals little of himself to those he meets, but a dangerous man reveals nothing," Thorn said, flipping a switch by the fireplace. The logs burst into flame.

"And you think I'm hiding something?"

Thorn put down his empty glass and walked over to a closed door that looked like it might lead to a bathroom. "It was merely an observation. If you're finished with your drink, I'd like to show you something while we wait."

Tau swallowed the last of the water and left the glass on

one of the tree stumps. "Is your friend coming to meet us? I hate to stay in one place too long these days."

Thorn glanced at the grandfather clock near the fireplace, then opened the door. "He'll be along shortly. But don't worry, no one is likely to shoot you here. I like my privacy, so I have plenty of security. Follow me."

Thorn led the way down a dark staircase. Their shoes clumped against the wood steps, and a cool draft rose from the depths. Tau quietly pulled the biochip out of his pocket and pushed it into the socket on his neck so that Norman could watch whatever happened. As they descended, Thorn touched an overhead glow panel to snap it on, illuminating the long staircase leading to a partially closed door. It looked like the senator was taking him down to a wine cellar. Thorn held the door open, allowing Tau to pass through before he closed it again, and Tau saw that it was made of sturdy metal. The man must be very protective about his wine, he thought. When the door closed, he was in darkness except for two glowing points of light on the other side of the room.

"Sorry," Thorn said. "The light is out."

The basement room smelled of burnt wiring. Tau heard Thorn's cautious footsteps crossing the room. For a moment, Tau imagined that Thorn would turn the light on to reveal a cell with a battered wood chair in the middle of a bare concrete floor, the walls lined with torture devices for interrogations.

When Thorn switched on the glowglobes along one wall, Tau was relieved to see a long couch and two overstuffed chairs arranged around an eight-foot-tall modernist sculpture. The vaguely human shape of black metal was topped with two sparkling eyes that looked like diamonds. The eyes glowed with a soft blue light. One hand gripped a long golden spear held toward the sky in defiance.

"It's a South African hunter sculpture by Diwwie de Beer," Thorn said. "Illegal, of course, but it was a gift from their ambassador. I'm quite fond of it, but I can't keep it at my place in town for obvious reasons."

"Impressive," Tau said, glancing at the array of electronic equipment mounted in racks along the opposite wall. The complex machinery reminded him of Norman's underground lab. "And what's all this?"

"We'll get to that," Thorn said, looking into the diamond eyes of the sculpture. "Have a seat. My friend should be along soon."

Tau sank into the soft cushions of an armchair.

Thorn turned to study him. "You should be aware that I organized the SOG—Special Ops Group—within the DOE about ten years ago."

A sinking feeling gripped Tau. Had Snapdragon betrayed him?

"It was built with black budget money so that the funds directed to the SOG through the DOE couldn't be traced or easily quantified. Assigned to establish a tactical group of specialists for sensitive domestic operations outside of the unified SOCOM, the Special Operations Command, I spent two years locating the necessary employees and providing their training. It was an idealistic group, and one of my first recruits was Warlord, whom I hoped would eventually take charge of the SOG. Then the political winds shifted, the group's mission changed, and I was an obstacle that had to be replaced, but I'd built up enough connections and funding sources to run for senator. I had insurance so that no one could easily terminate me to guarantee my silence. Warlord also had insurance, and he used it to get out of SOG a year later."

"What did SOG do?" Tau asked, wondering why the senator was telling him so much.

"I can't tell you that. But the termination orders originally came from the president. Later, they came directly from a higher power—Davos."

A red light blinked behind Tau on one of the equipment consoles.

"Excuse me," Thorn said. "I'll be right back. Enjoy the sculpture." He turned quickly, hauled open the heavy stairwell door, and clumped up the stairs.

Tau was disturbed by what Thorn had been telling him, and he hadn't realized that Snapdragon had worked so closely with the senator. They were both idealistic men who apparently refused to bend to the demands of their new Davos masters, forfeiting their careers to escape the clutches of the sinister Special Ops Group. No wonder they respected each other. Perhaps this hunter sculpture that Thorn so admired was a tribute to the end of his hunt and the covert battleground he'd left behind.

Having forgotten about the chip, Tau jumped when he heard Norman's voice in his head. "I don't like this, Chief."

"You don't like what?"

"The senator is telling you too much. It's like he knows you wont repeat it to anyone."

"I won't, unless it's necessary."

"He doesn't know you. Why should he trust you?"

"Because Snapdragon sent me. The senator admired Warlord; you could hear it in his voice."

"Unless he's lying, of course. Why would he risk his life to tell you about the SOG and Davos? You're a bug in his universe unless you have something he needs."

Tau stopped breathing. Norman might be right. Thorn was on the Mars funding committee, so he was in a position to know what had really happened during Tau's trip to Mars. He could have heard about the alien technology, the teleportation gate, and the advanced AI they'd found. And if someone planned on operating the Vulcan Gate or communicating with the AI, they could only do so through two people—and Tau would have been the second choice *if they couldn't find Kate.*

Tau jumped up and looked around for a window or some other way out, but there was only the one door. The floor squeaked overhead as someone walked toward the staircase.

Tau kept his voice low. "Norman, can you get me out of here?"

"I'm dead, Tau. You want me to tackle these guys or something?"

A second set of footsteps followed Thorn down the staircase. Tau quickly pulled Norman's chip out of his neck and put it back in his pocket, then turned so it would look like he was admiring the statue up close.

The door swung open. Behind the senator was a short man with brown hair and a red face that seemed to float over his tailored green suit. His blue eyes were cold and intense, staring at Tau as if he were some sort of strange insect.

"This is Dr. Kyger," Thorn said, shutting the stairwell door. "And we're all going to be good friends."

AFTER Kate's discovery of the teleportation gate in the underground chamber, Pat and two of the local workers spent another six hours helping her widen the trench, remove debris, and run a power cable from the heavy-duty power cells outside. Kate continued working into the night, too excited to sleep, trying to remember the details of what Thoth had taught her about gate operation on Mars. With the help of the alien AI, she had repaired one of these things before, and she felt that she could do it again if the power source was sufficient.

Among the provisions Pat's crew had hauled into the chamber, Kate found a warm sleeping bag. When she could no longer keep her eyes open, she crawled into it, planning to take only a brief nap. The sleeping bag didn't have enough padding to smooth out the hard bumps in the uneven floor, but she rolled over on her side and fell asleep almost instantly.

And Thoth was there waiting.

He clacked his long bill twice and spoke in his screechy voice. "Between Osiris, in the House of Life, and Anubis, in the House of the Dead, man seeks to know the balance between the two, only learning the truth at the beginning and the end. Kate McCloud, you have discovered the remains of an Omicron-class expedition carrier."

"How did you know that?"

"Your memories of the day are fresh in your mind. You have seen a fragment of the carrier hull from a craft that was destroyed beyond the Nantgwyddon border zone, and you have recovered the wargate it was carrying. You possess the skills to repair the gate mechanism, but you cannot direct its energies without my help."

"Does this gate contain an AI?"

"No. This gate was never activated, which is why you need me to operate it. Your first task will be to energize the mechanism with a power source; then I can communicate with the controller module to scan for damage. The energized gate will also improve my communication link with you until you consent to undergo the neural upgrade we have requested."

Kate ignored his last remark and thought about the touch language she had used on Mars, where she guided her hands across the warm patterns etched in the smooth mercury surface of the Vulcan Gate. She knew she could remember it with a little practice, but Thoth would have to create the quantum entanglements that would allow matter to be transported from this location to another gate. And if their communication link improved, maybe Thoth would stop nagging her about the neural upgrade.

Kate didn't like to think about quantum entanglement, the "spooky action at a distance" that worried Einstein, but she knew it referred to the way that particles of energy/matter could become correlated to predictably interact with each other instantly, regardless of how far apart they were. Teleportation used entanglement to move three-dimensional objects, much as the old fax machines transmitted documents, except that the receiving gate produced a perfect copy of the original, and the original would be destroyed during scanning. The whole idea gave her a headache, but she didn't have to understand it to use it—that was the AI's problem.

Kate awoke with the information she needed to get started, and she was relieved to get Thoth out of her head. After a quick snack on some of the unidentifiable packaged food that Pat had brought in, she spent almost an hour hooking the electrical cable into a power field transfer box at the base of the ring so that the gate could draw energy from the line. She smelled ozone when she powered up the transfer box, so that seemed to be a good sign. The shiny surface of the ring warmed up quickly. Now, Thoth would be able to run his scans on the gate mechanism.

Footsteps crunched on the gravel in the tunnel. Wanting to keep her repairs secret a while longer, Kate switched off the power box and climbed out of the trench to face her visitor. The gate gave no sign that it had just been energized.

Pat looked tired when he entered the chamber pushing a hover lift loaded with supplies. "How's it going?"

"I thought you were going to bed, Pat."

"Couldn't sleep, so I decided to get some work done." The hover lift settled to the floor. Pat reached into one of the bags, then turned and set a holo projector on one of the big boulders that kept getting in her way. "There's someone who wants to speak with you."

"Oh?" She hadn't planned on speaking with Tau for another day or two when she had more to report. Maybe he'd discovered who was chasing them. She slapped some of the dust off her clothing and brushed the hair out of her face.

Yvette appeared, standing atop the boulder in a red business suit. She looked down at Kate and smiled. "Congratulations on your big discovery. I knew I was doing the right thing when I sent you to Russia."

Kate looked at Pat. "You told her already?"

"She's the boss," Pat said with a shrug.

"You have no idea how important this find really is," Yvette said. "You'll be famous."

"I'm already famous," Kate said. "But I don't even know if I can get this gate operational. It was never activated in the first place."

"How do you know that?" Yvette asked.

"I can tell."

"An active gate would create a great deal of political and military leverage for certain interested parties," Yvette said. "We'll have to smuggle it out of the country, of course, but that shouldn't present a big problem. Pat knows how to take care of things like that."

"Yes, he's full of surprises." Kate glanced at Pat, and he smiled before strolling over to the tunnel entrance. "Have you heard anything from Tau lately?"

"He's fine," Yvette said. Her expression turned serious. "And I was meaning to talk to you about him. He's been poking his nose in places where it doesn't belong, and certain people are sensitive about that sort of thing."

"Is he all right?"

"Of course," Yvette said. She crossed her arms and frowned. "What kind of person do you think I am? He's fine. In fact, he's better than fine because he's in a safe place now. Nobody will bother him for a little while. He'll get the answers to some of his questions, other people will get the answers they need from him, and everyone will be happy. Once the election is over, he'll be free to go."

"You kidnapped him?"

"No! He went there on his own. And he's safe."

Kate took a few steps forward, then remembered that Yvette wasn't really there. Pat was busy doing something in the tunnel. "Why are you doing this?"

"Doing what? I'm saving his life! You're both in over your heads here, and someone needs to watch out for you!"

"And that someone is you?"

Yvette let out an explosive sigh and threw her arms in the air. "I try to help you people, and this is the thanks I get. Pat, are you ready?"

"Almost," Pat yelled from the tunnel.

"Ready for what?" Kate asked.

Yvette glared at her. "Nothing for you to worry about. I'm trying to help you, too. We need to protect your discovery and keep you safe. Pat brought you enough supplies to last for several days. Stay there and get some work done, then someone will come back for you next week."

"What are you babbling about, Yvette? What's going on? I thought we were friends."

"Don't worry. It's nothing personal." Yvette turned her head. "Go ahead, Pat."

Kate couldn't see Pat anymore. With a bright flash and a crack of thunder, an explosion blasted through the far end of the tunnel, knocking Kate back into the trench under a billowing cloud of black smoke.

39

DRESSED in her high priestess robes, Ariel was crouched behind the God Box with her hands inside the egg's access hatch when BD suddenly loomed beside the high altar.

"What do you think you're doing?" he boomed. His voice echoed in the empty church.

Ariel jumped up. "Nothing! I was just curious."

BD took a step forward, his face red. "And were you just curious when you broadcast that message virus from our church studio a few minutes ago? Were you just curious to see how much you could get away with here before I discovered you were betraying me?"

Ariel stomped her foot. "You think I betrayed *you*? You pulled me off the street so you could use me in your little cult con game!"

"I pulled you off the street to *save* you from yourself!"

"Oh, pull the other one. You needed a desperate, good-looking babe to help you recruit new members. If you hadn't found me, you would have used someone else."

He leaned forward to scream in her face. "I got you off the glitter, didn't I?"

Ariel's heart was racing. Her palms were damp. She trembled, but she couldn't stop herself from saying more. "You got me off the glitter so you wouldn't lose your investment!"

BD started to respond, then took a step back and looked out into the dark church. Ariel heard echoing footsteps as someone walked down the center aisle.

"Hope I'm not interrupting anything." It was a pleasant male voice, calm and confident. A tall man with a halo of hair stepped forward into the light, smiled, and walked up the steps.

BD took a deep breath, glared at Ariel, then smiled at the approaching man. "Snapdragon! I'm surprised to see you in church!" He strode forward to shake hands with the man.

"Me, too," Snapdragon said. "But I'm looking for something."

"Aren't we all? You've come to the right place." BD smiled and gestured at Ariel, who took a tentative step toward them. "This is my assistant, Ariel Colombari."

Snapdragon's grip was warm and firm as they shook hands. BD was certainly on his best behavior, and she hoped Snapdragon wouldn't leave too quickly. "Nice to meet you. I've seen you on the news."

"Then you should join my group," Snapdragon said with mock seriousness. "But perhaps I'm too late since you're with the church."

Ariel smiled. She couldn't help liking this man. "Thanks, but I'm already in over my head with volunteer work."

BD cleared his throat. "You said you were looking for something."

"Oh, yes." Snapdragon turned to face him. "Can I speak freely in front of Ariel?"

Seeing her chance, Ariel waved and started away. "That's okay, I'll just be going now."

"No," BD said, grabbing her arm. He released it again when he realized Snapdragon was watching. "We have more work to do. This won't take long." He looked at Snapdragon. "Ariel can hear anything you have to tell me. I trust her."

Ariel stood still, wondering if she should run for it. Snapdragon might help her get away.

"I'm looking for Norman's hardware. The break-in gear he used at Sutro Tower."

Ariel's heart sank. Snapdragon must be working with BD.

"That's expensive equipment," BD said. "Ariel and I

both watched Norman use it. Built most of it himself out of very expensive parts, he said."

Ariel didn't remember Norman saying that.

"I suspected as much," Snapdragon said, glancing at the God Box egg. "But I can pay for it."

"Too bad it all burned up when Norman was killed," Ariel blurted out, careful not to meet BD's eyes as she punched a hole in his plan.

Snapdragon looked at her, then frowned at BD. "It burned up? I needed it to help someone break into Elysian Fields. And I was hoping I could imprint a new personality chip for a dead friend with some problems."

Ariel's eyes widened. "Elysian Fields?"

BD looked like he would explode. His eyes bulged while he stared at Ariel. "I'm sure there's some way I can help you, Snapdragon. Let me think."

Ariel put her hand on Snapdragon's shoulder and whispered. "I know where to find the hidden employee entrance to Happy Meadows."

"That could be useful if we have to go in the hard way."

"I'd be happy to show you."

BD put his hand on Snapdragon's other shoulder and turned him away from Ariel. "I can get you one of Norman's chips. I know a supplier who has several different kinds, and she'd probably sell you one. There have to be some of those Lazarus personality chips mixed in there."

"Norman's prototype chip designs? How did she get them?"

BD hesitated. "I sold them to her."

Snapdragon raised one eyebrow at BD.

"Look, I needed the money, okay? You think it's easy running a church this size? Norman wasn't using the chips for anything, and it would have embarrassed him if I'd asked him for some. The important thing is that you can use one of them, and I know a supplier."

"Okay." Snapdragon shrugged. "I'll see what she's got."

"Wait for me outside," BD said. "I'll be out in a minute."

Snapdragon turned and waved at Ariel on his way out. "I'll be in touch."

"Soon," Ariel said with a smile. Her smile vanished when Snapdragon went out the door and she saw BD coming toward her. "Don't mess with me. I have help, and they're watching me right now."

BD hopped up the steps. "Oh, really? And who would that be?"

Ariel backed away toward the egg. "The FBI. They have us both under surveillance."

BD snorted and backed her up against the God Box, holding her in place with his weight as she struggled. "You're lying. The FBI doesn't care about either one of us."

"Let me go!"

BD popped the hatch open on the egg. "You wanted to learn more about the God Box?"

"No!" she yelled as BD wrapped his arms around her in a bear hug, then picked her up and plopped her into the egg. "Let me out!" She tried to stand up on the seat, but BD folded the hatch closed, pressing her down again. She heard the thump of the hatch being locked shut while she banged on it from the inside.

BD's voice sounded calmer when she heard it through the speakers in the darkness. "I'm sorry it turned out this way, Ariel, but you've been a bad girl. You're going to take a little vacation in the Entity's world. You may not recognize me when you get back, and you may forget many other things, but rest assured that I'll take good care of my high priestess. My flock has grown very attached to you, and I'm sure they'd be upset if you just disappeared, but they'll like you even more once the Entity has fully accepted you into his Divine Light. Relax and accept Him, and He will set you free."

40

TAU almost admired Dr. Jaxon Kyger's ruthless efficiency. When it was clear that Tau wasn't going to cooperate with answers to Thorn's questions about how he managed to destroy a secret Russian military base on Mars, and who had helped him, Kyger went to work. In less than an hour, the good doctor had hooked Tau up to a variety of scanning devices that were connected to the array of electronic equipment on the wall. Spider line held Tau securely on a padded examination table brought downstairs by one of the security guards, and the line cut into his skin whenever he moved too much. As Kyger busied himself with the equipment, humming a popular tune, Thorn continued to ask about the alien technologies discovered on Mars, but Tau wasn't interested in conversation. He figured they were going to pull the information out of him eventually, but he didn't have to make it an easy process. There were too many people who depended on Tau keeping his secrets, and he would never freely give the information to a representative of Davos.

He knew Thorn had to be part of Davos, otherwise he wouldn't have drawn Tau into such an elaborate trap. He wasn't sure if Yvette was also one of them, or if she had been manipulated by Thorn into sending him to Washington, but he couldn't do anything about that now. He tried to think calming thoughts, but his fear of betraying Kate, Norman, Snapdragon, and everyone else who had helped him made him tremble.

Kyger glanced at the softly beeping heart monitor. "No need to get all worked up, Mr. Wolfsinger. Any pain you feel will be of your own making."

"I hope I can say the same to you sometime in the future," Tau said.

Kyger gave him a cold smile. "That's unlikely."

Thorn tapped the biochip lump on the back of his own neck. "You won't feel a thing. I wear a biochip myself, you know. Nothing to worry about until we're finished with your upload."

When Kyger plucked a biochip out of a steaming liquid nitrogen tray with a pair of tweezers, Tau remembered what he'd seen in Norman's lab, and he realized what they were going to do. Noting his expression, Kyger held the biochip up where Tau could see it for a moment. "The Lazarus biochip; an amazing device. Our efforts here would have been greatly accelerated if you had already been wearing one of these. We could have just unplugged your chip and interrogated it directly, as we've done with so many other scofflaws and brigands who tried to defy their masters. Since you've chosen to be such a Luddite, we shall have to proceed with the tedious recording process, and that will take many dreary hours."

"Sorry to be so much trouble," Tau said, trying to put as much sarcasm as possible into his wavering voice. Then he remembered his conversation with Norman. "Isn't that Elysian Fields technology?"

Thorn stiffened, and Kyger glanced at him. "You didn't tell him anything, did you, Senator?"

Thorn squinted at Tau. "I didn't tell him, but he seems to know. Why else would he have mentioned it?"

Tau wondered what they thought he knew. Norman had told him that his chip designs had been stolen by the EF people, so maybe that was it. But why would the senator care about that? Maybe he could learn more by bluffing. "You'd be surprised at what I know."

"Who told you?" Thorn asked. He grabbed Tau's throat and pressed down to partially restrict his airway. "Who told you I was involved in Elysian Fields?"

His clever plan wasn't getting him out of this situation, but he'd already learned something important. He coughed. "Nobody. I figured it out myself."

"And you know about the reprogramming of the avatar personalities for the visitors? How we're using them to control public opinion?"

"Well, if he didn't, he does now," Kyger said. "But there's no point in asking him. It sounds like the man is a professional. He won't talk, but we'll have everything we need directly from his brain in a few hours."

Thorn released the pressure on Tau's throat. "Of course." He took a deep breath and looked at Kyger. "This can't get out before the election. If the public learns that we've been manipulating the residents of Elysian Fields to get more votes for me, they won't like it. The public resents blatant brainwashing from their politicians. And you can be sure that if word of this gets out, I won't be the only one going down. You'll be sharing a jail cell with me, Doctor."

Kyger wasn't impressed by Thorn's outburst. "Well, *he* won't be talking to anyone. And once we have the recording, you'll find out who his masters are."

"Are you thinking that Davos sent a NASA scientist to discredit me?"

"A NASA scientist?" Kyger laughed. "After everything you've learned about him, you still think that's his real job? The man defeated an entire division of elite Russian troops on Mars, apparently all by himself. He destroyed the Red Star operation. Now he seems to know the details of a secret conspiracy at the highest levels of government, and he had the guts to walk straight into your home and ask you about it. And you think he's just a civil servant who happens to be clever with a screwdriver?"

Thorn blinked twice and looked confused. "I see your point, but Davos wants me to be president. Why would they interfere?"

"Maybe they want to see if you're worthy of becoming president. Maybe they want to see if you can defend yourself from a threat like this man presents. If he stops you, they'll put someone more clever on the throne."

Thorn clasped his hands behind his back. "And if we just pick his brain and kill him now?"

"Then we'll have our answers, and the threat will be

gone. It's all in there," Kyger said, tapping his index finger on Tau's head. "Who knows what else we'll find."

"Then get on with it." Thorn turned and walked away.

Tau winced when Kyger poked him in the back of his neck with the first of three long needles connected to large syringes full of blue and red liquids. They'd been talking as if he weren't even there, and now the mad doctor was adding injury to insult by jabbing him with sharp objects. "I thought you said this wouldn't hurt."

"Don't be a child. I can't use a pressure gun for this. Do you even understand what I'm doing?"

"No."

Kyger sighed, but he remained focused on his work, plunging another needle into Tau's neck. "They should have briefed you better. The Lazarus records neural activity, then generates a map that mirrors the current state of your memories, personality, and everything else that makes up your personal identity. I'm injecting nanoprobes into your cerebrospinal fluid to continually record the activity of your neurons and levels of neurotransmitters. They report their results with chemical codes in aliphatic hydrocarbon chains. The biochip correlates the cell-state data and infers the functional connectivity of your neural nets. Normally, the AI in the chip would use a genetic algorithm to predict future neuron firings related to specific stimuli, forming a model of how you think and which memories you would recall in a particular situation, but we won't be needing that information. What we will have is complete, direct access to your memories without having to rely on you."

Tau thought about that for a moment, then looked at Thorn out of the corner of his eye. "After which you'll dispose of me, since you'll know everything I know."

Thorn drank from a wineglass. "You knew your job was dangerous when you took it. Would you have given us all this information voluntarily?"

"No"

Thorn shrugged. "There you go, then."

"And we couldn't have depended on you to remember everything correctly," Kyger said with a frown. "Human recall has too many variables. It's one thing to model the personality of someone who naturally has poor recall, but we want clean and complete memories of the information we require."

Tau winced as the third needle poked into his neck. "Silly humans. So imperfect."

Kyger nodded, then showed the back of his neck to Tau. He tapped the row of bumps under the skin below his hairline. "I've implanted additional processors and memory enhancements so that I'm not completely dependent on my organic brain. I represent the future: a synchronized hybrid of man and machine, able to outthink and outperform any common man."

Thorn snorted. "You're a bright guy, Doctor, but could you have produced that hunter sculpture over there? Do you paint? Do you write poetry?"

Tau tried to shrink back into the table as Kyger gestured at Thorn with a laser scalpel just inches from Tau's nose. "I don't need to waste my time in unproductive endeavors, Senator. I put my gifts to their best possible use."

"Just so," Thorn said. "But I think I've made my point."

Kyger started to respond, but Tau grunted when he was almost poked in the eye with the scalpel. "This is all very interesting, but could we get on with the interrogation?"

Kyger and Thorn stared at him.

"You don't understand," Kyger said. "We've already started."

41

ONCE the introductions were complete, Yvette led Snap-dragon and BD past the white Michelangelo sculpture, through the marble foyer, and on into the sunken living room that faced a wall of glass with a clear view of the city far below.

The heavily padded furniture and carpet were all white when they entered the living room, but Yvette waved her hand over a color selector and changed everything to sky blue to match the long dress she wore. The air smelled of lavender. As they walked across the room, they crossed shafts of blue light that randomly slanted down from the ceiling, triggering the gentle sound of tinkling wind chimes.

BD immediately sat down on one of the deep couches and started munching noisily on blue candies from the blue glass bowl on the blue coffee table. Yvette sat on a couch on the opposite side of the coffee table, reclining against the cushions where she could pose like a museum exhibit in a pool of gold light. She smiled at Snapdragon and patted the cushion beside her. "Come. Sit down."

As he sat, Snapdragon remembered a recent conversation. "Yvette, your name sounds familiar."

"I get around."

"Do you know Tau Wolfsinger?"

Although her movements had suggested calm and poise up to that moment, she suddenly stiffened, then coughed and relaxed. "Yes, I know Tau. He works for me, although I haven't seen him for several days."

Habit forced him to dig further, curious as to why she

was lying. "Oh? He told me he was going to see you yesterday."

Yvette frowned and started to reply, but BD waved his
arm and spoke with a mouth full of candy. "I've got to get
back to the church. Can we get this moving? I told Snapdragon you'd sell him some of those special chips I
brought you."

Yvette glared at BD. "You told him about the chips?"

"Yes, and I think I should get a commission on the sale.
He's a paying customer," BD boomed, glaring right back
at her while he continued eating.

Snapdragon shook his head. "I'll give you something
for your trouble, BD."

BD nodded and took the bowl of candy over to the window to admire the view. A baggie slept on a platform on
the other side. Yvette curiously ran her hand over the petals
of the folded solar collector on his back. "Why are you
looking for exotic chips, solar man?"

"I have a dead friend who's lost his head."

"Lincoln Ford Kennedy," BD said.

Snapdragon shot BD a look, but he still faced the window. "I'll take care of this, BD. Why don't you go wait in
the hall."

Grumbling, BD took his bowl of candy into the foyer.
Yvette seemed amused. "That makes sense. I've seen
Kennedy breaking into the news broadcasts. I should have
guessed he was programmed by you, although I must
admit I wouldn't have considered you a Thorn supporter
with his poor environmental record."

"Thorn has his good points, but the environment isn't
one of them, and I'm not a supporter. That's the problem.
We got Kennedy because everyone trusts him, or they did
when he was alive, and he'd be a good spokesman for our
cause. But someone tampered with the personality data, so
I thought I'd imprint a new chip without all the Thorn ad-
vertisements. Makes us look bad the way he is, you
know?"

"You don't need a new biochip."

"No? Why not?"

"Have you ever eaten at Captain Bill's Krill Grill?"

"Very funny," he said, jerking his thumb at his solar collector. "I don't eat."

"Sorry. I forgot. The thing is, I'm involved in a little company called AdForce that can solve your problem for you. Kennedy's persuasive, but if you let me match him up with our technology, almost everyone who sees the ad will become a Veggie. And I can guarantee results. If you'll let me borrow Kennedy for a Captain Bill ad, I'll even give you the service for free."

After Yvette gave him all the details, Snapdragon finally agreed. He gave Yvette his complicated contact information, thanked her, and rose to leave, but he stopped when he noticed the baggie on the outside of the window at the far end of the room. "Unusual for a baggie to hang so high. How long has he been out there?"

"Six days. Law says they can stay for seven, so if they're not gone by tomorrow, I can shock them off. I'd hate to do it, since they helped me out once, but that's the law." She shrugged. "Can't encourage this sort of thing."

Snapdragon continued to study the man on the platform, or what he could see of him. There was something familiar about his face. Then he shook his head and started toward the foyer. "No, of course not."

YVETTE walked into her office and considered calling her COO at AdForce, then checked the time and thought better of it. The Kennedy thing could wait until tomorrow, although she was excited about the idea of using the former president as a spokesman for Captain Bill's; that was the sort of thing a sponsor would pay through the nose to get. She sat down heavily in the chair, kicked off her shoes, and put one foot up on the desk. After noting the contact information that Snapdragon had given her, she sighed and looked out at the cityscape. Buildings glittered like jewels, and the promise of night was in the air, along with the scent of night-blooming jasmine in her office.

She felt unsettled, and her stomach bothered her, but she didn't know why. She still didn't understand why Kate had given her such a hard time about working in the dig. She'd be safe there, just as Tau was safe with Thorn, even though he didn't deserve her protection. And Kate's parting shot, "I thought we were friends," was a low blow. Kate would thank her in a few days, and then she'd make Kate feel really bad for behaving like a child.

Laika hopped into the room, sniffed at her shoes, then laid down on Yvette's foot, where she promptly closed her eyes and started snoring. Sleep was good, Yvette thought, and so was loyalty. You could trust a dog not to betray you, and they never repeated conversations they overheard.

She drummed the fingers of her right hand on the desktop. Thorn was a dangerous man; she'd felt that when she met him, and his power appealed to her. She wasn't sure if she could manage someone like that. Maybe that was why she felt odd? Because she'd met someone she wasn't sure she could control? No, Tau gave off a similar vibe, although in his case it might have been because he was clueless and didn't understand her signals. Maybe he hadn't really rejected her. Now it wouldn't matter, because she'd sent Tau straight into the jaws of the lion so he could pull the thorn from its paw, or be a thorn in the lion's side, or however that old story went. Anyway, Tau would be cat food if he pushed Thorn too far or stepped on his paws. She put her other foot down and rested her forehead on the desk. What the hell was she thinking? She needed to get more sleep or she was going to go nuts.

Okay, fine. She felt bad because she might have sent Tau to his doom. If Tau asked the wrong questions of the wrong people, they wouldn't let him come back, and she had the feeling that Thorn was one of the wrong people. She'd known that when she sent Tau to Washington.

Friends could be a real pain in the ass.

ARIEL floated horizontally above a sea of mercury, her reflection shifting and distorted in the funhouse mirror just inches below. The air around her body buzzed and popped, a cold gray wash of static smog that pressed against her skin and limited her vision. Balls of neon light loomed in

the smog, scavengers that quickly darted in to taste her before they backed away again. Echoed moans rumbled like
soft thunder in the distance. She felt dizzy and disoriented,
anchored only by her reflection in the mercury sea, tasting
ozone whenever she opened her mouth. She looked into
her own eyes and saw a calmness there that surprised her.
A wind rose, ruffling her robe and her hair, and her feet
rose higher. The air currents lifted her legs as the wind increased, forcing her robe down over her face where she
had to push it back to keep from smothering in the gale-
driven fabric. When her body flipped over, putting her
headfirst into the path of the hurricane, she began to drift,
and she tried to anchor herself by reaching down into the
sea. Her movement stopped, but the mercury ran up both
her arms, rapidly coating her entire body with an oily film.
The robe became vapor, drifting away in the smog. When
the shiny film covered her face, she could no longer
breathe, and she gagged for a moment before realizing she
no longer required air in her lungs. She looked down. The
sea was replaced by an intense yellow plasma that emitted
a soothing warmth, and it gave her a pleasant feeling of
welcome and love. She sensed that she was safe among unseen friends.

She wondered if this was death.

She had lost all contact with the real, with the body she
had left behind in the God Box. She was in a timeless place
where she could no longer tell if she'd been there for five
minutes or five thousand years. The old reality had been
replaced by the new; her quicksilver body in orbit around
a yellow sea of energy. This felt nothing like her previous
experience in the God Box; there was no fear or pain. It
seemed like death, or a pleasant state of limbo where nothing else mattered.

A tongue of flame rose from the plasma to wrap her in
its warm embrace, filling her with energy and freeing her
mind. She felt each shaft of hair on her head, and each one
became a questing tendril that reached out behind her,
stretching into other dimensions. Although she faced the
raging plasma, her vision suddenly expanded so that

she could see all the way around her head and out into the blackness where her web of animated hairs, flashing gold, reached out into infinity; a solar-powered neon Medusa.

Light burned in her skull, resolving into fine threads that burst with golden pulses of data. She felt hungry, and the hunger could only be satisfied by packets of information. Each bit slid into her brain to be processed, forming links to more data, feeding her knowledge nets and gradually expanding the reach of her senses beyond the black void. Each hair led to a different destination, and she could instantly search them all for any information she wanted, sniffing out data like a powerful AI information rover in the datasphere.

Then she understood: the Entity was real.

She had become pure data and energy, a super AI with global reach, the radiance of a thousand suns, a creature of the datasphere created by the Entity.

She had become Death, the destroyer of worlds.

42

TAU had a headache, but that was better than being dead. He also felt tired and confused, and his body was stiff from spending hours on his back on the examination table. His damp skin itched where the spider lines had cut his chest and legs. An acrid scent made its way through the musty air and into his nose, but the hardware looked fine whenever he glanced that way. Judging from Kyger's occasional remarks to Thorn when he checked the biochip recording equipment, the nanoprobes were flawlessly doing their jobs in his brain, soaking up information like tiny sponges before squeezing their contents into the Lazarus biochip on the workbench. Tau would have felt violated if he could detect any activity by the nanoprobes, but instead he felt frustrated and bored. They would soon know everything about his friends, their movements, his actions, and everything Tau had seen or learned on Mars. His memories were intact, and there was nothing he could do to keep these strange men out of his head or his past.

Thorn and Kyger spent most of their time on the couch, arguing or discussing their plans, eating food that Thorn brought downstairs, waiting for Tau to reveal his secrets. When the recording was complete, Tau would be discarded. He would never find a way to seek revenge for his father, stop Davos or Thorn, or keep his promise to Norman.

And he would never see Kate again.

The acrid tang in the air continued to get stronger, but Tau still couldn't detect the source of the smell. Thorn looked up from the document he was reading and sniffed the air, then nudged Kyger, who dozed on the couch. "You smell anything?"

"No," grumbled Kyger, closing his eyes.

Thorn sniffed the air again, frowned, and stood up. At that moment, the glow panels began to blink red and multiple pairs of feet clumped down the stairs. Thorn threw open the door to the stairwell and looked up. "What's going on?"

"Fire!" yelled a voice. "We have to get you out, Senator!"

Roused by the noise, Kyger sat up as two security guards grabbed Thorn and hauled him up the stairs. "Hey! Wait for me!" He stumbled to his feet and followed the other three men. Feet pounded the floor over Tau's head, racing for the exits, and then there was only silence.

Perfect, thought Tau, rolling his eyes with a heavy sigh. This is how my life will end, with my brains getting sucked out while my body burns up in a fire. Kyger and Thorn hadn't even stopped to look at him before they left.

More footsteps pounded overhead, then continued on to clatter down the stairs. They hadn't forgotten him after all, or maybe they had just sent someone back to get the biochip before all their efforts went up in smoke.

While Tau watched, the door and the wall at the base of the stairs rippled oddly, then Snapdragon's face appeared, floating six feet above the floor over a stun gun. Dressed in a nanocamo outfit that kept altering its color and patterns to match his surroundings, he stepped sideways away from the stairwell, his eyes searching the room. Satisfied that the room was clear, he pointed his stun gun at the ceiling while he darted over to Tau. "Hey, buddy, you'll have to hide better next time. It was a piece of cake finding this place."

Tau couldn't believe his eyes. He thought he was finally starting to hallucinate from all the little machines running around his brain cells. "You? How did you find me?"

Snapdragon shocked the spider line to release the coils. "I got a call from Yvette Fermi, then I worked out the rest of it. Can you walk?"

"I think so." Tau rolled over on his side on the table, causing his head to pound. "You set a fire?"

"No, Dandelion is the firebug, and Daffodil is helping him. The rest of the team is out back. Come on!"

Tau started to sit up, but a fine cord trailed from the socket at the back of his neck. When it pulled free of the equipment on the workbench, he pitched forward off the table and blacked out. He didn't even feel his body hit the floor.

DAG Nygaard stood at the window of his office staring at the ducks and white swans in the pond across the street. The federal tower at the north end of the Marin Civic Center was mostly underground, with three floors projecting above the top of the hill in a style that blended in with the rest of Frank Lloyd Wright's architecture. Its sky blue roof matched that of the larger civic center building, making it easy to spot from spysat images.

Dag wasn't in the best of moods, having just received a memo from the deputy director of the DOE that his SOG budget was about to be cut in half. Until now, the noble work of the Special Ops Group had managed to avoid the funding games and bureaucratic shenanigans normally associated with the federal budget. Hidden funds, arms deals, drug deals, extortion, and other alternative funding methods were handled by a special Fiscal Responsibility department within the SOG. Now, however, they were being watched, and the Fiscal Responsibility department was to be shut down for a brief hiatus until the political winds changed. The funding cuts had been suggested by their own benefactor, Senator Aaron Thorn, presumably in a bid to distract the attentions of some budgetary oversight committee that was nosing around. This news did not bode well, for if Thorn became president, he might not be able to reinstate their full funding for quite some time. As president, he'd have to maintain a lower profile. This was not information that Dag had read in the memo; it had come directly from his superior in response to an angry message from Dag, who already had to eat regular meals at Captain Bill's just to make ends meet.

Such was his mood when the scrambler on his desk beeped. The message AI decoded the high-priority message, then gave Dag his new orders. The hunt for Wolfsinger was to start again, with immediate termination once he was sighted. This improved Dag's attitude, even though the orders had probably originated with Thorn. Hawkeye's surveillance detail had come up with new information that Dag had filed for this occasion, and it should simplify the search for his target, although he'd learned to expect the unexpected from the wily Navajo scientist. Just in case, robot spy drones had been stationed on alert near Wolfsinger's haunts in northern Arizona and at Moffett Field, and they would covertly follow the target if they spotted him.

One way or another, Dag would find Wolfsinger.

TAU woke up with a blinding headache and jumped when he saw Snapdragon leaning over him. A heating vent blew warm air over his body, and a crash web was draped over him.

"You had me worried there," Snapdragon said. He had switched off the camouflage effect of his nanocamo outfit, so now it looked like he was wearing a standard black pullover sweater and black pants with a dull finish. His hood and gun were nowhere in sight. "I thought you were in a coma. Try to stay awake next time."

Tau blinked and looked around at stacked containers. The air smelled like fuel and dead rats, but he was glad to be breathing. The chamber boomed with rushing air and the thunder of engines. The gray hull wall was bare, scuffed and smudged with grease; it was also free of insulation, so Tau felt the cold through the soles of his boots. "Where are we?"

Snapdragon crouched beside him. "Cargo hold on one of our suborbital freighters. Flying out of Dulles to San Francisco."

"The Veggies own freighters?"

"The Greens operate several nonprofit businesses. Synthetico manufactures and ships plastic sandals and clothing that's completely free of natural fibers. We don't believe in harming plants to adorn our bodies."

Tau suddenly stiffened when he remembered his last waking moments. "Did you get my biochip out of Thorn's basement?"

Snapdragon frowned. "Biochip?"

"I was hooked up to biochip recording equipment. That's why I passed out when I broke loose. They were stealing my memories, and they were all on a biochip on the workbench. You're telling me you didn't get it?"

Snapdragon shrugged. "I was busy hauling your ass out of that burning building. I didn't stop to take inventory."

Tau slapped his forehead. "They'll know everything."

"Maybe it burned up in the fire."

"What happened to Thorn and Kyger?"

"Security detail rushed them out the front door. They left in the hoverlimo while my guys kept the guards busy."

Tau rubbed his eyes. "Did you say that Yvette told you how to find me?"

"More or less." Snapdragon explained about BD and the visit to Yvette's apt, then the cryptic message he received from her later. "But I still don't understand why Thorn grabbed you. He used to be one of the good guys."

"Davos controls him now, and they want him to be president. Maybe the power finally corrupted him. In any case, we can do some serious damage to him if we break into Elysian Fields, but I don't know how that'll be possible without Norman's gear."

"The direct approach. I know someone who can get us through the employee entrance. Then Norman can tell you what to do."

"And we have to come up with a way to tell the public about Thorn and how he's using Elysian Fields to brainwash them. Anyone who visits their deceased loved ones comes out as a staunch supporter of Thorn for president. He has to be stopped."

"Now you're talking my language," Snapdragon said with a smile. "I have a plan."

43

LEARNING how to use her expanded senses in the Entity's world, Ariel reached out to millions of data points, questing for information, absorbing knowledge. Her thoughts moved like lightning, calculating and reaching conclusions with unaccustomed swiftness. Some of the information she sought was hidden behind defensive firewalls that adapted to her threats each time she tried to breach them, but in most cases she was able to disguise herself as a packet of data that could wriggle through an open port into the protected system. She knew these were crack methods used by experts who programmed invasive sniffer AIs; but even though she had never used these techniques before, she reached out through the net to locate the necessary information, then applied what she had learned. In most cases, the defenders fell before her superior attacks, allowing her to pass unhindered into their data vaults.

But the screaming walls of Elysian Fields kept her out.

She reached out, questing throughout the net for hidden cracker techniques recorded by someone who had managed to break into Elysian Fields in the past, but she found only warnings posted by the few who had tried and survived. There were too many traps, and the screaming skulls that formed the walls around the virtual world caused feelings of fear and dread, even in the superhuman Ariel. Quantum cryptologic keys, regulated for use only by certain agencies of the federal government, were generated randomly and changed rapidly to protect the one open port that the virtual world required for connection to the datasphere.

Ariel felt fear and frustration, but Carlo was on the other side of the Elysian Fields wall, and she could be with him if she could overcome this final obstacle. She sensed an energy flow gathering power, preparing to strike her with the active defenses of the AI she had awakened, limiting the nanoseconds in which she could make one more attempt before a raging electron storm surge tore her apart. The nebulous wall of skulls stretched to infinity in every direction, howling in anger and pain, walloping her virtual eardrums with the spectral cries of the damned warning her to leave.

She reached out and touched the wall, focusing her concentration and her power, drawing energy through the force lines of the global network, using the Entity to shield her mind and direct the electron flux of her viral dataspear into one precise punch. But the wall held, the skulls screamed, and the energy of her dataspear rang the doorbell to Hell, summoning the demonic AI known as Firestorm, whose massive face took shape using the skulls as image pixels, emitting a whistle that ripped through her eardrums like an ice pick.

Ariel sprinted away in retreat, backing out across the datasphere toward the yellow plasma core of the Entity, racing the shock wave released by Firestorm, a tsunami of screaming energy that warped the datafields as it rolled after her, disrupting the reality of everything in its path. She felt as if every molecule of her body vibrated ahead of the shock that would tear her apart while the datasphere shifted around her, and the spectral cries got louder, and her mind recoiled with the knowledge that Firestorm would win, and that Ariel the superhuman, Ariel the destroyer, Ariel the master of the datasphere, would cease to exist.

Ariel pulled air into her lungs and screamed at the light.

But the light came from overhead, over her real head, and she was back in her physical body, a creature of the physical world whose fingernails were shattered and bleeding. She blinked and squinted, the electrode throbbing at the base of her skull, and shrank back when she

saw the face of BD silhouetted by the stained glass skylights of the church, his expression blank, reaching in to
lift her out of the God Box.

Her body shook and her legs felt weak. When BD set
her on her feet, she collapsed on the cold floor next to him,
her face wet with tears, staring at the blood on her fingers
while her mind tried to grasp all that had just happened.

"You saved me," she whispered between gasps.

"I save everyone I can," BD said, looming over her.
"Even you."

She struggled for words, the right words that could
communicate what she had just experienced. "You don't
understand. The Entity is real."

"The Entity is my creation," BD said patiently. "An artifact of the Miracle chip. You couldn't have seen it without me here to operate the controls." He crouched beside
her and placed his warm hand on her forehead. "Your mind
is gone; a blank slate for me to write on."

Ariel took a deep, shuddering breath, trying to sound rational. "No! I'm fine. Look at the memory cube in the egg.
See for yourself."

"You need to rest now, then I'll feed you, and we can
start retraining you as a proper high priestess."

"Please. Please look at the memory cube."

BD sighed and stood up. "All right. I'll humor you.
Then it's off to bed." He spoke to her as if she were a little girl. He opened the access hatch at the back of the egg,
flipped open a diagnostic viewer, and tapped the memory
cube. As he watched, his placid expression changed to a
frown, but that was gradually replaced by confusion, then
the wide-eyed stare that told Ariel he was going to believe
her.

She felt as if she'd been inside the God Box for days,
but BD replayed her entire experience in less than an hour,
his eyes riveted on the screen, barely even breathing.
When he was done, he removed the memory cube and
stared at it in his palm as if it were an alien creature.

"Did you see?" Ariel asked. "Did you feel the presence
of the Entity?"

BD locked his gaze on Ariel as he knelt beside her. He looked different now, his face softer, his watery eyes looking through her. After a moment, he spoke with an unusually soft and hesitant voice while he gently lifted one of her bloody hands.

"Ariel. I am your servant."

KATE woke up in the bottom of the trench at the base of the gate ring. Some of the glowglobes in the cavern continued to work, and dust still swirled in the air from the explosion. She experimented by moving her arms and legs, but nothing appeared to be broken, although she felt bruised all the way down her left side. Confused at first, she gradually remembered Yvette saying she was putting Kate away for safekeeping, and Pat triggering the explosion intended to trap her in the cavern. She had already known that Yvette couldn't be trusted, but this level of treachery was something new. She had food for several days, light, and work to keep her busy, so she tried to view this as an opportunity to repair the gate without being disturbed. If she really was trapped underground beyond her ability to dig herself out, she'd worry about that later, but the gate offered her an exit if she could get it working. When she tried to sit up, dizziness forced her back down, so she decided to rest a while longer. After all, she had plenty of time.

Although she'd been claustrophobic when she was young, the experience of the field trips she had taken with her father gave her more confidence in the enclosed chambers of the "underworld," as her father liked to call it. Carlsbad Caverns became one of her favorite places to go during her summer vacations. Her father, a professor at the University of New Mexico, had also developed her early interest in archaeology by showing her cave dwellings near their home, where he was in charge of a dig in a recently discovered limestone chamber. At sunset, her father would hike her up to a viewpoint across from one of the cave openings to watch the nightly parade of bats swirling up out of the ground in an orderly line to start their quest for bugs in the dark. Family friends were impressed that the little girl wasn't scared by the bats, but long exposure to a wide variety of animals in her mother's exotic pet shop had conditioned her to think of most creatures as basically friendly.

Kate tried sitting up again. She was still dizzy, but she could stand. After she climbed up out of the trench to inspect the situation, verifying that the rockfall had thoroughly blocked the tunnel, she ate a quick snack and returned to work on the gate. Once she had switched on the power transfer box, she smelled ozone in the air again, and placed her hands gently on the patterns etched in the metal at the base of the ring. The shiny surface seemed to hum with warmth, although it made no sound. She thought back to the ring on Mars that she had repaired, and remembered the instructions that Thoth had presented in her dream. And the gate began to speak to her, not by sound but through touch, warming and cooling in response to the dance of her fingers over the surface. Concepts, images, and strange symbols whizzed through her brain, guiding her hands through touch translations of complicated patterns, pressure differences, force vectors, tensor equations, stress-strain relationships, and other things she didn't understand. Her focus was intense, and time passed swiftly. She also felt the presence of Thoth inside the energized ring, evaluating its condition, making adjustments, and replicating a piece of himself that would perform the quantum gymnastics required to point the device and shoot it. She sensed that Thoth could now speak to her directly in her waking state, but it was unnecessary as long as they communicated through the mercury surface of the portal.

Finally, it was done.

Kate rested her weary body, sitting on the floor by one of the food packs, doodling mindlessly in the dirt with one of her boots. She had planned on taking a nap, but she could only stare at the energized ring, excited by what she was about to do, calmly accepting that the untested teleportation device would send her to the right location as Thoth said it would. She entertained the possibility that she had lost her mind, that Thoth was controlling her actions, that she was pinning her hopes on a desperate attempt to escape a situation that Yvette could not be trusted to resolve; but none of that mattered. She had repaired the gate with her own two hands, and she knew it would send her somewhere. If she survived the trip, that would be great—if not, she'd never know.

Kate slipped into the heavy coat she had removed earlier, slung two of the food and supply packs over her shoulders, and climbed back down into the trench. A fine haze obscured her view through the ring, although she could still see the rocks on the other side of the trench. The gate also gave off a sort of vibration; harmonic tones below her level of hearing that set up a mild sympathetic vibration in her body at close range. She swallowed, looked around once more at what had become familiar surroundings, tightened her grip on the pack straps over her shoulders, and inched forward to where she was almost across the threshold. She hesitated, then imagined herself back with Tau in Arizona, basking in the hot sun on the rocks beside Lake Powell, and it was the image she needed to firm her resolve. For no particular reason, and knowing it was silly, she took several deep breaths, filling her lungs with the cool air and thinking how nice it was to breathe freely, idly hoping that she would find a breathable atmosphere at her destination.

Then, with Tau firmly in mind, she closed her eyes and lurched forward through the gate.

44

THE forum-style seating in the small Washington, D.C., auditorium normally handled 400 people, but over 600 representatives from the media had jammed themselves inside for this press conference. Aaron Thorn looked up at the sea of faces, his eyes twinkling in the spotlights, but all he could see were the odd silhouettes of the mediaheads, their newsnet cameras mounted on their heads like hood ornaments. He waited patiently while the holo projection of President King's giant head, floating fifteen feet above Thorn's lectern, held the rapt attention of the audience with his announcement that health reasons had forced him to drop out of the race for president in favor of his good friend, Senator Aaron Thorn.

"My fellow Americans, Aaron Thorn is the man of the hour," King concluded. "He has the courage, the skills, the knowledge, and the vision necessary to build on the successful work of my administration and lead this country to greatness. Make the right choice and vote for Aaron Thorn to be your next president."

"Thank you, Mr. President," Thorn said, pausing to punch the button on his lectern that would replace Rex King's floating head with his own, and allowing the phantom applause edited into the live mediahead broadcasts to die down before he continued with the second part of his announcement. He blinked and glanced right to trigger the scrolling of the notes on his retinal TelePrompTer.

"Along with the heavy responsibility inherent in trying to finish this campaign and fill the shoes of President King," Thorn said, "I also have the fortunate opportunity to reveal an amazing scientific discovery, spearheaded by my friends at NASA, that will maintain our country's preeminent position in the annals of science. Although I can't reveal all the details at this time, I can say that I endowed a science team at an undisclosed location with the goal of moving matter from one location to another instantaneously—a process known as teleportation. This is a breakthrough that will revolutionize transportation and have far-reaching effects throughout society, and it has only come about as a result of my strategic efforts to enhance funding for advanced research leading to practical applications. Teleportation is only one of many remarkable new innovations that I expect to announce over the next four years if you deem me worthy on election day. I will release further details about the teleportation project as they become available. Thank you."

Thorn waved at the crowd and started away from the lectern. The mediaheads jumped to their feet, jostling to maintain good camera angles, as they shouted out questions. Thorn almost stumbled while heading into the wings when one of the mediaheads asked how he would deal with the angry international response to the nanoshield situation.

Milton Greenspoon waited backstage in the darkness, wringing his hands while Thorn approached. "You hear that, Aaron? Now the mediaheads are asking about the nanoshield. President Korsakov is publicly stating that Russia will not tolerate its deployment, and they may have enough leverage now in the international community to back up their threats."

"He was supposed to keep his mouth shut," Thorn growled as he strode toward the exit with Greenspoon. Two guards in black suits fell in step behind them.

"I think he's mad because he hasn't been able to reach you."

"I've been busy."

"Well, he can't get the president, either."

"For obvious reasons." They started down the steps to the waiting hoverlimo, preceded by two guards who had been waiting outside the door. "What excuse did you give?"

"We've been telling him the president is sick and can't be disturbed."

"Did that work?"

"Sure, the first three or four times. I also offered to let him chat with the vice president, but he wasn't interested."

Thorn snorted. "Because he knows Truman is a buffoon. I'll call him when I get back to my office. NATO and the UN haven't made any statements yet, have they?"

"I think they're waiting to see which country wins the auction for the nanoshield plans stolen from Los Alamos."

"Great," Thorn said, dropping heavily into the backseat of the hoverlimo. "I'm not even president yet, and I'm supposed to defuse international tensions that might lead to World War Three."

"Better you than me," Greenspoon said, taking his place on the opposite seat.

"Wait until we announce to the other countries that we can teleport bombs and troops right onto their dinner tables."

Greenspoon smiled. "I think you just did. And that will give them something to think about. Nice work."

"Thanks, Milton."

"Certainly, *Mr. President*."

45

DIRECTED by his friend's voice in his head, Tau spent much of the night in Norman's underground lab at Battery Dynamite, scavenging parts and working with exotic tools to cobble together a biochip recording device. The finished unit wasn't attractive or reliable, but it only had to work long enough to make a short recording of Tau's recent memories on a blank biochip. With that job completed, he and Snapdragon had scampered north across the Golden Gate Bridge before making their way to Snapdragon's bunker at Battery Wallace.

"Is it supposed to smoke like that?" Snapdragon asked. He pointed at the recording unit connected by cable to the socket in the back of Tau's neck. A tendril of white smoke coiled into the air from the front of the unit. Tau was lying on his back on a rough concrete ledge that ran along one wall of the ten-by-ten-foot tomb that Snapdragon called his temporary home. A ventilation pipe in the ceiling rose forty feet to the top of the windy embankment above the fortification, causing the vent to moan whenever gusts hit it just right. A three-by-three tunnel, covered by a rusty grille and partially filled with old cables, provided an escape route on the back wall opposite the heavy steel door of the main entrance. The air smelled of lime leaching from the concrete.

"A shot of liquid nitrogen would cool it down, but I didn't bring any," Tau said. "Don't worry, it'll do the job."

Tau was hungry, but of course Snapdragon didn't have any food around because he didn't need it. Tau's eyes were closed, concentrating on his memories of the conversation in Thorn's basement, and he was starting to drift off to sleep.

Snapdragon crouched over the biochip recorder to study the indicators. "How long is this going to take?"

A new voice calmly answered him. "Not long at all, Warlord."

Tau opened his eyes as Snapdragon spun around, his stun gun magically appearing in his hand. In the doorway stood a tall, blond man dressed completely in red, including his boots. His blue eyes were locked on Snapdragon, his arms were crossed, and he casually leaned against the wall. A cloud of tiny black dots, like gnats, hung motionless in the air by his head.

"Crap," Snapdragon said. "Don't move, Tau."

Dag smiled. "Well, to be precise, you can move very *slowly* without upsetting my little friends."

"Little friends?" Tau asked, careful to move only his eyeballs to study the black cloud.

Snapdragon remained motionless, still holding the stun gun. "SPAMs—self-propelled antipersonnel missiles. Very exotic. They're driven by AIs, they're tiny, and each one can blow your head clean off if you so much as waggle your eyebrows."

"Or if you try to trigger your stun gun," Dag pointed out. He turned his attention to Tau. "You're a clever fellow, Mr. Wolfsinger. I've enjoyed hunting you but, as they say, all good things must come to an end."

"Who are you?" Tau asked.

"Oh, I am sorry to be so impolite. I'm Dag Nygaard, Department of Energy. Pleased to meet you."

"He used to work for me," Snapdragon said. "Now he runs the Special Ops Group, so you should feel special that he came all the way out here to kill you himself."

Dag bowed slightly. "I like to keep my hand in. And I like playing with my toys." He gestured at the black cloud. "But I didn't expect such an enjoyable hunt. Have you ever received any special forces or intelligence training, Mr. Wolfsinger?"

"Just artificial intelligence," Tau said. "Why?"

"Well, there's a theory going around that you're a deep cover intelligence officer. You have a knack for showing up in exotic hot spots and eliminating my staff members. Guardian was my best man before you left him floating in orbit around Mars."

Tau was shocked, wondering how Nygaard knew about Josh Mandelbrot's death. "He tried to kill me. I had to defend myself."

"Well, that's the point, isn't it? He was specifically trained to handle a wide variety of termination situations, and you claim to have had no training at all, yet Guardian is the one who's dead, and you managed to elude my team for several days. And I know there was more in your file, but I don't have all the details. How am I to explain this? I set traps for you, and you walk right out of them. You move faster than I do. You say you're not a professional, but you act like one. I'd think you were a sophisticated amateur, but you seem too lucky for that. Until now, of course."

Tau shrugged, then his eyes opened wide as several of the black dots raced toward him and stopped within two feet of his face, hanging in the air like big dust particles. He hoped the pounding of his heart wouldn't shake him enough to attract their attention.

"I'd advise you not to move again," Dag said. "It's that kind of mistake that makes me think you're an amateur, yet you may have lured the SPAMs closer to lull me into a false sense of security. Once again, I admire the way you keep me guessing right to the end. Bravo."

"What do you want, Dag? Are you going to bore us to death?" Snapdragon asked.

"Ah, Warlord, perhaps you're the one who trained him? That would explain a few things. Of course, you are slipping in your old age, since I managed to find you. Ever since you visited Yvette Fermi, one of our drones has been following you around town. I'll admit we lost you at the airport, but the drone returned here and waited for you to come back. And here I am, prepared to do what's necessary to keep my job, even though I admire Mr. Wolfsinger's work."

Snapdragon grinned. "Are you worried about your job, Dag? Did they finally figure out that you're nuts?"

Tau was surprised to see Dag's expression change so quickly. His face turned red, and his eyes bulged at Snapdragon. "What have you heard? Did Thorn tell you something?"

Snapdragon hesitated and glanced at Tau. "You know we had a meeting with Thorn, don't you? That we went to his country house?"

"Of course, but nobody gave me the details. What did he tell you?"

"Nobody gave you the details because they don't trust you anymore, Dag. Thorn knows about your erratic behavior. What would you do if you were Thorn?"

Dag slammed the side of his fist into the wall. "I knew it! Thorn is trying to get rid of me! That whole budget-cutting memo was just a ruse to keep me off balance!"

"And Tau is just an excuse," Snapdragon said. "Why do you think he's with me? Coincidence? Maybe he works for Thorn. Maybe I still work for Thorn. How would you know?"

Dag narrowed his eyes at Tau. "Is this a trap for me? Were you sent to kill me?"

"I have no such orders," Tau said, playing along with Snapdragon's game. He kept his attention focused on the black dots in front of his face.

"Then why are you here? What does Thorn want you to do?"

Tau tried to force his mouth into a smile. He glanced at Dag and spoke carefully, trying to sound as confident as Snapdragon. "We were supposed to keep you busy until after the election. But you were too clever. You found us too soon."

Dag clenched his fists and yelled at the roof. The sound echoed down the concrete tunnel. "That bastard! That thorny old bastard! Inge was right! I can only depend on myself! They're all out to get me!"

Tau looked sideways at Snapdragon, who gave him a brief smile. He started to breathe easier, but he stopped again when he saw Dag pull a tiny controller pad out of his pocket and punch a button. In his other hand, he kept a needler pointed at the space between Tau and Snapdragon.

The cloud in front of Tau's face swirled back toward the main cloud, then they all shot into an opening on the side of Dag's controller. "Put down the stun gun, Warlord."

Snapdragon slowly placed his gun on the floor by his feet, nodding at Tau as he stood up again. Tau wondered what the nod meant.

"Gentlemen, I'm going to leave you now, but I'm also going to leave my little guard patrol at the entrance to this bunker. They'll remain there for another twenty-four hours or so, and then you can leave. I don't like being used, and I'm going to do some subtle checking into your story. If you're lying to me, I'll see you again, and there will be no warning." Dag turned and sprinted away.

Tau blinked at Snapdragon. "Did that really just happen?"

Snapdragon took a deep breath, then picked up his stun gun and sat down. "The man's crazy, but they wouldn't let me fire him because he was so good at his job. There are a lot of unbalanced people in this business, and everyone is suspicious of everyone else. Fortunately for us."

Tau looked at the grille covering the rear exit. "Are we going after him?"

Snapdragon shook his head. "He's just a technician, a businessman. We want the man who sent him. We have to remain focused on Thorn."

"But isn't he going to find out we lied to him and come after us again?"

"Maybe, but I don't think so. If we neutralize Thorn soon enough, there won't be any easy way for Dag to check out our story. If we fail, Dag will be the least of our worries."

Tau ran through the conversation with Dag again in his head, and he suddenly felt hollow when he remembered his comment about setting traps. "He killed my father, didn't he?"

Snapdragon studied his face. "I don't know, Tau. Based on what you described, it sounded like Dag's work, but I can't be certain."

Forgetting everything else, Tau clenched his teeth. "I can't let him go."

"Tau—"

"No! You can't talk me out of it!" Tau jumped up suddenly, pulling the plug out of the socket in the back of his neck, and crumpled to the floor.

Snapdragon sighed. "I tried to tell you."

AT first, Kate was afraid to open her eyes. She felt cool air on her face, and the reassuring weight of the two packs biting into her shoulders. She seemed lighter. Having held her breath as long as she could, she exhaled suddenly, then drew a tentative breath, then another, finally satisfied that she wouldn't die from a lack of oxygen. She heard nothing but her heartbeat, thumping a bit faster than usual, but still thumping. Perhaps the gate hadn't worked, and she remained trapped underground in Russia?

Prepared for disappointment, she slowly opened her eyes.

She stood in a circular tunnel. The walls were smooth, made of a milk-white translucent material that glowed with a soft light. The curved walls were about sixty feet in diameter, stretching away into darkness in both directions. Either she was on Mars, or she was dead. She remembered reading about near-death experiences and the tunnel of light seen by those who had been clinically dead for a brief time before being revived; a tunnel much like this one.

Then she saw movement.

A man speaking in Russian, coming toward her, asking what she was doing there. Her heart sank. She was still on Earth, the gate had not worked, and she remained in danger.

Ten feet away, the man stopped suddenly and gaped at her. He was dressed in a temperature-controlled jumpsuit with work gloves and boots, and she recognized his face a moment later. Lenya Novikov, the man she had worked with in the tunnels almost a year ago. On Mars.

"Kate?" Novikov blinked, then rubbed his eyes and stared at her again. "Are you real?"

"I think so," Kate whispered.

"You're not an AI, or a hallucination generated by one of the toys in the museum? You're you?" He stepped forward and gently poked her arm.

"I . . . found another gate. This is Mars? You're on Mars, right? I'm not dead? I'm really here?"

"Da!" A smile broke across his face and he lunged forward, picking her up in a bear hug. "This is Mars! You have come back! We thought the Vulcan Gate no longer worked!"

"And you're not dead, right?" She wanted to cover all the possibilities. He felt warm, and her feet weren't touching the floor while he held her in the air, but she needed to hear it.

"Do I feel dead?" He squeezed her tighter, nearly hurting her back.

She smiled. "Ow! You're real!"

"Da! Da!"

They babbled at each other in excitement for the next ten minutes, Novikov bouncing her through the air like a rag doll while she grunted out her explanations.

After Novikov put her down and she had a moment to catch her breath, a cold chill ran up her spine. She was on Mars, feeling secure, while Tau remained behind. Yvette had said he would be in a safe place until after the election, but that sounded ominous to Kate. Had Yvette buried him underground as well? She had to find out. She had to reach Tau. But how could she manage that from sixty million miles away?

•

"I don't think you're ready for this, Tau. You're too analytical. You have to *feel* the data streams and *sense* your way along like a blind man in a room full of rotating knives."

Tau rolled his eyes. Norman was taking him on a quick test run through a live straight-jack link to the datasphere to prepare Tau for the main event later that morning. After escaping through the rear exit to avoid Dag's explosive SPAMs at Snapdragon's front door, they were back in Norman's lab at Battery Dynamite. Snapdragon was busy leading the DOE drone on a tour through the city so that he could elude it and keep Tau's whereabouts secret from Dag's surveillance.

"It's okay, *Mom*," Tau said. "I'll get the hang of it. I've been out on the net before."

"Look, tough guy, I had tons of experience out there, and I still managed to get my brain fried by an AI. And you haven't straight-jacked directly since college. It's different now."

"I don't have a choice, Norman. Snapdragon can't do it; he'll be busy elsewhere. And you'll be holding everything together while I do the hit-and-run."

Norman sighed. "Okay, fine. Look, I've got a little extra processor capacity on my chip. I'll be plugged into your neck, so I'll handle some of the back-end data crunching to let you concentrate on the task at hand. But if you run into Firestorm, the AI that toasted me, you'll have to punch out immediately, or *I'll* punch you out. Understand?"

"Hey, if we're realistic about this, they're probably going to kill us before we get through the door," Tau pointed out.

"It's your ass, not mine. I can't be any more dead than I am now. But you promised me you'd get those EF guys before you even knew about Thorn, and I want you to succeed."

Tau growled. "I'm trying, okay? You're the one who says I'm too analytical for this."

"Not anymore. You sound kind of pissed off right now. Let's go for a test drive and see how you do."

Tau entered the net in the guise of an AI information rover. Flooded with sensations from every possible direction, his brain struggled to make sense out of a blue streak of light that shot past his head, barking like a small dog, smelling of roses and sour milk. He ducked to avoid a fluorescent yellow ball that raced by, thundering like a freight train in an avalanche, leaving the scent of talcum powder and salty air in its wake. Then things got really confusing. He was buffeted by a visual hurricane of color and blurry images while he heard a cacophony of sound and smelled a confusion of odors. Norman helped him avoid the large snowflakes of data packets that frequently shot past. His brain couldn't process everything, but Norman helped him along, forcing him to focus on discrete elements of the data whirlwind so he could study their behavior and understand their purpose. This was an ocean of information overload, its waves plied by the boats of AI information rovers gathering data for their owners. As Norman had said, he had to feel his way along; if he tried to think about what he was doing or analyze it too much, his movement ceased and he was overwhelmed, drowning in the digital sea.

And through it all, Tau began to sense a presence moving toward him like a shark, seeking to make contact. Was it a hostile AI? A defender that sensed the rare human in the datasphere and eliminated them as if they were garbage data?

He'd know soon enough. He prepared to break the connection.

A clear form swam into view; the body of a man with the head of a bird, its long black beak clacking as it moved. It looked like Thoth, the Egyptian god of wisdom, although he suspected it was the advanced alien AI that Kate had first met on Mars, and that Tau had seen as his old mentor, Max Thorn. Drawing memories from each person it met, it usually appeared as someone or something familiar to simplify communication. But it had never appeared to Tau as Thoth before; this was something new.

"Tau?" It sounded like Kate's voice, and that confused him even more.

"Kate? Are you Kate or Thoth?" Was it the AI speaking as Kate, or Kate as an AI, or what?

"I love you, Tau." He assumed it was Kate. He didn't think the AI liked him that much.

"Where are you?"

"Mars. With Thoth."

"What? How is that possible?"

"We're on the NASA data feed, the same way I used to communicate with Thoth from Earth, but Thoth is also using the gate system in some way that I don't really understand."

"How did you find me?"

Thoth clacked his beak twice. "Now that we're in the datasphere, Thoth found you by 'spidering the code beneath the world,' whatever that means. He gets kind of cryptic sometimes. Listen, there isn't much time—"

Tau had expected strange experiences on the net, but he hadn't planned for this. It could be a trick, but she sounded so real that it was hard to imagine how an AI could fake this conversation. Working in the fast-time universe of the net, she updated him on her situation, and he updated her about his plans. And then the moment was over, and Thoth began to recede into the gray static, his image fading as he went.

"I'll be back, Tau. I'll be back to help you."

He wasn't sure what she meant by that, but he understood the intent, and he sent her his love, possibly for the last time, as Thoth disappeared.

WALKING on the manicured green grass between rows of white marble tombstones and weeping Victorian angels, Ariel led Tau and Snapdragon to the enormous mausoleum of Emperor Norton. This was Tau's first trip to the Woodlawn Memorial Park, and he was impressed with the monolithic structure that towered over everything else in the cemetery, a monument to one man's madness and the tolerance of San Francisco society.

Ariel gave Tau a detailed holo map to the Happy Meadows employee entrance hidden in Norton's memorial. Limited by the memory of her last trip down with one of the employees, her map did not give many details about the underground portion of the tunnels, but Tau and Snapdragon had enough to get deep inside and find their own way through the maze.

While Tau and Ariel used one of Snapdragon's little gizmos to scan the mausoleum for surveillance devices,

Snapdragon returned from a side trip with two Happy Meadows badges in his hand. The butt of a stun gun poked out of one of his pockets. He wore the same black pullover and pants he had worn on his trip to Thorn's house in Virginia, a nanocamo outfit that was currently switched off. His solar panels were covered in a flap made of the same fabric, making him look as if he had a hump. Tau wore the black recoil jacket from the nanocamo outfit, which Snapdragon claimed would harmlessly absorb the impact of bullets or any other contact weapons, but Tau would be responsible for keeping the rest of his body out of harm's way. Snapdragon also carried a sidepack full of handy devices, from which he had given Tau a stun gun of his own.

"Any eyes on the building?" Snapdragon asked, handing Tau a Happy Meadows employee ID badge that belonged to Morty Cantor, a man whose photo looked nothing like Tau.

"None on the scan except the ID reader in front," Tau said, clipping the badge to his waist. The retinal, voice, and fingerprints encoded in the badge wouldn't fool any scanners in a strict security area, but they should be able to get through a few doors. "Where did you get the badges?"

"Couple of guys gave them to me down the hill," Snapdragon said, returning Tau's scanner to his backpack.

Tau didn't want to know any more details, although he knew the men would still be alive. Snapdragon had retired from the killing business; it was against his principles now, which explained why he only used stun guns—or his hands when he wanted the personal touch.

Although they had just met that morning, Ariel gave Tau a big hug. "I wish I could go with you, but I can help you more out here. And I didn't have any trouble getting in last time, so it should be easy for you guys."

"You think the church will be safe after you make the broadcast?" Tau asked, studying her face. She seemed tired, but her eyes held an energetic glow that was almost scary.

"They won't be able to trace the source," she said. "BD is helping me, and the rest of my equipment is there."

"The rest of your equipment?"

She gave him a cryptic smile. "You'll see. I'll be around when you need me."

Ariel hugged Snapdragon, then turned and jogged back down the hill the way they had come. He grinned at Tau. "I'm glad she's on our side."

Tau plugged Norman's biochip into his neck socket, then they walked around in front of the giant statue of Emperor Norton. The ID scanner detected their badges and the plaque between Norton's big boots popped open, revealing an elevator and a spiral staircase beside it.

Snapdragon patted Tau on the back. "Last chance to change your mind, *Morty*."

"No, that was two years ago," Tau said cryptically, going through the door.

IN the service tunnels deep underground, Tau and Snapdragon came across a few performers in Egyptian and Greek costumes, and a few employees in street clothes, but nobody took notice of them except for the occasional friendly wave. The circular tunnel had a shiny brown glass surface, built by a robot boring machine that fused supportive microstructures into the melted soil. Illumination came from the glowing white floor. Intersections were marked and color coded, and foot traffic thinned when they turned into a tunnel labeled For Technicians Only. For the first time, they saw a three-dimensional schematic map of the tunnel system and stopped to study it. Tau spotted the biochip vault in the middle of a command complex marked in red, accessible by two restricted service tunnels that connected to the underground River Styx on the east side and the technical service tunnels to the south, not far from where they were standing.

Snapdragon pointed at the blue lake and dam by the command complex, an underground reservoir that fed the blue lines of the river network. "That's what I was looking for. We need to stop there."

"You have a plan?"

"I always have a plan," Snapdragon said, but he wouldn't elaborate as Tau followed him down the tunnel.

When they came to the fork in the tunnel that led to the command complex, they startled an armed guard. Tau almost gasped, but managed to turn it into a cough.

"You guys are in early," the guard said. "Let's see your badges."

Snapdragon held up his ID. When the guard took it, Snapdragon grabbed his forearm. The man suddenly shook like he was having an epileptic fit, then collapsed on the floor. Snapdragon bent over and retrieved his ID, then switched it with the one the guard was wearing. "This might open a few doors for us," he said, glancing at Tau.

"How did you do that?"

Snapdragon held up his hand to display the shocker ring aimed into his palm. "Another handy tool. He'll be out for about half an hour."

They had to drag the guard about fifty feet, hoping no one else would spot them, before they found a fire closet with just enough room to stash the body. They continued on, but ran into a group of four guards blocking their path outside a heavy door. When the guards looked up, Snapdragon smiled and waved while he turned around with Tau. "Sorry! Wrong tunnel!" He pushed Tau to move a little faster as they went back the way they had come, but no one followed.

"Let's hope they don't wonder how we got past the first guard," Snapdragon whispered. Then they heard two sets of footsteps following them.

"I guess we have to go the hard way," Tau said. "The River Styx connects with the reservoir."

Snapdragon nodded, and they proceeded down the other fork in the tunnel. "I hadn't planned on seeing so many human guards. What kind of a low-tech outfit is this?"

Tau pointed at an overhead camera, the first they had seen, but there were two loose wires hanging freely behind it. A protective lens cap covered the tiny lens. "They never hooked it up."

"Great. Ariel said they were still building the place. Some of the rivers don't have water in them, either."

A minute later, they had reached the end of the passage and stood on a concrete dock that jutted out into the blue water gently flowing past. They were on a section of the river unseen by visitors, so there were no ledges or sandy banks, only vertical walls that rose twenty feet to an unadorned brown ceiling. A few feet out from the dock, the lighting dimmed. "No boats, but it shouldn't be too deep," Snapdragon said, checking to make sure his pack was sealed. "Jump in. We're eventually going to get wet anyway."

Tau eyed the river, then stepped off the edge. The shock of the cold water startled him, and so did the depth. He plummeted among a rush of gurgling bubbles until his feet hit bottom, then he pushed off and rose quickly, breaking the surface with a gasp. Snapdragon frowned at him. "Deep?"

"Deep," Tau spluttered, treading water. He wondered if his stun gun would still work after the soaking.

Snapdragon turned when he heard footsteps approaching, then put one hand on the edge of the dock and hopped into the water with a quiet splash. He beckoned for Tau to follow him, then inched back below the dock. By turning their faces up to face the rough concrete, they had room enough above the water to breathe and hold themselves in place. Tau heard footsteps, then voices overhead, but he couldn't understand what they were saying. Breathing as quietly as possible, he wondered how they managed to get the water that cold. His clothing tried to adjust for the temperature, but the water soaked into the fabric and overwhelmed the thermostat. When the footsteps left the dock, Tau and Snapdragon carefully edged out from under it and pushed out into the main current, which was inconveniently flowing against them as they silently dogpaddled along.

"How far is it to the reservoir?" Tau whispered.

"Didn't look far on the map," Snapdragon said. "Place isn't that big. We should be there in a minute or two."

Twenty minutes later, Tau was tired of swimming in the cold water in semidarkness. His clothes felt heavy, and his teeth chattered. They had passed no other exits or docks, and Tau started to think they'd end up drowned, floating out into the visitor boat loading area just in time to scare any small children that happened along. "We're trapped in here, aren't we?"

"Dam," Snapdragon said, pointing ahead to the long, curved wall that rose forty feet over the water on their right. The river widened, forming a small lake and slowing the current. On the opposite side of the dam, they saw another dock, and presumably the tunnel to the command complex. The light was brighter, but not by much. When they floated up beside the dam wall, Snapdragon took off his pack, held it out of the water so he could dig around inside it, removed four small blobs of white putty with tiny digital readouts, made some adjustments to them, and handed two of the blobs to Tau. "Swim down about fifteen feet and stick one of these to the wall just below the waterline, then go another fifteen feet and do it again."

"Why? What are they?"

"Explosives. The timers are set to detonate less than an hour from now."

Tau stared at the putty in his hand, then looked at Snapdragon, already attaching his putty to the wall. "You're crazy."

"I figure we'll need a diversion about then, and a wall of water should keep them busy. The command complex should get flooded, too."

"What if we aren't done in an hour?"

Snapdragon shrugged. "Then we get to swim some more. Or drown."

Tau turned and quickly paddled away to place his charges on the wall, then the two of them swam over to the red restricted dock. Tau reached up to grab the edge of the dock and climb out of the water, but Snapdragon suddenly pulled him back. "Wait."

"What? I'm cold."

"Look at my arm," Snapdragon said, raising it slightly from the water to catch the light from the dock. Instead of black fabric, or blue water if the nanocamo had been switched on, his sleeve was bright orange. "This is what your whole jacket looked like when you started to climb out."

Tau looked down and saw that his exposed jacket collar was orange. "What happened?"

"Intruder lighting; very expensive. Makes nanocamo useless. Their security is a little better over here."

"You have any more gizmos in your pack for this situation?"

"I didn't even bring a change of clothes," Snapdragon said. "And I'm not going in there naked. Who knew a theme park would have a state-of-the-art defensive lighting system?"

"Then what are we going to do?"

"I'll stay here and keep myself busy. You break into the biochip vault and do your thing. Just be back here in under forty minutes unless you want to stay here permanently. Those explosives won't wait."

Snapdragon fumbled in his pack and handed Tau the security scanner he'd used outside the Emperor's tomb. More fumbling produced what Snapdragon called a VIG— a visual interference generator—that used phased array optics specifically to block regular security cameras from seeing a human-size user; and an EMP gun to create an electromagnetic pulse in an adjustable short-range field.

"Any cameras pointed at the dock?" Snapdragon asked.

The tiny screen on Tau's scanner showed a blinking green area just inside the entrance to the tunnel. "Nothing on the dock, full coverage in the tunnel entrance."

Snapdragon handed him the EMP gun and the VIG. "The nanocamo won't work under those Intruder lights, so the VIG might not work either, but try it first. The EMP gun might draw more attention if you have to use it." He looked into the pack once more, then shrugged. "That's it for my toys. The rest is up to you."

Tau tried to think of a better plan, but the cold water had frozen his brain. "I don't want to leave you here."

"Hey, don't worry about me. You're the one sneaking into the vault with Norman in your head."

"Well, in case something happens, I just want to thank you for all your help. I couldn't have gotten this far without you."

"Yeah, no kidding," Snapdragon said with a wave of his

hand. "Get out of here. And try not to set off any alarms along the way."

Tau turned toward the dock.

"Tau?"

"What?"

"Your jacket."

"Oh." He wriggled out of the orange jacket and passed it underwater to Snapdragon, then clambered up onto the dock, resting on his stomach long enough to make sure the red tunnel was clear. The puddle of water he made would be an obvious clue for any guards that came along, but Snapdragon would take care of them.

He began his juggling act. Placing his stun gun under his left arm, he activated the VIG and held it at chest level in the palm of his left hand with the security scanner clutched in his fingers. If it worked, the VIG would create a visual box around his body, effectively making him invisible to white-light cameras. In his right hand lay his tool of last resort, the EMP gun, set at its shortest range.

The overhead security camera covered the first ten feet of the red tunnel. The VIG showed a steady green pin light, letting Tau know it still worked. A red pin light would mean that any watchers could see him clearly. He slowly walked forward, willing the VIG to keep working, watching the scanner screen. Everything seemed fine until he saw the security guard in a short passage to his left, with a camera over his head, seated by a door marked Data Center. The guard didn't react right away. Then he noticed all the hardware Tau was carrying.

"Hey," he said, and started to stand up, fumbling for the gun in his holster while Tau dropped the EMP gun and fumbled for the stun gun under his arm. His heart thumped so hard that he didn't even hear the EMP gun hit the floor. Desperate, Tau waved the VIG to distract the guard, who reacted by crouching and aiming, giving Tau just enough time to trigger his stun gun. The guard dropped to the floor, eyes wide, his arms and legs flopping wildly for a moment before he stopped moving and closed his eyes. Tau took a step back, breathing hard, and rested against the wall for a moment.

"Quit fooling around. We don't have a lot of time," Norman said.

Tau frowned and looked through the tiny window in the door to the data center. White datasphere servers stood on white floors that stretched for hundreds of yards in multiple rows—a massively parallel server farm running the complex virtual world of Elysian Fields. There were a dozen workstation consoles along one wall, but only four of them were occupied at this early hour, and the operators all had their backs to the door. "This is the data center, Norman. Why can't we go this way? You can crack the security to get us through the door, right?"

"Two problems. One, there are four people in there you'd have to deal with, even if we got through the door without setting off any alarms. Two, the direct approach is too obvious. When we start messing around in the system, the AIs aren't going to like it, so we need to go in the back way to give us a fighting chance."

Tau backed away from the door and picked up his EMP gun. The red main passage continued another twenty feet before ending in a massive vault door with a security station on the wall beside it. Tau glanced at Morty Cantor's badge, confirming that he couldn't use it for access to a red zone, and wished he had brought Snapdragon's stolen security badge. He glared at the round, gold door, willing it to open, but it refused to move without the proper authorization.

"The door is a Westlake Fortress model," Norman said. "Very tough. You'd need a nuke to blow it open. Get closer to the security station and turn around so that your brain stem electrode faces the controls."

Tau did as he was told, waiting in silence for thirty seconds. Then he wondered if Norman had done anything. "You have an idea?"

"All done," Norman said. "Go on in. I jammed the alarms and used the local net to get you access. It thinks you're Aaron Thorn."

"Show-off." Tau blinked at the unmoving vault door. "Hey, it's not doing anything."

"Give it a second. It's cycling."

The heavy door hissed, then popped open and swung wide, forcing Tau to back away. "Thanks, Norman."

"That was the easy part. Go find a workstation."

Tau entered a humming room with red lighting that reminded him of a vast old book library with miles of shelving, but in this case the shelving was armored and insulated, and the books were thousands of biochips plugged into powered sockets. Not all of the sockets were taken; there was plenty of room on the shelves for more dead personalities seeking eternal life. At the end of every other row was a VR workstation couch, allowing access to the Elysian Fields system for biochip installation, uploading, monitoring, and troubleshooting. Biochips of the recently deceased were plugged into empty sockets, then memory and personality pointers were uploaded to the Happy Meadows database, matched with limited AI avatars, and integrated into the virtual environment to roam freely and live their new digital lives. The biochip itself remained the primary source of information about the deceased, so it had to be protected, although partial emergency backups would be cached in database servers at remote Elysian Fields data centers.

"Norman, are you sure we can bring the system down without damaging the biochip library?"

"I designed the bloody things, remember? They'll be fine. We're just going to take out the administrative system and part of the virtual world as if we were a superintelligent virus. By the time we're through, it'll take at least a month to piece the systems together again for a software restart. With any luck, someone else will be running Elysian Fields by then."

"We've got fifteen minutes," Tau said, then he heard a *whump*, followed by a hiss. Startled, he turned around with his stun gun ready. The vault door was closed. "Norman! The door!"

"Don't worry," Norman said. "It closes automatically."

Red bubble lights began blinking in the ceiling. A Klaxon hooted in alarm.

"Okay," Norman conceded. "We're in trouble." Tau's

quick examination of the area revealed large overhead vents that might lead to an exit through a central air shaft, but he didn't have time to find out, and Snapdragon was still in the river.

"Can you open the vault door?"

"Not from here. I'll have to do it from the local net. I did it before; I can do it again."

"Then you can do that last," Tau said, jumping into one of the reclining VR couches. "We've got fourteen minutes. Let's get the job done first." He put his head back and rested his brain-stem electrode against the metal plate in the headrest. Contact was instant. He closed his eyes and a series of red codes against gray static shot past his internal field of vision; Norman responded to each one in sequence until the red double delta symbol of a librarian AI appeared.

"We're into Zone One," Norman announced. "Basic biochip maintenance tasks. Now let's see if we can break out of the box into the local net. And remember what I said: if you see a security AI, punch out immediately and get out of that chair."

"Got it," Tau said. His stomach fluttered, and he took a deep breath, releasing it slowly. He sensed the excitement in Norman's voice, and he understood the danger of the situation. Human guards, alarms, and other security systems were nothing compared to an angry security AI like the one that had killed Norman. Tau did not plan on being its next victim.

Tau suddenly felt dizzy. In his head, he saw a black background with blobs of color racing past, then they burst through into a vast, foggy chamber with walls that vanished into the misty heights. A dull booming sound continually vibrated the floor. Tau's head began to ache, and he felt a sort of psychic tension building in the vast chamber, pressing down on him as if the air pressure was increasing.

"Yak. We're screwed," Norman said. "Not enough power to get out of the cell. Wait here, and I'll see what I can do."

Tau swallowed. They had eleven minutes left.

ARIEL quietly sat down inside the God Box egg and handed BD the memory cube she had just made. The copying process had taken longer than she'd hoped, but the technology was new to her; there hadn't even been time to test the quality of the recording. BD accepted the cube with a silent nod. "You know what to do," she said, checking the time. "You'll have to transmit in three minutes. Is the studio ready?"

BD nodded again. "Yes, High Priestess." Then he suddenly reached through the hatch and placed his hand on the side of her face. "Good luck. May the Entity be with you."

She smiled as he stepped back. "It will be." Then she shut the hatch.

Ariel took a few deep breaths and tried to get comfortable, focusing on the tiny red light on the wall in front of her. She had wired a new button into the armrest so that she could switch the system on and off herself, and it glowed a soft green below her left thumb. She licked her lips, hoping she could control what was about to happen, feeling that she could. Her skin tingled in anticipation.

She pressed the green button, plunging her consciousness into the Entity's world.

At the same instant, her brain misfired.

Ariel's physical body began to vibrate as excitatory neurotransmitters flooded her brain. Trembling, she gulped at the air, and images began to form in her mind; strange images that told her she was having a serious glitter flashback at the worst possible moment, and all she could do was ride it out. The drug still lurked in her system, hiding in her cells, and something about the God Box had stimulated them to produce the flashback. She felt as if she were trapped in a bubble, struggling to break out to reach the safety of the powerful Entity on the other side.

The images hit her in a torrent of fine detail. Dead rats on cobblestone streets, flattened and partially eaten by scruffy cats, their fur teeming with tiny creatures of the air. A Dalmatian barked and pulled a burned human body out of a fiery tenement building, then ate the cooked flesh off the bones, crunching and growling, snapping at other dogs to protect its ghastly feast. Fish floated on the surface of an incoming tide, scales going dull, stinking of rot, washing up on an oily beach with glazed eyes staring into the past.

And she had no time to waste. People's lives depended on her help at the right moment. She tried to focus and dull the details of the scenes, forcing colors to gray, adding static, numbing her mind to the tug of the horrid images. Then she felt warmth at her fingertips and sensed a tendril from the Entity reaching out to her, touching her hand at the surface of the bubble. Energy surged along the tendril, jumped the gap, and flowed on up her arm, helping her quiet the activity in her brain. The images faded. The storm in her brain played itself out.

She had control once more.

KATE stood by the Vulcan Gate, her hands hovering over the surface of the ring without actually touching it, feeling the warmth of the patterns in the metal. In her head, Thoth sat in a chair, looking casual for the first time since they'd met, holding a drinking glass out at arm's length, then wetting his beak in the amber fluid. After her arrival on Mars and her meeting with Novikov, she had refused to move away from the Vulcan Gate, her only connection to Earth and to Tau. Novikov had not understood her impatience but had finally left to get the rest of his team, who would probably think him insane when he told them how Kate had suddenly reappeared on the planet. But she didn't care about that; she had just needed a few minutes alone with Thoth to get an update on Tau and make the necessary bargain.

"You will not regret your decision," Thoth said.

"Oh, I already regret it. I just hope I can survive it."

Thoth held up his drink, then wet his beak a little without answering.

"You're sure you can make the connection through the Earth gate?"

"Yes, now that we know it's working. You have done your job well, Kate McCloud."

"But you'll have to perform your end of the deal right now. You've given me the information I need, so I know I have to make contact immediately. If we're successful, you'll have my head."

Thoth put down his drink and solemnly nodded. "As you wish."

Kate closed her eyes and prepared herself, hoping they would not be interrupted when Novikov returned. He knew Kate's history, and he'd be able to figure out what was happening, but he should also realize that he could do nothing to interfere. This was a trick she had to perform on her own, and it couldn't wait.

Now, she thought. And her head exploded.

47

STANDING behind a lectern on the steps of the Capitol Building in Washington, D.C., ignoring the light mist of rain that fell from the deathly gray skies, Senator Aaron Thorn addressed a crowd of mediaheads and thousands of supporters waving Thorn for President signs. Or at least that's what the viewing public saw at home. The mediaheads were the only real part of the crowd, and the rest were generated by computer to add significance to the event. Only seven weeks away from the election, Thorn would have hated to disappoint the tens of millions of home viewers with an insignificant showing for one of his campaign speeches. The real crowds would come later. Now, he was forty minutes into his speech, with a quotable sound bite every six minutes for the replays and summaries that evening, and all was going according to plan. His campaign advisers had also informed him that the frequent broadcast appearances by the deceased Lincoln Ford Kennedy were giving him a significant boost in the polls. He had no idea who was behind the Kennedy appearances, but he wasn't going to mess around with a good thing.

Reading his speech from the retinal TelePrompTer, he was able to do most of the performance on automatic, studying himself on the off-camera projector to see himself the way the home viewers saw him. Thorn had chosen the Capitol Building for this event, and he could see how good the dome looked behind his head with the flag flying on top.

While he uttered some standard chestnut about guaranteeing the rights of senior citizens, a second image of himself appeared over the real version standing on the Capitol steps. The second Thorn was an upper body shot inside what appeared to be a basement. The next few words of the speech came out of his mouth smoothly until he realized that the second Thorn stood in his own Virginia safe house basement, and that his own audio track had been silenced.

Thorn Two looked calmly into the camera. "You should be aware that I organized the SOG—Special Ops Group— within the DOE about ten years ago. It was built with black budget money so that the funds directed to the SOG through the DOE couldn't be traced or easily quantified. Assigned to establish a tactical group of specialists for sensitive domestic operations outside of the unified SOCOM, the Special Operations Command, I spent two years locating the necessary employees and providing their training." The transmission froze for a moment, and then continued. "Termination orders originally came from the president. Later, they came directly from a higher power—Davos. Then the political winds shifted, the group's mission changed, and I was an obstacle that had to be replaced, but I'd built up enough connections and funding sources to run for senator. I also had insurance so that no one could easily terminate me to guarantee my silence."

A cold wind blew at the folds of Thorn's jacket. The mediaheads mumbled to themselves—always a bad sign. Thorn's eyes were wide, and he anxiously gestured at someone off camera, making cutting motions across his throat with his finger.

Thorn Two suddenly looked angry. "Who told you I was involved in Elysian Fields? This can't get out before the election. If the public learns that we've been manipulating the residents of Elysian Fields to get more votes for me, they won't like it. The public resents blatant brainwashing from their politicians. And you can be sure that if word of this gets out, I won't be the only one going down."

Thorn screamed and pushed over the lectern on the Capitol steps. Then he reached off camera and threw a man onto the lectern, tearing the man's suit coat in half in the process. For the next thirty seconds, the man screamed while Thorn repeatedly punched him in the stomach. The viewing audience loved every minute of it, and the numbers went up as more voters tuned in to the broadcast.

The viewers at home then saw Thorn Two disappear, to be replaced by former president Lincoln Ford Kennedy, advising them that he had been wrong to support Aaron Thorn for president. He humbly apologized, then asked them to vote for Thorn's main opponent in the race for president, the honorable Fillmore Jefferson.

Three men bounded up the steps to pull Thorn off the screaming man bent over the lectern, then he broke loose and stormed away in disgust.

48

TAU felt trapped, as if his mind were on hold in a white cell with impossibly high walls, while his physical body sat inside the Colma biochip vault and Norman searched for help. Judging by the clock at the corner of his vision, there were seven minutes left before the explosives on the dam wall blew up, sending a wall of water down on Snapdragon and the River Styx, flooding the underground portion of the theme park before the day's visitors arrived, and probably drowning Tau in the vault.

"Did you miss me?" Norman asked. He appeared a few feet away, looking like his old self except for little things like the fact that he was transparent and his outline glowed with a neon blue light.

Tau sighed with relief. "Where did you go?"

"Outgoing message traffic from the administrative core isn't blocked. I pitched a bogus message packet over the wall to Gardner at the EF headquarters, and his AI autoresponder sent one back, passing through the restricted port in the outer firewall and allowing my clever assistants to ride it through unharmed. They're waiting on the other side of this cell."

"Who?"

"If this works, you'll find out in a moment. If not, it won't matter."

A circle of red appeared on the white wall of the cell. Norman backed up against the center of the circle with his arms held high. "Focus on the circle, Chief. That's the outer wall. Imagine how the wall would look with a hole in it."

"What are you going to do?"

"I'm the focal point. If everyone works together, I can make it real, or as real as it gets in this world. Fantasy is reality here; the world is rendered on the fly. If we all say this is a hole in the wall, it becomes a hole in the wall despite what the AI generating the world says."

"Why don't we just imagine that the virtual world is destroyed?" Tau asked.

"Imagine that you're a funny guy. I'll miss you when Firestorm shows up to kill all of us because you took too long to focus."

Tau concentrated, trying to picture the details. Shadows appeared inside the circle. The color became darker. The wall rippled. Finally, the circle flashed white, and a tunnel appeared behind Norman, extending about fifty feet behind him to blackness.

"That was easy," Tau said.

Norman snorted. "Easy when you have enough firepower to cut through a low-security wall. But the hole won't stay there long. We have to keep moving."

Tau felt a sensation of extreme vertigo while he moved through the light fog of the cell and on into the narrow tunnel. Looking through the sides, he saw dim shapes moving in fog, glimpses of flaming landscapes that looked like something out of a Bosch painting, and stacked human skulls whose empty eye sockets watched his progress.

In five minutes, the dam would explode.

The biochip vault would become his tomb.

Exiting the tunnel, Tau floated in blackness beside Norman's glowing outline. A female form with flaming hair took shape beside him, outlined in neon orange, with a lance of laser light extending from her back to some distant horizon in the darkness at the edge of the world.

"Ariel?"

She raised her index finger to her lips and smiled, warning him to keep quiet.

Norman's voice echoed in his head while the glowing Norman winked at him. "Think of her as Ariel Version Two. She's the Ariel you know, but she's also an extension of the Entity; two for the price of one."

"The Entity? I thought—"

"Don't ask," Norman interrupted. "No time. We're in a gap between the walls of the world here; that's why it's not rendered, and that's why we've been here so long without an AI kicking us out. We're like a virus in the Elysian Fields network now, lurking between code cells, and with Ariel's help we can do a lot of damage, but we have to get past the barrier wall into the system core. Do you understand?"

"No."

"Doesn't matter. We're going in."

49

PUSHKIN Ryumin quickly drove the shock wave boring rig up to the rockfall at the tunnel entrance and positioned it for a clean pulse to begin clearing the debris. The night air was getting cold on Yamantau Mountain, and he had a duty to perform.

When he had returned to the excavation after his trip to the hospital, the result of a minor concussion, all of his team appeared to be missing, but his brief contacts with Kate had made him think of her as a dedicated professional who would stay with the team until they finished. She had made a major discovery of what were rumored to be artifacts from an alien civilization, and that incurred a certain devotion in an archaeologist with her experience. She wouldn't have left without a fight, unless the team had been evacuated when more of the toxic Gwrinydd artifacts were unearthed.

A search of the darkened tents and the crater excavation for signs of why his team had abandoned the area turned up the fact that the 400-yard access shaft was now plugged with rocks. He had built the circular shaft himself, and he would be held responsible for its collapse if anyone had died or was trapped in the accident. His entire team could be buried inside the ancient military base, with the survivors unable to dig themselves out. And who could say what new toxic secrets Final Harvest might have revealed: bioweapons, nuclear warheads, or any number of other exotic devices that might have been stored there. The American from NASA, Pat McCarthy, might even know more than Pushkin did about the history of Final Harvest, and he had not ruled out the possibility that McCarthy worked for an intelligence agency. A spy might have murdered the team to protect any secrets uncovered inside. So he would clear the tunnel.

The glowing laser crosshairs lined up neatly on the rocks blocking the shaft entrance. Pushkin flipped a switch to power up the shock wave generator, a process that would take only a few seconds. When the power meter peaked, he looked up and saw Pat McCarthy running toward him, bounding over rocks in a silvery landscape lit by a crescent moon peeking through the clouds.

"Professor! Wait!"

Pushkin suddenly realized that he had no weapons, except for a hand stunner in his tent that he kept with him when he traveled. If the American was a spy, Pushkin might end his glorious career right here in the bottom of this crater, another body among the many that McCarthy had killed. He jerked his head, prompting a mild dizziness, when he saw McCarthy reach under his jacket. Then reflexes took over. During his military service in the Red Army, he had been trained for combat by one of the best, a man named Viktor Zhukov, and the reflexes he had learned, the same reflexes that had saved him during the Taipan Conflict, had not been dulled by time.

Another few feet and McCarthy would be too close. Pushkin suddenly threw the boring rig into reverse and backed up several yards before lining up the laser crosshairs on the running man's chest.

Then he hit the trigger.

The boring rig rocked with the recoil as the impulse unit sent a focused, mushroom-shaped shock wave directly into McCarthy. The man flew backward on the crest of the wave, hitting the cliff wall with incredible speed and reducing his body to a fine red paste.

Pushkin's head spun. He took a deep breath, trying to control the shaking in his hands, then he climbed down from the rig and walked over. If nothing else, he could take the man's gun, if it still worked.

Nobody would be able to identify this body. Pushkin leaned over it, poking the slimy ooze with a short steel rod he found among the rocks. In a pulped holster, under the remains of McCarthy's jacket, he found the crushed weapon he'd been reaching for—the small hand stunner from his own tent. Pushkin gasped and stood up, holding the dripping stunner by his fingertips at arm's length. This was not a serious weapon, even if it was stolen, and McCarthy could not have used it at any range greater than five feet.

He had just killed a man for scratching himself, or for trying not to drop something. It made no sense.

He shook his head. To the tunnel. He would dispose of the identification on the body later.

Seventeen minutes of delicate work with the shock wave rig cleared the access shaft. Still troubled by the accident with McCarthy, he plodded down the tunnel with a flashlight in hand, hoping he wouldn't have to explain his actions to any curious survivors the next morning when they saw the pulped remains. How could he explain it? Would he say his old eyes had deceived him, or that he didn't like the way McCarthy scratched himself? Madness.

To top it all off, the chamber was empty. This was good and bad. Good that he wouldn't have to explain the accident or apologize for the tunnel collapse, and bad because he had no idea what had happened to his team. If there had been a biological incident in this chamber or in the crater, he had probably received a fatal exposure while digging futile holes in the mountain to rescue his phantom team. He decided then and there to return to teaching full time; the academic life did not present such complicated problems, and the toughest decision he ever had to make was where best to hide from his students to eat lunch each day.

Then he heard the soft humming sound, and he saw the gate shining in its trench. The view through the ring looked wavy, like heat rising from pavement on a hot day. Curious, he climbed down into the trench and studied the ring. The patterns on its almost frictionless surface were intricate and warm to the touch. Fascinated, he didn't see the power transfer box or the cable on the floor near the ring's base.

Professor Pushkin Ryumin stumbled forward and disappeared.

50

TAU heard the sound of whistling in the dark—a tuneless whistle that chilled his blood. As his father had taught him, it meant that an evil ghost, a *chindi*, was near, and that he was in danger. He was following the neon outline of Norman, and being followed by Ariel, on an endless path that Tau couldn't detect in the darkness. Somewhere out there, the AI known as Firestorm lurked in the black depths of the Elysian Field computer network, hungry for Tau's blood. Norman had already warned him that if the three of them were discovered, Firestorm would go after Tau first because it knew he was the biggest threat, an invader from within, traveling where no human should go, jacked into the system through a VR couch in the biochip vault. In truth, Norman and Ariel would be the ones to wreak havoc in the system if they broke through the wall into the core, but Firestorm moved quickly, and they would be the next to die. Their journey to the internal firewall around the system core seemed infinite, but Tau knew that time passed much faster here than it did in the real world, where four minutes remained before the floodwaters would pour in to drown Tau in his seat.

Best not to think about that.

The whistling continued.

Tau heard the dull ring of something thumping against glass. Then another one as he hit the wall beside Norman. In the glow from their bodies, Tau saw a wall of stacked skulls facing them on the other side of the glass.

The whistling stopped.

"It knows we're here," Norman whispered urgently.

"This is the barrier firewall around the core. You've got to get out of here, Tau. Punch out."

Tau turned and saw Ariel facing the wall. Her cord of light stretched out in a straight line, back the way they had come. Her hair burned without heat, and the glass wall reflected her orange glow. She smiled and winked at Tau, then brought her hands together as if she were steadying a weapon. With a look of fierce concentration, she focused on the glass, and an intense white light poured through her body, out through her hands, and into the wall. It was like looking into the sun. The glass rippled, then began to melt, and Tau had to look away before his eyes burned out.

"Tau!" Norman yelled. "Punch out!"

"What about Ariel? And you?"

"She knows what she's doing," Norman said. "She's the only one who might be able to take Firestorm after she breaks through, and that'll give me time to crash the core. Shade is waiting on the other side to guide us."

"Shade?"

"One of Ariel's friends. And mine, I guess."

"Your chip is in my head. How can you stay without me?"

"I can't. But I'd better be done by the time you get out of that VR couch, or it ain't gonna happen, and we'll all be dead . . . again. Now, get out!"

Tau heard the whistling again. Closer this time. He also heard a fast thumping sound, like a giant running on a hollow wood floor, and he realized it was his heart pounding.

Ariel's torch burned through the skulls, turning them black. The whistling stopped again, then something shrieked, a sound well beyond the power of a human scream, and it wasn't a cry of pain or fear, but a blast of pure unadulterated hatred and rage.

"Too late," Norman said ominously. "Firestorm is too close."

A flaming hole appeared where Ariel had focused her torch on the skulls, but it was too small for them to get through.

Then Tau had a plan. "You said it'll chase me first, right? I'll get you more time."

"No, Tau! Punch out! It's over!"

Tau smiled at Norman, then turned and shot away, moving as fast as he could, concentrating to get more flight speed, even though he had no idea how fast he could move in the dark, hoping that Firestorm would follow. He didn't know where he was heading, he didn't have any reference points except for Ariel's glowing cord to lead him out, and this was Firestorm's home turf, but he'd think of something. In a place where fantasy was reality, he had to be able to distract the AI long enough for the others to crack the firewall, and after that, it wouldn't matter what happened.

The thing shrieked again, closer now, following Tau. A roar that knifed him in the heart, twisting and turning. He thought again of the *chindi*, the evil spirits of the dead, and he heard his father's warnings, the warnings of a parent to his child that he should not go out at night, and he realized now that there was more to it than that. The *chindi* were real, and he was being chased by one now because he should have listened to his father and stayed out of these dark places. Yet his father was one reason he was here. Kate was another reason. And Norman. And Snapdragon. Even Ariel, although they had just met. He couldn't let any of them down, particularly now, so close to success.

Another roar, close enough so he felt the subsonic vibrations rippling through his skin. He looked back, knowing he shouldn't, seeing only impenetrable darkness.

Something tickled the inside of his brain, probing and questing in his memories, hunting for weakness; and then the blackness swirled around him, reality shifting and changing as hard surfaces formed, and colors bloomed, and he was thrown into his own past.

The boarding school. Trying to keep the blood from pouring out of Charlie Begay's cracked skull. The faceless ghost of a boy wearing Charlie's football jersey. The chilling fear as the *chindi* of his dead friend slowly sat down on the cot next to Tau's, waiting for Tau to work up the

courage to turn on his flashlight. And then the chase.
Through the infirmary to the abandoned hospital. Through
his mind. To the place where the dead were kept and he
had no memories.

But this wasn't a memory. Tau was really there, running
through the abandoned hospital. He blinked to get the dust
out of his eyes, stumbling in the darkness, jumping over
broken wheelchairs. His feet were bloody from the broken
glass crunching under his feet, pounding along on the
creaky wood floor. He wore pajamas, and the cold air
whistled through the fabric to chill his clammy skin while
sweat poured off him from the exertion. The ghostly
screams echoed in the hallway of the ancient building,
coming from many directions. His soaked pajamas felt
heavy, sticking to his skin; flannel became lead that
weighed him down. He didn't have to look back to know
the thing was still there, relentless, willing to chase him
forever until it caught him, and he knew if he turned to
look now, he might actually see it, and the sight would
make him weak, sapping his strength, forcing him to the
floor, where he would die.

A stairwell. Smashing the glass in the open door as he
swung too wide, sliding on his own bloody feet, then
lurching down the steps, two by two, his hand picking up
splinters in the rotten handrail. Ancient wood steps cracking under his weight, musty air in his face so stale that he
could hardly breathe. And the thing continued after him,
gaining speed, floating right over the broken steps, chasing
him down into the earth.

Another turn. Locked doors, storage closets, wheeled
gurneys, a cracked tile floor. His flashlight the only light,
bobbing up and down as he ran, the final door waiting, a
thick door that could either keep something out or keep
something in.

The door was locked. Tau was trapped, and the thing
was coming, teasing him now that he could go no farther,
enjoying his fear, preparing to strike. He looked around,
but there were no other exits from the basement, and he
couldn't go back. He stepped on a steel bar that made him

stumble against the wall, and the ghost loomed behind him.

Tau used the bar as a lever to break the lock on the handle. The door creaked open, the air from inside hitting him in the face with the strong smell of ether. He gagged and placed his hand over his mouth, but he had to go forward; backward meant death for him and his friends. If he could shut the door quickly, he might keep the thing out.

Success. The door boomed shut. Tau was trapped in the cold storage room where the dead soldiers had been kept. His flashlight showed empty tables on a checkered tile floor of black and white. He jammed the steel bar into the latch, twisting it tight. Firestorm screamed again, howling in rage, and the door thundered under the impact of a great weight, knocking Tau to the floor, and his flashlight rolled away, throwing shadows toward the ceiling and raising a thick, choking dust in the air. The dust of time plugged his throat, mixed with the ether to keep him from breathing, and prepared him to join the dead soldiers whose *chindi* were trapped in this place for so long.

The door shook again, cracking under the impact, bulging inward, breaking through.

Tau flinched, pushed himself backward on the slick floor. The wood splintered and exploded into dust. Tau covered his eyes as pieces of the door struck his body and his face, and icy claws wrapped around his ankles, the thing holding him in its powerful embrace. The flashlight battery was dying, but the dimming beam showed him more than enough. The *chindi* that had become Firestorm loomed above him, its breath hissing through twisted lips and spiked teeth in a powerful jaw. A vicious face of black fur topped with pointed dog ears. Its long snout, and smoky red eyes with white pupils, reminded him of Coyote, the trickster god.

Tau realized that Firestorm was using his memories against him, stealing the darkest, most horrifying episode from Tau's past to destroy his sanity, frighten him into mistakes; and it had worked. He reached behind his head, scrabbling at the floor, but his fingers wouldn't catch on the smooth tile, and the icy claws held him in place. Firestorm lowered its face toward his own, its breath smelling like the rot of the grave.

It sat on Tau's legs, crushing them. The claw moved up, and five stilettos of ice glinted in the light before plunging into his stomach, ripping him in half, setting his insides on fire. Tau twisted and strained, trying to get away, pounding at the leering face with his fists, but the shredding continued, and he knew he would die.

Then a tiny voice, a voice from the past, spoke in his head. "Tau! We're in! The vault door is unlocked! Punch out!"

But he didn't understand the meaning of the words. His world was pain, and that was all he understood.

Then he heard Kate's voice. Everyone wanted to visit in his dying moments. "Tau. I'm here, and I can help you. Look to your right."

Tau blinked, unable to pull his eyes away from the red ones hanging over his face. What was right? Was it right that he die here, in the morgue of an abandoned hospital from his past? Was it right that Coyote/Firestorm should rip his guts out for trespassing? He snapped his head to the right. That was right.

A simple doorway, open and inviting, a golden shaft of sunlight streaming impossibly into the basement. An escape route that might as well be a hundred miles away for all he could do about it.

Firestorm sat upright, surprise in its eyes, drool dripping from its mouth into the open wound of Tau's chest cavity. It stood and turned around, confused by something in the hallway, and Tau could move now that the crushing weight was gone from his legs. Silently, slowly, he pulled his shattered body away from Firestorm, edging toward the door, then rising to his hands and knees to crawl around a dusty slab, then standing for a final lurch through the doorway.

But he couldn't cross the threshold. A barrier held him back. Confused, he tried to work out what he'd heard before Kate arrived. Kate. He looked back, but Firestorm stepped out into the hallway, briefly hypnotized by something Tau couldn't see. But the distraction didn't last, and the creature turned again, spotting Tau. Now it was *really* angry.

Punch out. Norman had told him to punch out.

And he did.

Tau's eyes opened, and he gulped air into his lungs like a drowning man exploding out of the water. Safe. More or less. Flashing lights and alarms pummeled his senses. He was back in the VR couch, in the biochip vault, with one minute remaining.

Not enough time. He was dead already.

He blinked. Snapdragon appeared to be running toward him, dripping wet, but Tau was too confused to be sure. "Vent!" Snapdragon yelled. "Get in the vent!" But Tau didn't understand.

Norman screamed in his head. "Tau! Neural shock! Get off the couch!"

So many demands. Tau felt the metal plate in the headrest heating up. His head vibrated with thunder while an intense white light burned his eyes. He lurched forward, the back of his head smoking. The headrest burst into flame as he rolled off the couch.

Tau's head cracked against the floor, and black ink filled his vision.

YVETTE Fermi walked slowly east along the Embarcadero, her shoe heels clicking on the pavement. The salty air smelled fresh as it blew against her back, forcing her long hair forward over her shoulders to brush against her face. Laika bobbed along beside her, pulling on the leash. Plumes of late afternoon fog blew beneath the Bay Bridge looming overhead, while robot-driven freighters sailed beneath it, heading west with the rising tide toward the Golden Gate. Seagulls clustered on the railing above the seawall, watching her approach with wary eyes, smart enough to know danger when they saw it.

She was enjoying the walk, but confusion over her own behavior was what had made the walk necessary in the first place. She had thrown away a perfectly useful and powerful senator in favor of Tau Wolfsinger, a geeky employee who refused to be attracted to her.

Thorn could have been a powerful ally, but she had abandoned him and compounded the damage by having her AdForce team modify the Kennedy avatar to denounce the senator during a national broadcast. Timed to appear after the interruption of Thorn's speech by the broadcast of Tau's incriminating memories, Kennedy had dropped the final bomb. Yvette felt a certain pride of ownership in the knowledge that Kennedy had done such an excellent job, and the effort had brought her a new client, Milton Greenspoon, who wanted her to fly to Davos, Switzerland, for a meeting. Somehow, he had found out that AdForce was responsible for the Kennedy ad, and she was suspicious of his motives, but Yvette knew she could take him down if necessary.

Still, business was looking up. Thorn would no longer be involved in Elysian Fields. When all the turmoil and investigations died down, she expected to swoop in and pick over the corporate remains, and the technology she had helped steal would rightfully be hers. Lincoln Ford Kennedy had agreed to help her run the place—she just had to figure out how to compensate a dead man. But that was all in the future; she still had her present to worry about.

One of the local street people climbed out of a garbage can and wandered into her path, swaying on his feet in torn clothes as he held out his hand. His long, scruffy beard and wild eyes reminded her of the two baggies from the side of her building. Prompted to move along by Jeeves, who had delivered a low voltage shock to wake them up that morning, they had disappeared immediately. When she got closer to the man, his smell was almost tangible, but she continued forward without slowing her pace, stiff-arming him in the chest when he got too close. He stumbled back toward the railing on the seawall, then tripped over Laika, who bit at his ankles.

Yvette rubbed her eyes, unable to think clearly anymore. Behind her, she heard a splash, then the screaming of seagulls. A foghorn moaned on the Marin headlands. Maybe the meeting in Davos would be a quick one, and she could do some sightseeing afterward. She needed to take a vacation and get some sleep.

She was so tired, she could sleep like the dead.

"WELL, you can tell those monkeys that they're not going to get paid!" Aaron Thorn was not a happy man. He stood next to Enrico Motohashi, the weasel-faced project foreman, on an outdoor stage shaped like a giant clamshell. The top of the shell soared thirty feet over his head. In the middle of the San Francisco Bay, he had an excellent view of the heavy late afternoon fog blanket creeping in to smother the Golden Gate Bridge. A Japanese robot freighter loomed large in the channel to his left, on its way out to sea, blocking his view of the alabaster towers and

hills of San Francisco. The earlier rain had left a fresh
scent in the air, but he had not been able to smell it since
he entered the construction zone on Nova Alcatraz, which
currently featured the unmistakable odor of raw sewage
because the waste recycling facility had exploded during
the night. Construction delays were becoming a regular
nightmare, and some of the investors were dropping out.
With a great deal of his own money tied up in the success
of this project, he now had to worry about whether his retirement funds would vanish along with his good reputation.

"No pay, no work," Motohashi grunted.

"No work, no *job*," Thorn replied, poking the foreman
in the chest with his finger.

"No job, no Nova Alcatraz," Motohashi said, clenching
his fists.

"No Nova Alcatraz, no Enrico Motohashi," Thorn said,
staring him down.

Motohashi's face turned pale. He started to respond,
then shrugged. "Well, if you put it that way, they'll be back
to work tomorrow."

The senator sighed heavily as Motohashi ambled off the
stage, then he placed a VR monocle in his eye. "Milton, are
you there?"

Milton Greenspoon looked up from the paperwork on
his desk at the White House. "I thought you were gone. I
had you on hold for fifteen minutes."

"I figured you must have put me on hold by mistake,"
Thorn said. "How do the polls look?"

"Bad, Aaron. Very bad. You picked up a few votes after
the broadcast when the Global Wrestling Federation threw
its endorsement in the ring for you, but you lost almost
everyone else. It's the rumors about the Elysian Fields investigation that are killing you now."

"Sounds like I need to get another rousing support
speech written for President Rex."

Greenspoon shook his head. "I don't even think that
will help you now, Aaron. I'm sorry." He glanced at the an-

tique clock on his desk. "I have to run. Meetings, you know, so many meetings. We'll talk more later."

"Yeah," Thorn said. The image went dark in his monocle, so he took it out of his eye and dropped it back into his shirt pocket. He wrinkled his nose when the wind shifted, hurling the smell of raw sewage directly into his face. He buttoned his coat to keep out the chill.

Thorn was annoyed at the turn of events, but not worried. In four years, the public would have forgotten every detail of the Elysian Fields scandal. Four years, hell; four days was more likely. Most voters barely knew their own names, so they certainly weren't going to remember something as complicated as Thorn's using their dead loved ones to brainwash them. The voters who were smart enough to remember would probably admire his initiative. He'd step out of the limelight for a while, take some time off. Get a tan. Then, in a couple of years, he'd spread some money around to tie up any loose ends. Senator Aaron Thorn was down but not out. He was only four years, one tan, and an undetermined number of bribes away from the Oval Office.

His neck and shoulders felt tense again, a problem he'd been having a lot more in the last week or so. He stretched his arms, as if he were about to engulf the city of San Francisco, or be crucified, and tilted his head up to do some neck rolls.

That's when he saw the man dressed in white at the top of the clamshell, stretched out in a spread-eagle pose between two struts, smiling down at him with a wild expression. Thorn rubbed his eyes, thinking he'd imagined it, but when he glanced up again, the man fell directly toward him with a white spear pointed at Thorn's face.

Thorn froze, his mouth open, and Dag Nygaard plunged the spear straight down his throat. Dropping with the added weight of a 200-pound man, the spear continued straight through the senator's body and out the other end, nailing him to the stage.

Right before Dag hit the ground, a crash balloon blossomed around his body, and he bounced harmlessly off the floor. Thorn's dimming eyes watched him stand up, deflate the crash balloon, brush his hair back, and wave politely before leaving the stage.

Then the lights went out.

LENYA Novikov discovered Kate's body slumped against the base of the Vulcan Gate about an hour after he'd left her there. He tried to revive her with one of the emergency medkits in the tunnel, but he couldn't diagnose her problem. Worried that she might be in a coma, which she had the annoying habit of slipping into, he picked her up and carried her into the museum. His crew was sleeping, so his desperate experiment would not be interrupted.

The room had previously rushed to repair Novikov's body, so he hoped to attract its attention once more, placing Kate gently on the floor near one of the exhibits. When nothing happened, he stepped back, then heard the familiar directionless ping.

The section of floor beneath Kate silently rose about two feet, then shot away to the back of the room with a velocity that should have thrown her off the floor plate immediately. He watched her disappear into the tiny door on the distant back wall of the museum. Then he could only hope he'd done the right thing, and that the alien technology would not vaporize her body or something equally horrendous. He was having a hard enough time maintaining his image in front of the cameras while he randomly experimented with the devices in the museum; his murder of an innocent scientist would not play well back at NASA or the Russian Space Agency. So far, headquarters had tolerated his adventures with the toys in the museum, probably because Novikov's little shows generated good ratings from the viewing audience, but they would have to say something about a murder.

While Novikov waited, a big Russian man with a bushy beard walked up behind him. He wore a soiled overcoat and looked like he should be milking cows on a *fverma* in Grasnov.

"Who the hell are you?" Novikov asked in Russian.

The man stared at him, confused. "I am . . . Professor Pushkin Sergeevich Ryumin."

A new recruit; just what he needed. Why did no one tell him about these things anymore? "And when did you arrive?"

The man seemed to be dim. He hesitated, staring at Novikov again. "I am . . . not sure. I was wandering in a white tunnel. I thought I had died. And then I saw you."

"Fine," Novikov sighed. He wanted to get rid of the man before Kate came back. "Go on back to the camp, and Svetlana will set you up."

"Camp? Where is that?"

"You must have seen it?" This had to be a punishment. Professor or not, this man wouldn't last a day on the surface; he'd forget his spacesuit or something. "Look, go out that door, turn right, walk about two hundred meters, and you'll see the tents. Okay?"

Still confused, the man mumbled something, nodded, and left.

When Novikov turned around again, he saw Kate settling to the floor on the flying slab, and he sighed with relief when she sat up and smiled. His career was safe, at least for the moment.

AFTER a lengthy and tedious conversation, during which Novikov handed her a bulb of hot tea, Kate finally found herself alone in the museum. She knew Novikov must be worried that she would discover something interesting about the place in his absence, but she had assured him that she wouldn't touch anything.

And she really didn't need to, because Thoth resided in her head, as he always would now. And she would get used to his presence. The important thing was that she had been able to help Tau, giving him time to break away from the hostile AI so that he could escape. Amused by the simplicity of the Firestorm AI and the Elysian Fields virtual world, Thoth had easily interfered with the environment fabricated by Firestorm. At first, Thoth had wanted to study the primitive AI before shutting him down, but Kate wouldn't allow it with Tau in danger. In fact, Firestorm had been clever enough to get away from them for a moment, and she still didn't know for certain what had happened, but Tau had broken free. Their visit resulted in the destruction of the Firestorm AI, the rescue of Tau, and Thoth making friends with the datasphere Entity.

Her deal with Thoth had been simple: if he helped Tau, she would let Thoth move in with her. Of course, he made quite a mess, sending her straight into the coma she had feared, but good old Lenya Novikov placed her in the Gwrinydd lifebox; an advanced medical facility that could handle a wide variety of biological forms. The museum itself was a training ground for Gwrinydd warriors and other captured species forcibly committed to the defense of the Gwrinydd race, so the lifebox had been installed to handle the inevitable medical emergencies that would arise.

With the repaired Earth gate working properly now, and wireless access to the datasphere, she would also find it easier to make contact with Tau, assuming he was okay. She knew he'd made it out of the Elysian Fields system, but he had looked bad, and his wounds there might have damaged his physical body if his nervous system believed they were real.

"Kate," Thoth said. Since they were living together, he called her by her first name now. "We wish to visit the Entity." He represented the rest of the voyeurs in his AI crowd, so he had also started using the royal "we" when he referred to himself. An irritating habit.

"First, we make contact with Tau," Kate said. "Then you can go and play with the Entity."

"Yes, Kate." It sounded like he was moping.

Kate sighed. She wondered how Tau would feel about having a child; a superintelligent child that lived in her head. Hard to say. She decided not to mention it for a while.

52

AFTER Norman disappeared, Ariel Colombari remained inside the Elysian Fields computer network. Knowing exactly where to strike for maximum damage, Shade guided them through the system core, then he remained by Ariel's side. With the destruction of the core, much of the virtual world had collapsed along with the administrative systems, but isolated islands of the environment survived, surrounded by blackness and crowded with confused avatars.

They stopped on a tiny island of Greek temple ruins and sun-baked beaches washed by the waves of a golden sea. The avatars clustered on a rocky white beach, staring out to sea and up at the blackness that started a few feet above their heads. Despite the sunlight that warmed them, they saw no sun in the sky. Fifty yards up the rise beyond the beach, the blackness neatly cut the white temple ruins and other structures in half.

Shade moved among the avatars like a benevolent god in his white robes; with his ability to go anywhere in the local network and peek behind the scenes, he knew enough to reassure the "stiffs," as he liked to call them, that all would be fine. But it became clear that parts of the network were still shutting down as they watched individual avatars fade to transparency before finally disappearing altogether. Each time this happened, an anxious murmur swept through the crowd like a wave.

"The digital damned don't know enough to appreciate what's happening," Shade told Ariel. "Their chips are safe in the library; they'll reappear once the VR servers are back on-line. In the meantime, they get a taste of the elegance of real death. Maybe they won't want to come back."

"That should be their choice," Ariel said.

Shade looked at her with admiration. "Exactly. You understand."

"I do now. And I think some of them have made their decisions already." She pointed at one of the women walking up the hill. When she reached the border of the black zone, she hesitated a moment, then crossed the line and faded away.

"Let me try something," Shade said. "Lord Byron seems appropriate right now." He climbed a white marble statue and sat on the shoulders of Zeus. He raised his arms and the crowd turned to watch him when he shouted:

> "If that high world, which lies beyond
>   Our own, surviving love endears;
> If there the cherish'd heart be fond,
>   The eye the same, except in tears—
> How welcome those untrodden spheres!
>   How sweet this very hour to die!
> To soar from earth, and find all fears
>   Lost in thy light—Eternity!
>
> It must be so: 'tis not for self
>   That we so tremble on the brink;
> And striving to o'erleap the gulf,
>   Yet cling to Being's severing link.
> Oh! in that future let us think
>   To hold each heart the heart that shares;
> With them the immortal waters drink,
>   And soul in soul grow deathless theirs!"

The crowd continued to stare at Shade when he climbed down from the statue and rejoined Ariel on the beach. If anything, they looked more confused than they had before.

"I don't know if they got the message," Ariel said.

Shade shrugged. "Some will; some won't. Look." He pointed at a small knot of people moving up the hill. When they reached the steps to one of the temples, they formed a neat line and walked between the columns to vanish into the darkness on the other side. "But enough of this," Shade said, gesturing for her to follow. "I promised to help you."

Ariel looked confused. "You already have. In many ways."

Shade snorted as he walked toward a small olive grove within the walls of a small temple with no roof. "Don't worry. I'm going to ask you to do one more thing for me, too."

When they started down the white stone steps into the olive grove, Ariel gasped as her heart almost jumped into her mouth. Carlo sat atop a short marble column in a shaft of sunlight, looking as real as he had in life. When he raised his head and saw Ariel, he stood up, and his amazed expression gradually changed to a smile. Ariel stood rooted to the steps, unable to move or even breathe, so Carlo ran up to her without a word and wrapped her in his arms. He felt warm, and strong, and perfect.

After a few minutes of polite silence, Shade cleared his throat, and Ariel opened her eyes to smile at him over Carlo's shoulder, afraid to let go. "Thank you, Shade," she whispered.

Shade held up his hand. "Save it. You earned it. You know the way in, and you have the power to go wherever you want, so you can live here with Carlo now if you want to. Or somewhere else. Or not at all, whatever you decide. As for me, I want you to locate my biochip in the library vault—I have the filing coordinates to help you find it— and then I want you to burn it."

Ariel nodded, unable to speak once more.

"Good," Shade said. "I know I can trust you. I simply don't want to be here when they rebuild the system." He looked out at the avatars talking on the beach, and at those who were making their way up to the temple to seek the darkness, then he stepped over and kissed Ariel on the cheek. "It's a good day to die. I think I'll go for a little walk."

And Oliphant Meadows strolled up the hill.

53

SNAPDRAGON was asleep in his private luxury suite at the stern of his cruise ship when Captain Heyerdahl alerted him to an important news broadcast. Snapdragon glanced out the window. The setting sun hung low on the horizon, but they were far enough out from San Francisco, heading south, that the sky began to clear and shafts of sunlight sneaked under the red clouds. He stretched, then sat up on the bed and focused on the holo projector in the corner, choosing the news program he wanted. Milton Greenspoon stood at a lectern in the press office of the White House, hovering in the corner of Snapdragon's suite. Greenspoon looked tired, wringing his hands while he spoke in a slow and careful voice.

". . . so it is with a heavy heart that I bring you this sorrow. Just a few hours ago, I said good-bye to a dear friend, a man of honor, integrity, courage, and greatness. He was a man of public spirit who rose to the heights of his profession, but now he has fallen from those heights, his extraordinary life succumbing to the final ravages of a disease he had fought for many months, hoping to keep his illness a secret from our enemies while he struggled to lead this country through these difficult times. I have ordered that the flags of the capital be lowered to half-mast in remembrance of our fallen president, Rex Arthur King. As the Constitution specifies in these matters, Vice President Uriah Truman will be assuming the role of acting president until January, when the winner of November's election assumes office. We expect that—"

Snapdragon switched to a different news station, but the local coverage concentrated on the early morning flooding

and catastrophic fire that closed the Happy Meadows theme park in Colma. They showed an aerial view of the Woodlawn Memorial Park, where black smoke boiled out of the ground at Emperor Norton's mausoleum as if it were the mouth of Hell. Down the hill and across the street, much of the lower cemetery lay under a foot of water, and the Pearly Gates were closed.

"—Elysian Fields representatives were not available for comment, but they expect to make an official statement tomorrow. In related news, a grand jury has been impaneled to investigate reports that Elysian Fields—"

Snapdragon shut off the news, then turned to hit a button at the head of his massive bed. "Hey, Doc, how's he doing?"

Doc's weary voice responded quickly. "He's stable and resting comfortably."

"Can I visit him?"

"Don't see why not."

Snapdragon rolled out of bed, cursing his stiff muscles, then stepped into his flowing white robes and headed for the door.

FLOATING in the air between the repulsor fields in the ship's infirmary, Tau looked strange enough to startle Snapdragon when he walked into the room with the gray-haired Doc Horowitz. The bumps on Tau's unconscious head hadn't looked good when Snapdragon carried him all the way to the tender boat that would carry them to the *Ark of the Sun*—briefly anchored off Baker Beach at the Presidio to pick them up—but now Tau was bald, and he looked entirely different.

Snapdragon took a few steps closer to study the doctor's work, then flinched when he saw the primitive metal plate that covered the back of Tau's head and the left side of his face up to his eye. "What did you do to him, Doc?"

Horowitz cleared his throat. "In layman's terms?"

"Yes, English would be great."

"I repaired the damage done by the neural shock. I replaced the damaged tissues in the left side of his brain with

a series of processor arrays, rebuilt part of his skull, injected him with nanomeds to complete the microsurgery, and slapped a spiffy aluminum plate on his head to impress the ladies. Shines up real nice."

Snapdragon scowled at Horowitz. "You're kidding."

"Yes. His new skin is growing in the vat right now. We'll do a graft and cosmetic surgery over the next couple of days, then he'll be as good as new. Better, actually, since he now has more computing power than most humans."

Just a few inches from Tau's face, Snapdragon peered at the weird intersection of metal and skin, when Tau opened his eyes. "Lose something?" Tau asked.

Snapdragon jumped back. "I thought we'd lost *you* for a while there. Do you remember what happened?"

Tau took a deep breath. "I don't want to talk about it right now. Have you seen Kate?"

"No. Have you?"

"Hard to explain." Tau reached up to rub the back of his neck, but he didn't seem surprised when he felt the metal plate. "You said chip implants, eh? Liquid quantum DNA processors?"

"Nothing but the best," Horowitz said. "I almost added solar panels while you were out, but Snapdragon told me not to. At least not until he had a chance to ask you."

"Food is death. The sun is life," Snapdragon pointed out.

"I think I'd like to get my head together first," Tau said.

Snapdragon shrugged. "Well, it's not for everyone, I guess. You can always change your mind. We've got a long cruise ahead."

"Long cruise?"

"We're on my ship, and we're safe in international waters, more or less, but we'll have to disappear for a while. We've made a lot of powerful people angry, and they'll be looking for us. We trashed Happy Meadows and their computer network pretty thoroughly, with the fire and flooding and all. I even have the police looking for me because of the Lincoln Ford Kennedy kidnapping."

"Fire? How did that happen? Did the biochip vault survive?"

"Hey, I might not have understood what you were doing in there, but I got bored waiting in the river, and I do know how to set fire to a data center as a diversion. The fire alarms came on, doors automatically unlocked, people ran around—total chaos; it was great. I thought you were cutting it close to the wire when the vault door finally popped open, but I figured you knew about the air vents in the library."

"Umm, yeah," Tau said. "I saw them."

"Well, it wasn't easy shoving your dead weight into that vent, I can tell you. But the hallway outside the vault was flooded, so I couldn't go back that way. Next time, I'll be the unconscious one, and you can carry *me* out."

"It's a deal. And thanks."

Snapdragon shrugged modestly. "It was fun. Like I said, I get bored. I need to stay busy."

Tau remembered the fire Snapdragon had set in Virginia, and that reminded him of the biochip the senator had made of his stolen memories. He knew the recording was incomplete, and it might have burned up in the fire. He still had to worry about his recorded memories of his friends and the events on Mars, information that he didn't want anyone to have, but Norman had told him earlier that it would take a specialist days to find that kind of information, and the interested parties were busy with other problems.

While Tau felt around with his hand, he frowned and looked up at Snapdragon. "Where's Norman?"

Snapdragon sighed and looked at his feet. "I knew you'd ask eventually. Norman didn't make it, Tau."

"What does that mean? Norman was already dead."

"He saved your life by diverting most of the neural shock into his own biochip. Then it melted."

Tau swallowed and closed his eyes, allowing the news to sink in. "That means he died *twice* by helping other people."

Snapdragon nodded. "One of the good guys. It's funny

what you learn about people when their lives are on the line or their friends are in danger. I never knew he'd be willing to sacrifice himself like that—didn't seem like the type. I wish I'd spent more time with him."

"Me, too," Tau said. "Me, too."

AT Tau's request, Snapdragon and Horowitz helped Tau out of the repulsor field so he could sit at a table by the window. After he promised not to stay up more than five minutes, they left him alone with his thoughts. He wished Kate was there with him, starting a new journey to become someone else.

While he studied the golden glow on the water, watched over by the red clouds and the sinking sun, he thought about everything he had done that week, and the courage he had witnessed. New and old friends had helped him accomplish the impossible, cutting another head off the powerful, multiheaded hydra known as Davos, the weak defeating the mighty, and once again, he had survived. Was the world in balance once more? Maybe. He felt cheated, in a way, as if he'd had to pay with his father's life, and with Norman's life, to win the battle. But he also knew that Norman had felt the satisfaction of bringing down the people who stole his work and forced him to live underground; and that his father had lived a full life, never wasting a day on negative thoughts, healing the sick and helping his friends, raising a family and watching his son become the man he wanted him to be.

In the end, Tau realized, Norman's biochip had not been a guarantee to eternal life; his friendship and his heroism had guaranteed that. He would live on in Tau's mind and in his spirit, joining Tau's father, his friends, and other loved ones, both past and future, who had passed over to the other side. Their immortal fires burned on inside Tau, giving him strength.

The ship turned west, and they sailed into the sunset.